Sam Sterk, Ph.D., is a sport psychologist, psychoanalyst, and a certified master clinical hypnotherapist. Dr. Sterk's practice, Peak Performance Plus LLC, is located in Scottsdale, Arizona. Additionally, Dr. Sterk also teaches medical hypnosis at a local medical university and is the immediate past president of ASPH (Arizona Society of Professional Hypnosis). Dr. Sterk has presented at national conferences including, the Association for Applied Sport Psychology, NGH (National Guild of Hypnotists) and Hypno-thoughts. In 2019, he was a judge in the Arizona Literary contest, sponsored by the Arizona Author's Association.

Sam Sterk's published works are as follows:

Sammy's Journey, a memoir about the author's early life struggles and triumphs in overcoming life-threatening asthma.

Win! Get the Mental Edge Skills in Martial Arts is a sport psychology manual for martial artists.
Win! Get the Mental Edge Skills in Golf is a sport psychology manual for golfers.
Win 2! Train and Master Sport Hypnosis is a how-to manual for doing Hypnosis with athletes.

Hannah's Visions is Sam Sterk's debut novel with Austin Macauley Publishing.

In his free time, Sam Sterk is an avid reader and writer who is always thinking about and inventing new characters and plots for his future novels. Family time is vitally important to him, highlighted by many memorable vacations with his wife Miriam Sterk, his children, and grandchildren.

I dedicate this book to my deceased grandfather, Jacob. As a young child in Israel, he created fictional accounts about a fierce, but caring dragon whose mission was to help me when I was ill with life-threatening asthma. These stories proved helpful in my daily struggles with this disease.

Sam Sterk, Ph.D.

HANNAH'S VISIONS

AUSTIN MACAULEY PUBLISHERS™

LONDON * CAMBRIDGE * NEW YORK * SHARJAH

Ordering Information:
Quantity sales: special discounts are available on quantity purchases by corporations, associations, and others. For details, contact the publisher at the address below.

Publisher's Cataloging-in-Publication data
Sterk, Ph.D., Sam
Hannah's Visions

ISBN 9781645363965 (Paperback)
ISBN 9781645363972 (Hardback)
ISBN 9781645363996 (ePub e-book)

Library of Congress Control Number: 2020906981

www.austinmacauley.com/us

First Published (2020)
Austin Macauley Publishers LLC
40 Wall Street, 28th Floor
New York, NY 10005
USA

mail-usa@austinmacauley.com
+1 (646) 5125767

I want to thank my wife, Miriam Sterk, LCSW C-ASWCM, who patiently listened to my evolving tale about Hannah's visions. Miriam is a talented therapist providing counselling, case management, and healthcare advocacy services. My daughter, Dahlia Maskin, and son-in-law, Erik, and their two children, Ava and Jacob, I hold very closely to my heart. My son, Ethan Sterk, and daughter-in-law, Anna, and their three boys, Evan, Elliot, and Asher, are also incredibly dear to me.

My grandfather, Jacob Wilshkovsky, has long passed on but he taught me to have imagination and to care about others. He's still my role model today. As a child, he narrated tales about a very kind, protective dragon able to smite any and all foes.

"Whenever you experience a bully, a kind dragon will protect you against any enemy."

When I was six, I asked him, "Can you show me some picture books about these nice dragons? Are there some pictures?"

He said, "No, but you can see them and create them in your own mind."

I further inquired, "Well, how and where can I find these stories?"

He said, "They're in your mind, Sammy. You can create as many of these dragons as you wish, and they'll always help and protect you."

That was the beginning of my use of imagination, which created inner strength and resiliency in the face of life-threatening asthma.

I want to thank Ms. Lisa Aquilina, owner of Green Pieces Press, for her guidance and support in my journey to publish this work. I am also thankful to Ms. Mary Holden for her editorial support.

Thank you to J.E. Kelley Snyder, a retired detective, who runs an agency called FIND ME, which helps locate missing people with the use of psychics. I am thankful to Austin Macauley Publishers, who have provided me the opportunity to publish *Hannah's Visions*.

Chapter One

Hannah roused in a cold sweat when she envisioned a young adult female victim, her throat slashed and bludgeoned to death. From the victim's throat, large amounts of blood pooled together, some still liquefied while the rest had congealed. Her blond hair, soaked and caked in blood, melded with the sandy gravel below. All around were ancient gravestones, as the body had been placed in an ancient cemetery. "Oh my goodness! What kind of animal would do this to another human being? How could anyone be so brutally cruel?" The victim's face revealed that her nose, cheekbones, and jaws were crushed, most probably from the poundings by a large rock. A blood-soaked note read, *"You f***** whore, you deserve to die. You bitch!"* No footprints were found.

Hannah became hyper-vigilant as she examined to see if her bedroom windows had been smashed. Hannah's face was now crimson-red and sweaty. Her breathing was labored and she hyperventilated, which made her feel even dizzier; her heart beat so rapidly, very much like a speedy locomotive pounding down on some old rickety tracks. She could hear the sound of the thumping pulse in her ears. 'I must find a way to collect myself. I'll try and slow down my breathing rate.' She wondered, 'Why am I having this vision now?' She inhaled deeply to catch her breath. 'This revelation, just like other in the past, means something to me. I must respect the inner messages that come to me. A mortal crime will be committed. A young lady will be murdered.' She concluded, 'But now I must find a way to relax myself before school starts. I need to get some shuteye. Later, I will have a talk with my parents.' She inhaled and exhaled deeply. She told herself, 'Inhale, exhale, and slowly relax my muscles.'

Unable to resume her sleep, she sat up in her bed and deliberated, 'Why now?' She concluded, 'You know what? I respect these inner messages and images that come to me. But who is this young lady? This victim… she can't be any older than twenty-one or twenty-two. Who is this monster who will commit such a gruesomely brutal crime?' She shook her head in disbelief. 'Oh my God, the victim and I are so close in age. Wow! That could have been me. The victim and I resemble each other – blond hair, about five feet, six inches, and blue eyes. Is this a telltale sign that I will become a fatality as well?' Near Hannah's bedroom was the family bathroom. Her face was still beet-red. 'Certainly, not all visions come true?' She tried to reassure herself. 'Perhaps, it's just a bad dream – a nightmare? I must first lie down and rest my troubled mind.'

That same evening at 9:45 p.m., Leonid Kozlov stepped into the Russian Volga sex nightclub in Tel Aviv. Several patrons rubbed their eyes from surrounding harsh smoke. Tonight, Leonid wore a sleeveless shirt, one that revealed his bulging muscles. Highly committed to bodybuilding, his physique looked like Michelangelo's 'David,' the master's hand-carved marble statue, well known for its anatomical details. The nightclub employed exotic dancers that originated from Russia and spoke Hebrew with a thick Russian accent.

Two almost completely nude exotic dancers were gyrating with sexually suggestive moves on the well-lit pole-dancing stage. He sat at a table with a candle and make-believe flowers. A blond, blue-eyed server with a well-toned body approached him. She could have been a Hollywood star with beautiful facial features, blond and blue eyes. "Vat you vant, Choney?"

"Double Vodka, little ice."

"Vat's your name, Choney? You look so strong, so manly. I viel call you my lion of Judea. I can bring you pleasure like you niever chad before. Okay? Vie can leave anytime you vant." She bent over, touched his face, blew air into his ears, and whispered, "You vant great sex? I make you chappy! I chave all kinds of tricks and skiels to make you chappy. I bring a big smile to your face, one you can chave for a long time."

"Chow much you vant?" One hand touched her buttocks while the other hand massaged her thighs.

"Four chundred shiekels. You von't regret it, my lion, my king of Judea. I viel bring you to the moon, the cheaven and back." She smiled seductively, massaging his inner thighs.

"Too much monie. Give to me better price."

"Okay, two hundred and fifty shekels." She now licked his inner ear.

"Okay, but first I drink my vodka." He lit up a cigarette – unfiltered Camel. She smiled and winked at him.

"Come back in five or ten minutes. Then, vie go. Good?"

Fifteen minutes later, they were in his gray van. She noticed a number of knives, some covered by a blood-stained towel, in the backseat of his van. The smell of marijuana permeated his entire van. He offered her a hit from his lit marijuana joint, one that resembled a narrow Cuban cigar. "Chere, chave a chit. Is good for you. Make you fiel good, all over."

Nearby the Volga Club, he parked his van. She took his invitation for marijuana smoke, inhaled deeply, smiled, and placed her hand on his groin area. She gently massaged and kneaded the area while she observed his bulge surge and swell.

He removed a sharp metal item from its leather sheath, held it in his mouth first, and then placed it on his dashboard where it would be easily accessible to him. She noticed the large knife, and with growing alarm and fear in her voice, she said, "Why do you need this knife? Are you going to hurt me?" As if paralyzed from fear, she stopped breathing for a few seconds. She took a deep breath and instead of buckling up, she took hold of her can of Coca Cola, shook it up, and splashed his face while she bolted out of his van. Before she jumped out, Leonid held his knife and tried to slash her left shoulder using his nine-inch silver shiny blade. But he felt temporarily blinded by the Cola fizz and missed her shoulder. She ran quickly towards the Volga Club. He took a towel to dry his face and attempted to run after her. Leonid ran a few meters in pursuit of her. She reentered the Volga Club and hid in the owner's office. A couple of exotic dancers rushed over to her. "Are you okay, Marina? We'll call the police."

He refrained from entering the club for fear that the police would surely be called. Instead, he proceeded to loudly curse her, "You f***** slut. You deserve to die, you cwhore! Vomen like you should be kielled." The look on his face revealed contempt and rage as if he were a wild animal gone rabid. Consumed by his fury, his eyes, mouth, and jaws appeared warped and contorted. He took out his most prized knife and licked off the fresh new blood. He cursed the girl who managed to escape his hateful desires. He waived his knife in the air as if this were a victory ritual. He whispered to himself, "See chow strong I am. There viel be a next time. I promise you no escape, bitch!" He resumed driving his van but needed to urinate. He found a secluded hidden spot where he parked his van. In the distance, he could hear the sounds of police cars' sirens. Behind several trees, he reached to pull down his underwear and felt some sticky fluid. He then realized that he must have climaxed. "Oh, I vanted her so badly. It would have been so great." He sweated profusely and repeated, "I chate you, bitch. You deserve to die!"

***

Hannah was an A-plus student, pretty, popular with her peers, and won several art contests for her paintings in Ashkelon, Israel, her residence, and birthplace. She was also one of the best archers in all of Israel, having won several high school competitions.

"I must tell someone. Police needs to know about this killing but who is going to believe a seventeen-year-old high school psychic? I could tell my father who is the chief of detectives."

Her parents had awakened after hearing the water pour from the nearby bathroom faucet. Sarah, her mother, came to the bathroom sinks to inquire, "It's 5:30 in the morning. Are you okay? Are you sick? What's the matter, Hannahle?"

"No, no, Ima, I'm okay. I'm fine. I'm going right back to bed. Before you know, it will soon be time for me to go to school."

"I am worried about you, my beautiful Hannah. Did you have a nightmare?" Concerned, Sarah placed her arm on Hannah's shoulder.

"No, but I had a very unsettling vision about a victim killed by a male murderer."

"What happened?"

"This man, in his early twenties, killed a young lady in such a gruesome manner; he stabbed her multiple times in the chest and smashed her face in, probably with a big rock. Violent enough, Ima?"

"Did you see the killer? What did he look like?"

"Somewhat. But I'm sure I'll have other visions that will reveal details about his appearance." Hannah inhaled deeply and said, "Boy, I really need to get some shuteye."

Sarah felt protective when she placed her hand on her daughter's shoulder. "Hannah, these so-called visions could be signs of your needing psychological help. As your mother, you know that I'm concerned. There could be some underlying issues that trouble you. How about if I call a psychologist or a psychiatrist and make an appointment for you? What do you say?"

"I know you wish to help. But I don't have any psychological problems other than normal teenage feelings, you know – school, boys, preparing for art contests, being in the army in a few months, girlfriends, and deciding on my future career goals. Ima, these are normal adolescent-young-adult concerns."

"Hannah, what about when you went to a party and you almost got into a physical altercation with Danni's new girlfriend? What about being moody, of late?"

Hannah now stood upright, folded both arms on her chest, and said, "Ima, now you're really annoying me. I feel really mad now. After Danni broke up with me in a party, his new girlfriend screamed out loud that I'm a tramp – a cheap whore. I never ever slept with him. How dare she try to belittle me and put me down? How dare she? Wouldn't that upset you if you were in my shoes? Don't you think I felt humiliated and embarrassed being called a tramp? That doesn't mean I have to see a shrink. Ima, you just don't understand what it's like to be a psychic – a Clairvoyant. Now, that's a real communication problem we have. You and Abba just don't get it when it comes to my being a psychic." With a hint of anger in her voice, she said, "Ima, I know you care but I don't need a shrink. But I do appreciate getting some sleep now." Hannah turned around and headed towards her bedroom. She lay in darkness. Finally, she let go of this strained conversation with her Ima. Hannah was overcome by slumber. Yet, it was a restless sleep, one that would leave her feeling exhausted for the rest of her day.

Her mother walked away with her head slumped towards the floor. Sarah looked as if she felt rejected. Tears meandered down her cheeks. She blew her nose and dried her tears using a handkerchief.

***

It was 6:00 p.m. when Yoni, her father, returned home from work. Sarah informed him about Hannah's 'being short and her lack of respect.' Yoni decided to have a talk with Hannah. As chief of detectives and his high rank in the IDF, he didn't take well to sassiness or disrespect.

He greeted her and said, "Hi, Hannah. Say, before dinner, can we spend a couple of minutes talking?"

"Sure. Where do you want to talk?" Hannah already knew why her father wanted to have a discourse.

"How about our study?"

They walked into the study which consisted of a computer, two recliners, an office chair situated right behind their computer, and a light brown wooden desk. The walls, painted a light olive green, created a relaxing ambience. The sight of the Ashkelon Beach and the Mediterranean Sea, still visible from both windows in the family's study, added to a peaceful feeling. The setting sun had not yet sealed its nightly curtains.

"So, your Ima was hurt by the tone of your voice early morning. What's the matter?" His look was one of concern when he added, "You can talk to me."

"I had a very scary vision of the murder of a young woman killed, with really gory details. To calm down, I washed my face and wrists with cold water. I don't need Ima telling me that I'm all messed up in my head and need professional psychiatric help."

"I see. But she's concerned and worried about you. Imagine if you're the mother of a teenager who has psychic visions. How would you handle that? It's a concern for parents. Don't you think?"

13

Hannah inhaled deeply and for a few seconds looked away from her father. She pensively thought about her father's questions. She understood the need to be respectful but added, "I think the real issue is that both of you don't understand what it's like being a psychic. You haven't come to terms with the fact that your daughter is psychic. In this respect, we're not on the same page. Every time I have a vision, you think I'm crazy, that I'm nuts and that I must see a shrink." She paused to think. "I happen to feel that I am a well-balanced young lady with wonderful friends. I get great grades in school and I love to paint. Maybe I did get short when Ima said I needed professional help. Both of you should understand that being a psychic is not a sign of being emotionally unbalanced. I wish that you and Ima understood that." She took a deep breath to sigh and think. Her eyes gazed toward the tile clay floor below, and as if resigned, she said, "Fine, Abba, I'll apologize to Ima for being short. Perhaps I could have had been more patient and display better control over my emotions, but really I wasn't fresh to Ima."

Yoni went over to hug Hannah. They smiled and walked towards the dining room. Yoni sat at the head of the table. To his right sat five-year-old Aaron, while on his left side sat Hannah. Sarah sat opposite Yoni, on the other side of the table.

"Ima, can I speak to you before dinner?"

"Sure, Hannahle. What's up?" They went into the living room to talk.

"Perhaps I was short with you at 5:30 this morning, but I didn't mean to hurt your feelings. You know I love you. Don't you?"

"I know that you do, my Hannahle." They reached over to hug each other.

Using his loud voice, five-year-old Aaron blurted, "Can we please eat? I'm starving. My stomach hurts. That's how hungry I am. It's making all kinds of weird sounds." Aaron pointed to his stomach for extra emphasis.

"Not until your father chants the traditional blessing over the bread," said Sarah.

***

After dinner, while in her bedroom, Hannah's phone rang. His voice was deep and Hannah could not identify it. "Hi, I heard and read about your wonderful art accomplishments. Would you be able to paint a picture of myself, of course for money? I'm in my twenties and I'm launching a new business. A painting of myself in the waiting room would be absolutely great, especially if it's tastefully done. Would you do that for me? I promise you as much money as you want for your time."

"Who gave you my phone number?" Hannah felt mistrustful and suspicious of the voice on the phone. Instantly, she felt very upset about his voice.

"In the local newspaper, I read you won several local art contests, including the King David Art Festival. I then Googled you to initiate conversing with you."

"What's your name again? I notice you speak with an accent. Where are you from?"

"My name is Chaim and I originate from Moskva, Russia. But I live in Tel Aviv."

"I do love to paint but I haven't done so professionally. I mean, I haven't charged money for my paintings." She thought a bit about the request and said, "I have to think about it, as I'm a senior in high school with lots of homework and I plan to enter a national art contest. This requires a lot of time, as this contest requires a sample of my paintings."

"Whatever you wish to charge for your time and talent is fine with me. Money is of no concern to me when it comes to your creative talent."

Hannah thought that while he spoke in Hebrew, he was trying hard to cover up his pronounced Russian accent. "Let me think about it and I can call you in a few days with an answer. What's your phone number?"

'Chaim' provided her his number. She tested it by calling the number and found he had provided an inaccessible number. By now, Hannah became more suspicious than before. She felt tense and fearful. 'He tried to deceive me, that bastard! Why? He had no intention of providing me his correct phone number.'

Suddenly, Hannah felt sick to her stomach as sweat dripped down her face. She was disturbed about this call. His sinister, creepy voice created a red flag for Hannah. She felt the caller had malicious ulterior motives but she was yet unable to ascertain why. She felt rattled by this caller. Her hands began to tremble. She felt fearful and her face looked ghostly white and pale. She wondered, 'Why would this phone call have such a profound effect on me? First, I have a scary vision involving a murder. Next, this creepy-sounding stranger calls me. Hmm, that can't be a coincidence. There must be a connection here.'

She lay down for a few minutes and closed her eyes. She cuddled her favorite down-feather pillow and held onto a still-intact ragdoll that had been given to her by her grandmother, Sapta Chana. Her eyes soon fluttered and then they moved from right to left and back as she was catapulted into an entirely new vision. Her inner voice revealed, "His name is not Chaim. It's Leonid Kozlov. His voice is not deep, yet he is able to conceal his true vocal tones. He's not a businessman launching a new business. He is a dangerous killer." It suddenly clicked and dawned on her. "Leonid is the murderer of the twenty-two-year-old whose face was bashed." His previous vague-like appearance became unmistakably clear:

Five foot, ten inches, a deep scar on his left cheek, very muscular physique, closely cropped curly black hair, long black eyelashes and dark brown eyes, a muscular physique, and he originated from Russia.

Hannah suspected she had seen him before but was yet unable to recall where and when. She felt terrorized by this man in her vision. Her hands shook. "He called me right after I had the vision. Wow, I feel like he's begun to stalk me." Hannah felt vulnerable and her hands turned from mild shaking to trembling.

She asked herself, 'Why me? That's really creepy.' Her eyelids continued to flutter rapidly. 'Yea, I realize you'd like to kill others. You've placed me on your kill list. Why?' The answer came to her. 'You know that I'm a detective's daughter. You've done your homework and realized that he's assigned to all major homicide cases, just like the one you'll commit. Consequently, you're aware that my father will be assigned to lead the investigation team to capture you.' Her breathing rate increased, similarly to a full-blown anxiety attack. Her face was drenched with profuse sweat. She drank some cold water. She poured some of the cold water on tissues and padded her eyes and face. 'I must disclose this information to my father and mother. But now is not the right time to share these gruesome details because my Abba has been called to serve in a war. He'll be going off to Gaza any day now. I care enough to not want to add any additional burdens on his back.'

Hannah received a call from her best friend, Elena. "Oh, by the way, rumor has it that Yigal is really crazy about you. He's let people know that he really wants to date you."

"Well then, he can call and ask me out directly. You know I'm easily approachable. Yigal is handsome, athletic, and cute but he hasn't brought up dating with me." She paused and said, "Yea, so let him call me directly." Hannah smiled, knowing that Yigal intended to ask her out.

"Okay, I'll let it be known. See you later. Bye."

Chapter Two

Hannah's paintbrush slashed a broad acrylic ribbon of lilac across the top of a stretched canvas perched on an easel in her bedroom. From a small window in her bedroom, she watched the setting sun melt into early September's dusty orange glow over the rooftops of houses in Ashkelon. By now, she'd lost patience with the idea of painting the colors of dawn. Hannah rinsed the brush and left it in the can of water. Then she sat on her bed and bit her nails. 'This doesn't help,' she thought. 'Biting my nails just makes it worse, and besides, I'm tasting paint. Ach – it's disgusting!' She went to the washroom, brushed her teeth, rinsed her mouth, and placed a piece of gum to rid herself of oil-paint taste.

Hannah had been having visions of something other than reality for as long as she could remember. One day, while at school, Hannah reported to a teacher about an accident that was about to occur. Soon after, two boys ran into each other and had fallen to the ground. Both required first aid for their scrapes; the other required stitches. She'd get bad or good news about people she knew. When she was sixteen, she anticipated that Dani would break up with her, and indeed it did happen. She predicted a major head-on car collision near the Tel Aviv Police Station and suggested that her father take a different route in his ride. Undeniably, the area she envisioned had a head-on collision which resulted in the death of both drivers. Fortunately, her father listened to Hannah's prediction.

Despite her gift of prescience, Hannah could not yet see herself dressed in the uniform of mandatory military service in just a few months. What should she do about this latest disturbing latest vision about a killer? She agonized about a way to disclose this to her parents. Her state of nervousness drove her to the bathroom twice in the last ten minutes.

Yoni, her father, a police detective and an officer soldier, was scheduled to leave that night for up to ten days of required military service, as a war had erupted between Gaza and Israel. She paced her bedroom floor back and forth. She thought, 'How will I share my gory visions when my Abba is off to war as a tank commander?' She felt alone and caged with her latest visions. A tear rolled down her cheek as she stood, straightened her skirt, smoothed her blouse, walked out of her bedroom, and went into her Abba's study.

Hannah saw him at rest in a chair, his feet on an ottoman, his kippah on his head, and eyes closed and quietly reciting a prayer. It appeared as if he were in a spiritually meditative state. She said, "Abba, can I speak to you, please? It's really urgent. I know it's not the best time… You're going off to war. Frankly, I have mixed feelings about sharing something with you. On the other hand, I absolutely must get it off my chest!" She inhaled and exhaled.

Yoni opened his eyes to see his beautiful blond daughter standing before him with a worrisome look on her face. He smelled her familiar scent of peach nectar from her hair conditioner. "Sure, what is it, Hannahle? What's the matter? Please have a seat."

"Oh, never mind. I'm so sorry to interrupt your prayers." Hannah changed her mind. She took a few steps away from her father, her head turned towards the floor.

"No, no, what's troubling you, my Hannahle?"

"Well, I don't want to put any additional pressures on you." Hannah was considerate towards her father and hesitant to share any further. "I know you have all kinds of pressures being a tank commander."

"Well, that's your choice, Hannah. But I care, you know. Please, tell… I feel protective and I care about you."

Hannah turned to face him again, and with a burst of energy, she raised her voice, "Abba! I had a vision of someone who will kill a young lady and he's begun to stalk me. I also envisioned myself as one of his victims. I saw the knife dripping in blood and the location of the first murder. Then, I got a highly suspicious call from a person claiming he's a businessperson who wanted me to paint a picture for him. He concealed his true voice, lied to me about his name, and provided me a wrong phone number. That's when I realized his identity is not 'Chaim.' His real name is Leonid Kozlov and he was born in Ukraine."

Uncontrollable tears dripped down her face. Yoni looked up at her from where he sat. He felt both helpless and protective of his beloved, gifted daughter. She wrung her hands from nerves, stood up, and paced back and forth.

"Hannahle, my Hannahle! No, honey. You will never be his victim! Not if I can help it. As a supervisor of detectives, you know this will never happen – ever! It's not an option! I don't understand how this information comes to you, but I've seen it long enough to take you seriously."

He loved his daughter greatly, but inwardly he thought Hannah might be overreacting. She had never come to him before with such advanced information regarding someone so sinister, so downright evil. He stood and wrapped her in his arms, a father's best attempt to calm her down.

She trembled from fear, gazed at the floor below, and began to shiver as well.

Yoni brought her a warm sweater.

"Hannah, don't worry, I'll help to protect you, but it will have to be when I return from war. Come with me to the kitchen and let me get you some water to drink. Your face… it's so red." He wiped away her tears with a strong but gentle hand and they walked to the kitchen. The scents of flavorsome seasons on the freshly made brisket permeated the air. Hannah heard her mother's voice in the dining room, speaking with her five-year-old brother, Aaron. Yoni poured Hannah a glass of water and motioned her to step into the hallway.

As the two stood just outside of the kitchen, Yoni waited for his cellphone to ring. "You know I'll soon meet up with a soldier who is giving me a ride to my Mirkava IV tank division. Fighting this war is a must but I hate to leave you, my family, especially at a time like this."

Hannah understood that her father as a commander was expected to lead his soldiers into battle. Even from her distant view of the kitchen window, Hannah observed black billowing smoke rise towards the sky and heard the faint rumbling of explosions. In 2014, the Gaza war had erupted after countless enemy rocket ships attacks penetrated civilian territories. Israeli Phantom jets buzzed the sky above. One could hear bombs explode in the distance. Distant smoke blanketed the sky above.

Hannah finished drinking the water and held her arms open to hug her father just as her brother ran up to Yoni, also wanting to give his father kisses and hugs. Aaron, dressed in khaki shorts, a white cotton shirt, and sneakers, grabbed his father's pant legs. Yoni, dressed as Colonel Yonatan Cohen, was dressed in army fatigues with military boots. His helmet, the *Tavor* semiautomatic submachine gun, not yet loaded, leaned against the wall near the front door. His unloaded Galil rifle also was also propped up against his nearby file cabinet.

Yoni's nickname amongst his friends was G.C., short for George Clooney, the actor. He had a distinct Hollywood-like appearance, with a masculine chin with a cleft, a six-foot-one frame, muscular body, and a full head of wavy black hair that had the very beginnings of pepper-gray near the sides of his ears. That summer, he had turned forty-four, but his youthful-looking appearance made his look more like thirty-four. In his free time, he enjoyed jogging and weight training. He always sported his gold wedding band and was very much in love with Sarah, his wife for nineteen years.

***

Tonight was the beginning of Sabbath, the Jewish day of rest. Sarah smoothed the tablecloth and patted it with feelings of love for Chana, her grandmother, who had stitched it many years ago. The cloth was hand-woven with red and blue flowers on a white background. Embroidered on the cloth's center were a Kiddush cup and a loaf of challah. While she touched the tablecloth, her eyes reddened as she remembered Chana. She'd prepared the Shabbat dinner: homemade chopped liver, chicken soup, a challah bread, a brisket, an Israeli salad consisting of finely chopped vegetables with olive oil and a touch of lemon, and a dessert of a layered sponge cake covered with chocolate frosting.

Earlier that day and in preparation for the Sabbath, Hannah accompanied her parents to purchase a brisket. They stopped at Sabre Meats – a butcher shop in Tel Aviv. A young muscular butcher with a scar on his left cheek and short, dark brown curly hair eyed her up and down while he held a large, sharp carving knife in his hand. He gazed at her with malice in his heart. He appeared sinister and hateful with evil thoughts and intent. She broke out in a sweat and her hands began to shake uncontrollably. Suddenly, he looked familiar to her. She struggled to pinpoint why he appeared so recognizable. Hannah concluded, "That's him – Leonid Kozlov – the killer."

Mr. Menachem Stern, the owner of the shop, asked Yoni, "Solved any murder cases lately?" Menachem Stern gazed towards the young butcher and added, "He's a topnotch detective, one of the best in all of Israel!"

Hannah recalled hearing those words and thought to herself, 'Yea, I'll bet he knows how to carve meat alright.'

Laying the apron aside, Sarah tucked her white blouse into the navy-blue skirt and caught a glimpse of her face in a small mirror that hung on the side of a kitchen cabinet near the sink. 'I'll soon look like her,' thought Sarah as she recalled Chana's blue eyes, white hair, wrinkly face, and bowed bulging finger joints deformed by devastatingly crippling arthritis. When Sarah was a child, she helped her grandmother bake challahs for the Sabbath. Her face reddened by the presence of this memory. Tears rolled down her cheeks as if they were miniscule streams dripping down a pristine wooded mountainside.

Hannah reached over to hug her mother and wondered, 'You're crying! Why?'

Hannah loved her mother and, with heartfelt concern, asked, "Ima, why are you crying?"

"When I look at the tablecloth, it makes me recall missing my Sapta. She was a wonderful grandmother to me. While my parents worked, it was my Sapta who took care of me." Her tears continued.

Next, tears began to run down Hannah's cheeks.

"Oh no! Why are you crying now, my Hannahle?"

"I feel so bad that you miss your Sapta. Also, you know, Abba is going off to war tonight." She pointed in the direction of her father who was in another room. "I'm scared for him being in a combat zone to protect us and Israel. I can't stand the thought of losing Abba." Hannah picked up her mother's apron and wiped her eyes.

Their conversation stopped when they heard Aaron's voice shout, "Come on, Abba, and let's go kick the soccer ball outside!"

Yoni replied, "Son, we are about to have our Sabbath dinner. Put the ball away. Come to me, jump up, and I'll carry you to the kitchen."

Aaron squirmed in his father's arms. As a sensitive child, he'd developed nervous tics and anxiety because of exploding bomb sounds in the distance. Whenever a nearby bomb exploded, he'd cover his face and begin to cry. Aaron picked up on the soft sobbing noises coming from around the corner. "Abba, why are they crying?"

Yoni noticed the lines of worry on his young son's face. Yoni's heart fell deeply into his gut. "It's a sad time, son. But we can make things better for them. Get ready to smile," he whispered into Aaron's ear.

As the father and son came into the kitchen, Yoni smiled and winked at Aaron. The child took the cue and said with a smile, "Can we eat? Please, Ima? I'm so hungry." He hugged his mother who wore an apron.

Sarah reached for her son and touched the sleeve of his shirt with her tear-stained fingers. "Yes, Aaron, but please change out of your gray shirt and put on your good white shirt. It's Sabbath. And, please wash your hands!"

"I think we should eat now. I have to leave soon," said Yoni as he looked at Sarah. The family sat themselves after Aaron returned, wearing a white shirt.

Hannah bit her cuticles and asked, "How long will the war last?" Before anyone could answer, she said, "Oh no, look, I'm bleeding now." She reached for some napkins and wrapped them around her two fingers.

Yoni spoke, "There's no way for me to know the answer to your question. But please stop your nail biting. It will not do anything to bring this war to an end. Your fingers are so talented… Do not chew them to bits!" There was a sound of irritation in his voice.

Hannah put her hands behind her back. She was on the verge of crying again. "Abba, I'm so worried about your going to war. Can't you tell?" In a huff, she ran off to her bedroom.

Yoni's eyes followed her as he thought, 'Her emotions! I know this is so typical for a teenage girl, but she feels them so strongly. Oh my God!'

Yoni walked towards the hallway and called out, "Hannah, we just sat down for dinner. Please come out of your room and join us." He was happy to hear her door open and he stood up to put his arms out for her when she came to the table. With tissues in hand, she patted her eyes and cheeks and gave him a sad smile.

Yoni said, "I'll be fine. Don't worry. I'm doing my part to defend our country."

Sarah handed a lit candle to Hannah and together they lit the Shabbat candles. Now the family sat blessed and welcomed the Sabbath. As Yoni chanted the traditional blessings over the bread, Hannah's face became a frown. She knew what was about to happen – some additional rocket ships landing in the vicinity.

"But Ima, at night I dream that we'll get killed by rockets." He pointed outside.

"Aaron, dreams don't come true. You won't die because you're afraid," said Hannah.

He asked, "Well then, why do my dreams not come true but yours do?"

Hannah kneeled down and looked him in his eyes. "Aaron, dreams are different from visions. We all have dreams like yours when we sleep. But I get visions that come to me when I'm awake. See, they're not exactly the same," said Hannah.

He still looked perplexed.

Yoni held Aaron in his lap as he continued praying, reciting the blessing over the bread. As a father, he recognized his son's vulnerable state of mind. He then recited the prayer over the wine. He took out his prayer shawl, the tallit, one that had been passed onto him by his own grandfather. He placed the tallit over Hannah and Aaron and blessed them by saying that God will provide them direction in life and that they should abide by the Ten Commandments. Yoni also blessed the state of Israel.

Aaron hugged Yoni and didn't want to let go. "Abba, please don't leave us, Abba… 'cause… I love you," said Aaron.

Hannah wiped away her tears.

"I love all of you. Prayers are over. Aaron, please take your seat. It's time to eat. Hannahle, here… take and pass the challah. Sarah, would you cut me a slice of brisket?"

Sarah revealed she had overheard her daughter's anxious conversation with Yoni when she asked, "Hannah, would you like me to make an appointment to see the psychologist you saw when you broke up with Dani?"

Hannah knew to be honest with her mother. "Dani dumped me when I wasn't ready to sleep with him. He was my first and only boyfriend and I thought he cared about me more than he really did. The psychologist was good about helping me with feelings of loss and abandonment. But in terms of clairvoyance and knowledge of psychic phenomenon, he has no comprehension about this subject matter. Most psychologists and psychiatrists don't know anything about psychic phenomenon and ESP. I won't go to any of them. My visions are real; they're not figments of my imagination. You can't convince me otherwise. Ima, I'm not a nut job and I'm not crazy!"

"Hannah, it's unusual for a young girl to have visions and be so convinced they're real," Yoni said.

Aaron piped up and said, "Yeah, Hannah, you're weird. You can't say what will be in the future."

"Oh, shut up, Aaron. You're just a baby. What do you know? There are psychic individuals who've helped solve crimes all over the world. You're just a pisher in kindergarten."

Yoni interrupted them. "Hey! Come on. We're a family. We care about one another. Let's treat one another with more respect."

Both Aaron and Hannah had deep feeling of veneration and respect for their parents. They settled down and ate the tasty homemade meal. Soon, Sarah asked, "Anyone wants seconds of my Sabbath cake?"

"Yes," Hannah and Aaron said in unison.

***

Hannah and Sarah cleared the dishes as Yoni's phone rang. "It's my driver. He's honking to tell me he's here." He went to gather what he needed and then called his family over to the front door where they said tearful goodbyes. Aaron was crying and shaking like a leaf in the wind. Hannah wept as well.

Aaron said, "Abba, please don't go."

Yoni removed a handkerchief from his pocket and helped Aaron blow his nose onto it. Yoni hid his emotions; he wished he could have cried out loud. He thought, 'My family needs me now. God, why do I have to leave them? It's really so unfair!' Automatically, his right hand tightened into a fist. His face appeared taut and pensive. The lines on his face appeared like old dried riverbeds, which hinted of his anxiety about being in this war. He remained quiet and thought to himself, 'Men aren't supposed to cry. I'll be strong for them.'

Sarah detected a faint tremor in his voice as if he were about to cry. She knew how distraught he was about leaving his family behind. After some final hugs and kisses, Yoni left but hid his own inner sorrow. As a tank commander leading his men into battle, he felt he needed to be in control of his emotions. In his wallet, a picture of his family would remind him of his purpose in life. He'd admire this photograph and smile lovingly about his family.

Hannah went into her room with the intent to complete a sketch. After drawing a few lines on her easel, she couldn't concentrate. Her sad feeling continued as she cried.

She turned to her mother and said, "I know we're both heartbroken about Abba's departure. Can we enjoy a mother-daughter hug? I know we don't agree about my being psychic but I still love you and I need you in my life."

"I love you too, my Hannahle. You're so precious to me." They hugged each other and remained motionless, as if time stood still. Their mother-daughter bond was strengthened by their healing tears. They continued their hugs, each sad about missing Yoni.

That night, Hannah was barely able to fall asleep and lay in her bed feeling terrorized by a vision. Her nightgown and pillows were wet from sweat. The words and the sound of his killer's voice kept replaying in her mind. "Yea, I will stalk you and make you one of my victims." She went to the kitchen refrigerator to drink a bottle of cold water. She looked around to make sure a killer was not present. She listened carefully. Since she had these frightening visions, hyper-vigilance took over, especially at night. She became super aware of her surroundings, listening to all sounds, house creeks, and anything out of the ordinary in her environment. Her instinctual feelings told her to hide but she reminded herself that these sounds were normal and thought, 'I must be overreacting.'

Chapter Three

It was a pitch-black night with winds of twenty-five miles per hour. He hadn't slept in days. There were dark blue rings under his eyes, his cheeks were sunken, and he remained unshaven. He sported a fairly thick beard. His family didn't know when he'd return. They were asleep. No one yet welcomed him back at one in the morning. Still wearing his army fatigues, holding his helmet, and his hair uncombed, he returned with considerably unpleasant body odors. These odors permeated all around and spread to his immediate surroundings. He headed for the shower, but Sarah roused from her sleep. "Yoni!" she said in a loud whisper. "It's you? You're back!" She smiled like a little girl opening a birthday or a Hanukah gift.

Sarah rose from the bed and threw her arms around him. She smiled and held him close. With heartfelt sincerity, she said, "I love you. We were so worried about your safety. The children were so nervous and asked about you daily." With both hands cuffed, she held his face close to hers. "Welcome back, my love. Oh, I'm so happy you're home." She reached to hug and continued kissing him. Quickly, her kisses turned into additional gestures of passion.

"Sarah, my love, I'm sorry. I haven't showered in ten days. I feel that my body odors are downright disgusting. I don't want to gross you out by these horrendous odors."

She ignored his sweaty, grimy stink. "You look very hot, honey, so sexy in your combat uniform," she said as she took his hand and pulled him toward their bed. With her other hand, she lifted her nightgown while she massaged his tender loins. "Oh, now help me take off the rest of my nightgown."

"Yes… yes…" he breathed heavily as the garment fell, "yes… and now, my uniform…"

As his uniform piled on top of her discarded gown, Sarah lay back and smiled, kissing her husband as if it were their wedding night. Their loving sounds confirmed the extent of their intimately deep-rooted feelings.

A bit later, while still entwined in a lovers' embrace, each slid into a deep and well-deserved slumber.

***

At first sight of daylight, Yoni awakened and took a long hot shower. He shaved and put on clean clothes. Then he went to awaken Hannah and Aaron.

Aaron wrapped himself around his Abba, much like a koala bear would. He continued to hug his father for several minutes while he whimpered as he spoke, "Abba, you're home. You're here. I missed you!" He continued to cling to his father while he sucked his thumb.

"I love and missed you too, my Aaron."

After Hannah embraced her father, she asked, "Abba, we were really worried about you. Are you okay? What was it like being cooped up in a tank during the war?"

"I'll tell you all about it over breakfast. How about we all have breakfast in our kitchen?"

Dressed in her pink robe, Sarah brought everyone some fresh squeezed orange juice while they each smeared jam on their toasts and consumed the freshly prepared scrambled eggs.

Yoni said, "Well, this was a very different experience. We discovered underground tunnels used to store enemy missiles equipped with warheads and weapons; we discovered actual underground tunnels into Israel so that our citizens might be easily kidnaped. We found that children and families were used as scapegoats by our enemy. In other words, children and families were placed in the likely targeted areas for our retaliation efforts. That was very sad for me to witness because children need to be spared from the spoils of war. We also blew up several enemy underground terrorist cells."

Yoni rested a moment. He was weary of war and changed the subject. "At long last, I'm home where I belong with you… my family." His emotions surfaced as he welled up with tears. His eyes turned reddish-pink in color with tiny pronounced veins. "I carried your pictures in my wallet and I gazed at them daily. I missed you so badly." He paused and then said, "Tell you the truth, I felt terribly heartbroken being away from you." Tears zigzagged down his cheeks. He took out his handkerchief and blew his nose. He reached for Sarah's hand and held it tight. Looking at his children, he said, "I'm so sorry to be crying in front of you."

His family surrounded Yoni, all huddling closely. Every member of the Cohen family cried as they reached for tissues to dry their eyes. Everyone hugged Yoni.

"I love you, Abba," said Aaron while eating his last piece of toast. "I love you too, Ima. Hannah, do you want the rest of my eggs?"

"Sure," she said with a smile.

"Finish breakfast and get dressed," Sarah told the children. "No school today, and no work for your father. Maybe we can take a family hike or go to a museum in Tel Aviv? What is your preference?"

Hannah indicated her preference to go on a family hike. "Maybe we can hike and swim at Sachna, or in the Galil mountains somewhere? I feel like that would be lots of family fun, especially if we can combine it with a picnic lunch."

Sarah and Yoni both said, "Yea, let's do it. I'll pack some sandwiches if you each pack your own waters. Find your most comfortable hiking shoes and I'll bring additional sun protection cream. Also bring your swimsuits along." Everybody smiled, looking forward to being together as a family.

"We can kick the soccer ball, Abba! Yei!" Aaron said as he handed his plate to his sister.

Yoni smiled and gave Aaron an approving look. "Yes, take your soccer ball with you on our hike. Better than that, we'll deflate the ball now and we'll bring the small portable pump. How about that?"

Aaron smiled and winked.

***

After the family hike and swim at Sachna, they returned several hours later. Yoni found Hannah at her easel in the bedroom. He asked if they could talk. When she nodded yes, he said, "My Hannahle, so tell me what's new with you." His tall body filled the doorframe.

She put down the paintbrush and sat on her bed. "Oh, I'm fine. I got together with a couple of my friends, finished another painting, and… I do want to share my vision with you. But you just went through a lot in this war. Maybe we talk tomorrow or the day after? I think you need to rest, have good home cooking, and get lots of sleep."

"Sounds good to me, Hannahle."

"But… Abba… I can share that since you're the assigned lead detective, your responsibilities will be to apprehend this killer. This will be a huge challenge for law enforcement."

"If that's the case, then I will do whatever I have to do. We'll talk more about this in a couple of days. Where is your brother?"

"Aaron!" Hannah called out as Yoni stepped inside the small room and sat in the chair at Hannah's desk, "Aaron! Where are you? Abba wants to talk with you!"

The boy came running down the hall with his soccer ball as Hannah stood up and reached for a paintbrush. "Can we go outside and play?" he asked.

27

"I don't know. Ask Abba!"

Instead, Aaron rolled the ball under the desk chair where Yoni was sitting.

"Goal!" Yoni said and watched his son's smile widen. "How's kindergarten?"

"I h–h–hate k–k–kindergarten," Aaron said with a scowl on his face. "The k–kids are m–mean to me. They don't l–l–like me because I am too u–upset about the w–war. Abba, I m–missed you when you were a–away. School wasn't g–good for me when you were g–gone. I thought you w–weren't going to c–come back. There are k–kids that call me very b–bad names." It became apparent that Aaron's stuttering condition was pronounced.

"I missed you too, my Aaron." Yoni returned to the subject matter of his adjustment issues at school. "Now that I'm back, I'll talk to your teacher. You shouldn't be made fun of. That's not right and it's not fair! I'll arrange for you to get help with your stuttering issues. You're a wonderful boy and we'll get to the bottom of it. Don't you worry, okay?"

"Thanks, Abba."

Tomorrow, I will talk to your teacher."

"Okay, Abba."

Yoni made it a point to visit Aaron's teacher later. And he also gave some thought to Hannah's visions as he powered down for a nap with his son. It was good to be home, yes, good, but…

***

Later that evening, Yoni found Hannah sitting on the couch, reading a novel. "Hannah, let's talk now, not in a few days," he said, "I'm all ears. Let's talk about it, I mean, your vision."

"Abba, I don't mind sharing my recent vision but it would probably make more sense to converse the day you're actually assigned the case. At that time, you'll have some description of the murder. Does that make sense to you, Abba? You'll probably want to take notes or even make a video of my statements. Can we postpone this conversation until you're actually assigned this case? You're dealing with a very disturbed psycho. Abba, promise me you'll be careful. I don't want anything bad to happen to you."

"Yea, it's better to talk about it when I'm actually assigned the case. That's fine, Hannah. Oh, how's your art coming along? Are you working on paintings that interest you more than others?"

"Abba, I've entered a contest for the best high school painting in all of Israel. It will be judged by the Letzior's Art College faculty. I hope I can be in the final round, maybe even win." A pensive look overcame her as she added,

"Well, I'm sure there will be some tough competition in this art competition; the very best high school kids, in all of Israel, will be there."

"Ima and I both think you're such an amazingly talented young lady. You should win. You have such incredible talent."

"Thanks, Abba. I hope the judges will feel that way."

Chapter Four

Yoni drove to his Tel Aviv police office. On the way, a white sandy beach coastline, several colorful sailboats that darted the Mediterranean Sea, and the crystal-clear blue sky caught Yoni's attention. Inwardly, he smiled, appreciating Tel Aviv's natural beauty. He drove past a neighboring historic city of Jaffa, an appendage of Tel Aviv and an area where Jonah was swallowed by a whale. Yoni still felt so exhausted from all his sleepless nights living and fighting from a tank. He wondered, 'This will be a tough first day back. How will I concentrate on my first day being at work?'

He let out a deep breath, and with partly closed eyes, he powered on his computer. Over sixteen hundred emails awaited him. He managed to reply to some before his scheduled meetings.

He was assigned to the case of apprehending a serial killer, as had been predicted by Hannah. Yoni read the brief description of today's latest case assignment:

*"A young lady, drugged and raped, estimated to be twenty-one or twenty-two, was strangled and stabbed to death. Her entire face was so badly smashed; it was hard to identify her. Her head lay in the blood-soaked sand. A handwritten note scripted in the victim's blood stated, 'You f***** whore,' you deserve to die!"*

It would take some laboratory time to ascertain for sure but it appears as if the victim had been raped."

He was overcome by shivers as he read and reread these words of his latest assignment. 'My goodness, who the hell could have perpetrated such a sadistically cruel act?' He shook his head in disbelief that monsters like this exist.

***

On his way home, Yoni stopped at the local market and bought grapes, guavas, and oranges. He thought to himself, 'Hannah and I might have us a snack and talk about her vision when I get home. Maybe she'll want to talk with me before our family dinner?' On his drive home, he thought about how proud he was of his Hannah. How mature, artistic, and loving she was! Suddenly, a radiantly beaming smile appeared on his face.

Indeed, she was a beautiful young lady with a fair skin complexion, blue eyes, a cute pixie nose, and five-foot-six height with small freckles dotting her cheeks. One of the most striking aspects of her appearance was the cleft indentation on her chin, much like her father. She was highly responsible, never needing reminders about her homework or any school-related projects. She'd become immersed in her art projects, spending countless hours perfecting color tints, shades, and brushstrokes. Today, she worked on a biblical sketch theme of King David and his slaying of Goliath, the menacing giant.

***

Yoni's car turned into the driveway of the parking lot just as Hannah had also arrived home. "Shalom, Hannahle. How's my lovely daughter?" He walked over and gave her a big hug and planted a kiss on her forehead.

"Hi, Abba. I'm good. What's up? How was your first day back at work?" She smiled.

"I was assigned a high-priority case of a killer, just as you predicted. Can we talk about your vision? Let's go inside and have a snack. I brought home some fresh fruit, if you'd like."

"Sure, Abba."

"I'll write some notes while I listen to your narrative. I'll also record our conversation on my cellphone. These notes can be crucial and helpful in solving this case."

The father and daughter agreed to meet in the living room after each changed into more comfortable clothes. Moments later, Yoni washed fresh fruit which he carried a fruit bowl into their living room. "Hannahle, it's time for our talk. Would you like some fruit that I just picked out at Simon's market?"

He hugged Sarah. "Honey, can we wait to have our dinner, maybe a half an hour or so?"

"Yea, no problem."

Hannah held a glass of lemonade. "Yea, I might just help myself to some fruit. I know you want to know the details of my visions." Hannah sat on the recliner while Yoni sat on the light sandy-colored living room couch. He had a notepad, a pen, and had turned on his cellphone for video recording.

Hannah took a long sip of lemonade and closed her eyes. Within a few seconds, her closed eyes fluttered as if she were in a dreamlike state. Her eyeballs seemed to travel from side to side, first from left, then to right, and from right to left. She seemed to be in a deep trance. Her face reddened and her breathing became labored. Hannah's eyes were now closed. "He's maybe twenty-two or twenty-three… with a tan complexion and a scar on his left cheek. He's about five foot, ten inches in height, and has a very muscular appearance. He looks like a bodybuilder – big muscle with evil intents but fit-looking. His black hair is shortly cropped and curly. Eyes… his eyes are dark brown with long, almost black eyelashes. And he's evil… sinister-looking. His stare is frightening with malicious, evil desires." When Hannah described his sinister-like demeanor, she asked if her father could bring her a blanket. She became cold, more like shivering.

Yoni stopped writing when Hannah stopped speaking. He brought her a warm blanket. He looked at his daughter who appeared to be in a trance. Her rapid eye movements were indicative of being in a deep trance. They both sat in silence for a moment until Hannah said with eyes still closed, "Abba, are you sure you want to hear all of the gory details?"

"Well, yes. I'm a detective and I need to know all the details and clues pertaining to this case. Hannah, I see you're nervous, so take your time and sip your lemonade, honey. We'll get through it." He handed Hannah her lemonade.

"It's not good, Abba. It was two days ago at about 11:00 p.m. in the evening. He had picked up a woman in a Tel Aviv sex bar, the Volga. She's seductive and wants to do sex tricks for Leonid. They discuss money for that purpose. I hear his voice clearly. He has a distinct Russian accent, although he tries to hide it. He hates all women. That night, he has evil intent in his heart."

Hannah sipped her lemonade and instinctually sensed that her father appeared worried and upset. Yoni's face is taut like a wound-up rubber band, with clenched jaws. His right hand was clasped stiff. Yoni broke into a cold sweat and his heart pounded as if he was sprinting an all-out race.

"Abba, this is hard to tell you. Are you okay?"

"Yes, I'm fine. Well, not really. Israel's never ever had a killer like this; he'll be a challenge to capture. I can see it already. But go on. Keep telling me more, Hannah. I'm all ears."

"They enter his van. It is an American-made gray SUV. I see them smoking marijuana. She sniffs white powder. Next, he chloroforms her. He injects her with a more powerful and deadly drug – heroin. She's unconscious by now.

Next, I see him place a towel over her face. Her chest and body bounces up and down. She's having full-blown seizures. She bites her own tongue in the process. He punches and slaps her in the face, over and over again. She's bleeding profusely from her nose and mouth. The entire towel is blood-red. Then, he ties her hands. And then… oh no, Abba, he rapes her, over and over again." Hannah now covered her face with both hands as if she was terrorized by reliving her vision. Hannah's breathing became erratic as she appeared noticeably frightened. Her eyes remained closed while she relived her vision. Tears emerged from the corners of her eyes. Hannah begins to emerge from this trance. She cried about what had happened to this now-lifeless victim. She said, "Abba, could this become me?"

Yoni's heart began to race. "Hannah… Hannah, that's a horrible thing to see in your mind. No, this will never happen to you! NEVER! How about we take a bit of a break?" He got up and reached out to hold her hand. "I want to get some cold water. Hannah, come with me to the kitchen." She put her arm around his shoulder. He carried his cellphone, notepad, and pen.

As they walked to the kitchen, it dawned on Yoni that Hannah had stated that she too would become one of his lifeless victims. He looked frightened and this thought automatically triggered him to reach for his holstered gun.

Yoni filled a glass with cold water. "Let's sit here and talk." They each found a kitchen chair, the ones with pastel colors and floral decorations. "When you're ready, tell me more of your vision." They now sat in their kitchen breakfast nook. A small glass table separated the two as they ignored their hunger pangs for dinner.

Hannah closed her eyes. Within seconds, they fluttered once again. "Abba," Hannah said as she sat at the table, "he's a very bad man. He yells evil things to the now-unconscious victim. These words I never heard my friends or family say. He screams in rage, he chokes her with his hands, and he shrieks vile words. Then, he starts his van and drives toward the mountain of olives, quite near the Jewish cemetery where he parks his van. There, he grabs an icepick from under the seat and repeatedly stabs her, again and again. He aims for her chest, breasts, stomach, and her ribs. Both his fists pound on her chest. I hear the sound of bones cracking!" More tears welled up in Hannah's eyes. She imagined her father's eyes glaze in horror.

"This… is… appalling. Disgusting! Terrifying!" Yoni's voice conveyed feelings of anger and fear. "My daughter, why does God allow you to have this gift… and this curse?"

"I know, Abba, I know. It is not easy. But you must know this information as I do. God allows you to be my Abba; He allows you to do your work. We must be here to assist each other. Right?"

"Yes. With your gift, you were given wisdom, Hannah. Tell me as much as you can, but only as much as you're able to. I know how difficult it is for you to deliver these messages."

"I'll continue," she said.

Yoni nodded with a, "Yes."

"After he's stabbed her repeatedly, he writes a note with the victim's own blood. His hands… they're so bloody. No gloves, Abba. There is so much blood all around. He repeatedly screams, 'You're a f***** whore, you slut! You deserve to die!' Then he places the bloody note on her chest diaphragm. He will allow her naked body to burn and rot in the blistering Middle-East sun. The blood on her face, neck, and hair pools together. It blends with the sand below. Abba, he takes some brush branches and attempts to sweep away any evidence of his now-bloody sneakers. He wears a mask as he darts back to his van. That is the exact vision, Abba."

Hannah emerged from her 'trance.' She needed to wash her face with cold water. She was mentally and physically exhausted. Yoni gave her tissues to dry her crying eyes. In the meantime, Yoni finished writing every word on paper and he had a recording of Hannah's vision narration. She reached over to snack on a few burgundy-red grapes.

"Abba, in appearance I resemble the victim, as I'm also blond, have blue eyes, and am five foot, six inches in height. The thought of being his next victim scares the hell out of me. This case is going to present enormous challenges for you, Abba." Hannah began to bite her nails.

"Hannahle, I know you saw what you saw. I feel troubled, both as your father and as a detective. But I will do everything I can to protect you and others from this murderer. YOU WILL NOT BE HIS VICTIM! Believe me – your father. Please do not spend any time in worry. Keep up with your studies, your painting, and with your good friends. Oh, one other thing. Please don't discuss this case with anyone, as it could easily jeopardize this case outcome and your own safety. And if you are to have any other visions, let's talk. It would be very helpful if you could come up with where he lives, his occupation, and some additional van identification. I'm going to invite one of our forensic artists, Moshe, to draw the killer's face. How about if Moshe comes tomorrow after school, after my work?" Yoni peeled an orange and offered Hannah some.

"Sure, Abba."

Yoni's right eyelid began to twitch. "You know the information we discussed is highly confidential. You must not speak about this to anyone – only Moshe and myself. Otherwise, it could easily compromise my investigation outcome."

Hannah got up from the sofa and moved towards the window. She paused to drink her lemonade. "Abba?"

"Yes, Hannahle?"

"This is very unusual. I am not like any of my friends. Most fathers and daughters don't have these types of deep conversations. I want to be a normal teen, Abba. As your daughter and being a psychic, I wonder, do you see me as normal?"

"Yes, of course you're normal. You're blessed with abilities that most of us don't have, including myself. I know you're worried, but as your father, I will do my absolute best to protect you. You know I love you with all my soul, my Hannahle."

"I'm going to go call Moshe and see if he's available to meet with us tomorrow afternoon."

"All right. I'm going to do my homework soon. I love you, Abba." Hannah got up to stretch her loins.

"How about you wash your face, take a couple of minutes for yourself, and join us for our family dinner. Okay?"

"Yes, of course. I love Ima's cooking! Oh, by the way, how does your boss feel about a psychic helping in this homicide investigation?"

"I'm not sure, Hannah."

Chapter Five

Yoni's cellphone rang and awakened him from a deep sleep. It was 6:00 a.m. and Commander Gidon Mordechai Levy was irate. He launched into a reproachful verbal tirade of criticisms of Yoni. "What on Earth are you thinking about when you have your clairvoyant daughter involved in solving crimes? What's gotten into you? Have you lost it, man? Are you stark-raving mad… crazy? We've never used any psychics to solve crimes."

Yoni listened and didn't yet respond immediately.

Levy continued, "Did you forget your forensic training? You rely on your daughter who claims to be a psychic? When Moshe told me he was coming to do a sketch and about your daughter being a clairvoyant, I couldn't believe it. I demand an explanation. What's gotten into you, Yoni?"

Yoni was quite angry at his boss but felt this emotion needed to be contained.

The commander in his early fifties was a no-nonsense kind of a guy. His rank was a leaf with two stars and he believed in facts, black or white, with no room for woo-woo speculations. He had served in the IDF Special Forces Unit in the Golani Brigade where he fought against Hezbollah in Lebanon. His bravery earned him the high rank of an aloof general. Levy's reputation for being a hardnosed, demanding IDF Special Forces Commander only followed him when he assumed the office of chief of police in Tel Aviv.

Yoni replied, "Commander Levy, I'm sorry I've angered you, but yes, my daughter is a psychic and feels she can be of help to us. This special type of gift has been used to help solve crimes in several countries around the world. Granted, this is not the usual forensic protocol, sir, but at this time, we don't have any other information about the killer or the victim. My daughter predicts there will be several other crimes he'll commit. Can you give me a chance? I believe I may be able to solve this crime, sir. Of course, I'll always keep you in the loop, sir."

"What's your plan?"

"Moshe will create a drawing of the murderer based on information from my daughter's visions. I'll meet with my detectives and police officers. They will go from club to club in Tel Aviv asking if they've seen a person who resembles the sketch. We'll interview the victim/victim's families for possible clues. I'll meet with a well-known forensic psychiatrist, Dr. Eliezer, who will provide additional psychiatric information. I'll speak to our IDF headquarters because they review psychological evaluations of IDF soldiers. Perhaps they can review their files for the last five to six years? I suspect that some IDF rejections due to mental reasons will emerge. I'll pick a handful of experienced detectives to assist me. Right now, that's the plan but I'm sure my strategy will expand because this is truly a work in progress, sir."

"Yoni, I've never heard of a decorated detective like you resort to such Meshugas like having a psychic solve a crime. Okay, I'll tell you what. I'll give you three weeks, that's twenty-one days, to come up with proof/evidence. No, better than that, I'll give you four weeks. If you can't meet this deadline, I'll have to reassign the case to someone else. I may also have to consider a demotion in your rank, that is if you don't come up with real evidence for arresting this killer."

"I'll do my best, sir. But I do have requests."

"Yes? Like what?"

"I'd like to choose three lead detectives of my choice. I want Raffi, Yitzchak, and Shmuel. I'm likely to need additional police manpower as well."

"Yoni, this is the first time I've ever allowed something like this to happen in my department and under my watch. Keep me up to date on this investigation and give me fair warning if you see any dangers that lie ahead. I trust you more now, but you are going to have to work hard to prove to me that you know what you're doing."

When Yoni got off the phone, he did push-ups and sit-ups to rid himself of his pent-up resentment. "That son-of-a-bitch boss of mine. I'll show him!"

***

Leonid, aged twenty-three, was still sweating from his intense workout. His biceps and deltoid muscles were pumped. Although he showered and toweled himself dry, beads of sweat still clung to his face, neck, and armpits. His breathing was labored from his workout. His physique appeared like a Gray's Anatomy chart, with every muscle and vein bulging like Michelangelo's statue of David. Freshly shaven with sweet-smelling cologne on his face, he now changed into a tight-fitting black shirt which only accentuated his bodybuilder physique. His tight shirt revealed the outlines of his abdominal muscles. His adrenaline pumped at a rapid pace. He appeared ready for action-kinky and sadistic sex.

He got into his van and drove to the Ben David Middle-Eastern Restaurant in Tel Aviv. While driving, he listened to Russian punk rock with heavy metal sounds – all in Russian. Today, his car's steering wheel served as his drums while he pounded his fists to loud rhythms. He sang loudly, largely off key as he lit up a big, fat marijuana joint. A cloud of gray smoke overtook his van which had become cloudy with marijuana fumes.

After a ten-minute ride, he arrived and parked near a Mediterranean restaurant called Ben David. He called over the meltzar, a server. Some water and Middle-Eastern relishes, olives in olive oil, a scoop of humus, tahini, pita bread, and pickles were placed on the table. He was handed a menu. After a few minutes, the waiter asked him if he was ready to order.

Leonid spoke with a thick Russian accent. "I vant chieken chabbab and Kiefka. Is good tonight? Vat you say? Is fresh?"

"Oh yes, it's very fresh and well done. We make it on the spot using imported spices. It's not shipped from elsewhere. It happens to be one of the customer's most favorite dishes," said the young server in hopes of pleasing his customer.

"Okay, good! Bring to me a taste before I order. Is good? Okay?"

"Normally, we don't do that, but sure. That won't be a problem. I'll bring you a sample."

As he left heading towards the kitchen, Leonid eyed him with great interest, with erotic ulterior motives. He peered at the server's behind, imagining how sexy he'd appear stark naked.

The server quickly returned with a piece of chicken kabab.

Leonid first smelled the kabab, took a couple of bites, and with a faint smile he said, "Is good, very good. Bring to me, please. Oh, vat comes vit Chabbab?"

"Basmati rice with raisins and almond slivers. Is that okay?"

"Yea, very good!"

Moments later, the entire dish was brought out with basmati rice seasoned with cumin, coriander, turmeric, ground cayenne pepper, slivers of almonds, and raisins. Leonid ordered a side portion of finely chopped Israeli salad. He belched a couple of times as if to say, "I'm satisfied. Is very good. I'm chappy."

The server intuitively felt there was something awfully malevolent and dangerous about his customer. He broke into a cold sweat and couldn't wait for Leonid to leave the restaurant.

It was 9:30 p.m. when he got into his van and drove to the Volga Club in Tel Aviv. Till he found parking, it was now 10:00 p.m. when he entered the sex club. He wore a disguise of a beard and mustache. The beard covered his left cheek's scar. He was least concerned about the garlic and Middle-Eastern spice odors on his breath and mouth. That night, he was obsessed with other intentions – sexy, hateful, and murderous ones. Just the thought of the seduction pick-up was so enticing that he instantly became erotically stimulated. He practiced the seduction pick-up many times in his mind and appeared to be focused on his goal – seduction pick-up, drugs, sex, violent rage, and a kill as the final chapter.

The Volga Club was known for pole dancing and erotic liaisons. The evening temperatures of two days earlier still hovered, around seventy-four degrees, perfect for Leonid to show off his muscles without needing a sweater or a wind breaker. Some individuals could easily conclude that he was a handsome young man, but without the beard, there was a presence of a well-defined scar on his left cheek.

Several customers were smoking. An odor of burning tobacco permeated the air. Lights were turned low, except for the well-lit stage which had two pole dancers gyrating in sexually provocative movements and poses. Leonid felt instant surges of adrenaline when a beautiful young server approached him. With sandy-blond hair and a well-defined dancer's body, she alternated between being a pole dancer and a server. She was there to satisfy his erotic needs and fantasies. Moreover, she was eager to add to her income by performing sexual tricks which provided her enough money for drugs. She smiled and snuggled closely towards Leonid.

"Vat you vant, choney? I'm here to bring you to cheaven, the stars, the moon, and nirvana. Vit me you'll chave the best time ever!" She took his hand and placed it on her buttocks. "Vat you vant, sweetie? I bring to you magic." Clearly, she originated in Russia and spoke with a pronounced accent. She stuck out her tongue and wiggled it from one side to another in an erotically suggestive manner. She leaned over to expose her opulently large breasts including their cleavage. She pulled his head towards her bust.

"You like vat you see? My boobs vant to be touched by you."

Leonid did not yet answer her to that but said, "Bring to me Russian Mule vit double voodka."

She returned shortly and whispered in Leonid's ear, "Vat else you vant? I'm chere to satisfy you, my Russian Czar, my king. You can never chave pleasure like I viel show you, not ever vit your vife, or vit girlfriend. Nobody else can give to you vat I do for you. Nobody! I promise you cheavenly ecstasy."

"How much?"

"Five hundred shekels for your heart's desire, my Czar."

"How about three hundred shekels and I supply veed and blow?"

"Vie got a deal. Any time you vant, my Czar."

He drank his Russian Mule and began to feel greater surges of excitement in his loins. "Vie go now," he announced.

"Okay, I tell boss. My Czar, you von't regret it. I promise you nirvana – great pleasure."

They entered his gray SUV. She sat next to him, massaging his inner thigh. Leonid pulled out a joint of weed, one almost as large as a small cigar. He lit it, closed his eyes, and inhaled marijuana smoke. He gave her the weed which she gladly inhaled. She rolled back her eyes with feelings of deep relaxation. She sighed and said, "Ooh!" Next, she closed her eyes and listened to a Russian heavy metal band. She banged the dashboard in sync to the loud metallic music sounds. They continued smoking their weed. As if he were an orchestra conductor directing musicians, he carefully observed her. With her left hand, she began to massage his private part. She unzipped his pants. Leonid's private part stood firm like a mountain in the Andes or Everest. Her mouth now cupped his private part. They now drove from Tel Aviv towards Jerusalem. He pulled out some blow and they both inhaled the white powder. With each passing second, he observed that she was unable to hold up her head. It drooped and dangled from side to side. Her speech was increasingly slurred and she was unable to hold onto a single thought. Her eyes were dazed. She asked, "Ven you vant sex, my cavalier, my Czar? Vant more oral? You tell me vat you vant." By now, her words were jumbled, incoherent, and barely audible. He ignored her questions as she drifted into a deep, unconscious slumber.

Next, Leonid placed chloroform liquid on a white towel and forcibly pressed it over her face. He pulled over to the side of a tree-lined road and transferred her limp body to the rear of his van. There, he repeatedly slapped and punched her while she appeared to be in a deep stupor. She had a broken nose, broken jaws, and she bled profusely. Her eyes appeared like those of a raccoon with black and blue circles. Due to his aggressive poundings, several of the victim's teeth were now lying on the van's carpet. He placed a white towel over her face, which turned bright red from the gushing blood. He removed her jeans and underwear. He removed his pants and underwear and raped her repeatedly. She was in a deep stupor by now – completely unconscious. He threw additional punches to her face and head. Next, Leonid injected her with heroin and she instantaneously convulsed. She bit her tongue repeatedly. Her breathing became shallow. He resumed his drive towards the mountain of olives in Jerusalem. He then parked his car and physically picked her up. He transported her to the Jewish cemetery. Her body was slumped over as if she were a ragdoll. There were many ancient gravestones with Hebrew inscriptions. He placed her face-up, and with his icepick, he now repeatedly stabbed her in the chest area. Gurgling sounds were heard. She now choked on her own blood. Her breathing, at first shallow and infrequent, was now absent – non-existent. He found an even sharper knife and stabbed her over and over again. A plethora of blood was everywhere. Some even streamed down towards the nearby weeds. To himself, he said, "See how powerful I am, you bitch!"

He opened his knapsack and took out a white sheet of paper. Using the victim's own blood, with his index finger he wrote, *"You f***** whore. You f***** slut. You deserve to die. You f***** bitch."* The blood, sand, and the victim's blond hair were now all clumped together. Except for a few stars, it remained stark dark outside. As if he were a gorilla in a wild jungle, he triumphantly pounded his chest and screamed out loud, "You f***** whore! You deserve to die!" He spat on the lifeless victim.

He found a number of wild desert shrubs and managed to cut a few of the branches. He swept away any traces of his blood-ridden footsteps. As if he were Zorro in the middle of the night, he quickly vanished. In his van, he smoked additional weed and sniffed additional blow. He appeared happy and proud of himself. Next, he raised both arms towards the sky as if to suggest he was the victor, a champion, like a prize fighter at the end of a successful fight.

He ignited his van and while he drove, he thought to himself, 'Mother, you're chappy now, you f***** bitch? You're a lowlife vermin. You piece of shit. I chate your guts. Yes, look at me. I'm the monster you created!' As his words gushed out of his mouth, he continued his fuming barrage of hate by cursing his mother and all women alike. He continued to hide feelings of emotional abandonment long forgotten about from his childhood.

By early morning, the Jerusalem Gazette newspaper reported: *"A young lady found savagely killed and her limp, lifeless body placed in the Jewish Holy Cemetery in Jerusalem. The victim was repeatedly stabbed with what appears to be a sharp dagger. A note written with the victim's own blood appeared on her diaphragm. The body has yet to be identified. If you have any leads, please contact your local police headquarters. This case has already been assigned to the Tel Aviv police force."*

Chapter Six

The sun beamed its warm fall rays of a comfortable seventy-six degrees Fahrenheit. A young man, a senior from the same high school, had asked Hannah out on a date. She liked Yigal, but right now her art projects and her visions demanded so much of her time. She felt overwhelmed with dreadful anxiety about these latest visions. Her previous sound sleeping habits had all vanished. Her erratic sleep patterns made her feel tired and sleep-deprived. Today, she sweated profusely and wondered if it was because of the increased outside temperatures or was it a part of her recent anxiety symptoms. She wondered how to best postpone dating Yigal. She asked him if it was okay that they go out in a few weeks' time due to her many art commitments. Truth be told, Yigal had been having a crush on Hannah for several months. He concluded, "What's another month or two?" Enamored by Hannah, he was inclined to agree to just anything she'd say. They had had heart-to-heart conversations about the recent loss of his grandmother to cancer. Cognizant about his parents' recent divorce, Hannah was drawn to Yigal's vulnerable state of mind.

She smiled all the way home with a skip and a hop to her step. She seemed ready for romance in her life but… held onto some questions about Yigal. She was unable to yet put her finger on it. Perhaps a vision would reveal more about him. Awed about the pristine crystal-clear blue waters of the Mediterranean Sea and its sandy beaches in Ashkelon, she entered her apartment complex. The sea was less than a block away from where she lived. The fragrances of salty seawater made their way to her nasal passages. Today, there were medium-sized waves, good enough for beginner to intermediate surfer level. In the distance, she saw a colorful sailboat regatta. She thought to herself, 'Wow! Look at the blue sky and the clear seawaters today. Oh, I'm so lucky to live right next to the sea where I can swim, get together with friends, boogie board, and sunbathe… anytime I want to. Maybe Yigal and I will have our first date at these long-stretching beaches. Maybe Yigal and I will even have a picnic lunch?' Then her logical mind crept forward and she concluded, 'I do need to know him better before I'd ever consider such a romantic beach date.'

Yoni came home early and he mentioned that Moshe will arrive shortly. He kissed her on her forehead. He commented, "You look so happy today."

Hannah appeared animated to share with her father. "Abba, you know what? Yigal asked me out on a date. He's so cool and handsome. He's on our high school swim team and dreams of being a doctor someday."

Yoni put his arm around Hannah's shoulder and said, "Ah, so that's why you're so happy today. It's so nice to see you smile, my Hannahle. Let's sit and talk a few minutes." Yoni suddenly looked more serious. He added, "Can I get you lemonade or Cola?"

"No thanks. I'm fine, Abba. Just to finish what I was saying, when things quiet down here, with all my art projects and we're done with this serial killer issue, Yigal and I might go out on a date."

"You sound and look happy, but do you have some reservations about him? I hear caution in your voice. Is that correct, Hannah?"

"Yea, you got that right, Abba. I mean, he's handsome, smart, ambitious, and athletic. I know I have to take it one step at a time. I'm not sure yet. But, he's really sweet and caring."

"Hannahle, be careful and always trust your gut feelings."

"Okay, Abba. I will, and thank you for your understanding."

They sat themselves in the kitchen, each grabbing a cold Coke to quench their thirst. Hannah had changed her mind about sipping a cold drink. Initially, they sipped their drinks with closed eyes, as if they had been in the Sinai Desert, feeling so dehydrated.

"Okay, well, that's something real nice to look forward to. Let's switch channels because I'd like to talk to you about my case. Can we change the subject and talk about the killer?" He didn't wait for her answer. "Did you know that an article appeared today about the murdered victim? What are your thoughts about when the next crime will take place?"

"Abba, while I was cutting our challah using our sharp ivory-handle serrated knife was when another vision appeared to me.

"Leonid is at the Jerusalem open-air market called Machanei Yehuda, wearing a new disguise, a full long, dark beard and long black hair. He appears like a Chasid wearing a long black coat and a large black stromal hat. The market is busy with many people shopping, tourists looking around and the general hustle and bustle of a large crowd. It's quite easy to blend into the crowd of a multitude of unknown faces. It's about 5:30 p.m. and the sun's beginning to set. A young religious lady, perhaps no older than twenty-three, wearing traditional orthodox garbs, walks alone unaccompanied in the market.

She wears a wig which according to orthodox Jewish interpretation makes her less attractive to the opposite sex. Unaccompanied, she looks to purchase Sabbath candles. There are police and soldiers conducting daily surveillance of the entire market area. Leonid follows the crowd but manages to creep close behind her. Suddenly, she falls to the ground with a dagger penetrating her upper back's scapula muscle region. While she now lies helplessly on the ground, she cries and screams, 'I've been stabbed. Help! Help! Help me!' Leonid quickly vanishes into the throng of the crowded market. Police calls for Magen David ambulance and they arrive quickly. Police and military shout instructions to the nameless crowd of people. 'Stop your running now so we can isolate the offender. Stop!' Some did while others, in a state of panic, disappeared. Leonid was one of those who disappeared.

"The victim is taken to Hadassah Hospital near Mount Scopus in Jerusalem. The doctors are busy working to save her life. The blade came one centimeter short of penetrating her heart. After surgery, the victim is placed in an intensive care unit and monitored carefully.

"Guess what, Abba? She's twenty-three, blond, blue eyes, and five feet, six inches in height. Just like me. Isn't that a coincidence?

"The police interview several shopkeepers to see if they can identify who the perpetrator is. Hour after hour, the police review their surveillance films. In the crowd, they've been able to locate the victim and a bearded man who wears a dark coat and a stromal hat and he's walking right behind the victim. They zoom in and freeze a number of his picture frames."

"Abba, it's him. I see him in his disguise. It's him."

"I'll send a detective and some officers to confer with Jerusalem police. The victim will be interviewed as soon as doctors tell us that it's okay and that she's in stable condition to be able to converse."

He paused and noticed she had relaxed a bit. He asked, "Hannah, is there any additional information in your latest vision?"

Just then, the bell rang at their residence. It was Moshe. Hannah went to the bathroom to freshen up.

Moshe Greenbaum, a police forensic artist, had just arrived. He was short, a bit on the plump side, wearing khaki pants, a white shirt with hints of his lunch – ketchup stains, and oily smells of French fries. His hair was curly and light brown with a markedly receding hairline. His artist kit included a variety of face shapes, pencils, acrylics of various colors, and a pad of drawing paper. Yoni asked him if he'd like some lemonade, Coca Cola, or cold water. He declined for now but said, "Thanks, maybe a little later."

They sat themselves in the kitchen, physically separated by a glass table. Moshe and Yoni grew up in Kfar Gildani, a kibbutz in Northern Israel. Moshe smiled, recalling the good old days when he painted outdoors, hiked the mountains of Northern Israel, like Mount Tabor, looked for mountain goats, patches of snow in winter time, and hints of spring time when red poppy flowers blossomed and carpeted the mountains with bright red and white hues.

"Moshe, one of the things I most admire about you is that you're a one-of-a–kind original. You say things that are so honest – from the heart. You're definitely the opposite of being a phony. And you're one hell of a funny guy!"

"Thanks, Yoni. I appreciate the compliment."

"But I know you have a job to do. So can we move on and talk about that?"

"Yes, surely."

Yoni introduced Moshe to Hannah who vicariously overheard bits and pieces of their growing-up stories in Kfar Gildani.

As she sat at the kitchen table, the first words out of Moshe's mouth were, "Hannah, you have such an amazingly expressive face. I'd be honored to paint your portrait at some future time."

"Thank you. I'm also a budding artist. I know you have a job to do but at the end, maybe we can talk about my art projects and how to further my skills?" She blushed a bright red.

"Yes, yes, of course. I'd be happy to."

Moshe began by showing her the facial types – long, round, and oval, etc. Hannah looked at a number of facial patterns and decided on a somewhat elongated square-jaw look of the face. She also decided about the type of forehead. Next, they talked about eye shapes and eye colors. The killer's eyes appeared dark brown with thick black eyebrows that came together in the middle of his forehead. His dark brown eyes were almond-shaped with long black eyelashes. Next, she chose a small mouth with prominent thick lips. The nose was straight, thin, and narrow. They discussed ears and came up with ones with long earlobes. She remembered the killer had one diamond stud in his right earlobe. Hair was discussed, and Moshe showed Hannah several patterns. She chose thick, shortly cropped black curly hair and a thinly covered black beard as if the killer hadn't shaved in a week. She mentioned the inch-and-a-half thick vertical scar on the killer's left cheek.

Moshe was able to draw that with his acrylics and create a three-dimensional look to the left-cheek scar. "And what about the size of the neck?"

She stated, "Thin, average-looking neck, certainly not a short, stocky one."

"Any other body characteristics?"

"He has big, powerful-looking hands with protruding veins – much like a brick layer, a cement worker, or a butcher. He wore a short-sleeved shirt with rolled up sleeves and bulging, well-defined biceps and triceps. His wide shoulders, a broad chest, huge biceps, and a thin waist with six pack of abs made Leonid look quite athletic."

Moshe quickly assembled all of the pertinent facial characteristics and came up with the killer's facial profile but he also added the neck, shoulders, chest, and the killer's muscular arms. This sketch would be broadcast all over television, police stations, post offices, and newspapers. The message would get broadcasted as:

"If you know anything about this murder suspect, please contact your local police department. He's intent on killing young ladies. He's armed and dangerous."

She approved Moshe's drawing and asked if she could have a copy. "Your picture looks exactly like the killer in my visions. Can I copy it?" She proceeded to their printer and copied his original.

Moshe signed the copy. As they stood up to say their goodbyes, Hannah asked him if he'd like to see any of her sketches and paintings.

Smiling enthusiastically, she stated, "Moshe, my painting made it to the finals in all of Israel. I might even win."

"I'd love to see your artwork."

Hannah ran off to her bedroom with excitement behind each and every step and brought out a number of sketches and paintings for Moshe to inspect. She looked for approval by studying nonverbal expressions of his face, much like a fledgling art novice looking for approval from a great master painter.

Moshe pensively studied Hannah's paintings and sketches. He stood up to look at them from different angles. Finally, he told her that she was extremely talented. He liked how she exemplified details and shading in her paintings; she had a knack for being able to create a three-dimensional look, with a keen eye for depicting depth of field. He added that she should definitely consider a career in art. His compliments made Hannah smile and she held on to his encouraging words. She blushed and turned red.

"You think I might have a chance of being accepted to Letzior Art College? That's where I really want to go. I think Letzior will be able to help me grow as an artist."

"Absolutely! Yes, I think you're a very talented young lady, and when the time comes, I'd be honored to write you a letter of recommendation."

"Oh wow! Thank you. Do you happen to have some connections to the Letzior Art College?"

"Yes, I do. I graduated from that art college and was quickly recruited by the police department as a forensic artist. I'm a part-time instructor at the college. At one point, they tried recruiting me for full-time teaching, but I enjoy being a police department artist."

"Thank you for your offer to write a letter of recommendation. I really appreciate it. I had no idea that you were one of their instructors. Thank you so much."

"No problem. It's my pleasure. At Letzior, you'll find considerable opportunities to expand your talent and art skills."

Hannah felt inspired by Moshe's supportive words. With a smile on her face, she ran off to her bedroom before saying goodbye to Moshe. Yoni stood up and shook Moshe's hand as they bid each other goodbyes.

***

Yoni quickly wolfed down a chicken salad sandwich and some coffee in Tel Aviv, near to Dr. Eliezer's psychiatry office. It was seven p.m. Yoni's blue rings near the bottom of his eyelids were visible – reminders of his sleep deprivation. The recent Gaza war and his latest work assignment created sleep deprivation. He arrived in time when Dr. Eliezer, in his mid-seventies, stretched out his hand to shake Yoni's. They had previously worked on murder cases but it had been awhile. Being tall, with evidence of advanced scoliosis in his back and crippling arthritis, he used a cane to help him ambulate. The office had a reclining couch and two well-padded reclining brown chairs. Clay figurines of past civilizations were set on a book shelf with an accent light shining on them. Hanging on one of his walls was a metal representation of a coin that dated back to over two thousand years ago. It was found in Jerusalem at the Temple Mount and read: *JUDEA* in early Hebrew writing.

"Please have a seat. This one here to my right is very comfortable. Would you like some coffee or water?" The doctor sported a mustache and a goatee that had turned gray.

"Water, yes, that would be great. Thanks."

"So I received your description of the murder scene and how the victim was murdered. I also have the facial appearance of the murderer as narrated by your daughter. From your email, I gather there was a second crime committed, a near fatal stabbing of an orthodox young lady in Jerusalem. I think the best way to use our time today is me to offer you my thoughts. Is that okay with you, Yoni? Oh, by the way, how stupid of me for forgetting to offer you a seat. This one here to my right is very comfortable."

"Thanks. Would you mind if I record our conversation? I intend to have it transcribed to make sure I don't miss any of your thoughts, doctor. Oh, before I forget, my daughter, who is a psychic, predicted how and where the crimes will occur. The first victim was stabbed multiple times and placed at an ancient Jerusalem cemetery. There was blood everywhere."

"Yea, it's fine with me for you to record. If it helps you recall pertinent information, that's all that matters. So let me describe what's going on. One murder has already taken place – very gory and violent."

Dr. Ben Eliezer found his most favorite pipe, one carved from reddish-brown cherry wood. Wooden swirling rose-colored rings on the pipe indicated the tree's life must have been old. Yoni enjoyed observing how the good doctor methodically packed his tobacco pipe. Although Yoni was a nonsmoker, he enjoyed the rich aromas which conjured up his early memories of his growing up in a kibbutz in Northern Israel. Yoni had grown up where there were many pine, almond, and cherry-blossom trees.

Dr. Ben Eliezer continued, "Serial killers are psychopaths with excessive needs to dominate and have total control over their victims. They kill without a hint of guilt or shame. They immensely enjoy, even to orgasmic heights, when their victims suffer and take their last breath. Sadism and cruelty are the most prominent dynamics. Most serial killers involve sexual contact with their victims. There is a thrill in their quest for dominance; the killer feels empowered and thrilled when his victims suffer. In the case of our killer, he seems to be obsessed with prostitutes, drugs, and sex with complete control, domination, torture, and killing. In his second crime, although sex was not the prime motivator, the elements of surprise and control were. He surprised the stunned victim by stabbing her in the back.
One wonders about the following:
Do the prostitutes share a similar background with the perpetrator? Were they born in the same country? I'll bet they are from the same country and background.
Does the killer look for a certain physique type?
Why does he choose holy sites to place his lifeless victims?
What's the background of this perpetrator?"

The doctor paused to smoke his cherry pipe as he admired his pipe. For a few seconds, he followed the smoke patterns – the round winding circles. He appeared in deep thought.

He added, "Whenever there's a killing or even an intended killing, one needs to look as the killer's mother-son childhood relationship. The first victim's bone facial structure tells me she was of Eastern-European descent, probably Russian. I also spoke to the coroner and was led to the following conclusion:
Her teeth of several gold crowns are more common amongst Eastern-Europeans. This killer is drawn to prostitutes of Eastern-European

backgrounds. Even prior to the first kill, he slashed a prostitute's arm which required many stitches. This murderer enjoys young, well-built, athletic-looking women's body for sexual intercourse while she is completely unconscious. He enjoys complete domination and surprise when he chloroforms them, has sex, and repeatedly stabs them. This metaphor is symbolic for how he feels about his mother. He disdains, hates her, and in turn, all women. I would not at all be surprised if the killer is a homosexual or even latently homosexual.

"Our serial killer was unable to have a normal attachment to his mother, that is, she was unavailable to him in his early years. It's likely that she lacked a maternal instinct. I believe he was the subject of extreme sadism as a child. He was a loner and probably cruel to animals or family pets. I maintain that in addition to being a psychopath, he suffers from an attachment disorder as a child and now as a grownup. This kind of psychopath could easily hang a family pet – a cat or a dog – dismember it part by part or piece by piece while maintaining a sadistic glee in his eyes. He feels victorious over these helpless animals the same way that he feels towards the women he kills. He also hates his father who he perceives as passive and accepting of his wife's sadism towards their child. The killer is also in a rage about his father's passivity and inability to stop his mother's cruelty.

"His two-and-a-half-centimeter scar suggests that he might have been stabbed by a knife, a belt buckle, or a chain when he was a youngster. He could have been struck with some metal object, like a chain. He was definitely an unwanted child, which is rare in a Jewish family. Undoubtedly, he's likely to repeat this type of a murder over and over again. I'd also predict that when he took psychometric tests for the IDF, he was refused entrance due to red flags indicative of serious mental illness (SMI). This reminds me that you should look at all the IDF records going back five to seven years ago. This might help you find your guy."

"That's quite a bit of valuable information you provided. We have a psycho nut job on our hands. I'm grateful to you, Dr. Ben Eliezer. Thank you for your time. I appreciate your comprehensive and complex personality analysis. I'll definitely have discussions with the IDF."

"I'm glad to be of service. Please keep me informed, especially as your case unfolds. You realize that your daughter is in a vulnerable position, since he knows you're the lead detective working on this case. He may wish to seek revenge for telling on him. After all, she has advanced knowledge about the killer because of her visions."

"Yea, that's a very scary thought which my daughter and I discussed. Certainly. I will also circulate a picture of the victim as well as the killer's face and see who knows her. With my detectives, I'll discuss the killer's psycho-dynamics. I will also have my detectives go to the various clubs around Tel Aviv to hopefully arrest this crazy dude. Thank you so much, doctor."

***

Yoni was to provide his detectives with several copies of Moshe's drawing. The detective's assignment was to go to all of the sex clubs or exotic dance clubs in the city and inquire, "Have you seen this individual? Is this person familiar to you?" The officers were to also ask if they'd ever seen the killer, based on the sketch provided.

Yoni's blue eyes had turned pinkish by the time he arrived home at 9:30 p.m. Utterly exhausted, he displayed pronounced blue rings around his eyes. He was too tired to eat but his better self-thought that he should eat some food. Since first learning about Hannah's visions, he developed erratic sleep patterns. He'd average three to four hours of nightly sleep which was hardly enough, considering his daily grind that consisted of twelve to fourteen hours of work six days a week. He'd often enough drink three to four coffees daily to stay alert and awake. Now, he had grabbed a sandwich from the refrigerator. Since no one stirred, not even a cricket, he concluded that everyone was asleep. He ate a cold turkey sandwich, and shortly after, he plopped into bed.

Chapter Seven

Yoni drove from his home in Ashkelon to Tel Aviv, enjoying a blue sky with temperatures hovering around eighty degrees but that was early in the morning. It promised to be a hot and humid day. At times, the highway would traverse in a parallel direction along the Mediterranean Sea. On the way to his office, a number of Israeli Air Force jets were on practice runs over the Mediterranean Sea. He wondered if his first cousin, Ruben, a decorated ace fighter pilot, a colonel in the air force, flew in the blue yonder above. He opened his car windows and waved his hand as if to say, "Hi, Ruben. It's your Cousin Yoni. Don't you recognize my car? Ruben, be careful. Hope to see you soon."

Ten minutes from his office, while still on the highway, he noticed cars involved in a fender-bender and immediately called his police headquarters in Tel Aviv. Yoni reported to his office at 7:30 a.m. During the summer months, it was common to have humid and warm temperatures. He wondered if his armpits' sweat marks became increasingly visible to others. He carried the day's newspaper, the Jerusalem Gazette, with a headline: *"Murder in Jerusalem's Holy Cemetery."* He contemplated the content of what he'd say to his detectives, his strategy, and his expectations in a meeting scheduled for 8:00 a.m. In advance, he wrote an outline of his main talking points with several bullet points, and he'd distribute many copies of Leonid's pictures to his detectives and police officers.

On the way to his office, he had stopped to get a hardy twenty-ounce Venti from Starbucks – a little cream, no sugar, please. He placed his nose closer to his cup, relishing the coffee's titillating fragrances. This 'Verona' coffee blend was his most favorite coffee. His cellphone rang unexpectedly. He recognized the number as Hannah's.

Breathless as she walked towards her school, she spoke, "Abba, it's me. I'm really sorry to bother you but I had another very disturbing vision that I think you should know about."

Yoni knew that the quiver in his daughter's voice conveyed that she was very near to tears.

She continued, "Last evening around 5:30, Leonid, our killer, stabbed, nearly killing an orthodox young lady at Machanei Yehuda Market in Jerusalem. She's at Hadassah hospital in their ICU unit. I predict she'll live, but guess what? We resemble each other. You'd probably want to send your law enforcement team there to discuss police efforts there and to interview the actual victim. Abba, I am already late to my class but I just had to let you know. You see the killer varies his tactics, in part to fool your team of detectives." She paused to collect her thoughts. "I think you might want to send some of your detectives to look at the sex clubs in Tel Aviv." She paused momentarily and then continued, "I was thinking of his muscular hands and the way he stabbed the first victim. It's then that I realized he's a butcher. Remember when you and I recently went to purchase beef at the Stern Meat Shop in Tel Aviv? I actually saw him slicing beef there. I sensed his sinister and evil aura. He looked at me with evil and ominous intent in his heart. Yes, he definitely knows how to carve meat, no pun intended, Abba. I must go to my class now. Love you."

Yoni wrote down all of the information. "I'll have my detectives at Hadassah Hospital and interview Jerusalem police. I will talk to my detectives and disseminate the information. They'll have copies of Moshe's sketch of the killer. Thanks for calling. I also have to go now. In a few minutes, I'll have my initial meeting with my detectives. In fact, I see them walking into our conference room. Bye. Let's talk later. And be safe, Hannah."

"Okay. Please be careful."

A police conference room could hold up to thirty-five people. Today, his three detectives, Yoni, and several officers were present for this briefing. Some went over to the coffee machine and got their fix of caffeine. Others wanted a smoke but this conference room was a smoke-free zone. He waited till every one of his detectives shuffled into work. It was eight a.m. His meeting would take as long as it needed. Yoni addressed the group. "Okay, gentleman, let's get settled now. We have lots to discuss. Save your cigarettes for later, and let's get seated now. I'd like to get started."

Three detectives and twelve select police officers were also present.

Yoni shared copies of his briefing outline, his psychiatric summary, based on his discussion with Dr. Eliezer. He disseminated copies of Moshe's drawing of Leonid. He was able to have a police photographer take a picture of the first victim's headshot with photo-enhanced copies of the victim's facial features. He announced his three lead detectives, namely, Shmuel, Yitzchak, and Raffi. Each of these detectives would help in the process of apprehending Leonid.

"Initially, we'll begin our investigation with these two major cities, namely, Tel Aviv and Jerusalem. Each of the detectives will have as many police officers to assist. Yoni's detectives would walk the streets of Tel Aviv and visit all of the sex clubs, with pictures in hand. Make sure you visit Moyshe Stern's Zion Meat Shop in Tel Aviv. Our perpetrator has been employed there. Make sure you cover all the sex clubs as well as talk butcher shops in Tel Aviv. To begin with, I'd like you, Shmuel, to find out more about the first victim and make contact with her family. I was informed that a second victim was seriously injured in Jerusalem. Yitzchak, I want you to take the lead with the second stabbing, near fatal injury that occurred at the Yehuda Market in Jerusalem. This second victim is currently recovering at the Hadassah Hospital. I would suggest you take several officers with you. I believe that David, one of our police officers was a highly decorated sharp shooter in our IDF. Just minutes before this meeting, Hannah, informed me that last night at around 5:30 p.m., the killer struck in Jerusalem's Machanei Yehuda Market. Check out all known facts, interview family members, and get photos of this second incident.

"Shmuel, you'll interview the victim's parents. One wonders if she had known the killer. Had they dated? Was there any evidence of any previous relationship with each other? What kind of a background did she come from? Perhaps the victim's parents can offer us clues about our killer. Why don't you interview them?

"Raffi, you and police officers will pursue Leonid, our killer. We need to secure additional information like where and in what gym he works out, where he lives, and with whom. Is he currently employed?

"I want daily reports by email of each corner and cranny you visit, names, addresses, and the details of every conversation you have. I want you to send me emails and call me if you find out anything. You know that I thrive on details. I insist on knowing every conversation and telephone exchange. In addition to verbal communication with me, I want you to follow up with emails that describe your daily activities. Do you follow my drift? Oh, one other thing, any person considered of special importance should be videotaped." He paused and sipped his coffee. Yoni reviewed the various types of forensic questions. Next, the detectives' role played types of investigative questions and answers. The detectives observed and participated in mock interviews.

Shmuel, Yitzchak, Raffi, and the officers all nodded their agreement to Yoni's orders.

Yoni continued, "You may discover the killer's best friend. Interviews of a best friend could lead to a killer's arrest. Okay? Any other questions or suggestions?"

Everyone assembled and scribbled furiously to keep track of all the details. The detectives and several police officers stood up unanimously and said, "Yes sir. We'll do our best, sir!" Yoni also handed out his outline of task assignments.

***

By eleven a.m., Yoni had an appointment to talk to General Ayelon, the chief psychologist of the IDF. The kind general had earned his graduate degrees in psychology at Yeshiva University in Manhattan, New York City. He was nearing sixty years of age with a full head of pepper-gray hair and sporting a goatee.

Yoni thought to himself, 'What a great guy! So unpretentious and willing to be helpful.'

A solid investigative plan took shape, much like a painting, adding new strokes with novel color embellishments. It had been four days since the first victim was discovered.

Yoni was about to leave for his appointment with General Ayelon when his phone rang. It was General Ayelon confirming their appointment.

"You want to know about IDF rejects due to mental illness in the last seven years. Is that correct, Yoni?"

"Yes, sir. And thank you in advance for your research, General Ayelon."

His office was in Tel Aviv, at an undescribed location. The building was built from old Jerusalem white-tan stones that helped create cooler office temperatures. General Ayelon was in his late fifties, short in stature, perhaps no more than five feet five, and in full uniform when he greeted Yoni. He still maintained a full head of hair and blue eyes which made the general appear younger than his true age of fifty-nine.

After exchanging pleasantries about family, the job, and the steaming hot and humid weather, General Ayelon said, "Let me show you what I came up with." He continued, "First of all, thank God that we've hardly ever had any serious mental illness in the IDF. It was a challenge to isolate rejects. But I did come up with a few profiles over a span of six years. So, here are five individuals who were rejected due to clear-cut mental illness. The first individual was rejected because of insurmountable anxiety issues. He was unable to be outdoors, had severe claustrophobia and agoraphobia, and still slept with his teddy bear."

"That's not our guy," added Yoni.

"The next person was so severely depressed that he cried when taking the psychological tests. He was unable to complete the testing procedure due to his incessant crying, anxiety, and severe depression.

"Our third guy was clearly schizophrenic, seeing visions, having auditory hallucinations, and having multiple conversations with himself. That's certainly not our guy.

"Our fourth guy is a likely candidate. He originates from Ukraine, of the former USSR. He never finished gymnasium but began training as a butcher. His Rorschach scales scores were highest in areas of violence and rage, especially towards his mother and women in general. The scales indicated psychopathic behavior tendencies, a severe detachment disorder with inability of being close to anyone he experienced severe sadistic cruelty as a child, and harsh physical punishments that no child should ever be subjected to. The MMPI confirmed the rage he has towards his mother. Dr. Ayelon noted that this individual behaves with extreme aggressiveness towards others, but mostly women."

"This individual's profile suggests he's a psychopath," said General Ayelon.

"Do you have any photograph of this individual in your files?"

"Yes, let me show it to you, but it was taken about five years ago." General Ayelon searched his file and found the picture.

Yoni held it up, bringing it closer to him. He looked at it from various angles and said, "You know what? This is definitely our guy! An oval long face with shortly cropped black curly hair, noticeable eyebrows that met each other in the middle of the forehead, long black eyelashes, dark brown eyes, and a prominent facial scar on his left cheek. This individual has a thick Russian accent when he speaks Hebrew. The record indicates he immigrated to Israel when he was fifteen." Yoni took a number of seconds to examine the picture. "General Ayelon, do you happen to have a magnifying glass? Also, might you have a physical description of this man? Perhaps another picture?"

The general found a magnifying glass. Yoni carefully examined the picture and the scar on his left cheek. He thought to himself, 'Yes, Hannah is absolutely on point about the size and the location of the scar. She was correct that he hailed from the former USSR.' Yoni noted the photograph was almost identical to Moshe's sketch. Yoni shook his head from side to side, left to right, and then right to left in amazement as he confirmed Leonid's facial appearance based on Hannah's vision.

General Ayelon provided a physical description and a mug shot of Leonid. He was five feet, ten inches in height. "Would you like to see and hear more about the other two individuals?"

"No, we have our guy right here." Yoni pointed to the picture in the file. "Can you magnify the picture to say an eight-by-ten-inch shot? And when was this picture taken? Is it possible for you to photo-enhance it so that our killer appears as he does today, rather than a young eighteen-year-old?"

"Yes, the picture was taken five years ago. Give me a couple of minutes to magnify and photo-enhance this picture."

The psychologist general came back with the picture of the suspect and a summary of his rejection from the military because of psychiatric reasons.

"Our photo lab department enhanced the picture so that he appeared like a twenty-three-year-old."

Yoni inquired, "Oh, by the way, what's his name?"

"Yes, his name is Leonid Kozlov."

"Yes, that's the information I have. Thank you."

A close look at the hands with a magnifying glass indicated the killer might be a boxer, a martial artist, a stone worker, or a butcher with powerful hands so capable of strangling anyone. Inwardly, Yoni was amazed that Hannah could perceive such amazingly detailed visions. 'How is that possible? But I do know to trust her information,' thought Yoni. He held and looked at the photo. "Yep, this is definitely our killer," Yoni said.

"He looks so close to our artist's sketch. By the way, I never had a chance to tell you, my daughter, Hannah, is a psychic-clairvoyant. She had this vision with the exact same physical features. I'm blown away each time I think about it. Isn't it amazing?"

"So your daughter envisioned his physical appearance and the murder all in advance?"

"Yes, she did. And with great accuracy, might I say."

"You must be very proud of her talents as a clairvoyant?"

"I don't fully understand how her visions come to her but yes, she's accurate in her predictions and I'm very proud of her. My commander has given me a month to come up with enough evidence to make an arrest. I'm on my fourth day but now we have additional information. General, I want to thank you for all you've done." Yoni smiled and appreciated Dr. Ayelon's help.

"I'm glad to help out. And by the way, I do believe in clairvoyance and vetted psychic individuals. I'd say this killer is extremely dangerous. In addition, this killer is quite elusive. He may even expand his killing spree."

They shook hands. Yoni saluted the doctor, a man of a higher military rank, and they bid each other farewell. "Thank you for your time. I appreciate your help, sir."

"You're very welcome," said General Ayelon.

On his way out of the doctor's office, his phone rang. It was Hannah. "Oh, by the way, Hannah, we have our man. He's exactly the way you described in your vision. Moshe's sketch and this official IDF photograph are almost identical." Yoni smiled.

Her breathing was labored. She sounded frantic with the pitch of her voice sounding much higher than usual. "Is everything okay with you, Abba? How are you holding up?" She thought for a few seconds. "Abba, I wish I was never born a psychic."

"You're a very special person, my Hannahle. I'll have police and detectives dispatched, based on the information you offered. As for my protection, I'll surround myself with undercover officers. I'll also call for undercover police around our house, mainly for your protection, Hannah. Okay?"

"Yes, he's armed with fire arms in addition to knives. He carries throwing knives and he knows how to throw them with pinpoint accuracy. Abba! Be safe. Okay? Love you."

"I love you too, Hannahle."

The following morning, the Tel Aviv Advance had Moshe's drawing displayed on Page One. It appeared to be a true-to-life representation of the killer. The photo-enhanced picture provided by Dr. Ayelon also appeared in the newspaper. The article asked people to call the Tel Aviv Police Department if they've seen, heard, or known the whereabouts of the killer. The article described the first victim as follows:

A twenty-two-year-old woman found murdered was discovered at the Jewish Cemetery in Jerusalem with multiple stabbings, and a blood-stained hand-written note was also placed on the victim. Yesterday evening, a twenty-three–year-old orthodox young lady was stabbed at the open market in Jerusalem. The knife stabbing was intended to kill, but fortunately she survived, although she's recuperating in an undisclosed location. The same perpetrator is thought to be responsible for both crimes.

The suspected killer is five feet ten, about twenty–three, with short black neatly cropped curly hair, brown eyes, a scar on his face (his left cheek), and armed. Strangulation and stabbings were his murder tools. Women should be extra careful. Keep this information in your purse or wallets. If you recognize and/or have seen anyone that matches this individual's description, please call the police at once. Trust your instincts and make police reports of anyone who resembles these newspaper pictures.

Moments later, while watching TV, a flash announcement came on about the killer, his appearance and about the innocent first victim whose life was robbed. Nationwide, there was considerable phone activity by women calling one another. This slaughter was the subject of considerable discussions among

Israel's populace. Mother and daughters discussed how to best recognize the killer based on his appearance. But who would have predicted that he'd use disguises?

Yoni picked up his cellphone and called Yitzchak. "Hi, Yitzie, I just heard from Hannah that the killer struck in Jerusalem with the stabbed victim who is clinging to life at Hadassah Hospital. Why don't you see if you can interview the victim as well as Jerusalem Police? See if you can get your hands on some of the surveillance pictures. "

"We'll do, sir."

Chapter Eight

A dark night with stars and moon lay hidden under a thick layer of dense gray clouds. Heavy downpours were predicted by all the major television stations. They wore their raincoats. Detective Yitzchak and his police officers went to talk to police officers in Jerusalem. Machanei Yehuda's surveillance photos were shared. They revealed Leonid's incognitos – full beard, mustache, a stromal hat, and a traditional long black coat worn by the Chassidics. As had been predicted by Hannah, he had numerous disguises to hide from being captured. Law enforcement was able to identify the prominent scar on Leonid's upper left cheek. Willingly, they shared their surveillance photos with Yitzchak. As they left Jerusalem's Central Police Station, there was a downpour of heavy rains and strong winds. Since Jerusalem is fairly hilly, small water streams were evident in the undulating hilly terrain. Yitzchak and his team of officers arrived at Hadassah Hospital at Ein Kerem. This healthcare facility is known as one of the largest in Israel, only second to Sheba Hospital.

He had prearranged to speak to the head of ICU, Dr. Sahlstrom, previously born and medically educated in Sweden. The kind doctor was tall, thin, and with a full head of blond hair. Outside the patient's room, a number of men with black coats and beards were chanting the Mishebeerach prayer for her recovery. Her husband, Nachum, also twenty-three years old, was present. Rachel was a mother of four children ranging in age from one to four years of age. Her arranged marriage to her husband was a customary in the Jewish orthodox community. She was married at eighteen years of age.

Yitzchak looked forward to eliciting information from the doctor, family members, and the victim. "Hi, I'm Detective Yitzchak. I'd like to talk to you about Mrs. Rachel Horowitz, the patient who was stabbed yesterday." He flashed his detective identification.

"What would you like to know about her, Detective Yitzchak?"

"Please tell me everything you know about her condition and whether or not she can be interviewed for a few minutes. As you know, this investigation is a police matter and here is my identification."

"Okay, Rachel is now in a stable condition. The stab was deep, close to her heart, but thank God, it hadn't penetrated any further. In terms of interviewing her, I'd suggest no more than ten minutes at a time."

"Okay. Thank you, doctor. By the way, how is her overall spirit?"

"She wants to get back to her daily routines so her children and family won't suffer."

The room appeared light olive-green with a window view of the Knesset in Jerusalem. Rachel Horowitz had a number of different tubes – one to assist in breathing, another in the forearm for keeping her hydrated with fluids. She had a continuous blood pressure cuff to monitor her pulse and blood pressure. These gages were visible to doctors and nurses in the front nursing station. Rachel appeared pale and sleepy. A barely eaten kosher lunch of chicken sandwich remained on her plate. Rachel had not resumed having a normal appetite. The detective and two officers entered the room. "Shalom, Mrs. Horowitz. I'm Detective Yitzchak. How are you feeling today?"

"I feel better than I was last evening. The doctors say it will take three or four weeks to recover. I was very lucky the knife had not penetrated my heart. Baruch Hashem!"

"Yes, of course. Baruch Hashem! God works His miracles. What do you recall about the perpetrator? What was he wearing? What about his facial features? Please try and recall as much as possible."

"I barely looked behind me as someone seemed too close to me for my comfort level. I saw a fully bearded man with a black coat. Then, I began to pick up my walking pace. Let me see. I'm thinking back to yesterday. Oh yea, he had a noticeable scar on his left cheek."

"Had you known him from any time in your past?"

"No, I never saw him before."

"What if any communication occurred between the two of you?"

"None whatsoever. Next thing, I felt something very sharp in my back and I fainted. I awakened in the hospital after under anesthesia they surgically removed the knife."

"So you never knew him when you were suddenly stabbed?"

"Yes. That's correct. In my orthodox community, women don't associate with men. The only exception is their husbands and the Rabbi."

"Do you know anyone who might wish to harm you?"

"No, I don't. In my community, women keep to themselves."

There were knocks on the door when her husband and their four children had come to visit.

In unison, they all said, "Hi, Ima," as they stood by her bedside. Mr. Horowitz carried the baby in his arms. They all wanted to hug and kiss Rachel.

A bouquet of red roses was placed on her bed. Mr. Horowitz brought along a crystal vase where he proceeded to neatly place the roses in water.

"Oh, your children, they're so lovely."

"Thank you," said Rachel.

Detective Yitzchak said, "It's a special family time for all of you, so I'll let you go for now."

Mr. Horowitz asked his wife, "Who's that?"

"Oh, his name is Yitzchak and he's one of the detectives assigned to capture the man who stabbed me."

"Well, we certainly hope you'll apprehend him. If not, he could easily harm or even kill more women."

Rachel looked at Nachum, her husband, and said, "Yea, for sure. He's got to be apprehended as soon as possible."

"I know this is an important family time, but can I ask you a couple of questions? Can we step outside the room?"

"Sure. How can I help you, Detective Yitzchak?"

"Are you aware of anyone who'd want to hurt your wife? For example, has there been a scorned boyfriend in her past?"

"Rachel never had a previous boyfriend. We got married at age eighteen and she was my one and only. Neither of us dated before. It's our custom in our orthodox community."

"Is there anyone who'd want to hurt you by stabbing your wife?"

Nachum thought pensively and said, "No, I can't think of anyone."

"How are things between you and Rachel? Might there be a reason that you'd wish to hurt Rachel?"

"No, absolutely not. We love and care about each other. We have children that need and depend on us. I'd never hurt my wife, Rachel."

"Okay, thank you for your time. I may call upon you in the future. Would that be okay?"

"Sure."

Outside the hospital, Yitzchak grabbed a smoke and, for a few minutes, sat outdoors at a Starbucks coffeehouse. He took out his cellphone and called Yoni.

"Hi, it's Yitzchak. I interviewed Rachel in the hospital and came to the conclusion that they had no prior acquaintance with each other. I also interviewed her husband and he does not appear to be a person of special interest. In the crowd of people, Leonid picked her as a victim because she fit the age, height, and appearance requirements. She's blond, five feet, six inches, with blue eyes, just like our first deceased victim. This crazy psycho has a fetish about picking young ladies with a certain height and appearance."

"Yea, no shit! We must get this son of a bitch as soon as possible."

***

By 10:00 p.m., Yitzchak and three of his officers were at the Volga Sex Club in Tel Aviv, one of Leonid's most favorite clubs known. All of the officers including Yitzchak were dressed incognito. Yitzchak wore blue jeans and a brown sweater. His face was covered with a beard. He wore his bulletproof vest. Yitzchak thought to himself, 'On two prior occasions, he picked up servers here. One's arm was slashed while the other one was killed. We must find this monster!' It was a smoke-filled large room with a brightly lit platform. Three pole dancers were erotically gyrating to poles on the well-lit stage.

He looked around hoping to notice Leonid. In the meantime, a server inquired if he wanted a drink.

Yitzchak said, "For now, I'll have a rum and coke." She sat on his lap and offered him sex for money. He waived the hand displaying his wedding ring. "No thanks. Save your sex for someone else. I'm already taken."

Yitzchak and his men waited an hour. They were about to leave when Leonid walked in sporting a gray suit, blue shirt, and tie. He wore a goatee beard and a mustache. He tried covering up his scar with a makeup cream.

But his height and musculature could not be hidden. Yitzchak instantly recognized Leonid and his now-faint scar. Detective Yitzchak's heart beat quickly as adrenaline poured into his veins. His breathing increased when he now lightly touched his hidden gun.

A server asked if he'd like a drink. He ordered a cognac with no ice. Leonid looked around and then he went to the bathroom. That evening, he never returned, as he recognized the puffy outline of Yitzchak's bulletproof vest and made a quick getaway. He ran quickly towards his parked SUV and took off. His unclaimed cognac sat on the table. After about forty-five seconds, Yitzchak and his officers bolted out of the club, pistols in hand. They noticed that Leonid was running fast at least eighty-five yards ahead of them. Yitzchak commanded, "Fire now!" A stream of bullets was fired in the dark, one after the other in quick succession.

Leonid made it to his van but recognized that a bullet had penetrated his right deltoid muscle near the triceps of his arm. His right calf muscle had also been scraped by a bullet. He pulled over with his van. His breathing was rapid. Sweat poured down his face. He found a used pillowcase. He clamped down with his teeth from a corner of the pillowcase and tore a piece from which he made a makeshift tourniquet to stop his blood flow. He resumed his drive.

Once in an apartment shared by his one and only best friend, he cleaned his wounds with alcohol and cotton swabs without any facial winces. His expression remained unchanged. His wounds were puncture-like where bullets exited his flesh. He wondered if the bullet injured his rotator cuff. Using an alcohol-drenched sowing needle with found black thread, he began to stitch his wounds, the calf, and his shoulder. When Leonid felt satisfied with his stitches, he placed antibiotic cream to the fifteen stitches twice. He marveled at his job with a smile on his face. He thought, 'Good job, Leonid.' He placed additional antibiotic cream on his wound. Inwardly, he thought to himself, 'Those f***** cops can't catch me. I'm smarter than those f******.' He inhaled deeply and uttered, "Losers!" He took his right hand and patted his heart region as if to say, 'Yes, I'm great!'

***

Detective Shmuel loved to work out in his own home-style gym which he had proudly set up in his apartment. This room consisted of dumbbells, barbells, a bench press bench, a Latissimus pull-down machine, a treadmill, and a stationary bike. He got into his car still trying to dry up from extensive sweating. Today, Detective Shmuel Weiss headed towards Tel Aviv in search of his killer. Considered by many a lady's man – a playboy, women flocked to him because of his handsome masculine appearance. His fellow police officers referred to him as a babe magnet. There had been instances where women left their names and phone numbers with a hope that Shmuel would call them. Being six feet one, passionate about his weight-resistance training, a muscular physique, a full head of wavy jet-black hair, and crystal-clear blue eyes made him appear Hollywood-like handsome. Last but not least, he enjoyed his Saturdays at the beach – swimming, playing paddle ball, and eyeing women wearing their tight bikinis.

He entered the police force after his army service where he distinguished himself as an expert marksman. His top marksmanship scores earned his way to be recruited to the Golani brigade where he conducted undercover intelligence work in the Syrian-Israeli border. The Golani brigade was a Special Forces Commando fighting unit of the IDF. He helped uncover several Syrian military build-ups, especially tank brigades that were actively planning an invasion into Israel. He provided classified information which helped avert life-threatening situations for Israel's citizens, especially those living in Northern Israel. He attended officers' training school and was quickly promoted to the rank of lieutenant in the Golani brigade.

His background was ideal for police department work when he was recruited by the police academy. Within five years working as a police officer, he was promoted to the status of detective.

Today, Detective Shmuel Weiss drove his 1966 red Mustang and was headed towards Tel Aviv in search of the killer. His red 1966 Mustang brought him lots of 'oohs and aahs,' especially from female onlookers.

He called Yoni, his boss. "Listen Shmuel, get a signed statement from Mr. Shlomowitz, the Volga Club's owner, and let him know that he may be called for a future court deposition. Please explain why. Ask the parents of Yilena if they knew the killer. For example, had their daughter been dating him? Had she ever brought him home to meet them?

"I'd suggest that you go back to continue your interview of Mr. and Mrs. Moskovitz. Get as much information about Yilena and why she left home at such a young age. What was their family life like? Ask if Yilena was acquainted with Leonid. Examine Yilena's room to see if you discover some kind of connection to our killer. Ask open-ended questions because they reveal more information. As you know, those questions tend to reveal more information. Of course, ask their permission to record their narrative."

"Yep, that's a good idea. I'll do that."

"Anything else, Shmuel?"

"No, that's it for now."

"Thanks for your call."

***

It was 5:45 p.m. when Shmuel arrived to interview the Moskovitz household – parents of the deceased first victim, Yilena.

They were in their mid-to-late forties, but they physically looked like they were in their late sixties – wrinkled, old-looking, overweight, and with noticeable gold crowns on several teeth. Mrs. Moskowitz's hair appeared oily and unkempt. Overall, they appeared disheveled.

"Hello, Mr. and Mrs. Moskovitz, I'd like to speak to you again. The more we know about your daughter, the more it will help our case. First and foremost, I need to record the material as part of our investigation. Recording is part of our police protocol when we do an investigation of this nature. For us as police officers, it's really hard to recall all the facts. That's why visual recording make it so much easier to remember things. That's okay with you, yes?"

They nodded a 'yes' and welcomed him into their living room apartment in Tel Aviv, a modest-looking two-bedroom apartment with old used furniture

64

and a musty smell. Shmuel noticed how the worn down brown couch was frayed. Mrs. Svetlana Moskowitz, Yilena's mother, wore a very faded gray-white light blue housedress, had no makeup, gray unkempt hair, and pinkish crying eyes. Her husband, Boris, wore wrinkled and stained khaki pants, a white undershirt, and house slippers. He was morbidly overweight with a distinct bulging stomach. Shmuel quickly noted the smells of their distinctly unpleasant body odors, most probably a sign of poor hygiene or not taking proper care of themselves due to feelings of grief.

Boris led Shmuel to their living room and asked Shmuel where he'd like to sit. The couch's springs had lost their firmness. The clay tiles were also soiled with dirt spots here and there.

Shmuel sat on a wooden chair.

Mr. Moskowitz stated, "Vel, you know vie grieve the loss of our Yilena, and it's more difficult being recorded ven camera is looking right at us."

"Yes, I understand, and I am very sorry about your loss. But since this is a part of a police investigation, we record our interviews; it's police protocol. Do you follow? Does that make sense to you?"

They shook their heads in agreement and quietly said, "Okay, it's fine. Is good. No problem."

"Okay, thanks for your cooperation." He placed the video camera and connected it to a tripod. Then, with a click of the play button, the video began.

"Can vie offer you something to drink? Maybe you're thirsty?"

"No, no, thank you. I'm fine. So let's begin. For the record, please state your full names and relationship to Yilena."

"I am Boris Moskovitz and I'm cher father."

"I'm Svetlana Moskovitz. I'm Yilena's mudder."

"Thank you. What made your daughter leave your home at such a young age?"

Mr. Moskovitz chose to speak. "Vie're unsure. She vas always a rebellious kid, very difficult and always chielanging to chandle. If I said it's a blue sky, she'd say, no, it's orange or red. If vie said she needs to be chome by eight, she'd come at eleven, or even later. Sometimes, she stayed out all night. Vie tried to punish cher but she'd never take us, cher parents, seriously. She opposed us on everything. There vas niever apology for any of cher bad choices or cher rebelliousness towards us."

"Sounds like it must have been difficult getting along with her." They both moved their heads in acknowledgment. "So when you punished her, what happened next?"

"Oh, she'd run away for a day, sometimes two, and vie didn't know ver she vas – no phone call, no communication, noting!" He paused momentarily and then added, "To tell you the truth, vie vere siek about the vay she treated us – no sleep, just vorries, all the time, continuously."

"Then, what happened?"

"She'd say you can't touch me any longer. I viel call the authorities on you if you try."

"What did she mean by, 'You can't touch me any longer?'"

"She accused me of fondling cher and touching cher in cher privates. She even said I chad sex with cher ven she vas six years old. Can you imagine sex with my own six-year-old daughter? That's such a disgustingly, unpleasant thought and a false accusation."

"What happened then?"

"There vas a big Ministry of Social Welfare investigation in Ukraine. For nine months, she vas taken away from us and placed in a group foster chome. Medical examination revealed that Yilena vas a virgin. Vie ver required to go for psychological testing, chave counseling, and on a monthly basis go in front of a judge as if vie ver criminals."

"What happened next?"

"After the judge declared that vie chad fulfilled our requirements, he stated vie can chave Yilena return to our chome. But to be on the safe side, he still vanted social vorker monthly reports for the next six months. Once a month, vie met with a social vorker who wrote monthly reports to the judge."

"How did that affect your family relationships? And what did that do to you personally?"

"From that moment on, vie never trusted Yilena because she vas such a big liar. She lied to the authorities about me, cher father. Chow can I fiel towards cher but be very churt and angry about cher lies? She vas an accomplished and very polished manipulator. Vie lost all trust in our daughter. Cher lies divided and ruined our family." He pulled out a handkerchief, wiped his tears, and loudly blew his nose. He added, "I was a failure as her father – couldn't get through to cher."

The mother, Svetlana, finally spoke and said, "My chusband chas bad cheart condition and che's not allowed to get this excited. Yilena shamed our family's name in the entire Russian community."

"What other repercussions occurred after Yilena returned home? What do you remember?"

Svetlana continued, "She told false stories about us to cher teachers. She ran avay for a day. She refused to learn and practice cher piano lessons. She vas defiant to us, often saying, 'You can't make me clean my room or I'll tell on you to the judge.' It's like she chad all the power and vie ver left vit no authority as cher parents. Chow vould that make you fiel?" Anguish and hurt feelings accompanied her now-quivering voice. Tears ran down her cheeks. The veins on her reddish face screamed out in agony. "Yes, vie ver failures as parents."

"Sounds like you're in a lot of pain."

"Oh yes! GOD only knows." She sobbed while trying to cover her eyes. Her husband took out tissues to dry her reddened eyes. He handed her fresh unused tissues.

"What happened next?"

"So, as time marched on, Yilena began to be interested in boys and drinking vodka."

"What did you do?"

Mr. Moskowitz answered, as his wife sobbed extensively. She coughed, barely able to catch her breath. "Noting, because she always threatened to call the authorities on us. Once you've gone through court, you're looked upon as a child rapist, a criminal. Vie did everything vie could to avoid getting cher mad. Vie tried to talk to cher about not chaving sex, not drinking liquor, but she didn't vant to chear about any of that. Vie talked to cher about the dangers of getting pregnant. She spat on us. She vanted to only do cher thing – bolt out of the chouse or storm into cher room. She'd lock her room ver vie couldn't enter. So you see, this is a diefficult case about us, cwho ver ineffective, basically failures. Vie felt chelpless and at the mercy of the courts. That's all! She chad all the power and vie chad none. She vouldn't cooperate vit anything," said Mr. Moskovitz.

"Mr. and Mrs. Moskovitz, what types of feelings or regrets do you have, looking back?"

"Ven she vas six, my vife and I vent out to the ballet and chad a male sixteen-year-old neighbor baby sit for us von evening. Vie had good feelings about chim and asked if che'd be available to sit for Yilena. Che said yes and vie agreed on a price. Since that day, Yilena vas never the same. She denied that che molested cher but the fact remained; she vas never the same. Vie asked chim but che denied any incident and said that Yilena vent right to her bed and fell asleep quickly. Because vie ver neighbors, Yilena saw chim several times, going up and down the staircase. My vife and I are convinced someting bad chappened."

"What do you think happened?"

"I think che tricked cher into accepting candy in exchange for being allowed to touch cher privates or perhaps che made cher touch chim for candy. Maybe che touched his private part on cher. I'm not sure one hundred percent."

"Can you tell me what other significant events occurred?"

"Ven she vas twelve, she got cher menstrual cycle. About one year later, when she vas now thirteen, she invited three boys from cher eighth grade class to our chouse. My vife and I ver vorking. Somehow, the boys got their chands on some vodka and they partied."

"What happened in this party?"

"They all drank vodka and each of the boys chad sex with Yilena by cher own admission. Yilena told us this and vas defiantly proud. And vie found several used condoms lying around – proof of cher sexual activity."

"What made you come to that conclusion?"

"Yilena told us that she had them over and she chad sex wit each one of the boys. And vie found several used condoms lying around – proof of cher sexually acting out."

"What did you do then?"

"I said that vie viel report this to the judge. And you know vat she said? 'Go right achead. I'll tell on you to the judge.' You see, she knew vie ver in a no-vin situation. She vas completely out of control and vie didn't know chow to chandle cher. Vie made many mistakes as parents." Mrs. Moskovitz took out a handkerchief and sobbed. Mr. Moskovitz put his arm around her shoulder while his crying continued.

"Did she know anyone by the name of Leonid Kozlov? Did you find any of your daughter's notes with his name?"

"No, I never cheard the name before, nor vas there any evidence of any ritten note viet chis name," said Mrs. Moskowitz.

"How about photos – pictures of him or them?"

"No, not at all."

Shmuel thought to himself, 'What a sad sight to see – parents being so helpless and powerless in raising their own child. Yilena must have been a master manipulator, able to emotionally blackmail her parents while refusing to accept any rules and limits they tried to create.' Shmuel, a bachelor, thought to himself that this was an excellent reason to never get married and have kids. He thought, 'My goodness, they're miserable! Look how they feel like failures.'

"Before I leave, I'd like to have a look at her bedroom. Can you point me to where it is?"

Shmuel took some time looking for possible signs but came up with nothing.

The interview came to an end. Shmuel said, "I want to thank you for your cooperation. I know this has not been easy for you. But I do have one additional question. Can you provide me with a list of any of her girlfriends or previous boyfriends and/or the male babysitter?"

Mr. Moskovitz answered, "She chad no girlfriends and because she vas so defiant and oppositional, no von liked cher. As far as the guy chow vas cher babysitter, che no longer lives chere and vie honestly don't know chis vhereabouts."

"Do you know his name?"

"Yes, I write it down for you but we don't know ver che vent."

"Okay, well, I appreciate that you shared your family life with me. I know it's not easy for you, grieving about the loss of your daughter. Try not to blame yourself because you made solid efforts to be good parents. I'm so sorry you had so many disappointments. It sounds like Yilena was impossible to get along with. If you think of anyone – contacts or names of anyone that had contact with her, please call me." Shmuel handed them his card.

They said goodbye to Shmuel, still wiping their tears away.

Chapter Nine

Raffi, a young police officer of age thirty-three, was elevated to the rank of detective three years ago. His tan skin and jet-black hair could have made him appear more like a Spaniard, Mediterranean, perhaps Italian, or Greek. Married for one year, Raffi and his wife, Shoshana, were expecting their first child any day now. Raffi patted Shoshana's belly while he made cooing sounds to their yet child. He was determined to be a great father, the kind his dad was to him. Raffi and Shoshana wanted to be totally surprised by the baby's gender and avoided amniocentesis. They felt that God's miracles were worthy of waiting for. Most of all, they wanted a healthy baby. Raffi's real name was Raphael ben Yosef Yardeni. His friends and work colleagues referred to him as Raffi for short.

As he reflected on becoming a father, for a brief moment he reflected back to his own family of origin. Originated in Iraq, his grandfather, Abraham, pronounced Avraham, made a five–hundred-mile trek by foot and donkey while his wife, Sahadia, was barefoot and pregnant with Raffi's father. Crossing a desert with unforgiving mountains, they survived extreme daytime heat but cold at night. A jeweler by occupation, he designed gold, silver, and copper, often augmented with the stone of Eilat-tanzenite. As a child, Raffi heard stories of how Jews were persecuted and killed in Iraq, the reason his grandparents fled to Israel. Raffi was told that when his grandparents arrived in Israel, Avraham kneeled down and kissed the ground below. He worked in Jerusalem, designing jewelry based on biblical themes. They were Sephardic Jews who spoke both Arabic and Hebrew. Raffi grew up eating Middle-Eastern foods like falafel, hummus, tahini, shashlik, shish kabab, and lamb dishes. They attended a Sephardic synagogue with unique melodic prayers different from Ashkenazi prayers. Raffi's father, Yosef, became a police officer.

It had been a long day. At 11:00 p.m., he called Yoni.

"Yoni, hi, it's Raffi. I want to tell you what happened when I interviewed Mr. Menachem Weiss, the owner of Sabre Meats. I apologize for calling you so late."

"No, no, it's okay. Tell me what happened."

"Mr. Weiss had called our local police, saying he knew the killer and that he wanted to help us in any way possible. His shop was just off Yehuda Street in Tel Aviv. I recorded the interview as you directed and I mentioned to Mr. Weiss that he might be subpoenaed to testify in the future." Raffi paused to recall his interview with the shop owner. "I'll play the main excerpts from my interview."

He began, "I'm going to need to record our discussion today. For the record, please state your full name and what you do for a living."

"I'm Menachem Weiss, the owner of Sabre Meats – a butcher shop. I am a butcher and carry a wide variety of meats in my shop including several cuts of steak, chop meats, brisket, and chicken, etc."

"You understand that you may be subpoenaed in a future court hearing?"

"Yes."

"What is your marital status? Any children? And were you born in Israel?"

"Yes, I'm married, have a boy and a girl, both all grown up. And yes, I was born in Israel. I'm a Sabre – born in Israel. My daughter is married and my son is in training to be a pilot for the IDF."

"Tell us how you know the suspect and for how long?"

"Leonid Kozlov is originally from Ukraine which, as you know, was part of the USSR. He immigrated to Israel when he was fifteen years old. He came to work with me about four years ago. He was then nineteen and I was so amazed how he learned to cut and slice meat with amazing speed. He seemed knowledgeable about cutting-carving techniques. His strong arms and hands and could easily pick up a seventy-five-kilo-slab of beef without even straining himself. He was as strong as an ox. I believed he might have had previous experiences in meat cutting. He was that skilled with knives. Although my knives are always kept quite sharp, he insisted on bringing his own. But I insisted he sterilize them on a daily basis."

"Was there any evidence that Leonid had any psychological problems?"

"Not until a few months ago. I wondered if he dated but he never confided in me. He was a handsome guy, even with the noticeable scar on his face, and I'm sure he'd have no problems getting dates. I know he liked to work out with weights for at least five days a week. Leonid's muscular appearance made him thinks about competing in body-building contests. He was always on time to work and did what was expected of him. That made him a great employee in my opinion. He never discussed his growing-up experiences in the USSR. He was a very private individual – never shared any personal feelings with me. In that way, he maintained his aloof distance from me."

"What happened in the last few months?"

"A couple of months ago, I noticed he appeared more fatigued and exhausted. He came to work with rings around his eyes, as if he hadn't slept. Then, about four weeks ago, he suddenly disappeared – no calls, no emails, nothing. I called him several times but his phone was now disconnected. I went over to the address he had provided me but the landlord said he disappeared and never paid his last month's rent. It's a real mystery to me, since he was a great employee. When he worked, he did the job of two men. He was as strong as a bull and never afraid of hard work."

"Can you provide me his last phone number? Do you have his email address? Do you happen to remember the gym he belonged to or where he worked out?"

"No, I'm sorry but I don't know the name of his gym. Yes, I'll be happy to give you his phone number, at least the one I have."

"Do you happen to know anyone who knew him, friends or family?"

"I wouldn't know who his friends are, but I do know his parents and where they live."

"What are their names and address?"

Mr. Weiss willingly provided the information.

"Did he ever mention anything about a social life, perhaps girlfriends?"

"No, never."

"Do you recall anything that he wrote, such as names, phone numbers, or about clubs he frequented?"

"No, not at all."

"How did you happen to know the information about his parents?"

"They're customers of mine. I see them, oh, about two or three times a month. They live no more than five to ten minutes away by car. They live in the Yehuda Hamaccabi street area of Tel Aviv. When we're done with the interview, I'll give you their exact address."

"Thanks. Is there anything else you might be able to offer us – any clues to his personality?"

"I can't think of anything except that he was a very private person, perhaps very shy."

Raffi was able to secure Leonid's parents' names, address, and phone number. Raffi gave Mr. Weiss his card. "Call me if you think of any other people that might know Leonid. And thank you for your time and your cooperation." They shook hands. Raffi was pleased with the interview flow.

***

It was eight thirty in the evening, the same day when Raffi had spoken to Mr. Weiss. A clear sky with stars and moon shining made the address easier to find as Raffi drove to Mr. and Mrs. Kozlov apartment. Raffi knocked on the door of their second-story apartment.

Behind the closed door, he said, "Yes. Cho is it?"

This is Detective Raphael Yardeni. I have a few questions and would like to talk to you."

The door opened and they both said, "Come in, detective," although shyly.

"Thank you, and before we go any further, I must tell you that this interview is part of an investigation involving your son, Leonid. A murder took place two days ago and your son, at this time, is our prime suspect. Your son is wanted for murder. I will video our conversation as part of our investigation. Most people are initially camera-shy but after a minute or two, you'll be completely unaware of the camera. You understand that you may be called in for a future disposition. Yes?"

"Yes," said Mr. Kozlov.

Mr. Kozlov was short, about five feet five, with a bent back and incessantly smoking unfiltered camels. The apartment carried a heavy smell of smoke, probably years of it. His beaklike nose, receding hairline, sloppy clothes, and his gray unkempt mustache contributed to his unfavorable appearance. Mrs. Kozlov wore a babushka over her hair, had no makeup, and wore a simple, faded, light blue housedress. Mrs. Kozlov had several gold teeth that were clearly noticeable. Although they were in their late forties, they could have easily passed being in their early-seventies.

Raffi set up his camera and said, "This must be a difficult time for you as your son is our prime suspect in a murder?"

Mr. Kozlov spoke. "Of course, chis picture is all over television. Chow do you expect us to fiel? Our friends and our neighbors, they all vhisper bechind our back. Suddenly, cwhoever vie thought ver our friends chave turned their backs on us. Our son vas always a dieficult child. Even ven vie lived in Ukraine, che needed lots of punishments as a child. LOTS!"

"Oh, what types of punishments did he receive?"

"One time, after che chung our cat and dissected the poor thing, vie put him in a shed for ten days vit no cheat, no electricity. There vas an outhouse near the shed. Che vas tied viet a chain and lock so che vouldn't run away. Vie vould bring him food and place the plate on the ground. That's it. Nothing else. No vords ver exchanged. And che never complained, just took chis punishments."

Raffi thought to himself, 'Oh my GOD! Even dogs get treated better.'

"You left him in the cold for ten days?" Raffi felt horrified to hear about their rejection.

"Yes, che kielled our cat. Che chung cher from a tree and then dissected cher entire body. Che deserved to be punished. Chis mother, my vife, even beat chim vit vouden broom."

"In the winter months in Ukraine, aren't the temperatures between thirty or fifty below zero?"

"Yes, sometimes they are, but che deserved to be punished. Von time, che took our sharpest steak knife and tried to stab chis mudder. Che vas tvelve then. I made chim do a chundred and fifty pushups and one hundred and fifty squats. Che did it vit no problem. In fact, che didn't even break into a sweat. It vas nothing for chim. Che could do two chundred pushups. Che was strong like a bull. Another time ven che vas caught masturbating to chis mudder's undervear, vie sent chim to our shed for two vieks. In addition, che vas vipped for doing it in chis mudder's underwear. Vie told chim that by masturbating like that, he disrespected chis mudder. In the shed, vie tied chim to chains so che vouldn't get away. Vie provided food on plates. Che vas oppositional and difficult."

Raffi tried to avoid being overly judgmental or critical and maintain his professional demeanor. "When you say he was whipped, can you tell me more about what you did?"

"Vell, first of all, it vasn't me who vipped chim. It vas chis mudder."

Mrs. Kozlov spoke up and said, "Che used to masturbate to my undervear. I vould tell chim to pull down chis pants, vhich che did. Then, I'd take my chusband's leather belt and vip chim. Sometimes, I'd chit him vit a vooden broom."

"More or less, how many times did you whip him?"

"Manie times, oh, maybe thirty or forty strong vips."

"What did you use to whip him?"

"A leather belt, of course."

"Belts usually have metal buckles. Is that the kind of belt you used?" Raffi pointed to her husband's metal belt buckle.

"Yes, of course!"

"And then what happened?"

"Che vould bleed, chave velts, but che vas niever apologetic. Che'd never say che's sorry. For being like that, I'd give to chim at least ten to fifteen extra vips. Once che turned around to scream at me. He called me a f***** cwhore. It vas then that I chit chim vit the belt and buckle on chis face. That's vhy chis face chas scar."

"About how many extra whips would he get for not saying he was sorry?"

"Oh, I vould give chim extra ten or fifteen vips."

"So is it fair to say that he'd get at least fifty or more whips, possibly sixty?"

"Oh yes. And che never cried, not once. Che never showed remorse or shame."

"And then what happened?"

"Che vouldn't cry or apologize for chis wrongdoings. He'd go to chis room. There, che cursed me out and told me che vished I vas dead. Che'd take a knife and stab a picture of me. Che vould scream from chis room with chis door shut tight, 'I chate you, mudder. You f***** cwhore. You mean nothing to me. You piece of shit! I chope you die! You're a slut cwhore! You bitch!'"

"What did you do next?"

"I put chim out in the shed for another veek vit a chain and lock around chis leg. I told chim that I vould speak to a judge about chis behaviors, like chow che killed and then dissected our cat, the poor thing. That's normal? I did speak to a judge and a social worker. Che vas placed in a foster chome for one year. It vas okay. Vie didn't miess chim. Che vas always troublemaker. Vie'd visit him once in a vhile, maybe once a month. The social worker told the judge that vie used vhips and placed chim in a shed for a veek or longer. The judge vasn't very chappy that vie took such drastic actions. Che made us take parenting classes and anger-management classes. Che also said that if our conduct didn't improve, che will permanently take Leonid avay from us. The judge also said that if that continued, che might even prosecute us as criminals."

"What happened next?"

"The foster home complained to the judge that Leonid molested their eight-year-old daughter. He snuck into her bed at night and played viet her. Che even chad her lick chis privates. Che'd rub his private against cher vagina. Che was thrown out of the foster chome for being a child molester, a pedophile. The foster home shared this vit us.

"Che was then placed in an institution for juvenile delinquents. Che did chorrible tings like seducing teenage boys to chave oral sex. Che also got into fights vit some of the boys. Che threatened to kiel them if che chad veapon. It vas vell known in the group chome that che chad oral sex viet manie boys by force or coercion. Che would go viet boys to communal bathroom and do oral sex on them. Che vas there for a little less than two years and released to our care as vie immigrated to Israel."

"Now that you were in Israel, what was your family life like?"

"A mess! Che got in trouble in school for carrying and displaying a switchblade knife viet a six-inch blade. Che liked a girl but she liked someone else. Che threatened to kiel the girl. Che vas asked to leave the school. Che quit school and niever finished his chigh-school education.

"Between the age of fifteen or sixteen and eighteen, che did odd jobs like sweeping floors and cleanup duties vile vorking in stores, did some gardening, and che vas a dish vasher at a restaurant. Chis room vas always a mess, like a tornado chit the area. On chis valls ver nude pictures of ladies vit parts of their bodies all cut up. Chis own family pictures chad a plethora of dart choles.

"When che turned eighteen, che vas refused entrance into the IDF because of chis psychiatric problems. Some years later, che sought employment to train and vork as a butcher. As far as dating, che never talked to us about nothing. Che chad chis own computer and I know che looked at porn sites. In fact, che'd spend hours on these sites. Our son chas many psychiatric problems. I don't feel guilty about vipping chim or putting chim in the shed. Che vas a bad rotten apple from the beginning."

"But it was well below zero degrees."

"Niever mind, che deserved it. Che vas bad boy right from the beginning. There vasn't even one positive quality about chim."

"Do you have any idea where he is now? He disappeared from his job and apartment."

"Vie chaven't seen chim in months."

"Do you know who his friends are?"

"No. Che chas none."

"Not even one?"

"No, che's a very private person. Never talked to us about chaving any friends."

"Might you have a hunch about where he might be? Can you provide us with a recent picture of your son?"

"No, vie chave none and vie don't know ver che is. Vie chave one picture of chim from two years ago. Sorry, vie can't be more helpful."

"Can I borrow that picture? I'll return it. Or better that that I will take a picture of that picture. Well, we might talk again. Thank you for sharing your family problems. I know it's not easy. Shalom." After this interview, Raffi felt sad and depressed about the lack of parenting experienced by Leonid. Surprised by the extent of his mother's cruelty, Raffi thought, 'Is it any wonder that Leonid became such a psychopath – so sadistic and detached?'

Before leaving, Raffi had asked to look at Leonid's room. There were no clues, like names of people. He did notice some graffiti with a saying, *'Die, whore, die!'* He noticed something else. He graphited his mother's name in Hebrew. Under the graffiti, he wrote, *'Die, whore!'* He also witnessed graffiti with the Hebrew letters *M* and *N*. Raffi took pictures of these and sent them on to Yoni by email. Raffi felt curious about the letters *M* and *N*. Pensively, he thought, 'I know they mean something, but what? Who can I call?'

It was quite late by now. Yoni thanked him for doing a great job. They both wondered, 'Where could Leonid be? Certainly, he must be hiding. But where?'

"Raffi, I had another idea. In a couple of days, return and interview them once again. Surely, they must have some leads about their son's favorite hangouts, perhaps a friend or two, maybe an ex-girlfriend. Yea, I think we shouldn't let up on them so quickly."

"Okay, no problem. I'll give them a day or two and make another unannounced visit."

"Thanks, Raffi. Much appreciated!"

That same evening, now with a cool fall-like breeze in the air, Yoni decided to case out the Volga Club. He was armed to the hilt and wore his bullet-free vest. It was a particularly dark cloudy evening when Yoni pulled up to the nightclub at 9:30 p.m. As a detective, he wanted to see if he could spot and arrest Leonid singlehandedly. In part, this decision was based on Hannah's visions, convinced she'll be killed by Leonid. Also, there was a continual threat to Hannah's life and a major disruption in their family life. Yoni felt compelled to act. 'How can my family be at peace when Hannah envisions she'll be one of Leonid's victims?'

He was able to find nearby parking and stepped into the smoke-filled nightclub at nine p.m. He was dressed in a gray suit, white shirt, and a navy-blue tie, sporting a grayish well-manicured beard and mustache. Yoni texted Shmuel and Yitzchak that he arrived at the club. He positioned himself towards the rear of the club with good dance stage views.

She couldn't have been any older than twenty-two, maybe twenty-three. She asked Yoni if he'd like a drink before the show. Yoni said he'd like a Russian Mule and that it be with double shots of vodka.

She was blond, pretty, and had blue eyes. Her body toned from dancing made her look even more sensual. When she leaned over, her breast cleavage was visibly apparent. "Ooh, vat's your name, choney?" she inquired, snuggling closer and closer to Yoni. "Vould you be interested in anything besides drink?" She didn't wait for his answer and added, whispering in his ear, "I can make you very, very chappy, baby." She had a big seductive smile as she stuck out the tip of her tongue and wiggled it around. She placed her arm on his shoulder and said, "You know I can make you fiel vonderful, from your chead to your tippy toes. Choney, chow about vie find nirvana? I viel bring you to the moon, the stars, cheaven, and back. You'll love it – unbelievable sex!"

"I'll just wait on that for a while." He put her off.

A moment later, she brought Yoni's drink.

"So, are you chere on business, choney?"

"Yes."

"Ooh, vat kind of business are you in?"

"Oh, I'm in computer technology."

"Vow, that's such technical work. Ven you're done with programing, I can show you chow to relax and enjoy amazing pleasure in your life. Vouldn't you like that?" She once again snuggled closely and stuck her tongue out. She gently slapped her nearly naked butt and winked at him. She blew air into his ears while she wrapped her arms around his shoulders. Yoni remained still and unmoved by the sexualized flirtation.

"Later. Oh, by the way, when does the show start?"

"It viel start in about forty-five minutes. Okay, choney, just let me know about your dreams and passions and I'll take you around the vorld and back. At the end, you'll agree that you never chad such pleasures ever before. Remember, I'm chere to please you. Your sensual wishes can all come true, baby."

"I'll think about it." Yoni tried to appease her by making that statement. "Oh, by the way, have you ever seen him?" Yoni showed her a picture of Leonid.

"No, I niever seen chim before. Vat, you police officer?"

"No, just a family friend looking for him. If you see him, please call me." And with that, Yoni gave her his made-up 'international technology' business card. Yoni waited for one and a half hour and then left. On this night, Leonid did not show up.

Chapter Ten

Bluish-red bloodshot eyes characterized how physically drained and exhausted Yoni felt when he returned home. Indeed, it was a very long sixteen-hour day. He opened the refrigerator for a snack. After eating a sandwich, his warm welcoming bed awaited him. He closed his eyes and quickly drifted into a deep slumber. It couldn't have been more than twenty minutes when he suddenly heard knocks on his bedroom door. Startled, he awakened to the knocks and asked, "Yes, who is it?"

"Abba, it's me – Hannah. I'm sorry to wake you up but I must talk to you."

"Okay, let me put my robe on and we'll talk in the kitchen. I'll meet you there."

Hannah had already seated herself at the table. She bit her nails, a sign that she was worried and anxious.

"Okay, what's going on? What's up, Hannahle?" Her face had reddened. By now, Hannah's breathing was labored.

"She was only twenty-one or twenty-two, and Russian. Look how close in age we are. That frightens me a lot. Will I be his next victim? I'm so sorry for waking you up. I hope you're not mad at me for interrupting your sleep?"

"Hannah. Please, don't worry. You did the right thing. Now please go back to bed. Okay?"

"Oh, one more thing. I love you, Abba."

"I love you too, honey."

Yoni tried to drift into well-deserved sleep but his eyes remained ajar. Slumber's curtains remained wide open as he continued to feel hyper vigilant. He felt restless. He thought to himself, 'What if my Hannah does become a victim, a fatality? I can't let that happen.' He concluded by saying to himself, 'No, no way! That's not even an option. That f***** is never going to hurt my daughter. That will never happen!' Yoni was angry just thinking about it. Besides his anger, Yoni wondered, 'Will Leonid capture Hannah?' He shook his head in attempt to dispel these thoughts from his mind.

He was unable to resume sleeping, as he felt consumed by Hannah's worries. It was six a.m. when Yoni decided he'd head out and make an early start to interview Dr. Rubin Stern, the chief criminal pathologist who conducted an autopsy on Yilena.

"Shalom, Yoni. Okay, let me brief you. Thus far, it appears that she was drugged with heroine. Two vials were found at the Jewish Cemetery. We have evidence that he also chloroformed his victim into a deep stupor state. He killed the victim by multiple stabbings with an icepick. We found the same exact words written in the victim's blood: *'Die, you dirty, filthy whore! Die, you f***** bitch.'* We chalked the area where the victim was placed. Her body was taken to the morgue. We're taking lots of pictures. There were no footprints. There were no witnesses, just this horrendous, brutal killing." He thought for a few seconds and added, "This guy is f****** crazy. He's a psycho, a nut job, very dangerous to anyone scrutinizing his crimes, like us."

While driving to see Dr. Stern, Yoni's thoughts were preoccupied about the murder of Yilena. He also thought about Hannah's safety, who was not too far removed in age from Yilena. He concluded, 'No, this can't happen to my Hannah because she's just a teenager. She's not a prostitute. This would never happen to my Hannahle! After all, I am the lead detective on the killer's trail.' He felt instant relief when he came to this conclusion. Inwardly, he thought, 'One murder, one near fatal stabbing but no hints of where he might be hiding. That's totally unacceptable. Probably, Commander Levy will be real pissed at me for not solving this crime case yet.'

The sun rose as Mount Carmel and the shoreline of the calm Mediterranean Sea unfolded its sheer beauty. In the distance, he noticed a number of fishing boats that were busy hauling in the day's fresh catch. Yoni was killing time on Mount Carmel while waiting to speak to Dr. Stern.

He strolled to a nearby park, especially since he was early for his appointment. He needed a Venti and walked to Starbucks. He sat himself in a park which was near to major hotels like the Dan Ha Carmel and the Hilton. The park was near the Carmelit train which took people from Haifa up to the Carmel mountain.

A bench to rest on and pine scents created a feeling of relaxation. He leaned back on a bench as if to nap. With closed eyes, he suddenly regressed to a time in his life when he was an infant in a stroller. As the sun's rays peered out of its closed curtains, they began to emerge through the thickly enveloping tree branches. Mesmerized by the pleasant pine-tree fragrances, he concluded, 'I know I've been here before. But when?' He closed his eyes and took a few deep breaths, exhaling slowly. Suddenly, as if it occurred today, it came back to him. 'I remember my Ima took me here when I was about one and a half years old. This place was called Mothers' Park some forty-plus years ago.' He remembered that as a very young child, his mother pushed a stroller and would take him to this park. Forty minutes had passed, but he thought it was just a couple of minutes. He looked at his watch and couldn't believe his eyes. He thought to himself, 'I must have been so relaxed. Did I dream? And to go so far back in time? Wow! Perhaps I was in a state of self-hypnosis?'

While he had experienced a time regression to his infancy stage, as he now walked into the morgue, the unpleasant smells of formaldehyde overtook him. He couldn't stand the unpleasant smells.

"Hi, Dr. Stern. I'm here to talk to you about this latest victim." Yoni flashed his ID.

"Oh, hi Yoni, it's not necessary. I remember you from other cases in the past." He continued to work on the victim.

"Thanks, but you know it is police protocol. Say just as an aside what is that park called, the one with all the pine trees and benches? It's very near to the Dan Ha Carmel Hotel. In fact it's across the street from the hotel."

"Oh yes, that park is still called Mothers' Park."

Inwardly, Yoni smiled remembering a happy time in his past. Inwardly, he had a strong and loving attachment to his mother. Yoni thought, 'So unlike Leonid's encounters with his mother.'

There were cold temperatures inside, walls colored light gray, the site of lifeless bodies on freezer shelves, the smell of formaldehyde, and quite the morbid-looking environment in this morgue. Yoni thought, 'What a sad ending of a journey that just comes to a sudden halt. Are their loving family relationships connected to these corpses?'

"What can you tell me about this recent killing?"

He observed the victim lying on his table – gurney at the morgue. Dr. Stern had cut open her cranium as part of his comprehensive pathology report. Dr. Stern wondered if there was any evidence of head-brain trauma. The brainstem revealed trauma. The brainstem controls such life functions as respiration, heart pulse, and blood pressure. Dr. Stern concluded there was blunt object trauma to the brainstem which was fatal. For a few brief seconds, Yoni shivered. He wished he would have brought a sweater. He thought to himself, 'Oh my God, what a hell of a depressing workplace this is!'

"I found traces of heroin in her blood. Her blood chemistry revealed high levels of chloroform. She was strangled. Cotton swabs of semen were taken for further identification but there's evidence the killer had sexual intercourse with the victim. Was it before or after her death was not exactly clear. You can see abundant blood capillaries around her neck as well as black and blue fingermarks which indicates strangulation.

"She was stabbed twenty times with an icepick, several times through her heart and lungs. She actually died not only from being stabbed in the chest but due to her inability to breath. Her lungs filled with blood, and she ultimately suffocated. She choked from drowning in her own blood which collected in her lungs."

"What else can you tell me about the killer and his victim?"

"The killer appears to be extremely strong."

"What makes you say that, Dr.?"

"In strangling his victim, he also managed to crack several of her neck's vertebras. In fact, three were broken because of his powerful strangulation. And then, to add insults to injury, he cracked her neck by a sudden twisting movement of her head. Her cranium dangled by muscle fibers and skin. Her severed spine was so severe that had she survived, she would have been in a state of complete paralysis." He concluded, "The victim was killed in several ways."

Yoni said, "Such a nice guy we have on our hands!"

Yoni took copious pages of notes while Dr. Stern talked. He thanked him. "Can I put your comments about the killer in my notes?"

"For sure, but don't worry, Yoni. My report will be thorough for your forensic record and any future courtroom appearances if they're needed."

"Would you email me a copy of your report please? You could also email it to me as an attachment." Yoni presented Dr. Stern his business card.

"For sure."

They shook hands and bid each other farewell, for now.

It was now one p.m. and Yoni realized that his stomach gurgled from extreme hunger. He hadn't had breakfast or lunch. In Haifa, he went to a popular Middle-Eastern restaurant called the Ali Babba Café, where you can feast on a variety of gourmet Middle-Eastern dishes. The restaurant owner, with the name of 'Mazal,' was a young man from Tunisia, a 'Mizrachi,' with a full head of black hair, a mustache, and a tannish-brown complexion which made him look like he could have easily passed for being Arabic, but he wasn't. He was Jewish and Israeli. Yoni ordered a falafel, tahini, a side of humus, and a small skewer of chicken kabab. He asked for lemonade to drink. He sat down and grabbed a copy of Yediot Hayom Newspaper, which in Hebrew means 'the news of the day.' After he realized that much of the news described polices' failures in capturing the killer, he folded the newspaper and threw it away. The newspaper's first page devalued police efforts about not yet capturing the killer and ranted about the lack of police efforts. He was angry about biased one-sided news reporting. Being sleep deprived, he needed to relax and create some emotional distance from this case.

His food came out in two or three minutes. While he ate his lunch, he thought about Sarah and his children.

Every morsel of falafel, tahini, humus, and fresh pita bread tasted like amazing gourmet bites sent from the heavens above. It was so incredibly tasty. To date, he had accomplished a great deal. He thought to himself, 'Who cares what the newspapers have to say? They only want to sell newspapers by writing provocative, nasty comments. The hell with them. I'm going to solve this case no matter what.' This inner satisfaction and confidence helped him have realistic expectations and hope. He closed his eyes for a minute and took a couple of deep breaths, inhaling and exhaling to relax. Once again the thought about his children and Sarah made him feel more peaceful. He felt so lucky and blessed to have healthy and caring children. In a few months, Hannah was to turn eighteen and be in the army. He thought, 'Oh my goodness, how quickly the years have passed. Wow! Shortly, my Hannahle will be in the army. How quickly she's grown up! And next year, my Aaron will enter first grade.' He smiled having peaceful thoughts about his family. He ordered another side of humus, informing the meltzar that he was still famished.

***

In the early evening, Hannah called, saying, "I studied the latest pictures about the victim that was stabbed. I had a new vision, Abba. We need to talk as soon as possible."

"We can talk now. What is it, Hannah?"

"Okay. This latest vision made me so sick; I threw up my lunch." She cleared her throat and swallowed a swish of water. "My stomach was so unsettled about what I saw. Abba, can you see any pattern when you look at the pictures of the two victims?"

"Some. They were both young. They were blond with blue eyes. Both were five foot, six inches in height. They look alike – blond and blue eyes. Is that enough, or is there more, Hannah?"

"Abba, please take a closer look at their faces. What do you see?"

"They resemble each other."

"And?"

"Oh my God, I hadn't put it together till now. Yea, there's an uncanny resemblance to you." He inhaled deeply. "Oh my God!" Yoni was overcome by his own feelings of angst and fright. He inhaled deeply to quell his own inner state.

"Abba, the resemblance is there and I am terrified beyond belief. I'm beside myself because I know he'll come after me any day now." Yoni heard Hannah's labored breathing on the phone. Her voice sounded shaky and quivering. Yoni felt worried. His jaws got tensed.

83

"Maybe, I'll be his next victim? I could easily be his next victim, Abba. After all, I resemble them and I'm the lead detective's daughter." Hannah sobbed hysterically. Her entire body shook from feelings of uncontrollable terror to her life. Her stomach wreathed in pain.

"Hannah, please try and calm down. Maybe you can call one of your girlfriends? I'll have unmarked police following you, but don't worry, they'll be incognito; that is, they will not be in uniform. They will follow you to school as well as when you walk home. Hannah, I've got your back! I will have unmarked police cars in the neighborhood. You'll be protected. Don't worry, my Hannahle."

"Thanks, Abba." Her inner state found comfort in her father's words. "But before we hang up, Abba, another vision revealed that the killer is in our neighborhood and is stalking me. In the middle of the night, he breaks my bedroom window, chloroforms me, and hauls me away on his shoulders as if I were a slab of meat." She needed to inhale deeply and collect her thoughts. "He snatches me into his car and physically batters me so I wouldn't wake. He takes me to a secluded neighborhood, one away from you or any police station. You know the rest. Feebly, I try to resist, but I can't fight such a sadistic animal with cruel intentions. Ultimately, my fate is the same as the other two, being raped and killed. He shouts obscenities at me like, 'Die chwore, you f***** bitch. I gonna kiel you.' He repeats. When he's done, he drives towards Northern Israel, parks his car in a kibbutz in the Golan Heights, and disposes my lifeless body under an orange tree." Hannah got so nervous about this vision that she excused herself. "Abba, sorry, I have to throw up again." She put the phone down and quickly ran off to her bathroom.

When she came back, she sobbed out loud. Barely able to catch her breath, she asked her father to hold on while she paced back and forth feeling agitated, and patted her eyes with tissues. She then re-grasped the phone.

"Hannahle, please don't worry. I promise you that you'll have constant police protection at all times."

"Abba, you promise? Because I'm so beside myself."

"Yes, of course, Hannah. Have I ever lied to you? I promise you'll be safe."

"Okay, Abba. Thank you. I began to wonder if I should carry a concealed weapon. Last summer when I was in Gadna, you know, the army pre-training, I learned something about handling guns and rifles. Should I have a concealed weapon, Abba?" Her helpless demeanor gave rise to a more assertive voice. "Yes, I think I should, Abba."

"You're not eligible to carry a concealed weapon. You have to be at least twenty-one and have served in the military. Secondly, you need to formally apply and have good reasons, like self-defense. And you'll need extensive background checks, all when you're twenty-one years old. Hannah, I will call for police protection and I'll be home in a couple of hours. Besides, we're the police, so let us do our job! I'll let Ima know how frantic you are. But maybe you can have a girlfriend come over? You know, it's good for emotional support."

"Okay, Abba. I'll do that, and thanks for everything. What would I do if I didn't have a father like you? Abba, you rock!"

"Love you, honey. I'll get you lots of police protection." And they hung up the phone. Frightened for his daughter's safety, his own voice quivering, he called for additional police with unmarked police cars to surround their neighborhood.

During his call for additional police protection, he said, "Keep an eye on my daughter. Her life is threatened. The killer is illusive, smart, and cunning. He's bent on killing her. But this can never be an option!"

When Yoni got off the phone, he too had broken into a sweat. He went into the currently unused police conference room, got on the floor, and did two sets of fifty pushups, ran in place for five minutes, did sixty jumping jacks, and fifty crunches without rest in between. His way of relieving his own stress level was to work out, albeit a short one.

Although she felt some relief having additional police protection, Hannah contemplated that capturing Leonid may take considerable police time. She felt her life was suddenly filled with danger. She also felt that Leonid was street-smart and clever in a crazy kind of way. He'll be able to evade police. She had to develop her own plan to fight back and slow him down. 'How many more women will be killed? Will I be one of his victims?' Now, more so than ever, she felt compelled to protect herself. But she felt morally and ethically confused. 'Yes, it is a police matter, just like my Abba said, but if someone threatens to take your life, to rape or kill you, aren't there instances when you're in the right to injure or even kill the perpetrator no matter how old you are, especially when he's killed another young lady? Isn't that legitimate self-defense? There are several biblical instances that point to *an eye for an eye and a tooth for a tooth.*' She respected what her father said about needing to be twenty-one and have a background check… 'But? What if?'

Chapter Eleven

Detective Shmuel had just arrived to interview Nachum, the stabbed victim's husband.

He worked as a jeweler in a fashionable store in Jerusalem. Yitzchak asked Nachum if he could step into the hallway of the hospital, as he needed to interview Nachum. At age twenty-three, he had a full-length beard and wore a black coat and the kippah which rested on his head.

"Shalom, Nachum. I'm Detective Yitzchak. We met here yesterday but I need to ask you a few questions. How about we step into the hallway, away from family members who are praying right outside of Rachel's room?"

"Okay. That's fine."

"How did you and Rachel first meet?"

"We didn't formally meet or have a date. I did see her a few times at the synagogue, but as you know men and women sit separately. When we turned eighteen, our parents arranged the marriage. We were betrothed to each other by both sets of parents."

"Is there anyone in your network of friends and/or family that would wish to harm your wife, Rachel?"

"No, not at all. She is loved by everyone."

"Has she ever had a boyfriend who felt scorned, and if so, what's his name?"

"No, before we married, she never had a previous boyfriend. In Orthodox Judaism, it's not allowed to date. Women that have boyfriends prior to an arranged marriage would be looked down at and scorned for life."

"To get divorced, the Ghet is very difficult in Israel. Have you felt that she might have a boyfriend while being married to you?"

"No, not at all. We loved each other."

"Have you ever wished to harm your wife in any way?"

"No, I cared about her. Why would I want to harm my wife?"

"Trust me. It happens."

"Is there anyone who you believe wanted to harm Rachel?"

"No, not that I'm aware of. She was loved by everyone."

Yitzchak took out a picture of Leonid. "Do you recognize this person? Is this someone you've come across?"

Nachum looked at the picture and said, "No, but I did see a photo of him in one of the recent newspaper articles."

"Is he a member of your orthodox community?"

"Not at all. Never seen him at any of our synagogue's congregation chanting."

"Have you or Rachel received any letters from anyone who was suspicious?"

"No, no one."

"Okay, if you think of anyone that wanted to harm Rachel, here's my card. Give me a call if someone enters your mind. I thank you for your cooperation." He extended his hand to shake Nachum's and bid each other goodbye.

"I sure hope that you guys capture this animal. He's very dangerous. He might attempt to harm other females."

"Yes, you're absolutely correct, Nachum. We're trying hard and I'm sure we will capture him."

Yitzchak called Yoni to keep him informed him about his interview with Nachum. He believed that Nachum had nothing to do with the crime against Rachel. In addition, Nachum knew of no one who'd wish to harm his wife.

***

Shmuel and Leora had been seeing each other for a few months. Shmuel had never committed to any long-term relationship but had had many short-term flings. He loved his lifestyle – hanging out with his friends, enjoying a beer or two, going to the beach on Saturday and sunning himself in, clubbing on the weekends, physical workouts during the week, and being the very best detective he could be. Shmuel loved women, flirting and gaining their attention. Many of his male friends described him as a stud, a babe magnet. Some women even mistook him as a Hollywood movie star.

Leora, a teacher, was twenty-five, with jet-black hair of shoulder-length and stunningly crystal-clear blue eyes. An unmistakable hardcore body, giggly, and outgoing best described her. She was definitely a head-turner and had a toned body. Guys would often flirt with her.

Today, Leora discussed teaching elementary-school kids of age six to ten. Shmuel said that if he were six or eight years old, he would easily have a crush on her and would bring her a big red apple every day. She smiled from ear-to-ear, enjoying his flirtatious compliment. Shmuel met Leora at Club Gilboa when he asked if he could buy her a drink. This led to two or three.

Moscow mules, easy flowing conversation, mutual attractions, and flirtations led to much more. During a walk on a sandy beach in Tel Aviv, they found a quiet bench nearby. He placed his hand on her shoulder. She moved closer to Shmuel who initiated their first kiss. With her leg wrapped around Shmuel's, there were no objections when this kissing progressed to touching. Shmuel suggested she come along and they'd go for a ride to his apartment. There were no protests as they walked towards his car holding hands.

Shmuel drove his 1966 restored red Mustang convertible while the summer's salty sea breeze gently caressed their faces. They listened to the reggae sounds of Bob Marley who sang 'red, red wine.' They sang along, "Red, red wine…" In addition, they enjoyed Jimmy Hendrix's songs like 'foxy lady' while Shmuel drove his Mustang with one hand on her thigh. While he drove, Leora unbuttoned his shirt and licked his chest nipples. She blew warm, seductive air in his ears.

When they arrived at his apartment, the excitement of passions overtook them. In a mad rush, Shmuel accidentally tore two buttons of his short-sleeved shirt. Leora kicked off her shoes, with one crashing against the wall.

They made passionate love throughout the night. Leora said she had climaxed a number of times. All sense of time faded. Shmuel's alarm clock awakened them at six thirty a.m. He needed to begin his work. Even a warm, relaxing shower could not eliminate the black rings around his lower eyelids. Even more upsetting was his headache, most probably from drinking late hours and feeling sleep-deprived. Leora offered him breakfast but because he was late and in a rush to get to work, he opted for strong coffee instead.

"Sorry, but we'll get caught up later. Stay here as long as you want." He gave her a kiss on her cheek. And off he went. Leora got dressed and ready to commute towards her school. During her drive, she thought, 'Wow, what an interesting and handsome guy Shmuel is.'

They had seen each other weekly since their first passionate lovemaking date. It had been four months since their first fateful encounter.

***

"So, Shmuel, we haven't seen each other in a week but it seems a lot longer. What's up? How's your investigation going?"

"Can't discuss my investigation but yea, but yea all's well. How about you?"

"Back to teaching, I was assigned to a class I'm not so crazy about. They're five-year-olds, kindergarteners, pishers. You know what I mean? Their whiney."

"Yea, not yet curious to learn but having separation anxiety from their mothers."

"Listen Shmuel, we need to talk in person. Can you make some time when we can converse, you know, face-to-face? I need to do that as soon as possible."

"Yea, no problem. Why, is there some problem? Are you okay?"

"I prefer to talk to you face-to-face."

"Okay, how about tonight around 7:30 p.m. at the Alibaba Café in Haifa? I get off work around 6:30. How about we meet there?"

Shmuel wondered, 'What could be so urgent? Why does she have to talk to me as soon as possible? Does she want to end our relationship? Is she pregnant or is she in some kind of a legal jam?'

She appeared as if she had been crying, as her eyes were reddish. It was 7:30 p.m. Shmuel ordered for Leora after he asked her about her dinner preferences. The server looked quite tan, with long curly black hair, and Arabic in appearance – maybe from Morocco or Tunisia? Instead, he was an Israeli Sephardic Jew, born in Morocco, and therefore he was considered a Mizrachie. He spoke fluent Hebrew, Arabic, and French. After checking in with Leora, Shmuel said, "She'll have a shish kabab with lamb meat, a side dish of humus and tahina. Please bring us extra pita bread. I'll also have humus and a gyro sandwich with beera schorah, the dark beer. And she'll have lemonade."

Leora smiled and enjoyed how manly Shmuel sounded when he ordered for her. But she had some difficult words that needed to be expressed. Her face had turned red from embarrassment.

"Listen, I have to tell you something." She appeared a bit tongue-tied but took some deep breaths, inhaled, and exhaled as she began to speak. "Shmuel, I'm almost a hundred percent definite that I'm pregnant. I haven't slept with anyone but you, Shmuel." Her flood gates opened and she began to cry. "I can't believe I'm crying like a baby. Excuse me." She took out a handkerchief and blew her nose.

Shmuel put his arm around her shoulder. "Have you had any tests?"

"Yes, I went to the pharmacy and bought one of those pregnancy self-tests. It showed that I am pregnant. The pharmacy tests are pretty accurate. I intend to see a doctor tomorrow, as I have an appointment. I'll have a more official test. I am sure that I'm pregnant. I'm nauseous and recently threw up a number of times. By the way, don't be surprised if I can't eat. It's not you or your company. Shmuel, if you remember, we never used any form of precautions – no birth control. So, it's as much my fault as it is yours."

"But I pulled out a couple of times."

"Yea, but very infrequently, Shmuel."

"So, what do we do now?"

"Well, I wasn't expecting this news. Do you think we need to know each other better?"

"Yea, that's true. But look, a baby's on its way." Leora began to cry even harder. Shmuel continued to have his arm placed around her shoulder. She continued, "Look, this is a very difficult time for me. I was raised in a traditional Jewish home with a father and a mother. What will my family think? Are they going to think of me as a tramp who had sex while being unmarried? What will my colleagues think of me giving birth as a single girl? At this time in my life, how do I feel about being a single mother?" She continued to cry. "Shmuel, this is really a very tough time for me. And you're the father of our future child, but you haven't said too much. Why?"

"I'm in a state of shock, Leora."

"Is that all you can say?" She said this sounding hurt and angry.

"What else can I say? I feel stunned. I should have used protection, so I blame myself."

Leora became even more upset by his reaction and said, "Okay, since you don't want to assume more responsibility, I'm going home now." She took out a handkerchief and blotted her face to dry up her red eyes. "Goodbye. Thanks for the dinner," she said with an angry and hurtful sound to her voice. She rose from her chair. She appeared hurt. Her eyes were still red and her mascara was smeared because of her tears.

He gently grabbed her arm. "Leora, please, please don't go. Please sit. I feel terrible that you feel so alone. I do have very strong feelings for you. Please, don't go. Please sit. Let's continue to talk. Okay?"

She stopped and sat down again. "What did you just say?"

"Look, I'm so sorry. I see you feel all alone. I realize it's a crisis for you, for us. But I do have very strong feelings for you—"

She interrupted him. "Okay, but I will still have to bring up a child as a single parent. Don't you get it? Don't you understand?" Her crying resumed. Her mascara smudged and ran down her cheeks. She took out a handkerchief from her purse and blew her nose.

"Oh no, you won't."

"What do you mean oh no, I won't? Sure I will. Who's going to help me raise this child?"

"Me." He paused to think. "Leora, look at me. From the bottom of my heart, I love you. I've never loved anyone before. But I do love you." He paused and then repeated himself, "Yes, I'm in love with you."

Still stunned and confused by his words, she said, "It takes more than just feelings to raise a child." She began to stand up and wanted to leave. "I love you too, but… Nooh?"

He grabbed hold of her hand and said, "No, please, sit down." She obliged.

"What for? Look, you and I did a foolish thing by not using protection. I'm against having an abortion. I won't take the life of a living human being that's growing inside my body. Sorry, abortion is totally out of the question. That's just the way I feel." She continued to weep. Her eyes were red and swollen from crying.

"Leora, let's make it work. Honestly, I love you. I've never loved any woman before. But I am one hundred percent sure that I do love you. Please believe me."

Leora now cried even harder. This time, her tears were from joy, as they both got up to hug and kiss. These were now happy tears. Shmuel took her handkerchief and wiped her eyes while he kissed her lips. The entire restaurant crowd began to applaud and cheer them on. Someone from the restaurant staff shouted, "Nooh! So when is the wedding date, Shmuel? How about it? Are we invited too?" Everyone laughed.

The intensity of their emotions and passionate conversation blocked out the rest of their environment. They were both surprised and shocked when someone asked, "Nooh, so when is the wedding date, and are we all invited too?"

He turned to her and said, "I love you, and I care about you, Leora. How about we get married, okay?"

"Wow! I was hoping you'd want to marry me. Shmuel, I love you too. In fact, I loved you from the very first time we set eyes on each other."

"Let's go home – my house. Okay?"

"Yes, of course. Let's do that, my love." She smiled.

They walked hand-in-hand towards his car. She put her head on his shoulders. "You never asked me if I love you."

"Well, what do you think? I just asked you to get married because I know you love me."

"I believe that you do, and it's nice to hear it again from your own mouth. I don't want you to feel trapped in this relationship, baby or no baby. When I found out that I was pregnant, I felt insecure, not quite trusting what your response would be. But now I feel so much more protected by you."

"No, I think your pregnancy created urgency; we have to face what we've done."

"But look, if you don't want to be in a relationship with me, it's okay. I will survive and the baby will be fine, with or without you, Shmuel."

"Stop, Leora. I didn't grow up with those kinds of values where a man doesn't care for his child. And the best part of it is loving you and our future baby."

"But look, it's a new era. Women have babies and don't get married. No pressure. If you don't want me or our baby, it's okay. I'll survive. No worries!" She displayed a kind of false bravado and attempted to conceal how vulnerable and how in love she was with Shmuel.

He pulled her closer to him, looked her in the face, eyeball to eyeball, and said, "Stop, please don't talk like that. I love you with all my heart. I don't want to be with anyone else. I want to spend the rest of my life with you. The fact that there's a baby on the way, wow, that's wonderful because I adore you. God's miracles must never be tempered with. I want to spend my entire life with you, honey! And guess what? I love kids. At heart, I'm a kid myself. I'm playful, and sometimes like to do goofy things just like kids do."

"That's the Shmuel I love – fun-loving and playful. But in a few months, I won't be so sexy, especially when I start to look like a big house. Maybe then, you'll change your mind, Shmuel?"

Her eyes and cheeks appeared puffy from all the crying. Rivulets of tears swirled down her red face. This time, her tears were happy ones. Her breathing became more labored.

"No, I won't. Like I said, I'm in love with you. I'm happy when we're together. I've been a bachelor for a long time while most of my friends are married with kids or some on their way. You're a gem, one I've always dreamed of all my life. In two months, I'll be thirty-three. It's time. No?"

"Shmuel, but it has to feel right for you. I know I love you and I want us to build a future together. But–" Leora felt insecure. A previous boyfriend had dumped her. At that time, she felt brokenhearted. She recalled crying unexpectedly and just being in a sad slump.

He cut her off, "There is no but. That's what I also want, Leora. Honest to God, I've never been in love until you came into my life." I denied my inner feelings. But you helped bring out what I felt inside." He pointed to his heart.

She inhaled deeply and said, "Okay, why don't we move forward and have you meet my parents. They are traditional, so could you please ask my father if you can marry me? That would give him respect that he needs and deserves."

"No problem. I was planning to do that anyway."

"I also want you to meet my mom and brothers. I have two brothers."

She asked, "Oh by the way, where are we going to live?"

"How about moving in with me?"

"Sounds fantastic to me. I'll give my landlord the required two-week notice. Never mind that I may have to forfeit a month's rent because I'll have you for the rest of my life."

"If you're short of money, just let me know. We'll be living together in two weeks and making wedding plans." They embraced and kissed each other. He held her in his arms long enough to get into Shmuel's Mustang.

This time, they listened to 'red, red wine' while they arrived at his place. They undressed and Shmuel felt and kissed her stomach.

She said, "There's not much there to feel or see yet, but in about two to three months, you'll be able to hear the baby's heartbeat."

"Wow! I can't believe how excited I feel not just because of the baby but being with you forever. Wow, this is fantastic! So, can we make love or will we hurt the baby?"

"Yea, of course, let's do it. At this point, it won't hurt the baby at all. So don't worry, Shmuel." Shmuel initiated slow kisses and touched Leora's behind while she kissed his chest and belly area. They made sensuous, slow love as they discovered each other's new erogenous zones.

An hour or more had passed when Shmuel offered to make her tea or coffee, kissed her on the cheeks, and said, "You have no idea how much I love you."

Leora smiled from ear to ear and said, "Me too, honey. You're my love forever and ever."

In the morning while Shmuel was getting dressed to be ready for work, Leora stated that she'd call her parents and ask if she could come with Shmuel that coming Friday for Shabbat dinner. "I will tell them. I have a very special person in my life who'd like to meet them. How does that sound to you, Shmuel?"

"Great. Let's do it! Should we invite my parents as well?"

"I think there will be other opportunities for both sets of parents to meet in the near future. This is a very special occasion for just my parents to meet you. Are you okay with that?"

"Sounds good to me." He changed the subject. "I wonder the latest with Leonid. I'll check in with my boss, Yoni."

Chapter Twelve

It was in 1924 Ephraim and his wife, Sabrina, first immigrated to Kiryat Bialik. Since then, this picturesque suburban community, only five kilometers from Haifa, attracted thousands of new settlers due to its garden-like appearance with lush trees, grass, and flowers like gladiolas and roses. It was near enough to Haifa, had nearby beaches, and was also a gateway community to Northern Israel. The residents were mainly professionals, like physicians, engineers, educators, accountants, those in sales, and lawyers who lived in private homes with gardens. This was the hometown where Leora grew up in her parents' home.

Their older home with both Australian grass in the front and flowers in the backyard was a quaint three-bedroom house. From the kitchen, one could see the backyard garden with a variety of colorful gladiolas, purple irises, and roses, all so colorful and lush. In the backyard, there was a patch of land, perhaps no more than eight by eight feet with abundant tomatoes, radishes, lettuce, onions, kohlrabi, and scallion. All appeared to be healthy-growing crops. Leora attended a nearby elementary school and a high school, just minutes away from her family's home.

On this sunny late afternoon day, he parked his red, new, shiny Mustang in front of their home, which also caught the attention of Gideon and Yaakov, Leora's brothers. They came out to greet him and took an interest in his newly detailed 1966 Mustang. Shmuel arrived with roses, a challah, kosher red wine, and babka for dessert. He made sure that he went to a glat kosher bakery.

He was greeted by Leora who gave him a big hug and a kiss. She appeared nervous about introducing Shmuel to her parents, not because he'd be an object of their scorn, but announcing soon-to-be wedding plans made her feel tense. In addition, she also hoped her parents would approve of her choice of a husband. Leora frequently sought her parents' opinions and even looked for their approval. She'd never been married before and wondered, 'What will my parents think of my Shmuel? I hope they'd like him.' She introduced him to her family members, first her mother and then her father and brothers. She was also anxious about being pregnant prior to being married and wanted to keep it a secret just between Shmuel and herself.

Mordechai Stern wore a hand-knit blue and white kippah (a skull cap) and Shmuel was introduced to Chaya Stern, Leora's mother, and her two brothers named Yaakov (age seventeen) and Gideon (age twenty-two). Gideon just finished his Israel Defense Force commitment. He was now a student at the Technion, Israel's version of MIT, majoring in physics and engineering. Yaakov dreamed to score high in the pre-pilot training program through the IDF and he'd need to take the exams in a year's time when he'd be a senior in high school.

Shmuel shook everyone's hand and presented Chaya the bouquet of eighteen select long-stem roses – reds, orange-peach, yellow, and a few pure white ones. Chaya was appreciative and thanked Shmuel. In turn, Mr. and Mrs. Stern were also a bit nervous to meet Leora's love of her life.

The table was set with a challah, red wine for the blessings, and their very best of china. After all, this was a very special occasion. Mr. Mordechai Stern also still maintained jet-black hair which helped explain how and why Leora inherited such hair. Mr. Stern was college-educated and an accountant by profession who was employed by an accounting firm. His wife, Chaya, was an elementary school teacher. 'The apple doesn't fall far from the tree,' mused Shmuel as he looked at Leora and said, "Now I know why you became a teacher." He smiled.

"It's such a pleasure to meet you, Shmuel, and welcome you to our home. Leora has spoken a great deal about you," said Mr. Mordechai Stern. He smiled and welcomed Shmuel to have a seat in their living room. He added, "You've blessed our home."

"Would you like something to drink, maybe a glass of wine, lemonade, or Coca Cola?"

"Thank you. It's so nice to meet you. I'd love some lemonade. I see how Leora got her very special qualities from you, her parents. Your daughter is lovely. We care greatly about each other."

The Sterns welcomed Shmuel to join them at the dinner table. The meal began by blessings over breaking bread together and drinking the fruit of the earth – wine. Everyone stood while Mordechai chanted prayers, welcoming the Sabbath, the day of rest, into their heart, body, and soul, and thanking God for the bountiful food with Amen. Leora helped her mom by bringing the chicken soup with noodles. Following this, a salad was served and then a brisket and potatoes. Other vegetables were served like green beans and corn. Mordechai proudly mentioned that all of the vegetables grown were from his garden.

A conversation ensued as Shmuel shared that he was a detective working on a very high-profile case. The family intuitively understood to not be intrusive and avoided asking too many questions. They understood his need for privacy. Leora helped serve the food, such as soup. She helped cut the brisket and offered every one slices. Steam managed to escape from the freshly sliced meat.

Shmuel remarked to Chaya, "Wow, your cooking is incredible! You're such a fantastic cook!"

Chaya smiled from ear to ear.

Mr. Stern asked him, "So, what's it like being a detective, Shmuel?"

"Oh, it's very fast-paced and your hours can change from day to day. But I love what I do, solving crimes and arresting criminals. A rollercoaster of adrenaline rushes best describes the types of emotions I feel on a daily basis. My father was a policeman, so I guess it's in my family DNA. My mother is a legal secretary employed in a large law firm in Haifa. I was recruited to the police after I served in the Golani brigade. I worked as a cop for a few years and then got promoted to the rank of detective."

Chaya asked, "Are you an only child or do you have some siblings?"

"No, I have a younger brother and sister. My brother is in intelligence in the IDF. My sister is married and I'm an uncle to a boy and a girl, ages five and three. I love being an uncle and giving gifts to my niece and nephew. It's like Hanukah arrives monthly, instead of once a year."

Everyone laughed.

Shmuel stated that he appreciated being invited. "It's very nice when a family sits down and worships with some prayers that strengthen their belief in God. In my family, we don't pray or thank God for our bountiful food. It's just a given thing. I guess we're more like secular Jews. We do go to synagogue on Rosh Hashanah, Yom Kippur, and on Passover. I like the idea of thanking God for our bread and for the Shabbat. My grandparents were much more orthodox than my parents are."

Mordechai thanked him for the compliment about chanting prayers before eating. Leora winked at Shmuel. "So, when were you guys thinking of getting married?" Mr. Stern inquired.

Shmuel stated that they would like to be married in the next two or three months. "Hopefully, that can be arranged? If not, maybe three and a half months?"

Leora piped up, "What do you say, Abba?"

Mordechai stated, "Three months? Isn't that a bit on the fast side?"

Leora piped in. "No, Abba, we really don't want a big, super-fancy wedding. Maybe limit the number of people that will get an invitation – just immediate family and close friends. If we can keep it to under a hundred or even seventy-five people, that would be awesome. We're not looking for a super-fancy wedding – just something done in a tasteful traditional manner. But if you feel that it's an unmanageable timeframe, we'll go along with your way of doing it. Okay?"

One could see Mordechai's mind churning. He looked up while in deep thought. He wondered to himself, 'Hmm, what's the rush? Is my daughter pregnant? Does she feel that she has to get married because she's pregnant?'

Finally, he said, "Okay, well, I will try to make that happen. Let's think about dates and let me see if our Rabbi will be available. I'll choose a couple of dates close together. How does that sound?"

Leora came to her father and planted a big kiss on the cheek. "Thank you, Abba. I was thinking that we could have immediate families, his and ours – cousins, some close friends but nothing real fancy."

Shmuel asked Mordechai if he could speak to him privately, perhaps in the backyard.

Mordechai and Shmuel excused themselves but promised to come back for Chaya's exceptional dessert.

The backyard was surrounded by colorful gladiolas, roses, and a thick manicured carpet of green grass. They found a shady spot to stand. "I wanted to more formally ask your permission to marry your lovely daughter. She's an awesome person. I love and care for her. May I have your daughter's hand in marriage? Would you permit me to marry, Leora? We're really meant for each other and want to live a life of togetherness."

Touched by this traditional gesture, Mordechai's eyes began to well up with tears from the joy of deep respect being given to him. "Oh, yes, yes, of course. I see that Leora is very happy and that makes me feel grateful that you guys have found each other. Thank you for giving me this kind of respect and veneration. That goes a long way and means the world to me. Also, please feel free to call me Mordechai." Initially, they shook hands but Mordechai pulled Shmuel closer to him and the two men embraced. Mordechai took a handkerchief to wipe his unexpected tears. They smiled at each other.

They tried not to be overly nosy, but Chaya and Leora both noticed this warm exchange from the corners of their eyes. Mom and daughter both took out handkerchiefs and wiped their eyes as well.

Shmuel and Mordechai returned after a couple of minutes, both looking happy, relaxed, and peaceful.

Chaya said, "It's time for dessert, guys." She served a homemade rhubarb and cherry pie with vanilla ice cream and the chocolate babka. Who would like one or two scoops?"

Leora said, "Shmuel, you must try my mother's pies. They're absolutely amazing. She actually grows her own rhubarb in our backyard garden. My mom could easily win prizes for her delectable pie creations."

Chaya smiled from ear to ear. She waved her hand as if to say, 'Oh, come on. You're making my ears bigger and bigger. Thank you for the compliment, Leora.'

It was time to go. Shmuel thanked them for their hospitality, but before leaving, he overheard Chaya whisper to Leora, "Oh, he's so nice, polite, and wow, such a handsome young man! He looks like he was snatched right out of Hollywood. And he's so respectful! What a great catch! Where did you guys meet? Is he good to you, my Leorale?"

"Thanks, Ima. Yea, he's such a great guy and like you said, a terrific catch. We met at a club a few months ago. He's so romantic and sexy. And yes, he's very kind to me. He and I share the similar values about family." Details about their erotic love life were not discussed. Even though Leora felt very close to her mother, details about her pregnancy were too private at this time, as it was no one's business.

Chapter Thirteen

Today, he wore his favorite house robe, a blue and white one, and watched a few minutes of television. Yoni reclined on his favorite light comfortable tan leather recliner in their living room, watching the news. He received a scheduled conference call from Shmuel and Raffi at 8:00 p.m. to summarize their activities and the current status of the investigation. The killer's picture was well publicized, getting tons of newspaper coverage.

Leonid responded to the media and police reporting. At 4:45 p.m., Yoni was at police headquarters trying to finish up his day when he received a call. The voice was disguised, but the message was clear.

*"I promise revenge for your false reporting and chasing after me. You wiel niever catch me! You police and media are f***** sons of bitches, you bastards. I promise to kiel and siek vengeance against all of you police officers, especially Yoni. Vatch out! I'm coming after you!"*

Yoni knew it was Leonid's attempts to intimidate. "Leonid, we intend to catch you and bring you to justice. Ultimately, you'll rot in jail, that is, if you survive."

Click. Leonid hung up.

Yoni called Detectives Raffi and Shmuel. "Any clues or news about where this son of a bitch is? We must find this animal. We can't let him roam and kill young ladies. Continue your visits to the sex clubs, especially in Tel Aviv. Have another conversation with the butcher where Leonid was last employed. Get some additional ideas of where this bastard hides and where he lives. We don't even know where this f***** lives. This guy makes me nervous because of his threats to kill my daughter. He just called me and threatened to kill police officers. We've got to find this son of a bitch dead or alive! Guys, let's do whatever it takes to capture this son of a bitch dead or alive. It's my daughter's life that's at stake!" Yoni recognized his own feelings of desperation. He felt so keyed up and stressed. His adrenaline was churned up, making him feel like he needed to fight someone, preferably Leonid.

The detectives agreed, "Yes, boss. We'll continue to do whatever it takes."

Yoni was tensed and strained as he talked about this case. He got home late, at nine p.m. And Aaron was in a deep slumber in his bed. Yoni walked over and kissed Aaron's forehead, saying, "I love you, my son."

It seemed late for eating dinner but Yoni opened the refrigerator and thought about how a wonderful turkey sandwich would taste with mustard, onions, tomatoes, and potato chips on the side.

But Sarah wearing her bathrobe was a step ahead of her husband when she said, "Honey, I'll warm up the roast beef and potatoes. Don't worry. How was your day?"

He hugged her and sat so exhausted that his words fell short of being pronounced accurately. Still, he sported blue rings around his tired-looking eyes. "Well, we have not yet found our killer. One young lady killed, another one cut badly in her left arm, and a third victim stabbed in the back. The newspapers write that the police isn't doing enough, that we're not keeping our citizens safe. Today, our killer, using a disguised voice, called and threatened me. I have about two to three weeks left to apprehend this killer or I may face a demotion which would suck big time. If that were to happen, I'd face humiliation in my department and feel embarrassment. My boss is not very happy that Hannah is helping my investigation. He doesn't believe in psychics like Hannah." He thought for a few seconds. "That's how my day was. Nice, right?" In that moment of frustration and anger, he pounded his fist into his other fist.

He continued, "Now, I have another problem. Hannah feels she resembles the women who were killed and that she's next on the killer's kill list. In other words, Hannah has analyzed the victim's appearances. She believes she closely resembles the victims and that she will be his next victim to die. And you know what, Sarah? She's right. They do resemble each other. Moreover, she makes the argument that because she's the daughter of the lead detective on this case, she'll be his victim. Her breathing is erratic. She often hyperventilates. Her face is red most of the time. Maybe we should get her some professional help. So, that's the kind of stuff that's on my plate. Sarah, what do you think?"

Sarah came over and massaged Yoni's shoulder which had several rock-sized knots. He closed his eyes and allowed himself to relax. "You're great at what you do, and you'll figure this out," said Sarah. "I have the utmost of faith in you. As far as Hannah, I have great news to share. Wanna hear?"

"Of course. Yea, tell me."

"Okay, the great news is that our Hannah won the first place in the art contest in all of Israel. She was Number One as decided by a panel of art judges in all of Israel." She handed him Hannah's notification letter. "Take a look at this," she said with pride in her voice. She smiled and repeated herself for emphasis. "First place, Yoni!" She handed Yoni the official notification.

"Wow, how incredible is that! I always felt that our Hannah would become a great artist and now she's on her way. Wow! Our daughter! Can you imagine? Winning this title will certainly help her get into Letzior Art College. It's almost a done deal – a guarantee. Don't you think?"

"She will receive her prize in Tel Aviv in ten days. The panel of judges who are on the faculty from Letzior Art College will present her the first-place win. This win may even help her get into an art college. Isn't that great?"

"It's incredible. I'm so proud of our Hannahle. I will definitely want to attend the ceremony."

Yoni contemplated his next step. "Two letters *'nun' and 'mem'* written in a graffiti style were discovered when Raffi interviewed a victim's parents. These letters could hold important clues about the case. He looked through his contact list on his phone and there it was: Dr. Meir Shmira. He's the guy to call. He might decipher and find meaning in these letters." Sarah and Yoni slipped under their covers, and within minutes Yoni fell into deep slumber.

***

The following morning, Yoni called Professor Meir Shmira, a quiet, unassuming hunched over man with a graying full beard who appeared to be in his mid-fifties. He held a professorship at Tel Aviv University which had a partnership with the National Institute of Forensic Medicine. It was also affiliated with the Tel Aviv University School of Medicine. It was also known as the Abu Kabir Forensic Institute in Tel Aviv.

Professor Shmira's office was messy when he took a break from writing a criminal pathology report. He peeled an apple and took his first bite when his phone rang.

"Shalom, Dr. Shmira. I'm Detective Yoni Cohen and I am working on a case of the recent killing of a young lady and the stabbing of others. I'm sure you've read and heard all about it. I have some graffiti and would like to get your opinion on. Specifically, the killer wrote in graffiti the letters *'nun'* and *'mem.'* Can I forward it to you? It might hold some important clues to our investigation."

"Sure. I'll be glad to have a look at it."

"I'm on a deadline, so is there any chance you could get back to me as quickly as possible?"

"Sure. No problem, Yoni."

***

Next morning, Hannah was getting ready for school when she and her father had a few minutes of father-daughter time.

"Shalom, Abba. I'm still really worried but I do appreciate being protected by your team of police officers."

"Look, Hannahle. You're covered at all times. I have plainclothes police officers surrounding our building at all time. Please don't worry. I'm telling you that you're covered at all times."

"Okay, Abba."

"Oh, I almost forgot to congratulate you on winning the art contest and being number one for all the high school students in Israel. That's so huge and I'm very proud of you." He reached over to hug Hannah. We'll have to celebrate as a family."

"Will you be able to come to the auditorium of the Letzior Art School?"

"You know I will make every effort to be there. My work is such that in a heartbeat's notice, I can easily get called on an emergency to investigate something new. But I promise you that I'll try my hardest to be there. I want to be there for you and me. I've already placed it on my calendar. I'll have a sub ready to assist me in case a new emergency arises. I would never want to miss seeing you on stage getting this award. Number one in all of Israel! Wow! You've worked so hard to achieve this honor. That's so huge, Hannah! Keep up your great artistic work, honey." They hugged each other.

"Thanks, Abba and Ima, for your support." Sarah had overheard the exchange and smiled. Hannah hugged them both as she left for school.

"Love you!"

***

Yoni's phone rang. It was Professor Shmira.

Yoni said, "Boy, that was fast. How's your day going? What are your thoughts, professor?"

"So I was particularly fascinated by the acronym of two letters – nun and mem. I spun this around in many different ways which resulted in a question. Where does the killer currently live?"

"Well, there was a time he lived with his parents in Tel Aviv. Then, he disappeared. We talked to the landlord who did not have a forwarding address and the post office wasn't very helpful. So to answer your question, at this time we don't know where he lives."

"When I look at those two letters, here's what comes to my mind:

102

"The killer is trying to confuse you detectives by now being in a different place. He's clever and wants to generate a chase. I believe the two letters (N & M) are the Nahal Meiher, the caves of Wadi El Mughara, a region in the Carmel Mountain Range. These caves have historic significance since the remains of the Neanderthal man was discovered there. Now it's a beautiful hiking path, especially in springtime, kind of like a state park. So I spun these two letters in our computer software and came up with these caves as possible hideouts for the killer. Try it out. If he's out at the sex clubs by 9:30, you might want to go there earlier to apprehend this bad boy."

"Thank you, professor. It never occurred to me to think that he'd hide in caves."

"Well, give it a shot, Detective Yoni. Let me know what happens."

"Thanks for your time and effort, professor."

"Let me know if there's any way I can be helpful to you."

Chapter Fourteen

That following morning, Yoni had a conference call with Detectives Raffi, Shmuel, and Yitzchak. "Listen, guys, the killer left two letters scribbled on a paper in his parents' bedroom, nun and mem, written in graffiti style. I spoke to Professor Shmira from the Abu Kabir Forensic Institute. Dr. Shmira believes those letters represent a possible hiding place of our killer. He stated the killer was hiding out, possibly making his home in the caves of Nahal Meiar of the Wadi El Mughara in the Carmel Mountain Range. We need to go there with trained police dogs.

"Leonid may as well be hiding and living in one of the caves. So what I need from both of you is to organize perhaps five plainclothes police officers and snipers under your charge. Be there in the range of 5:30 to 9:00 p.m. and be fully armed. I'd suggest studying the area in advance and make a plan by dividing the areas. In advance, you can even use Google maps to explore the area, to get the feel of the topography. It's necessary that all of you and the police officers hike together. Okay? Any questions? I want you to begin this search at once. Oh, one other thing. Yitzchak, you've had experience working with trained police dogs, ones that can also detect and follow scents. I'd like you to visit Mr. and Mrs. Kozlov and have two police dogs smell the scents of Leonid's clothing, and maybe even his bed sheets or even old shoes."

"Yea, that's a great idea, Yoni. That sounds like a plan. I can easily bring two dogs and have them get samples of various items his clothing, shoes, and his bed sheets. We'll begin at once. Then, I will get our top dogs to smell one or more of Leonid's garments. I will make an unannounced home visit to Mr. and Mrs. Kozlov."

"Hey guys, communicate with me on how things unfold. Okay?"

They nodded in agreement and unanimously said, "Absolutely, yes sir."

Shmuel, Raffi, and Yitzchak made a time and place to meet the police dogs at the training center in Tzion, a Youth Village in the north of Acre, on the way towards northern Israel, the Galil.

A visit to Tzion Village, which was nestled in a northwest corridor of Acre, one felt an immediate connection with nature. On a clear day, the views from the youth village looking towards the Galil were spectacular. Mount Hermon over nine thousand feet high was clearly visible from the village. A variety of trees including lilac and pine trees along with well-manicured Australian grass adorned the property. The teens were provided unconditional acceptance along with defined roles and responsibilities in this campus facility. They failed in their academics and in their home life prior to being accepted to this therapeutic and educational group foster care.

Yitzchak, Raffi, and Shmuel teamed up with a police dog trainer and his canine specialists. That same afternoon, Raffi and the dog trainer went to Mr. and Mrs. Kozlov to get some samples of Leonid's most recent clothes he wore. The dogs also sniffed at his beddings and pillows. They indicated that he hadn't been home in at least a couple of months and wondered if his scents were still detectable. Yossi, the head dog trainer at Tzion indicated that it would still carry Leonid's body scents. Two dogs were selected. They smelled Leonid's clothing, his pillows, workout shirts, and even Leonid's underwear.

Ari, which means lion king, was a well-deserved name for this alpha dog of age three, a fully grown German shepherd having abilities to run with incredible speed, the fastest of the Tzion bunch, and easily able to explosively jump well over six feet in height. He was by far the most athletic one in the entire pack at Tzion, well trained, and aggressive when given commands like 'sikkim.' He had been used to sniff for bombs, heroine, and attack an enemy when given those types of commands. On this day, he was given that type of command, "Sikkim." To prep Ari, his face was exposed to several clothing pieces belonging to Leonid Kozlov. After these shmates were literally placed in the dog's face, they were now ready to go to the Naahal Meiar Caves in the Carmel Mountain Range. Regarding the killer, they were told, "Sikkim, go all out; attack and bite."

Avi, a second dog was endowed with a remarkable ability to smell well, which could prove to be an asset in this expedition. Certainly, he was not as aggressive as Ari but his abilities to detect smells were second to none. He was able to jump five feet. Both dogs were well prepped by smelling Leonid's clothing. Who ever said that dogs are not smart? Both Ari and Avi had a keen sense for detecting and following scents.

At 5:00 p.m., still seventy-three degrees Fahrenheit, they began their hike in the Carmel Mountains leading to the caves. To the west, they could view the Mediterranean Sea and the Stella Maris Monastery at the tip of Mount Carmel. To the east was a continuation of the Carmel Mountain Range. After walking a kilometer, the dogs began to pick up a scent. They increased their pace, heading towards a northeast direction. They were definitely on the hunt. It was nearly impossible for the team to keep up with the dogs that were running so unwaveringly fast in pursuit of scents. As the dogs ran, their tongues dripping saliva and open mouths facilitated increased breathing rates. The team of officers had let go of their leashes, as the dogs ran at a ten-to-fifteen-mile-an-hour pace.

The officers were completely out of breath. This made them think back to days gone by when they undertook their physicals for the police department. Today, Yitzchak, Raffi, and Shmuel had a hard time keeping up with the lightning-fast pace the dogs ran. Ari and Avi now dashed towards the caves, with saliva drops dripping from their mouths.

The dogs, well ahead of the men, approached the caves. Ari jumped and grabbed Leonid firmly on his left forearm. He bit down with full force. There were now deep puncture wounds and Leonid's arm bled profusely. A loud sound of bullets went off. The Uzi created a hell of a lot more carnage than the dog bites. Whimpering, Ari now fell to the ground but Leonid was still unsatisfied. He fired three more bullets to permanently silence him, once and for all. Ari's breath and heartbeat came to an abrupt end. The saliva flow stopped, as did his breathing. Then, Avi entered the cave, jumped, and grabbed hold of Leonid's right forearm. He chomped down. Leonid bled considerably from both arms with extensive deep puncture wounds and lacerations. Avi still bit and held on tightly to his arm. Leonid made his way towards the cave entrance while dragging an extra hundred and ten pounds of German shepherd. Leonid grabbed one of his daggers and repeatedly stabbed Avi. The cave's ground consisting of loose gravel was jam-packed with blood. He continued his stabbing motions. Finally, Avi let go of his arm and whimpered while he lay in a pool of his own blood. Two additional bullets quieted him down permanently. Both dogs lay in puddles of blood. The killer took his daggers, a knapsack and his Uzi. Off to the Carmel Mountains he went, leaving trails of blood in addition to several bloody tracks from his sneakers' tracks. Using desert brush, he was able to sweep away evidence of blood and sneakers' prints.

It was dark now, so the boys were unable to follow the blood trail. Twenty minutes elapsed before they set foot in the caves with flashlights in hand. There, they witnessed the killer's footprints caked in sand and blood and took a number of close-up pictures of Leonid's tracks. They'd have to wait till morning time to resume their search. They bent down to examine Avi and Ari who lay helpless and lifeless. They were Tzion Village's best trained dogs. Raffi silently whispered a prayer for the dead.

Shmuel called for assistance-police helicopters to help scan the area. Within fifteen minutes, three helicopters and several police snipers surrounded the area. They carefully listened for any unusual sounds and observed through night-vision binoculars to see if anyone was on the run. They covered distinct areas but were unable to find Leonid. Clever as he was, Leonid had studied the mountain terrain well in advance. He had extensive knowledge of all the caves, hiding places, and cliff ledges.

The three detectives opened up cans of food, pitched tents, and went to sleep. Disturbed, frustrated, and angry about their inability to capture Leonid, there were no Kumbayas sung that eve. There were no marshmallows being roasted over the campfire and no pretense that the mission was unsuccessful. In fact, it was a dismal failure.

By morning time, Leonid would have lost considerable blood due to his puncture wounds but he was clever enough to have ripped off shreds from his own shirt and used these shreds to tie them around his forearms to minimize his blood loss. Applying aloe cream provided temporary relief.

Three helicopters were out by seven a.m. but crafty Leonid knew where and how to hide within the hanging cliffs and ridges. He used desert brush to cover him as he hid in one of the smaller caves. They brought along two additional police dogs to cover any possible blood trails. The sanguine trail stopped a half a mile before the ridges. Why? When Leonid created slings, there were no more blood trails that could be detected. He also used desert shrub branches to sweep away his footprints and blood trail.

Additional police were dropped off by helicopters to provide help. They looked here, there, and everywhere but there were no traces of Leonid to be found. By noon, the mission was aborted. In the face of danger, Leonid knew how to survive. He had lost blood due to the sharp canine teeth of the puncture wounds by dog bites. Kind of like a modern-day Rambo with a demonic intent on killing young ladies, he knew survival techniques. He was clever enough to evade police capture, at least for now.

That next morning, the police search ended when they were unable to locate Leonid.

The helicopters returned to their home base in Haifa.

He walked towards a nearby gas station where he dyed his hair and eyebrows blond. He now wore a false blond beard and mustache. He thought this was a way of being less conspicuous and least likely of being recognized. His knapsack contained first-aid containers of alcohol which he poured over his puncture wounds. He changed from aloe to using an antibiotic anti-infection cream. He bought some long-sleeved shirts to cover his wounds. In one of the public bathroom, he applied alcohol to his wounds and smeared the antibiotic ointment. One of his puncture wounds was one and a half centimeter in length. His knapsack also contained a sewing kit. He began to suture his forearms as if he were a physician, a top-notched surgeon. All total his forearms brandished thirteen new stitches. To complete his job, he used antibiotic cream and bandaged his wounds as the very last step. He took out large Band Aids to also cover his stitched up wounds. He wore a clean, unblemished long-sleeved shirt which concealed all of his wounds.

Chapter Fifteen

The following morning, a dark gray sky and a fall wind's chill with rain drizzles blanketed the town of Ashkelon. Today, the sea waves had quieted down. It was eight a.m. when he had hitchhiked towards the seaside community of Ashkelon. He wore a khaki hat that helped disguise his facial features. His long-sleeved shirt covered his recent puncture wounds. His blond hair and beard added to his new disguise. He hitchhiked, weaving his right thumb in the air. Ashkelon was about sixty kilometers away. He continued to wave his hand and his thumb. Finally, a postal worker heading towards his post office job stopped to pick up Leonid.

"Your car broke down? Is that why you're hitching?"

"Actually, yes. I believe my transmission is shot. I'll have to look for an ATM machine to get some money so I can get it repaired."

"Where are you going? I need to get off at Ashkelon."

"Well, I'm heading past Ashkelon and will let you off. We'll shortly be on Highway Four that will take us to the town's border." He paused for a moment and then said, "You look very familiar to me, but I can't quite place where I've seen you before. Are you a television personality? Have I seen you before? Have we previously met somewhere?"

"I don't have the foggiest. I've never seen or met you before." Leonid became tightlipped and cautious about being discovered. They arrived at the town's border.

"You live there?"

"No, I have close family members in Ashkelon. Hey, can I offer you some money towards your gas for the ride?"

"Oh, no. It's okay, but thanks anyway."

***

Leonid walked slowly towards the beach town. In advance, he had studied a map and knew his way. In ten to twelve minutes, he'd arrive at the Bat Zion High School where Hannah was a student.

Hannah had gotten ready to go to school when she saw her father squeezing fresh oranges and making fresh orange juice. Her red face and her rapidness spelled trouble.

"Abba," she said, "I know the killer is coming for me today; he is close by. I had a vision that he was a passenger in a car, not his own one but that he was coming to kidnap me here in Ashkelon. Abba, I feel so terrified because I know he's stalking me. I see it so clearly in my vision, just the way I first saw him at the Sabre Meats Shop. Do you remember how sick I felt right after that?" She paused and added, "Abba, what do we do now? I know he's here in town." Sweat profusely poured down her face. Hannah was hyperventilating. She paced the floor and wrung her hands.

"Well, just remember, Hannah, I've got you covered at all times. There are eight plainclothes police officers surrounding the house, following you to school and following you home from school. We also have a swat team on the roof of our housing complex. In the evenings, they're around our home and they're in our neighborhood. I had requested from my boss a number of the best sharpshooting snipers to be perched on the roof of our building. If you weren't my daughter, you'd probably never receive this kind of protection. Please try to calm down. Go about your normal day as nonchalantly as possible. Okay?"

"But, Abba, he's going to get me. He's after me now. I know it. I see it."

"Hannah, you're protected. Please don't worry. Police are everywhere."

Hannah became irritated when she said, "Abba, I feel like you don't believe me. You're taking this much too lightly. But my life is at stake."

"Hannahle, I know you're frightened, but I've gotten you a lot of protection. I don't doubt you. So, what can you now do to help yourself calm down?"

"I'll try my best." The last few words from Hannah's mouth were ones she didn't believe in. She tried pacifying her father. She finished brushing her flowingly wavy blond hair. She drank orange juice and gobbled down yogurt mixed with berries. She left for school, hurriedly walking there. She looked around and past her shoulders to see if police were following her. She was unable to discern if they were. She felt frightened.

Wearing a disguise, Leonid entered Ashkelon. Hyper-vigilant about his environments, he was gifted by a kind of an internal radar; he knew when and how to recognize the presence of law enforcement. He was keenly aware of nonverbal gestures that were commonly used by law enforcement officers. Today, he disguised himself in such a manner that he would not be easily recognized. With dyed blond hair and eyebrows, a false blond mustache and beard, shoes that had over two-inch heels, he appeared much taller and different. With makeup creams, he hid the scar on his cheek. He trusted his own sense of intuition of being vigilantly aware of police officers. They were out there. But today, he also took out a small pallet with a canvas, brushes, and oil paint to add to his new disguise of being an artist. He pretended to paint on canvas.

For a few brief seconds, he thought about his childhood and remembered what he had experienced in the form of harsh physical abuse. He remembered how his mother looked when she was about to abuse him – her face, reddish eyes with rivulets of small veins, and a leather belt with a metal buckle. He recounted her look a million times over. To him, she looked like a monster – a fire-spitting dragon with huge fangs. He knew what to expect next by using his own internal radar antennas.

He wore a hat to partly hide his face. He had researched the nearby roads in advance and knew the whereabouts of Hannah's high school and her home address as well. His suspicion told him that it was poor timing to kidnap Hannah but that he was the artist with pallet and brushes in hand. He noted there were at least four police officers present. Even though they were plain-clothed, he could see the bulge in their holsters and discerned they all wore bullet-proof vests. He knew they carried one of several firearms, like a 45 Glock, a Tovar, a Desert Eagle, or the Jericho 941 caliber. He knew these pistols were semi-automatic. He decided to give one of Hannah's friends a handwritten letter sealed with his own sputum. It read:

"I'm watching you right now. I'm at your high school. I plan to rape and kiel you cwhore, bitch! You deserve to die! This viel be beautifully gory, you bitch!"

Gyora, one of Hannah's close friends, walked home nearby to where Leonid was painting, perhaps no more than six feet away from Leonid. There were several trees and brushes to provide shade from the sun.

"Chi. I'm a cousin of Channah Cohen but I don't vant to interrupt cher conversations viet cher friends. That vould not be good. Say, vould you do me a favor and give this note to cher from me? I am in the area on business and painting. I just vanted to say chello."

"Yea, sure. Can I tell her who you are? You know, who is it from?"

"Sure, tell cher it's from cher Cousin Leo. Okay? Thank you so much."

Gyora looked around and noted that Hannah was still talking to friends. Gyora decided to make a brief run for it and gave her the note as she headed towards the elevator at home building's entrance. In the meantime, Leonid disappeared like Zorro in the night. The adrenaline rush, the momentary feelings of excitement, and danger caused Leonid to get an erection and to climax. At that moment in time, he quietly whispered to himself, "Ooh, vow! This is awesome. It's so incredible! I fooled police. I can get to this chore – Hannah." He smiled and said, "Yes, victory is around the corner. YES!" Walking briskly towards the highway, he would continue to hitchhike towards Tel Aviv.

Surprised to see him, Hannah said, "Oh hi, again. What's up, Gyora? Do you want to talk or something?"

He arrived a bit out of breath with a note in his hand. "Your cousin was just here but he didn't want to disturb your private conversations with your friends. He spoke with an accent. Here." Gyora gave her the unopened letter. "Okay, thanks. See you later. Gotta go." Gyora turned around and took off.

Instantly, she felt tense. The sense of danger overtook her. She was unaware of having a grownup cousin. Hannah didn't wonder too long about who wrote this note. Before she opened the envelope, her heartbeat rate increased by leaps and bounds. She knew. She anticipated a lewd threatening message from Leonid. She feared opening this note.

With her Ima by her side, Hannah said, "See, you didn't believe when I said, 'He's after me.' Look what he says:

*Cwhore, you're next to die! You filthy bitch! I can't vait to rape you. I chave many surprises for you. See if your big-time daddy detective can chelp you now. See if che'll catch me. I viel kiel chim too. With Love. Yours truly. Bitch! F***** cwhore! Ve're going to have lots of fun. Get ready! I'm coming after your father too, you bitch, when he least expects it."*

Hannah now paced back and forth, hardly able to believe the note she was reading – from the killer himself. She tried to catch her breath but tears streamed down her cheeks. "Ima, I'm so frightened."

Sarah tried comforting her daughter. She held her and patted her hair but Hannah was beside herself, experiencing a full-blown anxiety attack. She hyperventilated. She broke into a cold sweat. Her face was beet-red.

She ran toward her father to announce this latest news while flapping the letter in the air when he came home, "See, Ima and Abba, I was right. I had a vision about his coming to Ashkelon and no one takes me seriously. *He is after me. He wants to kill me and I will be his third victim.* You see, I was right. Look, he was able to break through your police protection in our neighborhood." Agitated, she paced back and forth and then continued, "Abba, so what do we do?" She kept flapping the note in the air. She handed the note to her father. "Look for yourself. Nooh, so what do we do now?" Agitation and fear took over as she pointed to the note. "See, what did I tell you about being his next victim? I told you I saw it in my vision. Abba, I must tell you that I don't feel protected. Yes, you say there are officers all around, so how was Leonid able to get this note to me? How come?" Now more than ever she contemplated her option of some form of self-defense.

Yoni reiterated, "We have police officers around the house twenty-four-seven and they follow you when you leave the house to go to school and when you return from school. I will also call my boss and ask for additional manpower." As a father, he wanted to reassure her by placing his arms around Hannah and letting her vent. "I will look into what happened in not protecting you this afternoon."

He got up and began to walk toward his office when he reached for his cellphone and called Chaim, the lead police officer in the neighborhood.

"Chaim, it's Yoni. Did you see anything suspicious around the time my daughter left school? Was there anyone hanging out or near the school?"

"No, no one that looked suspicious to us. Just a long-haired artist with easel and canvas painting."

"Did you interview him?"

"No. Didn't think it was necessary because he looked like an artist, not a killer."

"Do you not realize that Leonid is a master of disguises?"

"Yes, but none of my officers felt the need to interview him. We thought the guy was an artist. I apologize if it was an oversight. Sorry, sir."

Yoni walked back towards her bedroom and explained the police oversight to Hannah.

Barely able to verbalize her thoughts, she now considered taking stronger measures to protect herself. She looked at her father, "See he wants to kill me as you can see in the note. I take this threat seriously. He was able to infiltrate your police officers and get this evil note to me." She rested a few seconds and continued, "I told you I was going to be his next victim. Now, it's going to happen. And that's not all, Abba. Now, he's also after you." She flapped the note in the air when she said, "See, it's in this letter. Look for yourself."

"Like I said earlier, I never doubted you, Hannah. You're right. The killer is clever and cunning. Do you want to live elsewhere… temporarily? I think it would help for now."

"With whom?"

"Maybe your Aunt Tante Rifka who lives in Tel Aviv, near Ramat Gan? I can give her a call."

"Yea, maybe. But Abba, how will I complete my school assignments? How would I take my tests?"

"I can talk to your school people and see about working out an interim arrangement with them. It was meant as a suggestion to get you away from here temporarily."

"Could we do that for... say a few weeks? I would get the homework assignments online, take my exams online, or even mail them back to my school. Can you or Ima arrange that for me? And we'll make sure that it's absolutely hush hush and that no one knows."

"Okay, no problem, but Hannah that means not telling your friends anything – just that you're at an undisclosed location. Don't tell any of your friends or teachers, not even your best friends. If your friends wonder where you are, and why they haven't seen you, what will you tell them? If you did disclose that you're temporarily residing with your aunt, it would easily jeopardize your safety and this case. Hannah, as your father, I will arrange it to happen with the utmost confidentially discreet manner. Okay?"

"I'll tell them I'm okay, but that I cannot disclose where I am." They hugged and kissed each other. Then Hannah said, "You're the best parents anyone could ever have. You make me feel safe and protected even when I feel like I'm going crazy. Ha! Ha! But one other thing, Abba, I will miss my friends by not seeing them for weeks at a time."

"Yes, I do understand. But it's a temporary arrangement. We must ensure that no one knows where you are. When Leonid realizes that you're gone, he'll eventually leave our neighborhood. You follow what I'm saying? The excitement of the hunt is driving his desire to kill. You get my drift, Hannah? If you disappear, there's no hunt."

"Yes, I do. But Abba, what about my schoolwork?"

"We'll arrange that you'll be able to do it via internet, distance learning, for a few weeks. Don't worry about that."

***

"Aunt Rifka was never married but just like her sister, your mom, she has a heart of gold. Her two-bedroom apartment overlooks a park. She loves you dearly and your brother, Aaron. She never forgets occasions, like birthday gifts, Hanukah, and other times when she can give of herself unconditionally."

"Shalom, Rifka. This is Yoni and I need a great, big favor."

"Sure, sure, sure, what is it?"

"We need to move Hannah to live with you for a few weeks. Hopefully, no more than that."

"Sure, is there a problem that I should know about? Did she get into trouble with a boy? You know what I mean. Tell me the truth, Yoni. I'm family and no matter what, I will always love our Hannahle."

"No, it's not what you think. I can't say more. It's a police matter. When it's all over, I'll tell you everything. So can she stay with you? Is that okay with you?"

"Oh yes, of course. I love my Hannahle."

"One other thing, please don't ask Hannah any questions because this situation is troubling her immensely. One day, I'll be glad to share it with you. And please don't share with anyone that your niece is staying with you. Will you do us that favor?"

"Yes, of course I will. There's no problem. So when will you bring her here?"

"Can we bring her tomorrow? Oh, one other thing, I'll arrange for Hannah to do her homework assignments online."

"Yoni, you can bring Hannah anytime. It's no problem whatsoever."

"From the bottom of our heart, thank you so much, Rifka."

"You're welcome, Yoni. Anytime."

***

Shmuel was on the phone calling Yoni. "Hi, Yoni, it's Shmuel. I want to ask your suggestion. Leora and I have just gotten engaged and I want to buy Leora a ring. You know, a diamond ring she'd wear with joy and pride. Do you know someone who could give me a good price for a diamond ring? Maybe you know a diamond dealer? She's such an amazing girl. She deserves a nice big bomb on her finger."

"Shmuel, Congrats, Mazal Tov! That's great news! I thought you'd never get married, you know, being the stud that you are. And by the way, who is Leora?"

"I met her a few months ago in a club and we fell in love. That's all. She's amazing in every way. Smart, a teacher by profession. Pretty, in fact beautiful and sexy. Great personality. Comes from a wonderful family. What else does a man need? Right, Yoni?"

"So let me think of who I know? I'll get back to you in a few hours after I've had a chance to think of my contacts. Okay?"

"Sounds good. Thanks, Yoni. I know I can count on you to come up with someone. I think you know so many different people with all kinds of occupations and that's why I'm turning to you."

"I'll do my best to come up with a name or two and will get back to you shortly."

"Oh, by the way in ten days, we're having our engagement party, maybe no more than forty-five to fifty people and you and Sarah are invited. It will be held at Café Andronicus in Tel Aviv on Saturday around seven p.m. It's owned by a Greek, and the food is amazing. Do you think that Sarah and you will be able to attend?"

"Yea, of course, we wouldn't miss this happy occasion. Thanks for the invite. I'll mention it to Sarah. I'll also get you the name of a discounted diamond dealer and either call you or text you the information."

"Thanks. I knew I could count on you, boss."

***

Five days passed when Leora and Shmuel had a day off. They planned on doing a hike at Banias National Park, near the foothills of Mount Hermon, where the Jordan River began. Beside the river, there were several creeks. They would see some of the Roman ruins. Shmuel planned on a four-mile round trip hike. Leora made some sandwiches for lunch. There was a stream at Banias National Park which meandered in a serpentine fashion, with waterfalls and slightly challenging river currents. Some were seen floating on their rubber floats. Along the several hiking paths, there were places to rest. Leora had no clue that she was about to happen.

'Today, her black hair and her blue eyes look so amazingly beautiful against the backdrop of fall trees and their changing colors,' thought Shmuel. There was a fall breeze helping them be cooler while they hiked. She was still under three months' pregnancy and already secured an OBGYN physician. The Cupat Cholim infirmary appointment had confirmed her pregnancy. Today, they felt ready for their hike wearing their hiking shoes and each having a camel of juices on their backs. Shmuel wore khaki pants with a matching khaki long-sleeved shirt as well as his hat. He had his Nike running shoes. He'd surprise her today but it had to be the right moment, the right atmosphere, and a picture-memorable environment, like a water fall.

They were now walking near the waterfall at Banias National Park. They found a nature trail that led to the falls. Incredible emerald-green water, like the stone of Eilat, with water that originated from Mount Hermon traversed in a southward direction. After hiking a couple of miles, they were both hungry. Leora commented that her stomach growled from hunger pangs.

They approached an area of green foliage near a waterfall. The sound of the rushing water relaxed them. "I have a surprise for you," said Shmuel.

Nearby, a wooden bench offered the opportunity to sit and rest. But Shmuel brought a big towel where they were able to leisurely sit or lie down. He removed his camel and reached for one of the zippered compartments. He looked for the small colorfully wrapped square box and card. She now sat up more erect and looked at Shmuel with curiosity. "Mah Pitom?"

Suddenly, he was down on his knees. With a huge ear-to-ear smile, he asked, "Leora, will you marry me, honey? I love you so much!" His voice quivered. The colorful box was decorated by drawings of flowers. He offered her the neatly wrapped box.

Shocked, Leora opened it carefully as if she were a little child getting a surprise birthday or Hanukkah gift. "For me, Shmuel?"

"Yes, of course."

She unwrapped the package and saw a ring box. She opened it and, with a big smile, said, "Shmuel, oh my goodness! It's so beautiful." Shmuel helped put the ring on her finger. She tried it on for size. "It's a perfect fit." She went over to hug and gave him a great, big kiss. "How did you know my size? Oh my God, it's so beautiful! It's so big! And what a brilliant shine! Oh my goodness!" Surprised and happy, she inquired, "How did you know my size?" The corners of her eyes were now filled with tears of joy.

"I asked your mother who looked through some of your rings and we both thought this size would fit you."

"Oh, it's so beautiful. I can't believe it. The diamond stone is so large and look how it sparkles. Wow! Thank you." She looked him in the eye and said, "Thank you, Shmuel. What a surprise! I kind of wondered if I was going to ever get an engagement ring but I didn't want to be too pushy and ask you. I also didn't want to put more pressures than you already have. But it's so beautiful, so big! It's so perfect. I love you so much! I only want to marry you. You're the man I've waited and wished for in my dreams and in my prayers."

Tenderly, they kissed and held on to each other.

"Oh, by the way, it's one and two third carats and a flawless stone." Shmuel smiled from ear to ear. Next, Shmuel asked some passerby if he'd take a couple of cellphone pictures, perhaps one sitting with a close-up and one standing with the waterfalls in the background. Leora showed off her new ring. She sent the pictures to her mom and her best friends by text.

Her cellphone rang. It was her mother congratulating her with the traditional Mazal Tov congratulations. She received a call from her father who also congratulated her. She received several calls from a few of her best girlfriends. They wanted to know all about the ring – how Shmuel proposed and if it fit just right. Leora smiled from ear to ear. In between, she managed small bites of her sandwich while she continued conversing with her friends.

She reminded them of the engagement party and looked forward to introducing Shmuel to all her friends and family.

Having eaten lunch, they felt full and continued their hike. Leora insisted on wearing her new engagement ring. Additional pictures and selfies were taken. More hugs and smiles were exchanged with one another. They continued their hike. Every once in a while, Leora looked at how pretty her new engagement diamond ring was. It sparkled so brilliantly. Shmuel stated it was the best of quality in diamonds – no imperfections. He thought to himself, 'Oh, my Leora looks so beautiful, so stunningly, exquisite! I'm so lucky to have her in my life.' Then, he placed his hand on her belly as if to make some nonverbal contact with the baby. Next, he placed his right ear to her belly, but the baby was not yet sufficiently developed to hear any movements or a heartbeat.

Leora stated, "Maybe, we should get it insured?"

"Yea, we should. Absolutely! It's a very high-quality ring and we must protect it."

They spent an unforgettably special day, one etched in their memory forever, just like an episodic memory. They held hands as they continued their walk towards their parked car.

Chapter Sixteen

Hannah's emotional mind state began to take its toll. The ominous note delivered by Gyora was proof enough that she'd be killed. 'I must get rid of this feeling of being his next casualty. I feel terrified and helpless all the time. Right or wrong, I must be brave and protect myself. I can't live knowing he'll rape and kill me. No, that's unacceptable to me. I know my dad is trying to hunt down this animal, but how much longer will that take? How many more lives will this animal take? Maybe, the detectives will never arrest Leonid? In the meantime, I have proof of his intention to kill me.' Her thoughts shifted to a need for self-protection and self-defense. 'I know these actions might hurt my parents' feelings and perhaps my future career. Were that to happen, I know it might bring shame to my father and mother. But I feel it's a case of self-defense. I certainly don't wish to be caught. If that were to happen, I can easily imagine the headlines:

Lead Detective's daughter is arrested.'

Reflectively, Hannah weighed the pros and cons of taking matters into her own hands. She reflected on the Old Testament when Moses killed an Egyptian after this man took the life of a Jew. What about when David slew Goliath? In the Bible, it says, "An eye for an eye and a tooth for a tooth." She would never become one of Leonid's victims. 'That is never going to be an option for myself. My life has been threatened. I have this note that states so. I've been stalked. What's wrong if I use self-defense measures to protect myself?'

She would stay with her aunt at least two, maybe three, weeks. Hannah had ample time to concoct a plan. 'First things first. Increase my fitness by daily runs, some to improve my speed, while others to improve my endurance.' In no time, she could easily manage six to eight miles at a fast clip of under an eight-minute mile, actually more like a seven and a half minute mile. She practiced running with her collapsible bow and arrow set which hung around her right shoulder and back. The Volga Sex Club, Leonid's favorite hangout, was only about three miles away from her Aunt Rifka's apartment. She Googled the Volga Club with Google maps and found the exact location and direction. During the day when her Aunt Rifka worked, Hannah jogged to the

Volga Club and back. Once there, she took notes about secluded streets close to the club. She considered shrubs, those ideal for hiding.

Hannah was a top archer on her high school team, earning first-place finishes in several competitions. When her high school competed against other programs throughout Israel, Hannah always took top awards. Her coaches wanted her to compete internationally but Hannah preferred her artwork. Hannah loved running and she determined the time Leonid entered the exotic sex club. It was usually at 9:45 p.m. She'd easily spot him from sixty or seventy meters away. She recognized his walk, his tough guy swagger, his height, and even his van. When she saw him, nausea overpowered and gripped her in the chest and stomach. She felt as if she was unable to breathe. This man was her enemy. Hannah's intentions were to hurt Leonid but not to kill him. She figured that were he hurt, he'd slow down his reign of terror of innocent young women. She promised herself that she'd never admit using her bow and arrows to hunt down this enemy of hers, even if she were to be questioned by police. But she'd need to have better control over her emotions to execute precise archery skills. She needed to control her breathing and heart rate as well.

She thought to herself, 'I can't accurately shoot a bow if my breathing and heart rate are off. I must slow down my heartbeat and breathing pace.' She remembered a sport psychologist that her coach brought in to teach archery team relaxation exercises of slowing down breathing and heart rate for improved performance results. She'd need to practice those techniques over and over again. She began to do those mental exercises nightly. One of the exercises was called progressive relaxation where you tense and relax each muscle as you inhale deeply and then let go and relax. This was followed by her doing visual imagery of her archery techniques and then 'anchoring' it. She also recalled how to reframe unwanted negative self-doubting kind of thoughts that interfered with good bow skill execution.

Leonid's pattern was to arrive every Tuesday and Thursday. She scouted the area, the least conspicuous area to hide, one where she'd be able to hide and shoot her archery bow arrows. Rechov Ben Gurion was across the street to the Volga Club. She was now about thirty to thirty-five meters away from Volga's entrance. A number of trees and shrubs provided ample opportunities for hiding. She'd hide behind a string of tall gladiolas flowers. She promised herself she'd never leave any self-incriminating evidence. Even sneakers' prints would be eliminated. The bow and any unused arrows must go with her. She'd wear her archery leather glove for support.

The use of visual imagery helped her recall and relive previous successful bowshots from start to finish. She'd focus intensely on her target, take a couple of deep breaths, and release extraneous thoughts. She told herself, "Relax," and then executed an arrow release with her bow. These techniques helped her perform at her very best. Soon, she'd have an opportunity to test it out. While her aunt worked, she found a nearby park and made a makeshift target to practice her archery techniques which she did on a daily basis. She practiced using her mental performance skills.

It was a clear night with stars and the moon illuminating Tel Aviv. The tall Migdal David Building was clearly visible. On this night, reflections of the moon on the still waters of the Mediterranean Sea were clearly visible. While Aunt Rifka had gone to bed early, Hannah, with bow hidden in a case, escaped using a rope that descended about 3.2 meters to the ground below. She wore camouflaged clothing and painted her face with dark paint. Effortlessly, she ran towards the sex club. She then placed five arrows next to her with a number of shrubs covering them. The exterior of the Volga Club was well lit on this evening. It was now 9:30 p.m. 'He might be here early,' she thought. For the past ten days, she had practiced daily quick relaxation, visual imagery, reframing any negative thoughts, target focused aim, and release techniques with her bow.

It was 9:45 p.m. when she spotted him crossing the street. He was now about six or seven meters from entering the Volga Club entrance. Hannah was now thirty meters away. She hid behind a number of tall gladiolas. Her heart rate increased, as did her breathing rate. With as very short window of time, perhaps no more than seconds, she relaxed herself, aimed, and released. She felt ready now. Her first arrow imbedded in Leonid's left shoulder. She quickly aimed and executed another shot – this time in his left bicep. It felt good and satisfying hits for Hannah. While he bent over with two arrows imbedded in him, another arrow lodged itself on his left bicep. Was he hiding or was he wreathing in pain? With the arrows deeply entrenched in his shoulder, bicep, and his left side, he flagged down a cab and directed the driver to take him to his private doctor. He always carried false identifications and disguises. He felt he was in great danger of losing his life. Hannah's intentions were to have Leonid realize that he was not invincible and to scare the daylights out of him. A number of patrons of the Volga Club screamed when they witnessed Leonid's injury. One called for police help, but Leonid quickly disappeared.

Hannah felt satisfied with her hits. Using her hunting knife, Hannah quietly sawed off a leafy branch to clear any sneakers' footprints. It was a dark night. She packed up her gear and darted off with lightning speed. By the time the police arrived, Hannah was long gone. She felt exhilarated with her hits and ran back to her aunt's house in twenty-one minutes – about a seven-minute mile. Tonight, her dark camouflaged running suit, much like a modern-day Ninja, served to disguise her. She ran carrying her bow and arrows. Using repelling rope, she climbed with ease. Climbing the ten feet to reach her bedroom was no challenge for Hannah. She found herself in bed by 11:30 p.m., proud of her accomplishment. Her adrenaline pumped hard. Turning off her thoughts and emotions was a challenge for Hannah. Eventually, she drifted into deep slumber. She realized she did the right thing. It was a case of self-defense. She slept deeply and soundly.

The following morning, Yoni called his daughter. "Hi, Hannahle. Did you hear the news? Did you have a chance to read the newspaper today?"

Curiously, Hannah said, "No. I haven't. Why? What's going on? You sound like you're in a good mood."

"Yes, I am. Leonid was injured last night but he was not apprehended."

"You mean one of your men shot him?"

"No, he was injured by three arrows. Then, he quickly disappeared from the scene."

"Well, I won't shed any tears about that. No, in fact that's the best news of the day. So, how was it reported? Were there any witnesses?" While they talked on phone, she heard him sipping his morning coffee in the background.

"There were no eyewitnesses. A couple of patrons of the Volga Club screamed from a combination of excitement and fear. The owner of the club came running out and saw Leonid quickly leave in a cab. He then called the police and the team of Tel Aviv Gazette Newspaper. He witnessed arrows deeply stuck in Leonid's shoulder, arm, and his side. He'll most probably need surgery to remove these arrows."

"Well, like I said, I'm not at all disappointed, as he's made several threats to end my life and hurt you as well."

"Hannahle, I've got to ask you if you've been practicing your archery lately?"

"Why are you asking me that question? Are you accusing me of shooting Leonid?" Instantly, she was annoyed.

"It was a fleeting thought because I live with you and know how upset you've been about this crazy perpetrator. I also know you're a terrific archer having taken top national awards."

"I can't believe the words I'm hearing. How dare you accuse me, your own daughter, of committing this crime?" Hannah was so angry that she hung up the phone.

He called her again, and before he uttered any words, Hannah said, "Yea, what do you want, now that you've accused me? For your information, my bow broke a couple of months ago and it was irreparable, so I threw it out. Is there any reason to keep a broken bow?"

"I said it was a fleeting thought. I don't want anything to jeopardize the integrity of this case. You know, police are frequently asked about being overly aggressive."

"But is it okay for your daughter to be killed by this maniac because you're so concerned about doing everything by the book? See, I see that his being physically maimed is a positive development. Maybe the victims' families are enraged about the loss of their daughters. Maybe someone else decided to hurt him, perhaps a vigilante? That might stop Leonid's reign of terror."

"Hannah, I'm conducting an investigation to apprehend the killer, and I don't want anything or anyone to interfere with that. We don't want any bad publicity about our police department."

"Yes, I understand, Abba. If I get a vision and any information about who injured Leonid, you'll be first to hear about it. So far, no visions."

"Okay, Hannah. Thanks."

The Tel Aviv Gazette's article read as follows:

"A male, age twenty-three, was injured in front of the Volga Club when someone shot arrows that penetrated his left shoulder, his left bicep, and one near the abdominal muscles. At this time, there are no suspects. After interviews with Volga Club's owner, the injured man has been identified as a likely suspect in the killing of one young lady and the near fatal stabbing of another one. The injured man quickly disappeared before police or medical attention could be called to the scene."

In the event that Hannah might be questioned by authorities, she decided to hide the bow and arrows by covering them with an additional plastic case. She'd bury them deeply at a local park and place broken twigs and leaves, all in the middle of the night.

She also had an alibi were she to be questioned by her father or other officers about where her bow and arrows were. She'd say that her bow broke beyond repair and she discarded it as garbage. She would also inquire if any of the victim's family members were questioned about their use of bows.

Leonid was able to find a doctor, also from Ukraine, who surgically removed the deeply imbedded arrows. The incisions involved a wide area. The doctor estimated that he'd need to cut deeply to withdraw arrows from Leonid's flesh. The doctor removed the arrows, but Leonid required both internal and external stitching. He was also given a tetanus injection and follow-up antibiotic pills for ten days. Leonid's shoulder, forearm, and abdominal areas were heavily bandaged – no bodybuilding for at least four to six weeks.

Yoni and Sarah sat on their living room couch watching the evening news. "You know, Sarah, this is the first time I've had some inner doubts about whether Hannah's been telling me the truth. Yesterday, the killer suspect was wounded with arrows in front of the Volga Club. I questioned if it was our Hannah who shot him. She got mad at me and hung up the phone. We spoke further and she said her bow had broken beyond repair and that it was discarded months ago."

"Yoni, my love, I think this case has got you super wound up. You need to relax a bit and not prematurely accuse our Hannah. She's a wonderful girl and she'd never do that. I really do think you're overreacting. Chill. Let's have a glass of wine and relax." She stood up and went over to where they stored a number of wine bottles. She brought over an unopened bottle of red wine, a Merlot, bottled in Northern Israel.

"Here," she said as she handed him the bottle and cork opener.

"Yea, you're probably right that I'm way too wound up about the case. Perhaps I overreacted because the suspect was injured with arrows. I know how Hannah feels about the killer and her need to use self-defense. It was kind of natural to assume she'd use her bow."

"You might just want to clear the air with her."

"Yea, I'll do that, my Sarah. Hannah is a wonderful young lady with a good head on her shoulder. And like I said, I'm probably overreacting. I'm all stressed out about this case."

"The fact that a rapist and killer was shot with arrows is a blessing. Maybe he'll stop his campaign of terror? I'm sure that public sentiment is totally in favor of his being injured, especially since he's killed and stabbed young ladies. I'm sure there will be no complaints from the populace. So my love, how about we relax?" she said.

They kissed, embraced, and touched each other in ways that husbands and wives should – amorously. She slipped off her housedress. They found comfort in each other's embrace.

Chapter Seventeen

Hannah's scheduled arrival was flawless. She was back at home with her family. Nearly four weeks had come and gone without new incidents. The previous weeks were difficult, as Hannah missed her family and friends. Hannah felt upset about being disconnected from her friends. Excited about coming home, Hannah sang along a happy tune, accompanying the car's radio song as she tapped her fingers to the heavy guitar beats. Yoni wondered, 'When will the killer strike again?' While driving home, Yoni asked if Hannah could sit for Aaron. Shmuel had gotten engaged with a planned engagement party. He added, "If you'd like to have a friend sleep over, that would be great. We could order pizza and some noshes in advance."

"Yea, sure, Abba. No problem, Abba. I'll invite Elena."

Café Hellena was adorned by paintings of Athens, beaches, and fishing villages. White table cloths on wooden tables were nestled near several grapevines in its back patio for whoever wished to dine outdoors. Vines of green and purple grapes grew were ready to be picked. Homemade red and white wines still in wooden barrels were available to the guests. Inside, a Greek band played songs like from Zorba the Greek, and some of the guests were dancing. The owner and his wife encouraged guests to dance and even led the way, instructing in various traditional Greek folk dancing skills. And of course at the end of each dance, it was customary to say, "Oppah." The guests were dancing and having fun learning Greek dances.

Wearing a canary-yellow dress with cutout sleeves just below her shoulders, Leora looked stunning. Shmuel wore navy-blue-colored pants with a short-sleeved white shirt with rolled-up sleeves. The top buttons were unbuttoned. His pumped biceps and popping veins were clearly visible. He wore his Star of David which lay resting on his chest. The bride's father wore a white-sleeved shirt with a matching vest. The bride's mom wore an elegant tan-floral outfit consisting of a skirt and short-sleeved tan floral jacket.

Shmuel introduced Leora to his parents once again. Mr. Doron Weiss was fairly muscular in appearance. His face was a tannish leathery-like skin. He had recently retired from the police force. He definitely had the look of a warrior-soldier type, being nearly six feet in height, muscular, and still sporting his black hair. Mrs. Eranit Weiss worked as a legal secretary for a prominent Haifa firm. At a local gym, she worked out at least five days a week. The future in-laws mingled and congratulated one another.

By the end of the evening Mr. and Mrs. Weiss made plans to invite the Sterns over for dinner. Both in-laws had instant positive rapport as if they had known one another for years.

Leora's girlfriends congregated around her, all curious to meet Shmuel and to look at her sizeable, shining new diamond ring. There was a lot of dancing and 'oopas' while Greek food was being served – gyros, kebabs, humus, Greek salad, and baklava, a sweet dessert.

Mania, the best childhood friend of Leora, just met Shmuel and whispered, "Oh, my God, Leora, he's so handsome. What a hunk! He's so hot! What a catch! He looks more like a Hollywood movie star. Maybe he's got a bachelor friend I can be introduced to?"

Leora, said, "Yea, maybe. When the time is right, I'll definitely ask Shmuel."

Leora was introduced to Yoni and Sarah Cohen. Shmuel was complimented for being such a courageous detective. Yoni was happy to meet the person who'd bring sunshine to Shmuel's life. Many people brought presents for the handsome young couple. Yoni complimented Shmuel when he said, "You have fantastic taste. Leora has brains and beauty."

Leora smiled. "Thank you, Detective Yoni."

"It's fine if you wanted to call me Yoni."

Shmuel made a Le-Chaim, a toast to Leora and her fine family. "I want to thank my parents for helping me grow up to be the kind of person I've become. For that, I am grateful. Most important are my feelings for Leora and likewise, her emotions towards me. I never knew what I missed all my life until I met her. She's helped make my life feel so rich. Leora has rays of sunshine into my life. I'd like to thank all of you for coming to share our Simcha today. And with that, let us raise our glasses and say, 'Le-Chaim.'"

Next, it was Leora's turn. "Wow! Thank you all for coming. We met about six months ago and we quickly fell in love with each other. With Shmuel, I feel totally complete. His sexy good looks help too." Everyone laughed out loud. She continued, "We can discuss areas where we may differ but at the end of the day, we're each other's best friends. I have never been as happy as I am with my Shmuel." She smiled while she became sentimentally tearful. She tried valiantly to guard against mascara that began to smudge around her eyelashes.

Shmuel reached over to give her a handkerchief. Leora smiled, although tears still managed to creep towards the corners of her eyes.

I also want to thank my parents for providing me love and opportunities, such as piano playing, dance lessons as a child, and help with my university studies. My parents have always been incredibly supportive to me." Leora began to shed additional tears. Shmuel once again reached for a handkerchief to help dry her eyes. Leora said, "See what I mean when I say that Shmuel is so understanding?" She took a couple of deep breaths and continued, "I'm so happy he comes from such a fine family. That also makes me feel even securer in the future of our marriage."

The couple kissed at the end of these beautiful reflections.

Everyone raised their glasses and repeated, "Le-Chaim," to life, while the Greek band played on and the guests danced and laughed heartily.

***

Hannah called from her bathroom. Yoni excused himself so he could hear Hannah's voice message. "Abba, he's back. I heard tapings on my bedroom window. Please call me back as soon as possible. I'm so terrified, even in Elena's company. I don't want to talk in front of her, so I'm calling from the bathroom."

Yoni missed the call, as the restaurant was quite loud and he was unable to hear his phone ring. He went outside to call Hannah. "So what's making you feel so unsafe, Hannahle?"

Her voice trembled. She was hyperventilating. "I heard some tapping on my bedroom window. I've never heard these sounds before. He's back and wanting to find ways to kidnap me."

"Have your girlfriend stay with you till we return. In the meantime, I'll send another squad car with plainclothes police officers."

Within fifteen minutes, there were four additional officers patrolling the house. No one found any clues. Yoni and Sarah arrived home at 11:15 p.m. When Yoni came home from the engagement party, he went to inspect the house and roof. He holstered on his Desert Eagle and Tovar firearms. He checked that his firearms were fully loaded. Frightened to sleep in her own bedroom, Hannah lay in a sleeping bag with a pillow in Aaron's room. Hannah was unable to sleep that night. Her girlfriend was about to leave, but Yoni saw to it that he'd accompany her to her apartment.

It seemed like his injuries were healing well after ten days. Throughout his life, he learned how to ignore physical pain, although as a child he endured a plethora amount of physical abuse. Leonid's indulgence in oxycodone and other drugs like marijuana and cocaine also helped reduce some of his stabbing and stinging pains, which were still present in his left arm. Tears streamed down his cheeks but he had learned to ignore pain. Indeed, he had traversed the building up and down using grappling ropes and equipment. He wore black clothes which blended into the dark night. He wore light Ninja-style sneakers, ones that minimized sound.

Upon Yoni and Sarah's return, Hannah franticly said, "Abba, look!" On her window, an imprint of the killer's hand and his lip marks were visible. The statement read, *"You're next, my darling whore! You slut. I'm coming after you, my dear! You f***** whore! You deserve to die! And your father, the detective, I'm coming after him too!"*

Hannah cried, "You see, I was right. The killer is following me. He wants to harm me and you. He wants to do to me what he's done to others." By now, Sarah began to also feel nervous and anxious. She began pacing back and forth. Although she tried comforting Hannah, she felt terrified, especially when she witnessed the writing on Hannah's window and her daughter's utter helplessness.

Yoni photographed the writing on the window. Aaron, now awake, aimlessly walked around carrying his blanket and sucking his thumb. He wanted to be picked up as he eyed his father.

"Abba, uppie?"

"Aaron, your Abba is busy right now," said Sarah.

Finally, Yoni picked up Aaron, placed him in his bed, and gave him hugs and kisses.

Aaron continued sucking his thumb.

Yoni had indeed checked out Hannah's window, and Leonid's writing on the windowpane was exactly as had been described by Hannah.

"Calm down, Hannahle. We'll find a solution."

She thought to herself about the bow-and-arrow incident, 'Gee, I should have aimed my arrows towards his heart. That f***** is continuously threatening me. I should have finished him off.'

The wind kicked up and could be heard through their entire apartment window panes. The rattling sound was loud. Aaron got out of his bed and hugged Hannah by her legs. Sarah went over to reassure Aaron. She gently massaged his back while he lay on the carpeted floor with the blanket caressing his face. After just a few minutes, Aaron fell back asleep.

Yoni called his boss. "Commander Gidon Mordechai Levy. This is Yoni. I'm so sorry to call you this late, but we've run into a much bigger problem than I had ever anticipated. Sometime last evening when my daughter was babysitting our Aaron, the killer left his handprint, his lip marks, and his threats to kill Hannah and myself on her windowpane. He's stalking my daughter and has written threats to kill her and me. I photographed his window writing and will text it to you shortly.

"Hannah had predicted this would happen in a recent vision. This hits way too close to home and I thought you'd have some ideas about what we should do next. To date, I've had some plainclothes police officers observing our house and neighborhood. I arranged for Hannah to stay with an aunt in Tel Aviv for three weeks, and during that time, I stopped the police patrol of our neighborhood. Upon her return from her aunt's, Hannah's friend, a boy in her class, had given her a letter that carried the same threats of intending to rape and kill Hannah. I then made arrangements to have her live with her aunt once again. So now that she's back home, there's an imminently distinct threat to her life. What do you recommend we do next? What should we do now? It's affecting every member of my family. It's the biggest family crisis we've ever had to face. What are your thoughts, sir?"

"Let's get some additional plainclothes police patrol. I would like to place a swat team of six officers on the roof once again, just in case. We'll keep them there at least two or three weeks and then reevaluate. Okay? You don't have to make any calls regarding the swat team. I'll take care of it all on my end."

"Thank you, that sounds like a sound plan to me. I appreciate your help, sir."

"You're welcome. We're a team."

Yoni felt extremely stressed out. His sleep pattern was interrupted over a period of time. This entire crime scene was much too close to home, especially since the killer was directly threatening his family. He placed his Desert Eagle and his trusted Tovar next to his nightstand. Although he was reassured by his boss, Yoni had a sleepless night worrying about Hannah's safety.

At 3:30 in the morning, he finally fell asleep but shortly after, perhaps an hour or two later, he awakened to the sound of knocking against his windowpane. He immediately leaped out of bed and realized that strong winds had knocked a tree branch against their windows. He attempted to drift into deep sleep once again. Yoni tossed and turned for what seemed like an eternity. Finally, he succumbed to deep slumber.

In the morning when they got up, it was Sarah who first noticed something unusual on their windowpane. Their screen had been torn and there was writing on their window. *"Your daughter is a filthy whore. She deserves to die. She's a f****** slut! I'm coming after you too!"* These were written in red lipstick. Yoni took out his Desert Eagle, loaded it, put his clothes on, and ran the stairs towards the building's roof. He looked to see if anyone had been there. He searched and did find a rope that had been thrown to the ground below. He was sure the killer must have hung from a rope when he wrote the tender love notes. He decided to take a picture of the writing and send it with an accompanying text to Commander Gidon Mordechai Levy.

Commander Levy immediately requested a twenty-four-seven swat team on their roof. He realized the dire and perilous situation that Hannah was in. "Don't worry, Yoni. The request was sent in, but I'll send another reminder now as we speak."

"I think you need to know that the killer has also threatened to kill me in his love note."

"Don't worry, Yoni. You'll have as much police force as possible and we'll get this SOB!"

"Okay, thanks. When this killer is threatening Hannah and my life, this is now totally unacceptable."

"Yes, I agree and I'll do whatever it takes to protect you and your family. Whatever it takes, Yoni," said Commander Levy.

It occurred to Yoni that since a swat team had not yet been placed on their rooftop, Leonid must have secured ropes making his way down to their windows and writing these threats. Yoni climbed stairs which led to the roof and found some grappling ropes, like the ones used by proficient rock climbers.

In less than an hour's time, several swat team members appeared on the roof. They told Yoni that they will be there for the three weeks and then reevaluate the situation. Yoni showed them the repelling ropes and the killer's window writings. Hannah had awakened with a need to get to school but saw the writing on the window. Immediately, she became fearful and said, "I'm not going to school today. How do I know he won't kidnap me?" She was tired of feeling frightened and anxious all the time.

"Hannah, there are plainclothes police officers monitoring every step you take. We also have snipers on our rooftop. Why don't you call a friend or two and tell them you'd like their company? If you wish, I'll walk with you to school?"

"That would be wonderful, Abba. If I had friends come over and walk me to school, that would raise too many questions like, 'Why the need to accompany you? Why are you suddenly so scarred?'"

"Can't you tell them that you're not at liberty to discuss things right now?"

"I don't know, Abba. You think it's so easy to withhold information from my friends? I mean, what does that do to my friendships, the trust and bond between us? Abba, it's not as easy as you think; it undermines my friendships and our trust as well. Can you see that?"

"Yes, I do."

"I'd appreciate it if you'd walk me to school today?"

"Yes, of course. No problem, my Hannahle."

Hannah inwardly reflected on Leonid's writing on her windowpane. "I should have killed that bastard with an arrow right into his heart. My problems would have ended by now."

Yoni felt considerable turmoil over this direct threat to both his daughter as well as his life. He carried his loaded Desert Eagle in his holster at all times. He'd walk her to school but didn't feel comfortable about going to work, as he felt that his home presence was needed. There was plenty for him to do at work. The swat team was now present as well as plainclothes police officers. He thought to himself, 'There's a killer on the loose and we're not yet an inch closer towards apprehending him. When will this case break? When am I going to apprehend this bastard?' Sitting now, he looked down towards his laps and whispered to himself, 'Oh no, killing my Hannahle will never be an option. No way!' He dropped down on the floor and knocked off sixty pushups and two hundred sit-ups. He added sixty jumping jacks and ran in place for five minutes. Now breathless, he uttered, "No, you f*****, you're not getting a hold of my Hannahle, nor me! You son of a bitch! I'm coming after you!" He felt furious. He wondered, 'What else can I do?' The answer was, 'Nothing!'

It was nine p.m. when his phone rang. Although he was reading the daily news, it was more important to speak to Shmuel. "Hi, Yoni, thank you for coming to our party and your most generous gift. I was so happy to introduce you to Leora."

"Leora's a wonderful girl. I'm glad you found each other. In the meantime, the killer wrote threats on Hannah's window last night. This killer also wrote a similar threatening note on our windowpane last night. We've got a swat team and plainclothes police officers. Round the clock. You know what, Shmuel? We must find this bastard killer as soon as possible. At stake is Hannah's life and my life. He's threatening to kill us both."

"I'm with you and I'll continue to do whatever it takes to get this monster. Also, Raffi plans to call you today because he returned to interview Leonid's parents. Expect his call."

On her way to school that day, Hannah heard a loud explosion which turned out to be IDF pilot jet maneuvers breaking sound barriers with their supersonic flying machines. She immediately kneeled, seeking to protect her head with her book bag.

These explosions triggered a new vision where she saw her father's car being firebombed by the killer. In addition, she felt her Abba was now in imminent danger while driving back and forth from home. When she arrived at her home from school, she called her father about her latest vision. She stated that now more than ever she felt worried about his life being threatened and cut short.

"Abba, I'm sorry to bother you at work but I had another vision which involves you. The killer wants to kill you and firebomb your car." The words were stated with great inner foreboding and a trembling shaky sound in Hannah's voice. She continued, "The killer intends to kill you, Abba. You must be careful, even in the police departments and certainly while driving back and forth to work. Abba, you should wear a disguise?"

"What? That son of a bitch. I'll kill him first." Yoni was angry and shouting obscenities. He banged his car's dashboard.

"Abba, please be careful. Like I said, maybe wear some kind of disguise?"

"Yes, and I will also drive a different car with an entirely different look. Thank you for the heads-up. I'll take care of myself, Hannahle. Don't worry."

Chapter Eighteen

Yoni drove a police car rental of a different make and a car model. He also wore a new disguise – a blond long hairpiece, a blond beard, mustache, and even changed his clothing style. Instead of wearing long pants, he now wore a long-sleeved white shirt and a tie without the detective shield present on his shirt. He appeared as if he was an educator or somehow connected to the music industry, maybe even a musician in an Israeli classical music ensemble. His new car was a convertible black Mercedes, instead of his older 2011 maroon Honda Accord. He secured an entirely new parking area for his rented car.

Although Sarah had been warned of his new appearance when he came home for dinner, she couldn't believe her eyes. Suddenly, Yoni appeared considerably older as if he were in his early fifties. Yoni quickly changed clothes and removed his hairpiece, beard, and mustache.

"Now, that's better. We have the real you now," Sarah said with a smile on her face. She kissed and hugged him.

Aaron said, "Ach," under his breath, disapproving of his parent kiss. He appeared repulsed by their overt kissing.

Yoni noticed his son's reaction. "That's what people do when they love each other, Aaron."

Hannah and Sarah smiled at Aaron because of his innocent reaction.

Hannah said, "Aaron, one day when you get older, you'll have a girlfriend, maybe a wife one day?"

"No, I'm only marrying my Ima. And why do you have to kiss like that, I mean on the lips? Ach."

Yoni said, "Son, one day you'll understand. When I was five years old, I also thought it was weird. I didn't understand why my parents kissed. When people feel close to each other, they love each other and kiss. Just like when we kiss you on the cheeks. Why? Because we love you. But let's not worry about that now. You have plenty of time. You're only five years old." He changed the subject when he said, "Who's hungry?"

Hannah and Aaron unanimously said, "Me."

"Okay, well then, let's eat," said Sarah as she began serving the family.

"Ima, let me help you." Hannah got up to help serve her mom's salad and homemade lasagna. The family menu cuisine tonight was more Italian – a plate of olive oil, freshly ground pepper, and grated mozzarella cheese were present for their bread dipping pleasures. A freshly baked rye bread was ready to be cut. Hannah had bought fresh flowers from a nearby flower stand. Yoni's erratic detective schedule made it difficult to consistently eat together as a family, but tonight was different. Everyone felt close and looked forward to spending wonderful family time.

***

Suddenly, she felt preoccupied and worried when Hannah said, "Abba, I just had this eerie feeling that he's in close proximity to our home. I think he's going to do something bad tonight. I saw a great big fire in my vision, like a car was burning. It made me think of your car, Abba."

"Hannahle, I've got so many cops patrolling the neighborhood and this seven-story complex. Let's not worry so much."

"Okay, I'll try but I just envisioned his being right in our neighborhood now."

"Our backs are all covered, Hannah."

It was near midnight. Leonid wore a new disguise. He had a goatee, jet-black hair, and showed thick caked-on makeup to conceal his facial scar. He sported a suit and tie while holding onto a black leather attaché case. Prepared for possible police interrogations, he had false identification papers pretending to be a newly settled French immigrant. His paperwork reflected his new alias as Mr. Francoise Payette Stern. He had practiced some basic French, just in case he was questioned. He looked like a successful attorney or a businessman returning to his neighborhood condo. He managed to slip by with nearly no suspicion.

Officer Simon Kahn questioned the man. "Stop, who are you and what are you doing here so late? Do you realize it's midnight?" Simon was in his early thirties. He placed his right hand on his pistol, just in case.

Francoise answered, "Yes, I do realize it but I'm coming home from an all-evening business meeting." Clearly, he spoke Hebrew with a pronounced French accent.

"Where do you live?"

Francoise answered, pointing to a nearby building and provided proof, "Here, let me give you paperwork-evidence of my immigration to Israel, that is, if you'd like to see it."

"Yes, I would. When did you immigrate to Israel?"

"I arrived in Israel sixteen months ago because France had become unsafe for Jews, you know, growing anti-Semitism and the increase of Moslem fundamentalists' presence in France. Some areas in Paris have Sharia Law. Imagine that?"

Francoise presented a copy of his lease and a copy of his driver's license.

"Thank you, Francoise. You may go now. Sorry to bother you."

"Oh no, no, thanks for doing your job. We need more safety here. You know how these Arab kidnappers swept up the three teenagers which triggered the recent Israeli incursion into Gaza. That could happen anywhere. So I appreciate what you're doing to protect us, the citizens of our community."

Alias Francoise walked towards the building where the Cohens lived. He displayed a radiant inner smile, proud of his cunningness and being proficient in how to deceive law enforcement. He entered the building and made his way to the underground parking garage. He was able to unlock the garage door by simply fidgeting the lock using a lady's hairpin. He looked for Yoni's car – the maroon Honda Accord. This poorly lit garage was on two levels, each consisting of two rows. He looked to see if there were any security cameras. There were some, but he now wore a facial mask which hid his features. He searched for Yoni's car in the lower level first. The first of two rows consisted of about fifty cars. After a careful search, he spotted Yoni's Honda Accord. It was the fifteenth car in the right lane. He looked around to ensure he'd be able to carry out his plan of destruction. He found his box cutters and slashed Yoni's tires. A gleam of joy was on his face as he watched the tires deflate instantly. He smiled. He carried lighter fluid which he placed under each of the tires and close to the area where the gas tank was located. He lit the tire area. A strong smell of burning rubber was evident. The fumes permeated the entire garage. He picked up a nearby rock and smashed Yoni's car's windows. He proceeded to apply lighter fluid in the car's interior. He then lit it. With each passing minute, the bright reddish-orange flames enlarged with swells of fire reaching the garage's ceiling. In the meantime, the fire caused several car alarms to set off. Leonid took off to the second level of the garage, expecting police any second now. In the second floor of the garage, he found a large car and managed to squeeze under it. The siren sounds of several cars were loud and piercing. Several cars were now burning as the fire spread and grew huger. The flames now reached the ceiling. Police arrived quickly and began investigating. Immediately, they called the fire department. They were able to retrieve license plate information which helped them locate the vehicle owners.

Yoni was called at 2:00 a.m. "Detective Yoni Cohen. This is Sergeant Avi. I'm downstairs in the garage in your building. I'm sorry to wake you up, but we're patrolling the neighborhood and several car alarms went off. Your

Honda car's tires were slashed and it's on fire, real bad. The damage is extensive. The fire department is in the garage attempting to retard any further combustion. And the blaze has spread to other cars as well. We'd like to speak to you. Can you please come down? We're on the first level of the garage. Again, we're sorry to awaken you under these circumstances."

"Yes, I'll be down in a couple of minutes." Yoni put on his clothes and ran all the way down the staircase to the garage. Yoni coughed, trying to catch his breath because of the intense fire's fumes.

Once there, he inquired Sergeant Avi, "Did you or any of your men see anyone who might have been suspicious-looking? I mean, did anyone enter this building in the last couple of hours?"

"I know that Officer Simon Kahn questioned someone in a suit around midnight."

"Can I speak to him, please?"

"Sure, let me call him right now and see if he might still be around." Avi called Officer Simon who came quickly to the scene of this massive fire combustion.

"Hi, I'm Officer Simon. How can I help you?"

"I'm Detective Yoni Cohen and I see that my car was completely destroyed by the fire. I was informed that you spoke to someone who claimed that he lives here, around midnight? You should know that I'm investigating the murder and stabbing of young ladies. That killer has also threatened to kill my daughter and me."

"Oh wow! I'm sorry to hear this bad news. To get back to your question, yes, I did question a young man wearing a suit. He had identification that he was a newly settled immigrant from France by the name of Francoise Payette Stern. He stated he was in an all-evening business meeting that lasted several hours. He provided me with an address."

"What did he wear, and can you describe his appearance?"

"Yea, he wore a business suit with a leather attaché case. His hair was black and he had a goatee beard. He spoke Hebrew with a French accent and reported that he had emigrated from France."

"About how tall was he?"

"Oh, maybe about five foot ten."

"Did he have a scar on his face?"

"Sorry, I didn't notice that." He paused and said, "No, come to think of it, he did – on his left cheek. But it was not very pronounced."

"Did you notice any other distinguishing features?"

"Although he was in a suit, he seemed very athletic-looking, maybe a bodybuilder's physique."

"You guys need to check this out. Call up the owners and management of these buildings to see if anyone by that name lives here. He's probably the killer who's threatened to kill my daughter and me, but he's clever enough to wear a disguise. My gut feelings tell me it's him. I'm informed that he wears different disguises. In the meantime, my Honda was so trashed that it's unrecognizable." Yoni appeared angry and disgusted, more like fed up. Yoni thought to himself, 'What a life! I have to wear a disguise fleeing from this crazy man, my daughter's life is threatened, and my car is demolished beyond recognition. F***! Is this my life as a detective? Maybe I should look for another career? I admit I am frightened.' Yoni was so furious. He banged his fist against the palm of his other hand. He ran up the building's staircase to burn up frustrations he now felt.

He returned and got into bed around 3:00 a.m.

Sarah asked, "What happened honey?"

"Our car was burned and demolished, I'm sure, by Leonid, the killer. I'm so tense and wound up about Leonid. In the morning, I'll have to call our insurance company about the car. Thank God I have a rented car to get around in."

"Honey, don't worry, you'll apprehend the killer. You'll get him. I have faith in you and your determination. Hey, it's only a car. We have car insurance. You're healthy and we have a wonderful family. Let's be thankful for what we have. Material things like a car… they can always be replaced."

"Yea, you're right. It's just that this son of a bitch is out to kill Hannah and me. I must admit that it's got me feeling so furious, but I'm also worried."

"Yea, I know how agonized you are, but the killer has no chance in the world, not with your officers and you and your detectives."

"You're so amazing. I feel like here I am so crippled with angst, and you're just so positive and well grounded. Thank you for being so supportive, Sarah, my love. That's why you're so special to me. I love you."

"My love, how about we get some shuteye. It can all wait." They hugged and kissed goodnight.

Next morning, Yoni wore a new disguise, but little did he know that Leonid was still stalking him. After he had his breakfast of yogurt and blue berries, Yoni walked towards his Mercedes. Leonid's new disguise was a handyman fixing some door locks on the outside of buildings. He was now completely bald but had a thick black mustache. His disguise made him completely unrecognizable. Leonid noticed the individual drive away in the Mercedes. He concluded it must be Yoni with a new disguise.

Leonid felt most certain that the person in the Mercedes was Yoni. He decided to follow him by getting into his SUV. He appeared to be about one hundred and fifty meters behind Yoni, in route to Tel Aviv. After a couple of miles, the SUV continued to follow him. Yoni noticed the same car and concluded that he was being stalked. He removed his Desert Eagle pistol from the holster and placed it on the nearby safe compartment of the car. He knew that his Desert Eagle was fully loaded. Yoni's adrenaline level raced out of control. His breathing intensified, becoming more rapid. He swore profusely by now. He called for additional police help, identifying his location on the highway. Within a few minutes, several police car sirens were heard. A police helicopter hovered above. The chase was on. Leonid abruptly turned around, making a three-hundred-and-sixty-degree turn, exiting hurriedly, crossing several cemented sidewalks. Recognizing he was outwitted, Leonid became furious and entertained ways to seek revenge against the entire Tel Aviv Police Force.

***

Leonid engineered another plan – the destruction of the entire headquarters in Tel Aviv. The following day, it was around 7:00 p.m. Yoni was scheduled to leave his office. It had been a long day with phone calls to answer. As lead detective, he spent considerable time interviewing many of new leads pertaining to Leonid. He was preparing to leave but had one additional phone call to return. Just then, the phone rang. It was Hannah calling with high-pitched urgency in her voice.

"Abba, you and your staff must leave the building now, at once. Evacuate! I just had a vision of a large explosion in your police building, a major explosion any minute now." Her voice quivered in fear of losing her father. "Abba, leave now! NOW!"

"Oh no!"

"Yes, you and your staff must get out now, at once!"

"Okay."

Yoni quickly took his attaché case, cellphone, and his family's pictures that were placed on his desk. He made the announcement for everyone to clear the building immediately. *"Get out of the building right now. Immediately evacuate! Leave everything behind and run. NOW! NOW!"* The power of his voice increased when he said 'NOW' for the second time.

Everyone heeded Hannah's warning. Within less than forty-five seconds, the entire police department was empty, almost ghostlike. Police employees ran with their laptops and pocketbooks considering the short time notice. Yoni ran to his Mercedes. A loud explosion rocked, shaking the entire building. Smoke and huge flames engulfed the building. The fire spread quickly, shattering windows everywhere; the police building was demolished into rubbles. Glass shreds from broken windows and pieces of wood flew everywhere. Some officers sustained minor injuries, like glass cuts. Police headquarters was a mess with broken glass and a fire that raged out of control. Sirens, police, and ambulances were immediately dispatched to the area. He turned around and looked back. He was now about hundred meters away. He thought to himself, 'Oh my goodness! Had I not been for Hannah, surely, others and myself would have been killed. Hannah was spot on once again. What a blessing to have her as my daughter! Hannahle, my Hannahle. What a gem!' That thought brought a smile to Yoni's face.

He was now in the car and called Commander Levy to inform, but he was already notified by other police employees. Yoni was absolutely convinced that this was Leonid's undertakings, especially since Hannah had predicted this outcome.

"Commander Levy, just for your information, I'm wearing a disguise and driving a rented car because Leonid slashed my tires, completely burned and destroyed my car last night. Have you heard that Leonid exploded our police station on Chaim Herzl Boulevard? I was tipped off by Hannah who had the vision of the bombing moments in advance of this occurrence. She immediately called me and said, 'Leave the building right now. Evacuate,' which we all did."

"Yoni, are you okay? I mean, are you injured?"

"No, no. I'm okay, some sustained small cuts from flying pieces of glass that got imbedded in my finger." He looked at his hands and noticed a sharp glass shred still lodged in his bleeding right index finger. He added, "Just a piece of glass that cut my finger. I guess I'm lucky. It could have been worse, sir."

"Thank God, you're not badly injured. I'll take care of everything that has to do with the police building. We'll need to see if the video cameras captured the assailant or assailants. I was just about to call if anyone found any identifiable information, possibly captured it on video. Don't worry, Yoni. We're circling the wagons. Just be careful. We need you around and your family needs you as well. Leonid's defiance of police has only increased because he's feeling threatened about being captured by us."

"Thank you for your concern, sir. I wondered what possible type of firepower demolished our building. This son of a bitch did one hell of a job!"

"We'll investigate it," said Commander Levy.

"Okay, we'll talk later."

And they hung up their phones.

***

Early in the morning of the following day, Yoni received a call from Commander Levy. Yoni, still in his pajamas, brushed his teeth while he answered the phone.

"I have some interesting news for you. I had our men review the videos beginning from a few days prior to the explosion. We found two suspicious men who were loitering around the police station. They appeared like landscapers who had come to trim our bushes. Their faces were masked. They placed small bagged packages in the shrubs around the building. Then, they evacuated the nearby area with lightning speed. To confuse us even more, they trimmed the shrubs as if they were landscapers. These packages were well hidden in the bushes, pretty much towards the front of our building."

"Can you estimate the sizes of any of these packages?"

"We froze some picture frames as we replayed the videos over and over. Our bomb experts looked at some fragments and estimated them to be the size of a large thirty-two-ounce coke bottle. The entire area was scoured and we concluded that there were two bombs that were electronically set off. We found the remains of electronic wires, although they were badly frayed and burned. Our bomb experts concluded there were sophisticated dynamite sticks placed in a container, which turned out to be bombs. Whoever did this must have been acquainted with explosives. It may have been Leonid and his partner in this crime, or both. Any thoughts about that, Yoni?"

"Sir, I wish I had additional information to offer. We do know that Leonid was refused by the IDF due to mental problems. We're actively pursuing his apprehension. I know Raffi is actively looking for clues. Raffi is interviewing Leonid's parents in search of hints, such as whether he has any friends who might be assisting in any of his crimes." He thought for a moment and then continued, "Sir, when I as soon have additional information, I'll inform you pronto."

"Thanks, Yoni."

Chapter Nineteen

It was late in the evening when Yoni called Raffi. "I just got off the phone with Shmuel and said you may have additional information about the killer." Yoni was eager to get as much information about the case.

"Yes, hi, Yoni. So I interviewed the parents once again because I think they've been covering up for their son. I thought that they could give me the names of his favorite sex/porn club. I also thought they would be able to provide me an address as to where he lives. Do you mind listening to the interview recording?"

"Yes, let's hear it."

While on the phone, Raffi played the interview.

"Mr. and Mrs. Kozlov, I'd like to talk to you again. As you know, I do have to record the meeting. I do think you know more about your son's whereabouts and didn't share some information I need. For example, where does he lives, what is his favorite club, and who are his friends, this kind of information is what I need. It's your turn to talk. What's his favorite sex club?"

"They appeared anxious because I was applying pressure for additional answers. I also told them that, 'Withholding information is a criminal act, punishable under our laws. So now is the time for you to come straight with me. Your son is the suspected killer of a young lady and nearly fatally stabbed another one. He also slashed another woman's arm which required twenty stitches. What's your son's favorite sex club?'"

"Once, our son once mentioned che vas going to clubs Sheere-Az and the Volga Club in Tiel Aviv."

"How often did he tell you that he was going to these clubs?"

"About once or tvice a veek."

"So, he told you that that he goes out more than just once a week, right?"

"Yes, che did."

"Did he mention what evenings he prefers to go to these clubs?"

"No."

"Where does he live now? You have to help me out on this? Don't hold back on me."

"Sir, tis vie don't know. If vie did, ve vould share this information viet you."

"Okay, give me the names of at least two of his friends, where they live, and what they do."

"Vie only know von friend and chis name is Moyshe Stein. Che lives chere in Tiel Aviv and che's a butcher as vell."

"Can you provide me his address?"

"Sir, tis vie don't know. Che's a butcher and che vorks at Zion meats in Tiel Aviv."

"Did Moyshe Stein serve in the IDF?"

"Sorry, vie don't know."

"Thank you for your cooperation."

Yoni thought to himself, 'Good, you got some information. We're getting somewhere now.'

***

Next, Raffi visited Zion Meats, with its owner being Matan Kernberg. Raffi turned on the video camera and began to record their interview.

"I need to record this interview, Mr. Kernberg. You're the owner of Zion Meats and we have a suspected loose killer on our hands. He's worked for you in the recent past. Thus far he's killed one lady and nearly fatally stabbed another from Tel Aviv. What do you know about this killer?" Raffi displayed pictures and gave Mr. Kernberg a copy of the pictures.

"Yea, he did work for me and he's a friend of Moyshe Stein, my lead butcher."

"Do you know where the killer lives?"

"No, I'm sorry but I don't have any knowledge of his address."

"I'd like to interview Mr. Moyshe Stein. Is he here today?"

"He'll be here in an hour."

"Okay, I'll wait. And you better not call to give him a heads-up call. If I find out that you did, I'll have to arrest you for aiding and abetting a killer. What do you know about the murderer?"

"He was fascinated with knives of all shapes and sizes. When he looked at one of his shining silver knives, it's as if he was mesmerized."

"The shop uses several types of carving knives. We don't use just one type."

Sure enough, in about forty-five minutes, Moyshe Stein arrived at his job. He appeared to be in his mid-twenties. He also kept fit by working out in the same gym as Leonid. He had that look of a bodybuilder with bulging muscles and pronounced veins to match. Yet, he seemed to have had an effeminate quality, like sporting light mascara shadows around his eyes and eyelashes.

"Mr. Stein, I'm Detective Raffi and I'm investigating a murder of a female and a stabbing and slashing of young ladies. We have picture of the killer and we know that you guys are friends that like to hang out." Raffi handed him a picture of the suspected killer. "What do you know about the killer?"

"We met at the gym because we both enjoy weight training, you know, working out together. We have the same occupation, as we're both butchers who worked at Zion Meats. Leonid told me about a number of after-hour sex/porn clubs and asked me if I was interested to come along. I told him no, because I'm in a steady relationship with a girl. If she found out that I attended any one of these clubs, our relationship would probably end immediately. I do know that Leonid was fascinated by going to this club known as Shere-Az in Tel Aviv. Like I said, we worked out several times a week but that was pretty much the extent of our relationship. Oh, by the way, you should know that Leonid is a very fast runner. He runs and works out daily."

"Did he ever show you or talk about his knife collection?"

"Yes, he did once. I'm not a collector, so it didn't fascinate me as much as it did him."

"Did you ever serve in the IDF?"

"Yes, I certainly did."

"In what capacity did you serve?"

"I was a corporal in artillery."

This was a red flag for Raffi who also worked in the same bombed police building. "What type of work did you do in artillery? And where does the killer reside?"

"I don't know where he resides. As for me, I was an explosives expert for the IDF."

"What were your duties as an explosives expert in the IDF?"

"I dismantled bombs and explosives."

"What type of bombs and explosives?"

"Hamas and Hezbollah bombs and Qassam rockets shot into Israel. Also, I was successful in dismantling drones packed with explosives."

"So you definitely know how to construct and dismantle bombs, right?"

"Yes, for sure."

"Did you know that a Tel Aviv police station was bombed?"

"Oh no! I'm sorry to hear that. I don't know anything about it."

"What about Leonid's knives?"

"He had several scalpel knifes, several daggers, at least two serrated knives with at least twelve-inch blades and some throwing knifes. He also had several switchblade knifes and some hunting knives with handles made of antlers."

"What's the name of the gym you guys work out at?"

"Olympia International in Tel Aviv."

"What time do you guys meet to work out?"

"It varies but it's usually sometime between six and eight p.m. five days a week."

"Do you happen to have a phone number of him?"

"I'm sorry, I don't have his phone number. I did have a number, but it got disconnected."

"Can you tell me more about how you dismantled explosives for the IDF?"

"I helped disassemble Hamas, Hezbollah bombs, and other incendiary devices like landmines. I know a lot about bombs and was even awarded citations for having done excellent work for our IDF."

"So, would you say that you're an expert in assembling bombs?"

"Oh yes, I certainly do, most probably one of the best in Israel."

"And is it fair to say that you'd be able to construct bombs?"

"Yes. I can see where you're going with these questions, but I want you to know that I had nothing to do with the police station bombing."

"We'll see about that."

When Moyshe Stein mentioned the phone number, it was the same number that had been disconnected. Raffi thought to himself, 'When criminals are on the run, one of the things they do is disconnect their phone numbers, find new residence, and even change their appearance. In some instances, killers on the run have even had plastic surgery to change their overall look.'

"Moyshe, has Leonid changed his appearance in any way in the last few months?"

"Yes, he colored his hair blond. Before, he had black hair and short curly hair. Now he's a blond."

"Did he color his eyebrows as well?"

"Yes, blond."

"Does he have a mustache?"

"Yes, and it's blond now."

"Okay, thank you for your time and the information provided. One other thing, can you provide me your address? It's all a part of our investigation protocol. Don't tell your friend Leonid that a detective is after him. That could mess up our entire investigation. Can you do that for us? If I find out that you told him about my questions, I'll arrest you for cooperating with a criminal. I'll have your ass in jail in no time. You follow me?"

"Yes, I promise. I won't utter a word." Moyshe proceeded to provide his address to Raffi.

"One more thing. I want your cellphone for now. At the end of our investigative search, I'll give it back to you."

Raffi intended to send Moyshe's cellphone to forensics and secure additional information like Leonid's phone number and/or anyone else who may have been involved in the police station bombing. Raffi went to get a cup of coffee and called for some police help – plainclothes officers, four of them on this eve to arrive with him at the Olympia International Gym in Tel Aviv.

It was now six o' clock in the evening. Raffi and four plainclothes officers were placed in strategic locations, two on the roof and two in the lobby near the entrance and near to street access. They watched everyone come and go till nine p.m. Leonid was nowhere to be seen. Raffi wondered, 'Could Leonid have been tipped off by his friend Moyshe?'

***

The following evening on Friday, Leonid entered the gym at six thirty p.m. It was a large gym, perhaps thirty thousand square feet. Several plainclothes officers were strategically stationed around the gym. Leonid wore shorts, an undershirt, and running shoes.

Leonid had just finished bench-pressing one hundred and twenty-five kilograms. Rafii spotted Leonid. A fast speed chase ensured as Raffi ran after Leonid. They headed up the staircase which led to the roof. At one point, Raffi was no more than twenty feet away from his assailant. "I'm coming after you, you son of a bitch. I'm right behind you. Stop or I'll shoot. I said stop or I'll shoot!" These statements were repeated loudly. Adrenaline pumped Raffi while he chased Leonid as fast as possible. Raffi, with pistol in hand, fired two shots, but missed Leonid by centimeters.

Leonid knew the layout of the building and ran rapidly up the stairs to the roof. Raffi and the police officers followed him closely. Leonid was swift and nimble, like a modern-day Ninja in action.

When Raffi was about twenty feet away, he shot once again. Instead, his bullets hit the steel staircase banister. Loud fire sparks lit the staircase as metal bullets hit the metal railing one after the other. Raffi thought to himself, 'It's hard holding a pistol, running, and aiming all at the same time.' He missed Leonid who was now on the roof. At one point, Raffi could swear he nicked his calf, but it was probably wishful thinking.

The gym building was about six to eight feet away from the nearby building. Leonid ran with incredible speed, jumped, and landed on the roof of the next building. Raffi ordered the officers to run down the stairs and search the next building. He called the police officer who was in the lobby to search the next building.

Leonid had jumped effectively, dodging the police officers. Raffi thought to himself, 'Wow, I'm so close and yet so far away. What a clever bastard we have on our hands! That f***** son of a bitch! How could I have missed him? So close, yet so far away! That bastard must have jumped at least six or seven feet from one building to another.' Raffi was convinced that Leonid was an athlete in great shape. Raffi ended his conversation with Yoni when he said, "Leonid is so fast. He's elusive, that f***** bastard."

Yoni indicated, "Raffi, you might want to look into his buddy a bit closer. Something tells me that he's hiding our murderer."

"Yes, I thought the same thing. We're on the same page. I also wondered if they have a gay relationship. Sometimes, these big muscles can be a cover-up for being gay. That's why I'll follow up on Moyshe Stein, now that I have his home address."

Yoni said, "Yea, that's a great idea. I don't trust this Moyshe Stein. I believe he's covering up for his friend. I wouldn't be at all surprised if the two are lovers."

"Yea, for sure. Moyshe is an expert in explosives and our police station was just bombed. I think he actively helped Leonid in the bombing of our police department and they're both involved in that crime."

Chapter Twenty

It was a rainy, windy fall day with strong sea gales beating the sandy coastline of Tel Aviv. People took their raincoats and umbrellas. Some even blew away because of the unrelenting and unforgiving winds. In the very far distance, one could see slight peaks of blue sky patches straining to be seen from the current morgue-like gray. The gloominess of this overcast day called for staying indoors, perhaps enjoying a hot chocolate drink or tea with biscuits or croissants.

Commander Gidon Mordechai Levy was a no-nonsense type of a guy, least interested in small talk or fluff – only facts mattered to him when he called Yoni. Although Yoni felt apprehensive talking to his boss, he needed to share the latest information in a succinct and factual manner. His boss only appreciated facts.

"Shalom, Commander Levy, it's Yoni. I want you to listen to a verbal recording of the latest about our killer. Do you have about a half-an-hour time, sir?"

"Yes, please go ahead and turn on the recording. It's fine on this end. Take as long as you need. Okay?"

"Thank you, sir. Here we go."

He had turned on the recording and his boss listened attentively to Raffi's recording.

At times, Commander Levy was heard adding his own commentary like, "Get that bastard. Shoot him again and again."

At the end, Commander Levy said, "Congratulations, Yoni. You're circling the wagons and making it harder and harder for the bastard to get away. That's really good news. I liked the way Detective Raffi asked his questions. Also, the relationship between Moyshe and Leonid needs to be further explored, especially now that we know Moyshe is an expert in explosives. I'm of the opinion that he's involved in Leonid's life and the recent bombing. I wouldn't be surprised if you'll apprehend Leonid shortly. You're doing a great job, Yoni!"

"Thank you, sir. We're trying. We don't yet have his home address."

"Ask the gym manager if they have an updated address on that bastard. Maybe they can help out?"

"Yes, sir. I had thought about that as well. Thanks for your suggestion, sir."

"Okay, keep me informed as you do, and have a good day, Yoni."

They both hung up the phone. Yoni called back Raffi and suggested he go back to the gym and elicit information on the killer – where he lives, his credit card payment methods which could have his latest address, and the bank he does business with, etc.

Raffi planned on visiting Olympia International Gym.

Raffi had to get ready for his workday. It was seven a.m., but it appeared darker due to the heavy rains and the dark melancholic sky. He made sure that he carried several extra magazine clips of ballistic power and called for four additional plainclothes police officers to assist him. This would amount to eight extra officers.

He said, "Okay guys. I'm going into the gym again and talk to the manager. The purpose is to get an address and Leonid's banking information regarding his monthly membership withdrawals. It would seem to me that they would have updated address and phone information on Leonid, our illusive killer." This last comment was made with intended sarcasm. I'll need your backup in the event of seeing him in the gym or visiting Leonid at his updated address. Any questions?" There were no questions. "I suggest you position yourself in key areas, just in case you see our killer. Some of you in the gym while others, outside. Bring some workout clothes, but make sure your weapons are concealed."

Mr. Gal Berany was the Olympia Gym's manager. "Hi, Mr. Berany. I'm Detective Raffi and I have a few questions for you." He flashed his detective badge. "Where is the best area to talk privately?" In the meantime, the plainclothes officers positioned themselves at important strategic positions, both inside and outside.

"Hello, please come to my office just down the hall. Okay, have a seat. What seems to be the problem?" Mr. Berany was in his mid-thirties, a handsome man who also appeared like a Mr. Universe, bulging muscles everywhere. He wore a suit of gray and blue stripes, a tie, and appeared like a manager/businessperson, but his bulging, clearly visible muscles drew considerable attention. Raffi wondered to himself, 'Shouldn't this body type be in a gym outfit, perhaps shorts and a tee shirt, or the lead picture of a magazine rather than a suit?' Oh well, Raffi had no control over Mr. Berany's choice of attire.

"We do have a serious problem on our hands. One of your gym members is a suspected killer, and he's killed a young lady and he's a suspect in the police office bombing." He handed Mr. Berany a copy of the picture. "Do you recognize this man?"

"Yes, I do. He's here frequently. Let's see. Yea, he's here at least five days a week." He looked up his record of gym attendance.

"What I need from you is his updated home address, phone number, and his banking information. You know, which bank he does business with?"

"Okay, let's see how I can help you. I see that he had a change of address, but he did not offer us his new address."

"What about his phone number? Do you have his phone number?"

"The only number we have is the one in our record."

"What is that number?"

The number provided turned out to be the same disconnected number. "Is it not your practice to get updated information from your customers?"

"Yes, it is."

"Can you get his updated phone number next time he comes to the gym? I will give you my card and I want to hear from you when he provides you an accurate phone number and an updated address."

"Okay. The address we have is such and such." It turned out to be the same address where his parents live – also an outdated address.

"I want you to ask him if he's got an updated address and then call me with that information. Okay? Does he happen to live with someone, perhaps another gym member? I expect to hear from you in the next couple of days."

"Yes, I'll call or text you in the next couple of days."

"Thank you, Mr. Berany. Time is of essence, as we want to capture this killer, like yesterday." Raffi handed him his card. "For today, my officers and I will hang out in the gym a bit. You are not to tell the killer that we're here searching for him. That would compromise our investigation and place you in serious legal difficulties. Is that understood?"

"Yes."

After an hour and a half, Raffi called his officers to leave and meet to the right of the gym. It was now seven thirty p.m. In the interim, Mr. Berany texted him where Moyshe Stein resided. He indicated that Moyshe and Leonid were friendly. This address was entirely different than what Moyshe provided. "He's about fifteen minutes away. We'll drive towards Stein's apartment and see what happens next. At first, I'll listen in at Stein's apartment. If I hear two men talking, I'll signal for you to provide me extra firepower, especially if I need to break in. Then, you'll have my back with extra firepower. Okay guys?"

They nodded in agreement. Unanimously, they all said, "Understood, sir."

Mr. Stein's apartment was on the second floor. Most of the apartments had balconies, albeit narrow ones. Raffi had asked that two officers to position themselves near his balcony at the base of the street.

Raffi listened carefully. He used a sound magnifying device which allowed voices to be heard considerably louder. Unsure if he was hearing television sounds or the resonances of real people conversing, he was about to ring the bell. But first he listened carefully to who was talking and how many people were conversing. He thought he heard the sounds of two people in a conversation. He rang the bell, and at first no one answered. He rang a few more times. Finally, Moyshe came to the door wearing a flowery burgundy housecoat. Raffi flashed his badge. Moyshe recognized Detective Raffi. Moyshe sounded fearful, as he began to stutter. He whispered in Russian to Leonid, "Run, run fast! Fast, now! Police are here."

Raffi had pushed his way into the room, but Leonid ran with all his might towards the nearby balcony. Raffi shot, ignoring the curtains fluttering in the breeze. Shots were heard from the street level below. Raffi fired again, most probably to make himself feel better, although he no longer had a distinct target – just a fading phantom shadow. Raffi ran to the balcony, but by this time, Leonid ran and jumped at least five balconies to the left, one at a time, with great speed and agility. Leonid knew the building's layout and was aware of the exact locations of emergency exit staircases. He jumped six to eight steps at a time, darting downstairs. Raffi thought, 'Man, this guy is lightning fast. It's as if he has jet engines attached to him.'

Before Raffi could shout his instructions, Leonid disappeared. He vanished from eyesight once again. His men did aim in the direction of his balcony, but it was too risky to take a chance due to inhabitants that lived in these units. Had they used firepower, they might have killed innocent people. Raffi called his men to come to the second floor. They came quickly. "I want you to arrest Moyshe Stein for aiding and abetting our killer. Take him to our security holding center."

Raffi asked, "Do you realize that you lied to me?"

"Yes, I did. I was protecting my friend. In my mind, he comes first. He's more important than your f***** investigation!"

"Even if a young lady was killed? He still comes first?"

"Yes."

"Did you know you're breaking the law by aiding and abetting a murderer? Are you lovers?"

"If you want to arrest me, go ahead. And yes, we are lovers. He's the best thing that's ever happened to me."

"So much for your pretense of having a girlfriend, lover boy! And your relationship goes way beyond just being butchers and workout buddies. Is that correct?"

"Yes."

"Remember the other day when I asked you for his address and you provided an old extinct address? Why did you lie to me, Moyshe?"

"Because I love my friend and I feel protective towards him. We're lovers."

"But do you understand that your friend is wanted for murder, a stabbing, stalking, blowing up the Tel Aviv Police Station, and slashing a young lady? Those are five separate crimes. You mentioned that you are an explosive expert? Two men were noted on the police station videos. Were you the one who helped Leonid in the bombing of the police station?"

"Yes, I was involved in the bombing. But I know there's a side to Leonid that no one knows, a very tender and loving one that we've have shared. We love each other."

"Oh yea? Well, he wasn't tender and loving with his crimes which included a murder. Yea, tell that to the judge. You protected a murderer, public enemy number-one in Israel. Do you understand the gravity of your actions? You've also assembled incendiary devices and bombed the police department." Raffi thought for a few seconds and said, "You're probably looking at twenty to thirty years in jail."

"Yes."

"Well, I'll tell you what, if he kills another woman in the next day or two, how will that make you feel?"

"Not good."

"It's going to be your fault, Moyshe, for not divulging your correct address where Leonid resides. And I hope the judge throws the book at you." He looked at his officers and said, "Now take this vermin piece of shit away. Lock him up."

"In a few days, you'll be represented by a court-appointed attorney, and guess what? I'll be there telling the judge about your lies, not telling us the truth that Leonid was staying with you, bombing the police, and your cover-ups for your lover boy, which in turn resulted in a murder. My friend, you're looking at some heavy-duty prison time. Oh, one more thing. You shared with me that you're one of the two men who bombed the police department. Is that correct? And that your position in the IDF was as an expert in explosives, right?"

"Yes, to both questions."

Raffi addressed Moyshe and his team, "Yes, it is your right to have an attorney represent you." Raffi looked at his officers and said, "Now that he's handcuffed, take this lowlife away. With handcuffs, take him to our temporary holding jail. The charges are aiding and abetting a murderer and an additional charge – the bombing and the destruction of police headquarters in Tel Aviv. Call the courts to set up a hearing date."

The rest of the day was a quiet one for Raffi. His wished he could have punched Moyshe right through the wall. He felt Moyshe was arrogant. 'Oh well, maybe there will be some occasion in the near future? But probably not. There's no room for police brutality.'

***

As he recounted his day, Raffi never ceased to be amazed at Leonid's speed and quick thinking. Raffi thought about Leonid, 'Just you wait. I'm still after you, you son of a bitch! You got away a few times, but remember I'm coming to get you, you lowlife bastard! You're going to get locked up soon.' Raffi could not forget the time Leonid got away and then killed Ari and Avi, the beloved well-trained police dogs.

Raffi called Yoni and informed, "Leonid's speed, contextual intelligence, and his incredible street smartness allowed him to get away once again. He's in a homosexual relationship with Moyshe Stein, the other butcher employed by Zion Meats. He's been arrested for aiding and abetting our wanted killer. He's an expert in assembling bombs. I've added the charges of planning and participation in the bombing and destruction of the Tel Aviv Police Station."

Yoni appreciated the information and said, "I had the feeling that they were lovers and that Stein covered up for Leonid. Just to change the subject for a moment. Raffi, about the police headquarter bombing, you just helped solve the puzzle parts, putting it all together. The video film indicated two people tossing objects in the shrubs which detonated hours later. Moyshe just admitted that he helped Leonid in the bombing. Did any of the officers hear that confession?"

"Yes, they did. They participated in the arrest of Moyshe."

"What else do you know about Moyshe?"

"Moyshe Stein is an expert in explosives and bombs. Those were his IDF assignments. In doing these job details for the IDF, he became a topnotch expert in assembly of bombs."

"You added some key missing pieces to this puzzle by arresting Moyshe Stein. Raffi, you just helped solve important pieces to the puzzle and putting them all together. The video film indicated two people throwing objects which detonated hours later. One person was Leonid. That second person was Moyshe Stein, our IDF bomb expert."

***

Raphael ben Yosef Yardeni was Raffi's full name. He had last left his home at seven a.m., and it was now nine thirty p.m. He hadn't had the chance to eat dinner and was famished. He gave his wife a kiss and a hug as he went to the refrigerator searching for food. Not bad, a fourteen-hour-plus-hour day. He missed his wife and had very little time to call. He proceeded to make himself a turkey sandwich. "What's new, my beautiful Shoshana? You're so cute with your big belly protruding." He proceeded to put his arms around her while he waited for the microwave to complete the warming of his turkey sandwich. He placed the side of his head to her belly area in attempts to hear baby sounds. All the while, he smiled.

"Well, Raffi. I went to the doctor today. Guess what?"

"Give me a clue. I've never done this before."

"The baby has dropped and is in the right position for birth. The doctor said it could be anytime, a day, a week, less, anytime now. Wow, it's so exciting – our first child!"

"Oh my God. Really? You mean it could even be tomorrow?"

"Yea, for sure. Any day now."

"What should I do, Shoshana?"

"You could tell your boss that your wife will be giving birth any day now. Put Yoni on some kind of a notice and that you'll need to take some time off from work. Right? You do want to be there when I give birth. No?"

"Yes. Absolutely. I'll call Yoni, my boss, now." He took out his cellphone and began to call him.

With his sandwich in hand, he called Yoni. "Hi, Yoni. Sorry to call you so late. My wife saw her OB/GYN doctor today and the baby is in place for birth. It could be any day now, our first, Yoni. I'll have to take some time off from work. Don't know how much time." He took a second large bite as Yoni replied.

"Don't worry. Do what you have to. I'll assign Yitzchak to help out. Whenever it happens, just let me know and I'll take care of things. Mazal Tov to you and Shoshana. This is such a beautiful time in your life, creating your own family from scratch, and I wish you only the best to both of you. If it's a boy, I'll come to the Brit Milah. If it's a girl, I'll come to the baby-naming."

"Thanks for your support, Yoni. I'll keep you informed."

Chapter Twenty-One

It was early evening of the following day when Leonid arrived at his parents' apartment in a rage demonstrating bizarre and confused thinking. He seemed hyper, agitated, and his dark mood reflected the gloomy skies above. He threw chairs across the living room, the ones he perceived were in his way. He was indifferent to the low outside temperatures when he walked in to his parents' house wearing a sleeveless undershirt. He needed to shower prior to going out to one of his frequented sex club. His boyfriend, Moyshe, had been arrested. Adrenaline surged and pumped throughout his entire body as if he were a wild, uncontrolled rabid animal. He was hostile towards his parents. Looking furious, he peered at them as if they were enemies in his way. If looks could kill, he would have torn their heads off. His rage was predictable, one they recognized many times before, and they were quick to get out of his way.

Showered and refreshed, he knew that if he used some hits of 'blow,' he'd feel so much better. Ready and excited to find his next victim, he felt a thrust of his elation all the way down his loins as he drove to the club. He formulated his evening plan. He'd pick up a sex partner, do sex, and then he'd rejoice.

It was now eleven thirty in the evening, and while the rains ceased, the chill air remained. However, warm or cold weather conditions would never deter Leonid. He was the alpha lion looking for an innocent, easy prey. He entered club Shere-Az, well known for its young exotic dancers, some of whom were prostitutes and drug users. But it was also a hangout for gay and bisexual populations. Tonight's disguise was a mustache, a beard, a wig of long black hair with sunglasses to mask his eyes. "Give to me a Russian Mule with double shots of vodka, please."

Near to where he was sitting sat a young man wearing long leather pants and a tight shirt. His body lines indicated he could be a dancer. A near naked server smiled and took his order. In less than two minutes, the drink was on the table. She leaned over, revealing her opulently large breasts when she said, "Besides the drink, I can take care of your needs, choney." She whispered these seductive words while she blew air into his right ear. The nightclub was smoky with lights dimly lit. Tonight, Leonid ignored her sexual advances.

The man with the tight leather pants eyed Leonid. They smiled at each other. He winked at Leonid whose adrenaline pumped harder and harder, thrusting into his muscles and veins; he knew he'd have to act soon, either have sex, jack off, or run a five-minute mile somewhere to get this fiery adrenaline out of his system.

He turned to the young man. "Vat's your name? I bet you have a big von. No?"

"My name's Yoval. Yes, no one ever complained. You want to try me out? We can please each other. What do you say, mister?"

"Call me Leo. I love to suck big vons."

"Me too. What about yours? What size?"

"Big enough!"

Leonid grabbed his thigh and massaged it near his private area, which quickly observed his private bulge. "I like vat I see and feel in my chand. You vant a drink?"

"Sure!"

"Vat you drink?"

"Double cognac, no ice."

Leonid waived the server and ordered a double cognac. "My boyfriend got into legal problems and che's in jail now. So I'm free and available now."

"Oh, it's too bad he's in jail. Why? But don't worry, I'll show you a great time. Don't worry." Yoval massaged Leonid's groin area. "I love what I see."

Leonid indicated, "Yes, good and plenty! Our fun is about to begin. Let's go to my car. It's just around the corner. I have a large SUV with lots of room to stretch."

"Okay, let's do it."

***

It was eleven p.m. when Hannah awakened, terrified by another vision. She reluctantly knocked on her parents' bedroom door, saying, "Abba, I must speak to you. I had another vision. Can we please talk? It's really important." Hannah's face was red and her breathing was labored.

"Leonid just picked up a guy for a homosexual liaison at the Shere-Az Club in Tel Aviv. They are now in Leonid's SUV. He pulls over in a deserted area in Tel Aviv, one with large trees that provides seclusion. Next, Leonid and Yoval smoke weed which they inhale deeply. They start kissing and being frisky with each other." She paused and said, "Ach, it's disgusting; these guys engage in sex. They do things to each other that are so unnatural to even think or talk about."

"Hannah, it's okay, we don't have to talk about the specifics of their sexual encounter."

"Abba, Leonid next reaches over for his shiny silver dagger still in its brown leather sheath. He wants to stab or kill his partner. His partner looks so frightened. His eyes are frozen in a daze. It reminds me when we were on a trip and driving in the evening through the mountains of the Galil. It was pitch dark when we suddenly stopped our car as a deer crossed the street. You remember how the deer's eyes looked – scarred and frightened? The deer stopped in his tracks as if he was paralyzed. That's the way this guy appeared. He recognizes that he's in extreme danger of losing his life.

"He turns to Leonid and asks, 'Is there anything I did to make you mad?'

"Leonid says, 'Shut up. I just fiel like kielling.'" His eyes are enflamed with rage and hate.

"'Why? What triggered this when we just had fabulous sex?'

"Leonid says, 'Just because! Don't ask questions. Are you a psychiatrist or something?'"

"'But I've got a present for you.' Yoval reaches into his pocket and he quickly takes out a box cutter and slashes Leonid's right forearm. Leonid, in turn, stabs Yoval in his left shoulder. Blood's everywhere. They're both bleeding profusely. But Yoval jumps out of the parked SUV and manages to escape. Abba, Yoval was nearly killed, but due to his quick thinking, he survived."

"What happened next, Hannah?"

"Yoval runs into a woody area and tears his shirt to create a tourniquet to stop his bleeding. Leonid, in turn, drives off to camp out in Caesarea."

"Oh, why there?"

"I'm not sure why. Maybe it's because Moyshe is in jail and he's afraid he'll get caught if he stays at his place."

Hannah felt distraught having this vision.

"Hannah, chances are this crime will remain unreported, since they both responded in a violent manner."

"But, Abba, wasn't Yoval's response a matter of self-defense? Had he not used a box cutter, he'd be dead by now. Don't you think?"

"Hannahle, when it comes right down to it, police would have to look at the facts very carefully. In other words, was it really a case of self-defense or could he have escaped from the SUV?"

"Okay, Abba why don't we try and get back to sleep?"

"Yea, let's do that."

Hannah returned to her bedroom.

It was now 11:30 p.m. when Yoni called Yitzchak, who was thirty-two years old, in the police force, since he was twenty-four, now a married man to Eranit, with two young children, Ness (meaning miracle), a boy of age six, and Yaffa, (meaning pretty), a girl of age three.

"Shalom, Yitzie, it's Yoni. I'm so sorry to wake you up in the middle of the night, but the killer has stabbed a man after they engaged in a homosexual liaison. He stabbed him in the arm but Leonid was also injured. I'm told he's camping out in Caesarea. I think you need to get there as soon as possible and call in a squad of six to eight police officers to assist you. Be aware that the killer is a fast runner, but he can't outrun a bullet. He's armed and dangerous. Keep me informed and I'll also come there a little later."

"No problem, Yoni. I'll get out in a heartbeat." Yitzie made sure to have his Uzi and his military Tavor and Galil assault rifles ready and fully loaded. He also made sure to wear his bulletproof vest. Yitzie made his call and requested ten additional police officers. He made sure his officers were well armed. He felt as ready as one can be for an assault on maniacal butcher.

Yitzie had been a lieutenant, an officer, in the recent Gaza war, also on reserves just like Yoni. He had also distinguished himself being in the Golani brigade, being a part of reconnaissance missions into Lebanon. Even though, he was an Ashkenazi Jew, he spoke perfect Arabic. He had earned awards for great marksmanship in the IDF. Upon the completion of his IDF duties, at age twenty-three, he became highly sought after as a police recruit. At twenty-eight, he was promoted to detective rank.

The stars and the moon were out as they all converged on Caesarea, the amphitheater area. Caesarea had a Colosseum-style amphitheater from the Roman days, named after Emperor Caesar. It was one a.m., still pitch dark, and Leonid's SUV was spotted parked in an empty parking lot. Yitzie talked to his police force. "Spread out. You all have night-vision goggles. Your rifles also have night telescopic scopes. Use them to get the best possible views if you suspect anything. We'll all crawl very slowly. If you shoot, send out an immediate text for all to lie down, but please, no volume. The text can be a simple two words like, *Lie down.* This last step is a must. Yes, it will take a few seconds extra, but it's essential to our men's safety. Got it? Any questions?" There were none.

The men spread out over fifty meters' diameter. They were all on their bellies, crawling with a rifle in hand. It was dark. The full moon was a saving grace for the officers, making sight and visibility a bit easier. They noticed the parked SUV.

Nighttime critters like crickets and perhaps some field mice were heard. The men listened carefully with their phones silenced. The only other sounds were crashing waves against the coral sandy shoreline of the Mediterranean Sea. A salty sea aroma permeated the surrounding air.

The officers quietly crawled with rifles in hand towards the amphitheater. Someone ran darting across the empty field of desert brush towards the SUV.

Yitzchak took aim and took some shots, aiming his Tavor while he ran towards the running individual. He sent a quick text. *"Everyone, lay your head and body flat on the ground."* Loud bullets exploded, making the quiet area sound more like a war-torn battle zone.

He continued his running with lightning speed across ruins and open fields. About forty meters away, Yitzchak shot again and again, aiming his Tavor towards the fleeing person. The sound of his running came to a sudden stop. They were quickly replaced by the sounds of a car's motor being ignited. Bullets found their mark, but the vehicle disappeared into the night.

Yitzie asked his officers to send out a police bulletin to all the surrounding police that the killer was nearby. The nearby areas were Acre and Haifa. "Let's also send out a description of the killer." An immediate alert was sent out to nearby police precincts. Sunrise came soon enough as Yitzchak examined evidence of his bullet shots. He saw a trail of blood leading toward where Leonid's car had been. The blood trail vanished where the killer's car had been parked. Pictures were taken, all a part of the ongoing investigation. Yitzie sent out another bulletin: *Suspected killer wounded by bullets. He's dangerous and armed.*

Leonid was shot in his hip and buttock area. He was rapidly losing sensations going down his right leg. This might even have meant that an artery or the sciatic nerve was hit, or both. Truth be told, this could permanently interfere in his ability to ever walk again and most certainly, never to run again. He was driving one hundred and thirty kilometers an hour when he noticed a sudden police barrier that had been set up, requesting all drivers to come to a halt. There were two cop cars with five police officers standing and talking to drivers. The officers all carried pictures of Leonid. When Leonid spotted this police stop area, he did a three-hundred-and-sixty-degree spin turn, spun around, and took off in the opposite direction. Two police cars chased him. He drove at an extremely fast pace, but the police were even faster. When they were a hundred-and-fifty meters behind him, Leonid made a sharp right turn going into dessert terrain filled with shrubs, cacti, stones, and ravines as he headed in a northeast direction. Leonid seemed to be familiar with the landscape terrain. His SUV could handle just about any type of topography. It was obvious that Leonid had practiced driving in this type of topography. The police were less capable because they weren't familiar driving in this terrain. One of the police cars' tire blew out. A gush of radiator steam ended the chase for the other police car.

Leonid was far away from any sign of police; he hid his car in an old riverbed, an underground hiding place previously used by the Hagenah in their 1948 War of Independence. He used desert shrubs to hide his vehicle. He knew the layout of the land, the whereabouts of caves, which served as a protective hiding environment. The cops called for police helicopter help. Within fifteen minutes, they were roaming and combing the area. After twenty to twenty-five minutes, the helicopter mission was aborted.

Leonid found refuge in a small cave, a relatively unknown area used by the early pioneers as a safe haven against Arab marauders. He quickly realized that he was barely able to walk. His right hip was shot badly with a bullet that traveled south toward his buttock area, exited at the bottom of his right buttock, and nicked his calf. Severe bleeding in odd spots made it more difficult to stop his bleeding. Leonid wondered whether nerves and/or arteries had been severed. He appeared to be keenly worried about his health. He was aware that if he had a severed artery, this could threaten his life. He made the decision that he had to see a doctor at once, but he was worried about being recognized. There had been several television reports about him.

***

It was six thirty a.m. It was a fall day with a sun that emerged from darkness. He knew that he was not very far from Kfar Vrad (village of roses), perhaps no more than ten to fifteen miles. He drove his SUV and soon found his way to this village, found a Starbucks, removed his nap sack, took out his PC, and plugged the cord into the wall. The power returned shortly. In the bathroom, he tried minimizing the bleeding by tearing off an old sheet and making a makeshift tourniquet. He had fake identification cards and health insurance information. His alias name was now David Allyinsky. Surely, he'd seek a private physician in this exclusive town characterized by roses and nestled in the lesser mountains of Northern Israel. He Googled free-standing surgeons in Kfar Varad (the town of roses) and several names appeared. The doctor's fees would be of no concern. He always carried ample amounts of Shekelim – all cash.

It was now 9:00 a.m. Barely able to walk from his car to the office, he arrived at Dr. Ben Eliezer's home office. He was greeted by the doctor's office manager. He was still bleeding profusely.

"Shalom, do you have an appointment with the doctor?"

"Shalom, no, not exactly. I'm David Allyinsky, and I had an accident. I was impaled by a rusty metal stake in the ground. I was painting the outside walls of a house and was on a fifteen-foot ladder. I slipped, falling backwards and was impaled by a rusty metal rod which kind of went through my buttock-hip area. I need to see the doctor as soon as possible. I'm still bleeding, as you can see, and would very much appreciate the doctor's immediate attention. I don't want to mess up your waiting room with my blood."

"Have you thought about going to a nearby emergency room at our hospital? I can call them that you'd be on your way. I can also call an ambulance or cab for you."

"Yea, it entered my mind, but I don't want to be waiting in a waiting room forever. Besides, I suffer from agoraphobia and can't stand being in a large enclosed place like a hospital. I get unmanageably huge anxiety attacks when I'm in an enclosed place."

He thought to himself, 'She's an easy pushover.'

"Okay, let me talk to the doctor and see if he has some time to see you."

"Thank you. Money is no concern to me. I have lots of cash on hand."

Chapter Twenty-Two

Dr. Ben Mordechai Shanan was in his early fifties, trained in trauma surgery, a professor of medicine at Rambam Hospital in Haifa. He practiced surgery, small and large procedures. His handsome appearance with pepper-gray hair made him look like the late but dearly loved movie star, Mr. Carey Grant. He had completed several years of trauma surgery residency at a university hospital in Toronto, Canada. His four years of medical studies were at Hadassah Medical Center in Jerusalem. Close to six feet tall and a thin mustache with slick-back hair made him appear quite fit for his age. Leonid, alias David, noticed that the waiting room had only three other patients but his situation seemed more immediate, requiring quicker medical attention. The waiting room walls were painted in a combination of light olive-green, more even avocado-green with some cherry wood tables and magazine racks. There were paintings of ancient Israeli coins and archeological digs of Israel. A relaxed ambience was created by dim lighting in the waiting room. David was seen at once rather than sitting and waiting while his blood dripped everywhere.

"Shalom, David. I'm Dr. Ben Shanan. I see you're bleeding. Tell me about how this happened to you and how long ago."

"It occurred about an hour or fifty minutes ago."

"Yes, I think you should be seen at an ER of our local hospital. I can make the arrangements for you. I'd be happy to call for an ambulance."

"Do you have X-ray facilities right here in your office?"

"Yes, we do."

"I'd rather have a first look approach right here at your office. I mentioned to your office manager that I suffer from severe anxiety and agoraphobia, and a large hospital would definitely trigger those symptoms for me."

"Okay, we can surely examine you. I just think that an ER would offer additional options and safeguards for you. Certainly, the ER would have more sophisticated scanning technology in comparison to what I offer. But go ahead and take off your pants. If you need some assistance, I can help you with that."

Leonid was prepped for X-rays with at least eight shots of a number of different angles taken. He had to stand straight and also lie down on the table to get the right angles for these X-Rays. After a few minutes, the doctor placed the films in the light and examined each of the X-rays, one at a time. He methodically examined the extent of the wounds on the X-rays. Next, he examined the patient.

"I see that your left shoulder and your left bicep have a recent injury. Looks like recent puncture wounds. How did that happen?"

I was hiking in Northern Israel, the Galil, near a creek when I slipped. I fell on an old branch which got lodged in my flesh. I had some stitches and a tetanus shot. My recovery was good. See, I can easily pick up my arm." He demonstrated raising his arm.

"Were you treated by a physician for that?"

"Yes, I was."

"Well, you're lucky because your wound's healing real well. In reviewing your X-rays, you're one hell of a lucky person. There are no fractures or broken bones. Your right hipbone looks bruised but no fractures – just lacerations and puncture wounds. The stake went through some muscle tissues. I don't believe that any of your nerves were damaged, but let's make sure of that."

David, alias Leonid, was further examined by the doctor with some reflex and nerve conduction tests. The doctor indicated there seemed to be no nerve damage. "You're one hell of a lucky guy. You did damage some of your piriformis and gluteus maximus muscles in your buttocks. But muscles can repair themselves for the most part. I will clean up all the areas but because the metal stake was rusty, you will need a tetanus shot. Also, I will place you on a ten-day supply of antibiotic. You also need a total of twenty-six stitches, twelve at the entry point and another fourteen where the stake exited. So let's begin with that." The doctor topically numbed the areas and then gave the patient additional injections of a numbing solution. He found his stitch needle and thread and began the stitching process.

Dr. Ben Shanan cleaned all the areas and began to stich all total twenty-six stitches.

"But a few days ago, I had a tetanus shot."

"Then, you won't need another tetanus injection."

"Why am I having such a hard time walking?"

"The stake went through your muscle tissues and created hematomas, severing some smaller and tiny blood vessels. I believe that in two weeks' time, you'll probably feel considerably better. If you're still having a hard time walking, I'd recommend some physical therapy. I want to see you in ten days' time when I'll remove your stitches. I have your antibiotics right here." The doctor gave him a shot of a muscle relaxer. He said, "See you in less than two weeks' time. I am also giving you Percocet pills for the pain. These are narcotics, so you can only take the pills only as prescribed. Do you follow?" The doctor pointed to the label which indicated caution. If you don't wish to take the Percocets, you can take a thousand milligrams of Acetaminophen three times a day. Understood? My office manager will schedule your next appointment."

"So you think I'll be okay, doc?"

"Yes, like brand new! You look like you work out. Refrain from any exercise for the next few weeks. Just be sure to follow my medication instructions. Okay?"

"Thank you so much. What do I owe you for this treatment?"

"My office manager will collect your cash. Okay?" And he extended his hand to say goodbye for now. "Remember, I need to see you in ten days to make sure you're healing well and to take out your stitches. Also refrain from any form of vigorous exercise because you can easily pop open the stitches. You may walk slowly."

"Okay, doc. I appreciate you taking me in so quickly. Thank you." He stood up to shake Dr. Ben Shanan's hand.

After Leonid, alias David, left, as well as all of the other patients, Miriam, the doctor's office manager, discussed her concerns about David. Miriam was a thoughtful person committed to maintaining an efficient and flawless medical office practice. When she saw Dr. Ben Shanan, she said, "There's something weird about your last patient, David Allyinsky. He came here rather than go to an ER, and I find his entire story suspicious. Call me paranoid or overly critical, but David made me feel very uneasy, you know, uncomfortable. I can't quite put my finger on it, but I've seen him before."

"Where did you see him before?"

"Well, that's the part I can't quite figure out yet."

Just then, an all-out bulletin came on TV in the waiting room. The news reporter narrated, "Leonid, the suspected killer of a woman and the stabbing of another, was wounded by police near Caesarea. A chase ensued, but he managed to escape. Police followed him, but he's hiding somewhere in Northern Israel. He's thought to be very dangerous and armed with knives. Anyone knowing the whereabouts of Leonid should immediately call the police." Leonid's picture was flashed on TV.

Miriam turned up the volume, called Dr. Ben Shanan, and said, "See, I knew he looked familiar. Look, he came to us with blond hair instead of his natural black hair."

"So, he has been shot, not impaled as he had presented to us. I have a moral and legal obligation to inform authorities that he's been here. He's dangerous. I'll call right now," said Dr. Ben Shanan.

The doctor called and explained the circumstance of his coming to the office stating that he had accidentally impaled himself while doing some exterior home painting and falling off the ladder. The doctor explained that he had no idea of his true identity and he must have presented himself with an alias name, David Allyinsky. The police asked about the doctor's office address. When they heard that he was located in Kfar Varad, the police said they will dispatch police cars to the area and that the doctor should wait for them to arrive. The doctor said that he had a follow-up appointment which might be a good time for them to ambush Leonid.

Within fifteen minutes, a police squad car pulled up. The physician was interrogated. The officers wondered why the suspected killer was not referred to an ER at the local hospital. Dr. Ben Shanan explained that he did suggest the ER, but the suspected killer refused due to agoraphobia and preferred to be treated at the doctor's office. He added that, "Because of his disguise, my staff and I didn't recognize the killer. Moreover, the patient suffered from severe anxiety and panic attacks triggered by being in a large enclosed facility such as a hospital. Also, I felt I had a responsibility to stop his profuse bleeding." The trauma physician also reported that X-rays were taken and there was no evidence of broken bones. Had that been the case, the doctor would have insisted that the suspect go to an ER. He described the suture procedure and all the medications prescribed.

The officers asked for a physical description of the patient. He had a facial scar on his left cheek. An internal police bulletin was sent out, stating that the killer was now in Kfar Varad.

Yitzchak was driving in an unmarked car with two other officers patrolling the neighborhood. It was dark and hilly. The town was formed in 1984 and hosted somewhere between six thousand to seven thousand inhabitants. Many of the homes were embellished by rose gardens and gladiolas that appeared like a Matisse painting. It was not uncommon to have snow dustings during the winter months. The average elevation was about two thousand and five hundred feet above sea level. Later in the evening, any evidence of someone walking or running the streets was completely absent. Leonid had skipped town and was traveling to another city, perhaps back to Tel Aviv.

***

It was now ten p.m., and Yoni had gotten comfortable on the couch watching TV when he received a call from Raffi. "Guess what, Yoni?"

"I bet you're a proud papa of a baby boy."

"How did you know?"

"Just a guess. I knew that Shoshana was ready to give birth any time now."

"Yea. So we'll have a Brit Milah in a few days and we'd love to have you and Sarah attend."

"Oh, of course. We wouldn't miss such a happy occasion. Just let me know where and when. And by the way, Mazal Tov. What's his name?"

"Ephraim Ben Raphael Yardeni."

"Wow, sounds authentically biblical. How much did he weigh?"

"He weighed three and a half kilos."

"That's so wonderful. And your wife is doing well?"

"Yea, everyone is well. So I'll call you again after we decide on when the Brit Milah will take place. Sounds good to you?"

"Sounds good to me, and congrats again. Mazal Tov to you and Shoshana!"

Chapter Twenty-Three

A sunny day with fall tree leaves turning to orange and yellow hues spread across the land with temperatures that hovered around fifty-five degrees. Dressed in a yellow and green floral blouse and a matching skirt with light khaki long pants and tan sandals, an inch-and-a-half heel, and accentuated by the tanzanite stone of Eilat on the sandal straps made first-place-finisher Hannah look exceptionally stunning. She sprouted a smile, being just moments away from receiving her first-place award for her painting at the Latzior College for art. Her long flowing blond hair with large wavy curls were accentuated by a bright yellow-orange hibiscus flower picked from the Cohen's family garden. Yoni, Sarah, and Aaron were all present at the ceremony where Hannah would be presented a plaque for being the first-place winner in the Israel National High School Art Competition. Several honorable faculty members of the art college were invited to the podium, each providing information about the college's art programs.

Realizing she'll be called to a podium to say something, she resorted to nail biting. At that instant split-second timing, Yoni and Hannah looked at each other. He smiled as if to say, 'I caught you this time.' Hannah quickly withdrew her index finger from her face. They shared a split-second smile with each other.

Aaron was getting restless and bored and said, "Why all these speeches?" He whispered to his mom and dad and then added, "Oh, it's so boring, all these speeches. I'd rather play soccer outside or even have a play date."

Yoni gave him a dirty look and said, "Aaron, this isn't about you. Your sister is getting the highest award in art among all of the high school students in Israel. Be quiet and be proud of your sister instead of whining. That's not a very good choice, Aaron."

"Okay, Abba. I'll try harder." His restlessness stopped.

In the meantime, Hannah had rehearsed what she might say when called up to the stage to receive her award.

The dean and president of the faculty, Dr. Abramowitz, said, "And now for the awards you've all been waiting for. We decided to give three awards this year, a first, second, and a third prize, just like it's done in the Olympics. You have a gold, a silver, and a bronze. The third and second awards will be presented first. We'll leave the gold for last."

The third and second place prizes were announced and the high schoolers went up to receive their awards which consisted of certificates of accomplishment and medals – bronze and silver. The winners were each presented a bouquet of flowers.

"Last but not least, I want to announce our first-place winner, Ms. Hannah Cohen from Ashkelon. In this instance, all of the judges unanimously voted for her as our first-place winner. Hannah, please come up to be honored for your excellent art piece." A faculty member escorted her to her first-place spot. She stood in the middle of a slightly elevated platform which highlighted her appearance.

Hannah was presented a large plaque inscribed in gold letters; she was also presented a gold medal and ribbon to wear around her neck. The gold medal depicted a student artist engrossed in her work. Her first-place art contest certificate read as follows:

"For creative excellence in art, this first-place award is presented to Ms. Hannah Cohen. The faculty decided that your painting best embodies creativity, color sophistication, three dimensionality, and your use of depth of field. Congratulations!"

Dr. Abramowitz added, "Hannah, your artwork is a remarkable display of your fantastic talent. The review process consisted of several esteemed faculty members that decided your painting deserved the title of first place in all of Israel's high schools. Would you like to say a few words, Hannah?"

"Yes, thank you very much for this award. I would like to thank the Letzior committee. Thank you for having faith in my work, and I appreciate this recognition. Sometimes artists doubt their own abilities, but when you see creativity in my art, that means the world to me. One day, I hope to apply to your program and to be able to learn and grow as an artist. Your curriculum is incredible. And last but not least, without my parents' encouragement and support, I would not be standing here today. And Aaron, my brother, thanks for being here today. My family means everything to me. In closing, I want to say that many very fine artists never achieve any formal recognition. I am truly appreciative of this award and I will always have Letzior very close to my heart. Thank you."

And with those well-timed, heartfelt words, the committee also presented Hannah a bouquet of flowers. Everyone cheered and applauded especially

Sarah, Yoni, and Aaron. They were all so proud of Hannah. Even five-year-old Aaron clapped and shouted, "Hannah, you're the best in the whole wide world!" After the formal presentations, the three winners were also congratulated by the Letzior's faculty committee. Several newspaper reporters and photographers were on hand to interview and photograph Hannah and her parents. The reporters indicated that Hannah's story and pictures will appear in the newspapers, probably the following day.

Yoni asked, "Hannah, where would you like to eat to celebrate your wonderful accomplishment?"

"In Tel Aviv, there's this Greek restaurant called Café Andronicus which I heard great things about."

Sarah said, "Yes, let's go there. As a matter of fact, your dad and I went there recently because Detective Shmuel and his fiancé had their engagement party there. The food is great, plenty of it, delectable and huge portions. Opah!" Everyone in turn laughed.

Hannah ordered gyro and babaganush with pita bread. Aaron was happy with a falafel, pita bread, and humus. Yoni ordered chicken kabab with gyro, and Sarah ordered lamb kabab and kafka. Hannah also a Greek salad with lots of Feta cheese. Yoni ordered an extra-large platter of humus for the family. Aaron ordered falafel, pita bread, and Tahini. There was plenty of food to share. For dessert, they all enjoyed the sweet dessert of baklava. The restaurant served large portions and the Cohen family wound up taking boxes of food home.

They were in the car, driving home after everyone ate to their hearts' delight. Yoni got a call from a police officer patrolling the neighborhood. His voice sounded urgent. "Sorry to bother you but three of several of your house windows were shattered, most probably by rocks. Your neighbors called your local police station and out we came at once. My name is Officer Dan Gamlieli."

"Thanks for letting me know. We were in Tel Aviv, as my daughter won first place for art in all of Israel. We're now on the way home and we should be back in about thirty minutes." Yoni became pensive and asked Officer Don, "Oh, by the way, how did you get my personal cellphone?"

"One of your neighbors had your phone number, just in case of an emergency. I'll wait for you and meet you at your house."

"See you there shortly."

When Yoni announced the window breaking, Sarah, Hannah, and Aaron immediately believed it's because of Leonid. Upset, Hannah inhaled deeply, but she kept her feelings to herself; she didn't want to ruin the wonderful time she had with her family. Finally, Yoni asked, "Why are you so quiet? It's so unlike you."

"We had such a wonderful time as a family in the awards ceremony and then lunch. Abba, I think this is another reminder that he is still a menace who threatens and creates drama in our lives. Frankly, I wanted to enjoy the time with you, Ima, and Aaron. I really had good feelings and then this. That son of a bitch rears his ugly sinister demeanor!" Hannah's face reddened and her eyes welled up with tears. "How dare he ruin our good times as a family? I'm so sick and tired of being reminded of him. Enough is enough! His presence in our lives is just so unacceptable. It's time he's captured or killed."

"For sure. Let's continue to enjoy the day and your wonderful accomplishments, Hannahle. We're so proud of you, honey. And the faculty of Letzior College believes in your talents. Wow!"

"Yea, me too, Hannah!" shouted Aaron from the car's backseat.

When they arrived, Officer Dan handed Yoni a note enclosed in an envelope found scotch-taped to the door. So here's my written report that you can present to your insurance company."

Yoni asked the officer, "Was there anyone in the vicinity that was suspicious and have you talked to any of our neighbors?"

"Yes, I did talk to your neighbors and toured the neighborhood. No one was seen. I was unable to come up with anyone. I'm sorry, I'm not able to be more helpful about who vandalized your property. Do you have any thoughts about who might have it out for you? I think we'll send our unmarked cars to patrol the neighborhood. Also, here's my card and if you need me, so please don't hesitate to call."

"Thanks," was said with a discouraged-sounding voice.

In the meantime, Yoni opened the envelope and the message read as follows:

"You're next, Hannah, my filthy whore! I'm coming to get you when you least expect it. I'm going to get you, bitch." The note had bloodstains as a reminder of this brutal killer's blueprint logo of his kill spree. He ended by writing, *"You filthy whore. You're next to die!"*

Hannah began to cry hysterically and wrung her hands from anxiety, fear, and terror. In a meek frightened voice, she asked her father, "We had a beautiful family time at the art awards ceremony and then lunch. What do we do now, Abba? See, how determined he is to kill me. What do we do now?"

"I'm calling Commander Gidon Mordechai Levy, my boss." Yoni took a few seconds to collect his thoughts and then placed a call to Commander Gidon.

"Good afternoon, Commander Levy. We had a beautiful day with Hannah, our daughter, who won first place in all of Israel for her painting. She received her prize at the Letzior Art College. Then, I received a call from Officer Dan Gamlieli of the Ashkelon Police Department that several of our house windows had been smashed. When we arrived, we found a note from the killer that was handwritten to Hannah. It read as follows:

"'I'm coming after you when you least expect it. You're next! You slutty, filthy whore! Die bitch!'

"He's still actively threatening to attack my family and I won't stand for it. He wants to kidnap, rape, and kill our Hannah. What do you suggest we do now, sir? A couple of weeks ago, he wrote similar threats on our windows. I must tell you that my entire family is so frightened. There's no way I can be around for twenty-four-seven to protect my daughter and my family. I can't begin to tell you how disturbed I am. What do we do now, boss?"

In the meantime, Yoni had broken into a cold sweat. Sarah gave him some tissues to wipe his brow. Talking about the danger Hannah was facing made him also feel incredibly anxious.

"I'm so sorry you're going through this, Yoni. I'll have round-the-clock undercover police officers, day and night, including when Hannah walks to school. I'll also have additional plainclothes police officers on patrol. I'll have snipers hidden on your rooftop.

"On another note, congratulations to Hannah for being the number-one student artist throughout Israel. That's quite an honor. And congrats to Sarah and you for raising such a fine artistic daughter."

"Thank you, sir. And how soon can we expect this added protection?"

"Immediately. When you and I end our phone call, I'll make all the necessary calls. Yoni, I've got your backs."

"Thank you, sir. That will give us some added peace of mind."

When Yoni ended the conversation with Commander Levy, he called Hannah to their kitchen and told her of his discussion with Commander Gidon. "Hannah, don't worry. He's got our backs covered." Hannah nodded her head, acknowledging her father's communication, but she still felt startled and insecure about Leonid's threats to murder her. She looked towards the tiled floor with her head hung low. Yoni also said, "And now, I'll also call our insurance company and have them replace our windows." He stopped what he was about to do and asked Hannah to come over. He stood and hugged her, saying, "I love you, honey. I know you're terrified, but we're taking care of this problem."

"Okay, Abba. I believe you."

***

It was eleven p.m. when Hannah felt restless, unable to fall asleep. Her eyes appeared red as if she was crying. She knocked on her parents' bedroom door, saying, "Abba and Ima, I'm sorry to wake you up but I can't fall asleep because I'm terrified of his threats to kill me. Would you mind if I sleep in your bedroom until things settle down and the murderer is found? I can sleep on the floor in my sleeping bag. Is that okay?"

Sarah and Yoni unanimously said, "Oh, of course, Hannah. Let's get your sleeping bag and some blankets and pillows. Of course, it's never a problem. What else did you want to say?"

"I'm so terrified that he tried killing you by bombing your car and demolishing the Tel Aviv Police Station. I'm so horrified about thoughts of losing you, Abba."

Sarah said, "Come over here, honey." They sat on the bed while Sarah stroked Hannah's blond hair. Hannah began to cry even harder. But for Hannah, letting go of her pent-up emotions was helpful.

"Why me, Ima? It's so unsettling. It's taken over my entire life. I haven't had any time for friends. I haven't told anyone, which sucks because I'm the kind of person who is not secretive. I'm very open with my friends. This threat to my life interferes with the way I communicate. I'm hiding this big, fat secret." She rested and thought for a moment. "I've never been so petrified and scared about being killed like I am now. What do you suggest?"

Yoni, who was exhausted, yawned a couple of times, placed his right hand to his chin, and thought hard about Hannah's feelings. Finally, he said, "It seems like you felt safest when you stayed with your Aunt Rifka in Ramat Gan. How about you stay with Aunt Rifka indefinitely, that is until we catch this maniac?"

"What about my schooling? What will we do about that? What about my friends? It's hard not being able to see and communicate with them daily. How will it be for me to be away from my family for a long time? Abba, are there any other options?" Hannah wept while she contemplated making additional changes in her life. She felt upset to be away from her friends. Sarah placed her arms around Hannah and gently patted her back.

"Honey, no, I can't think of any other options. At least with your aunt, you'll be safe. I'm sorry. I will make arrangements with your school to be able to finish all your assignments online. I do think we're getting closer and closer to catching the murderer. We'll visit you weekly. We don't live that far away from Ramat Gan. As far as your friends, you can email, talk by phone, text, and even Skype if you'd like. Something else, you can't tell your friends where and why you're away. This has to be kept a secret. Keep in mind, Hannahle, this is a temporary arrangement."

"What do I tell my friends?"

"You can tell them that a member of your family has some health issues and you need to help out." He paused for a few seconds and said, "You can say it's a temporary situation and you'll be back."

"But what if my friends want to visit me?"

"You'll have to decline. You'll need to tell them that your family member needs your company and she can't have any visitors at this time. Instead, offer to Skype, text, or talk by cellphone, or even email them. Honey, that's the best I can offer. It's temporary. I am sorry you have to go through this mental upheaval. But at least you'll be safe. Isn't that the most important thing – being safe?"

Hannah noticed that her father's eyes had reddened and tears ran down his cheeks.

"Abba, why are you crying? First it was Ima, then me, and now you. What's the matter?"

"Well, I feel sad for you, for us as a family. I'm sorry you won't see your friends and attend your school for a while. I also can't stand what he's done to our family." Additional tears meandered down his cheeks. "You know, I realize how taxing it's been for you. That's why I feel so sad. I'm sorry I'm crying. It doesn't help our situation. Right?"

"Abba, I love you and Ima. Don't worry about crying in front of me because we're all sad. I think it will all work out, all for the best. I had a vision that it will all end soon. So when do we leave for Aunt Rifka?"

"It's now 12:30 in the morning. When I get up, I'll call and make the arrangement with her. There are many officers surrounding our apartment building and along the way to school. But I can walk you to school in a few hours. Would you like to sleep an hour later and I'll walk you to school?"

"Yea, that's sounds like a plan."

"As long as I'm walking you to school, I'll make an arrangement of getting your assignments by email. Cool?"

"Thanks, Abba. You're number-one." They both hugged, and Hannah got into her sleeping bag next to her parent's bed. Finally, Yoni, and Sarah fell into deep slumber.

Chapter Twenty-Four

Weary of these unrelenting problems, Yoni arranged that Hannah receive her daily homework assignment by online email. Aunt Rifka was pleased to help her niece. Yoni drove while Hannah sang a song, snapping her fingers to a radio tune on the way to Ramat Gan, a suburb of Tel Aviv.

"Abba, do you think I might be ready to date Yigal, that guy I mentioned about a week ago?"

"I'm not sure. I think you're in a better position to answer that. What do you think?"

"I'm way too preoccupied to get involved right now. This problem with Leonid has really drained all my mental and physical energies."

"I'm so proud that you exercise such great judgment. Continue to listen to your own feelings. You'll know when you're ready."

"Thanks, Abba. You've always believed in me."

Yoni appeared exhausted, with his face taut and tensed. His back and shoulders ached from nots and fatigue related to this case. While he continued to drive, he received a call and asked Hannah to turn the radio to a lower volume. She switched to her headset and reduced the radio's volume.

"Yes, it's Yoni. What's the reason for your call?"

"I'm Dan Shlomowitz. About ten days ago, one of your detectives, a Mr. Shmuel Weiss, came in and showed me a police sketch of the murderer. I just want you to know that Leonid has frequented my porn club in Tel Aviv for the past couple of nights. For all I know, he might visit my club tonight. So I'm letting you know of his whereabouts. I also sent a text to your Detective Mr. Shmuel Weiss."

"Thank you for letting me know. Is there anything else you can say about Leonid's appearance?"

"Yes, even though his picture indicates black hair, he must have dyed his hair and eyebrows blond. Lately, he's also sporting a reddish-blond goatee."

"Anything else, Mr. Shlomowitz? Approximately what time does he arrive at your club?"

"Yes. He had a fresh sutured shoulder. The wound looks like recent stitches because there was still some redness around this shoulder wound. Also, it appears that he's walking with a limp. Perhaps he was injured? He most frequently arrives at my club between nine thirty and ten p.m."

"What is the name of your club? I appreciate your call and these new clues."

"My club's name is the Volga; it's a Russian exotic porn club."

"Thank you for letting me know." Yoni realized that Mr. Shlomowitz owned a sex club but tried to make it sound classier by calling it an *exotic porn club.*'

He pulled his car over to talk. Hannah overheard the conversation. Yoni looked at his cellphone and immediately placed a conference call to Shmuel and Yitzchak.

"Shalom, guys. I need your ears and attention to this. I just heard from a Mr. Dan Shlomowitz, owner of the Volga Sex Club in Tel Aviv. He called me to say that for the past two nights, Leonid has frequented his establishment. Leonid still sports his new blond hair, blond eyebrows, and a reddish-blond goatee. He walks in wearing a suit." He paused for a minute to collect his thoughts. "You guys need to be there around 8:45 p.m. with disguises because Leonid arrives around 9:30 p.m. He's had some stitches in his arms and it was noticed that he walks with a limp. If he doesn't show up tonight, go there tomorrow and even the following day. Take several plainclothes officers, but be completely incognito. You guys also need to be there incognito. Be armed to the hilt, but see if you can first arrest Leonid. If he runs, shoot to kill. Bring down that miserable bastard once and for all! He's made numerous threats to kill my daughter, Hannah. He just notified us that she'll be his next victim. He's even written death warnings on our bedroom windows. He shattered our windows. But keep in mind, Leonid's always makes clever getaways. I'd suggest that you have a few officers stationed outside the club, the two of you and a few of the undercover officers inside the sex club. I think the two of you should sit apart, not next to each other. Any questions? Oh, one more thing, I will also be there to add additional firepower support, also dressed incognito. This time, let's go all out and get this f***** bastard once and for all."

They unanimously said, "Oh, yea, we'll take care of it, all right! We'll have your back covered. We'll make sure that Hannah once and for all is protected and free of this menacingly violent monster."

"Thanks guys."

Hannah took off her headset and inquired, "Abba, so what was that about, because I heard my name mentioned?"

"I was tipped off by the owner of a sex club in Tel Aviv that Leonid frequented his club. So, I arranged for two of my detectives to bring additional several police officers to finally ambush this bastard. I'll be there as well, wearing a disguise."

"Oh, I'm praying to God that our troubles end quickly. Abba, I know you're trying your best. I appreciate what you're doing to keep me and others safe. And you know what? I got a good feeling about this ambush plan."

"I'm hopeful too." He paused and then added, "I appreciate you, Hannah, because I couldn't ask for a better daughter."

It was time to drive towards Ramat Gan. They arrived at Rifka's place around 10:30 in the morning. Hannah gave her aunt kisses and hugs, as did Rika in turn. Rifka placed her arms around Hannah and was supportive towards her niece, Hannah.

"Every day, I have thought of you, my pretty blond ketzale (kitten)."

Hannah smiled and hugged her aunt.

"Would you like something to eat? Maybe you're hungry?"

"No thanks. I'm still stuffed from the big breakfast, but maybe in an hour or two?"

"Sure, no problem. So, how are you guys?"

"Rifka, we appreciate your help in taking care of Hannah. Thank you so much. Your sister also sends lots of regards and thanks you as well." He gave her a big hug and presented Rifka with some freshly picked roses bought at the Tel Aviv open market – the shook. He also provided a box of chocolates made in Safed, Israel.

"Thank you, Yoni." She found a vase and placed the flowers on the dining room table.

"I'll be off and running. Hannah, call me and let me know if you need anything from us. We'll visit you this coming Saturday." He reached over to give Rifka another goodbye kiss.

Driving toward his office, he began to feel agitated about Leonid. "This f****** bastard has taken over our entire life. This SOB is trying to kill my Hannahle. I'll show that f*****!" He decided to once again have a conference call with his detectives.

"Hey guys, it's me again. As I mentioned earlier, I'll also join you tonight at the Volga Strip Club. I'll wear a beard and mustache with a sports jacket and tie, pretending to be a businessman from Haifa. I'll also be fully armed to help you. I think we need to all wear bulletproof vests under our disguises. You never know if he'll be armed with firearms."

"Good idea, boss. Will you be speaking a foreign language as part of your incognito look?"

"No, I'll speak Hebrew."

"Cool, well then, we'll see you later, Yoni."

"We'll communicate ahead of time just to position ourselves at the club? Don't tell Mr. Shlomowitz that you're detectives on a mission. In fact, sit separately as if you're strangers to one another. If he inquires why you're visiting his club, just say that you expect to meet up with some friends for entertainment."

"Yes, absolutely. You're right, Yoni."

"Okay guys, see you later. Once we're at the club, let's not communicate, as it may tip Leonid off. But we can text and/or speak by phone ahead of time."

"Yes, sir. We will. Also, remember that you guys should also dress incognito. And be armed to the hilt."

"Yes, boss!"

***

It was a particularly dark cloudy evening with cooler temperatures that had plummeted downwards, heralding the onset of fall's torrential rains. The winds picked up in speed with a number of palm trees bending and swaying. Yoni pulled up to Club Volga in Tel Aviv. Able to find a nearby parking space, Yoni stepped into the nightclub at eight forty-five p.m. He was dressed in a gray suit, white shirt, and a navy-blue tie sporting his well-manicured beard and mustache. To look even older, he grayed his hair and sported a gray beard. He looked at least fifteen years older. He walked bent over with a cane in hand, all part of his disguise. In advance, Yoni texted Shmuel and Yitzchak about his choice of disguise. He positioned himself towards the rear of the club but still had good views of the pole-dancing stage. It was dark and smoky throughout this club. The smell of liquor and smoke permeated the air. The well-lit stage had two young ladies gyrating to the sound of music while traversing up and down and humping red and white candy-cane red poles.

She couldn't have been older than twenty-two or twenty-three, almost completely naked, save for a string Brazilian bottom. Her big bear-breasted nipples were covered by tiny fig-tree leaf patches.

She asked Yoni if he'd like a drink before the show. "Chow about it, choney?"

Yoni said he'd like a Russian Mule. "And make it with a double shot of vodka."

"So vat's your name, choney?" she inquired, snuggling closer and closer to Yoni. "Vould you be interested in anything besides a drink?" She inquired with a big seductive smile as she stuck out and wiggled her tongue around. She placed her arm on his shoulder and said, "You know I can make you fiel vonderful from your chead down to your tiepy toes. I'll bring you to cheaven and back, choney. Chow about it?" She sat herself on Yoni's thigh as if they had been intimately acquainted. Seductively, she rubbed his inner thigh. She moved closer towards his face and blew air in his right ear. "You von't regret it, choney. No, not viet me."

"I'll just wait on that for a while." He put her off, displaying a lack of interest.

A moment later, she brought Yoni his drink.

"Chere you are, my chandsome one. You chere on business or fun?"

"Yes."

"Ooh, vat kind of business you in?"

"My main two businesses are computer technology and the development of new arms used by military and police officers throughout the world."

"Vow, such tiechnical vork. Ooh, you must be very smart? Ven you're done vit your business, I can show you chow to relax and chave amazing pleasure in your life. Vouldn't you like that?" She once again snuggled closely and stuck out her tongue. This time, she also gently slapped her almost-naked butt and winked at him. "Ooh, I'd love to show you the moon, the stars, and the cheavens. I'm sure you von't regret it."

"I'm happily married. Thank you, but I'm not interested. Oh, by the way, when does the show start?"

"It viel start in about forty-five minutes. Okay, choney, if you change your mind, just let me know vat your sensual fantasies and passions are. I viel take you around the vorld and back. At the end, you'll agree that you niever chad such sensual pleasure in your entire life. Niever! Remember, I'm chere to please you. Give me a chance." The twenty-two year old was incredibly sexy – a greatly toned body, blond hair, and blue eyes with definite Hollywood looks.

He touched his wedding band, thought of Sarah, and smiled. He concluded to himself, 'Nope, I'm very happily married. No, this ain't for me. Some guys may cheat but not me. I'm happy with the love of my life – my Sarah.' He contemplated this verbal exchange and concluded, 'She's probably no more than four to five years older than my Hannahle, and wow, they really do resemble each other and have a strong physical resemblance to each other."

Within twenty minutes, he noticed Yitzchak, Shmuel, and Raffi entering, each separately. They positioned themselves, sitting on each side of the stage and across from one another. When no one looked, they nodded to Yoni. About five minutes later, five plainclothes police officers also entered Club Volga. Tonight, everyone wore their disguises. Shmuel made himself appear overweight and also had a long wig of gray hair, a gray mustache, and wore a brown sport jacket and tie. Yitzchak wore a bald wig-like thing to cover over his hair. He wore joggers, navy-blue long pants, and a windbreaker jacket. He also sported new blue and red Nike running shoes. Raffi wore a navy-blue suit and a blue tie with brown newly shined shoes. He had a full beard as part of his disguise. Four undercover police officers also grayed their hair and sat at various strategic locations in the Volga Club.

Outside the club, four plainclothes police officers strategically positioned themselves, each wearing a disguise. One of the sharp-shooter officers was on the roof in a crouched position ready to shoot. He was their very best sniper. All of the detectives and officers concealed mini earphones hidden either behind hair or their earlobes.

At nine forty-five, in strutted Leonid walking with a limp. Tonight, he wore a tight black dress shirt, black pants, and appeared completely muscular and fit. He wore orange Nike running shoes, had dyed blond hair, blond eyebrows, and a reddish-looking goatee.

The same server approached and welcomed him, saying, "Chi, choney. The same as usual viet double shots of vodka?" She recognized Leonid.

"Oh yes. Give to me double shots of vodka." He spoke with a thick Russian accent.

Yoni turned on his earphones and gave a prearranged cue to his men. When he took out his comb as if he was about to comb his hair, this was the prearranged signal for his men to turn on their hidden earphones. When Yoni lit up a cigarette and blew smoke towards the ceiling above, that was time for his men to pounce on and arrest Leonid.

Yoni combed his hair and his officers turned on their earphones. Yoni eyed Leonid like an eagle in flight looking for its next salmon fish prey. Next, Yoni took out a cigarette and lit it. He blew smoke in the form of rings towards the ceiling. Raffi, Yitzchak, and Shmuel jumped to apprehend Leonid from his rear. They pounced on him as if he were a wild animal that needed to be subdued. Shmuel got him into a strangle hold from the rear – a Nelson hold. Although Leonid was strong, he was no match for Shmuel. And there was the element of the surprise attack on Leonid which took him completely off guard.

"Yitzchak, hand me the handcuffs," said Shmuel. Strong as a lion and nimble as a fox, Leonid tried to wiggle himself away, but tonight he was incapable.

"You f***** police, can't you see I'm injured? Vie you so ruff wiet me?"

"Because you're a sadistic homicidal killer. Isn't that enough of an explanation, you son of a bitch?"

Yitzchak said, "If you make another move, I'll blast your f****** brains away. You hear me?" Yitzchak flashed his Jericho 941 pistol and once again warned Leonid. "Calm down, you son of a bitch or I'll blast your f****** head off. This is my last warning to you. If you try anything, I'll shoot you on the spot."

Low and behold, Leonid was finally handcuffed with his hands behind his back. While Shmuel held Leonid in a rear choke hold, Yoni placed Leonid in foot shackles with a heavy metal chain, ones that offered additional protection. Shmuel and Yoni were now in front of him while Yitzchak and the plainclothes officers had encircled Leonid. The officers had their hands on their guns, just in case. Yoni had called for additional police squad cars to assist and they arrived within minutes' time.

When Leonid saw Yoni making a call, Leonid attempted to free himself by throwing his body at the officers. By this time, Shmuel had already lost his patience and said, "Stop, or I'll shoot you. Don't you dare throw yourself at anyone of us or else!"

Leonid ignored the warning, as he attempted to lunge at the officers. Shmuel shot him by placing two bullets, one in each one of his thighs. Shmuel was sure that at least one of Leonid's Femur bones had been shattered. Leonid went down. Leonid was no longer able to stand upright. He fell to the ground and bled profusely. One of the officers placed tourniquets around Leonid's thighs to slow down his bleeding. Another officer applied his own bodyweight to keep Leonid down. Shmuel could have easily killed Leonid, but according to police protocol, he used considerably less extreme measures of shooting Leonid's thighs.

Yoni instructed to have Leonid taken to a local hospital for emergency treatment. The squad cars carrying several police officers and detectives arrived at Ben Yamin Hospital within a few minutes. Excelling in their treatment of trauma casualties, this facility distinguished themselves in emergency and trauma treatments. Once inside, Yoni instructed the doctor and nurses to not remove his feet shackles or his handcuffs. The hospital staff was told to not temper with police matters. The doctors and nurses nodded their heads in agreement. Yoni insisted that two officers be placed in Leonid's room, prepared to shoot. This measure would be used only if Leonid attempted to escape or if he attacked any doctors or nurses.

The doctors administered emergency anesthesia, cleaned his wounds, removed the bullets which were still lodged in Leonid's quadriceps muscles, and stitched him up. Leonid had not sustained any broken bones, only bruised ones. The doctors concluded that Leonid was to be hospitalized with a constant drip of antibiotics, still shackled and handcuffed. There were two police officers in his room at all times as well as two officers guarding the entrance to his room. After six days, it seemed as if Leonid had begun to recover, especially since he was now in modified physical therapy. On the sixth day, the two officers in his room took a brief cigarette break and stepped outside the room. They told the other officers stationed in the hallway to be vigilant. In the meantime, Leonid pressed a button needing help to go to the bathroom. A young attractive nurse, perhaps no older than twenty-three, her first professional job, arrived to help Leonid. He asked if she could stay close by his side as he was afraid of losing his balance. To himself he thought, 'She could easily become vone of my victims – great body, pretty face. Vow!'

"Please stand near me so I von't lose my balance vhile I pee. Oh by the way, can you help me pull down my pajama pants?" he asked. "See, I'm still in handcuffs."

The young nurse obliged by pulling down his bottoms and stood in close proximity to him. As he stood, she noticed that his private part was large and erect. His thighs were muscular.

Leonid positioned his arms and instantly grabbed her in a death-hold choke. He maintained a vigorous hold with the metal handcuffs pressing against her windpipe. She tried screaming but was unable to. Instead, she made gurgling choking sounds and was about to lose consciousness when the police officers returned. They heard suspicious-sounding noises and bolted into the bathroom. The officer took out his gun and pistol and whipped Leonid on his forehead. He quickly released the nurse. She fell to her knees and needed immediate CPR resuscitation. Her Adam's apple and windpipe were severely bruised and had almost instantaneously turned black and blue. The officers hollered for additional police help. Two of his partners came to help out. A doctor quickly appeared and helped resuscitate the nurse. She felt terrified and panicky by Leonid's attack. She refused to care for Leonid, insisting he needed armed guards at all times. Now lucid and conscious, she was still dizzy and in a state of shock. She could not quite fathom what had just happened. Her throat area had reddish-black and blue marks of being strangled.

Initially, she felt ashamed of herself. She felt she mishandled herself which created a life-threatening adverse incident. Her supervisor asked about the details of what happened. She suggested the young nurse to take the rest of the day off to recover. Additional attendees were needed to lift Leonid back to his bed. Leonid required five stitches where he had been pistol-whipped in the head. The doctors had called Yoni about this adverse incident. Yoni in turn asked to speak to the officers who went out for a smoke.

He stepped in the patient's room, sounding angry. "As long as you're on this case, don't you ever leave Leonid's side or you'll lose your job at once."

He looked at them eye-to-eye. "Yes, you'll be let go from the police department. You see what a dangerous piece of crap we're dealing with? I'm also going to call your supervisor who will give you a written warning notice. You almost messed up our entire capture mission with Leonid, something we've worked on for a long time. I'll have you know this piece of shit has made several death threats to my daughter and me. He blew up the Tel Aviv Police Station and he brutally killed a young lady. And you compromised this entire capture mission by going out for your smoke. How dare you? Because you wanted a smoke, you almost foiled our entire strategy of apprehending this lowlife piece of shit. Where was your common sense as officers of the law? Your supervisor will know of your reckless and careless actions." Yoni was furious.

"I'm very sorry. That will never ever happen again. I am truly sorry, sir." A sorry explanation was also stated by the other officer.

"From now on, I demand that two officers stay in his room at all times. Another two officers will remain outside his room at all times. Is that clear?" Yoni made sure this statement was heard by all of the other plainclothes officers. Yoni was physically and emotionally spent, a combination of tiredness, weariness, disgust, and anger. In the last few days, he'd averaged only three hours of nightly sleep. He developed dark blue rings around both eyes and he sounded more irritable than ever before. Yoni thought to himself, 'Boy, as a detective, I have never had such a difficult and threatening case.' He felt worn out, both physically and mentally, even more so since Hannah's life had been threatened.

After seven days, Leonid was about to get transferred to the Carmel Haifa Prison, a facility for hardened killers.

Chapter Twenty-Five

It was eight a.m. of the following day. Leonid showed signs of recovering, and on the eighth day after his arrest, still in handcuffs and ankle shackles, he was now transferred to a maximum security jail in the Carmel Haifa region. Pine trees surrounded the prison which was located at a high point on Mount Carmel. Leonid needed to be partially hand fed, assisted to the toilet, and helped with personal hygiene care. The prison warden would consider unshackling and un-handcuffing him in a few days, but right now his behaviors were still being observed. This prison was old with previous stones that had faded into age-worn tannish white.

The weather changed with a cold front and rains were coming in from the east. He wore a raincoat and arrived with an umbrella in hand and an attaché case. He had advanced clearance from the maximum security director who led him into Leonid's cell. He appeared to be young, perhaps no older than twenty-nine or thirty and a fairly recent law-school graduate. He tried to have an older appearance by sporting a mustache and a goatee. He wore a blue shirt, reddish tie, and brown pants that matched his auburn-color hair. He sat down on a plain wooden chair. "Is it okay to sit here?" He waited for an answer, but his question fell upon deaf ears. "By the way, I'm Chaim Davidovich and I was assigned as your public defender attorney." He reminded Leonid that in Israel, the death penalty did not apply. "So we're probably looking at a life sentence."

Leonid smiled and then said, "Cho cares? I don't really give two shits! Justice? There's no righteousness in this world! It's a vaste of your time to represent me. Vat you think, I deserve to be free man? I've done bad things. I kielled a vomen, stabbed another. Vhy represent me? Give to me poison or a bullet in my head. Don't bother viet me."

Chaim felt nervous talking to Leonid, a physically intimidating killer. He wondered if Leonid would flip out, become violent, lose control, or even strike him. Chaim grew up being raised and loved in a normal family. He wondered, 'Would I be able to understand the mindset of this murderer? What went wrong to make Leonid the killer he is?' He pondered over these difficult questions.

"Can we talk?"

"Vhy should I talk to you? Vat you vant from me?"

"If you don't talk to me, there's a strong chance that you'll spend your entire life in jail."

"So? Cho the chell cares? F*** the authorities! The young lady cwhore deserved vat they got. All vomen suck! All vomen are lowlifes!"

"Do you realize that before we go to trial, you're in a maximum security prison cell?"

"Vat's the purpose of a trial? I am guilty and all of Israel knows it. I kieled a vomen and stabbed another. Oh, vat fun it vas!" A smile overcame his face as he recalled those events one by one.

Chaim wondered how someone like Leonid enjoyed killing. "You're leaving out a number of other charges, namely slashing the young lady that you met in a sex club, stalking and threatening to kill the lead detective's daughter, burning and demolishing his car, and last but not least, blowing up the Tel Aviv Police Station. But under the law, you're still entitled to have your day in court. A successful trial might give you fewer years in prison. You're still young. What are your thoughts about that?"

"Oh, I don't care. In a vay, the longer I stay in prison, the better it viel be for society and myself. Trial? It's a complete vaste of time. Better, a bullet in my chead."

"Have you ever had any personal counseling, you know, therapy?"

"My parents sent me to a shrink once, but it vas a vaste of time. The shrink chimself chinted that che vanted a blowjob from me."

Chaim wondered if Leonid was schizophrenic or delusional. He decided to ignore Leonid's last comment about blowjobs. "Why is it a waste of time, Leonid?"

"Because I can't be chelped. Psychiatrists can't chelp people like me. They pretend they can, but they can't. You chave to vant to be chelped, but all I vant to do is rape and kiel young p****. That is my big pleasure in life. I'm not a nice guy and I can't be rehabilitated. Psychiatric medication just make me out of it – fiel like zombie."

"Yes, you need to want to be helped. If you feel like it's a waste of time, then you're not motivated to be helped. Certainly, if you were helped, the court might look more favorably about your case. The court might have greater leniency."

"I don't give two shits about chow a court vit judges views my case. You and I both know that psychiatry can't cure people like me. I'm chopeless. They can only medicate me to feel like a robot or give to me electric currents to my brain or institutionalize me forever. A bullet to my chead vould end all my problems. One, two, three – much better for me, society, and cheaper for Israel's economy."

"But it would be good for you to share feelings with a therapist, someone who cares."

"My feelings are too disgusting, very chateful. I can't imagine anyone caring about me. Nor do I give a shiet. I'm not a person cwho deserves to be cared about. I don't need or vant any sympathy from anyone. Just look at vhat I've done, the vay I killed the cwhore, the f****** slut. If you had a son cwho did that, vould you stiel love chim? No, I don't think so."

Chaim didn't quite know how to continue this conversation. He recognized that Leonid was clearly a sadistic killer, one that also refused psychiatric care. He also recognized that Leonid felt unworthy of being cared about." Chaim felt worried about the depravity of his client's mental state and his horrific crimes. He also felt that it was sorrowful and heart-wrenching when a person, like Leonid, felt unworthy of being helped or cared about. He thought, 'My goodness, how sad is that?'

"So, now that you know chow I feel, vhat you propose? Tell to me vat?"

"You're still entitled to a trial. And I'm here to represent you in court. We're going on a defense of insanity and mental illness based on your childhood traumas. Therefore, even before you stand trial, you'll be examined by more than one psychiatrist. The prosecution will have one and we'll also have a separate psychiatrist testify. The psychiatrists will most probably insist that you also have psychological testing. In court, I will try to paint a picture that you were severely physically abused as a child, which led you to feelings of hatred towards women and society. I'll also need to choose jurors, hopefully the types of people who can be somewhat sympathetic and open-minded to a mental-illness/insanity plea. And I will need to demonstrate that you were the victim of physical and emotional abuse. Can you share with me about your early childhood experiences in Russia?"

"Vat you vant to know? That I vas beat up viet chains and belts? Vipped with belt and metal buckle forty to sixty times, left outside viet temperatures of negative forty-five in our backyard dog kennel, tied viet metal chains for two veeks at a time? That my mudder vas sadistic and crazy, like me? That she vas cruel to me? Is that good enough for you?"

"I appreciate you shared that with me."

"I stiel tink a bullet vould be quicker and save Israel many shekels."

"So the worst-case scenario is that you'll get life in prison. The best case scenario would be fewer years in prison. But you're entitled to a trial and to have your day in court. To change direction for a moment, how are they treating you here?"

"Much better than vat I chad at chome. The food is shit chere – total crap! The good ting is that I'm allowed to do my veight training outdoors. There are many handsome chunks in this prison. Each day, they release me from my shackles and handcuffs for one chour so I can vork out. Guards chelp get me up and down from the bench press."

"Are your wounds and stitches healing okay?"

"Yea, the stitches viel be removed in a couple of days. Are vie done yet? Soon it's time for my vorkout, vitch I don't vant to miss."

"Yes, yes. I understand how important it is to you. I'm going to give you my card and contact information. They'll allow you to speak to your attorney."

"Okay."

Chaim bid his client goodbye and stated he'd visit him again in a few days.

***

The following day turned out to be a sunny day with an ideal temperature, a high of seventy-six degrees, with northeasterly breeze in the air. The weight training was in the middle of the courtyard. It also included a basketball court. The walls were high with armed guards with loaded weapons. Visible at the very top of the walls was barbed wire. It was a kind of day where people were seen playing basketball, jogging, and walking outdoors. Today, many of the prisoners conjugated outdoors, some to establish homosexual liaisons with other men, while others, like Leonid, were more committed to working out. Others like Leonid enjoyed bodybuilding opportunities with barbells and dumbbells. Armed guards mingled and observed the prisoners. Leonid was fairly new and he didn't yet partake in any conversations with others. But it seemed like everyone knew about him. Even though Leonid had not yet communicated with other inmates, he was feared and hated. Outdoors today, there were other killers working out. Others warmed up doing some rope-jumping. Leonid had not lifted weights since he had been shot. Today was his first day back to weight training.

He made eye-contact with no one, although several prisoners were attracted to him. Ephraim was forty-five years old with two grown children, a son aged twenty-one was finishing up his IDF requirements and his eighteen-year-old daughter was in an inpatient psychiatric facility. Ephraim had pepper-gray hair and a bulky muscular appearance. For the last year, his daughter had been psychiatrically hospitalized after she was brutally raped. Her internal lacerations were so severe; she required two internal reparative surgeries. She would never be able to bear a child. She had a nervous breakdown and her prognosis for a complete emotional recovery was guarded. When Ephraim discovered that rapist/killer Leonid was a fellow inmate, he became incensed enough to seek revenge against killer/rapist Leonid. In jail, raping and the killing of young ladies were scowled upon, since several of the male inmates had daughters.

Ephraim was five feet nine in height and weighed two hundred and fifteen pounds of solid muscle. He could easily bench-press two hundred and ninety-five pounds and dumbbell curl with seventy-five pounds in each arm. Leonid, in comparison, appeared emaciated and weak. Immediately after the rape of his daughter, Ephraim stalked his daughter's rapist. One day, when he least expected it, the rapist was beaten into unconsciousness. His recovery involved several surgeries and months of physical therapy before he'd ever walk again. Apparently, Ephraim broke the rapist's arm, his legs, and several of his ribs. The rapist also sustained a severe concussion. The manner in which the rapist had fallen resulted in three disc herniation in his spine. Eventually, he'd walk with a cane. Ephraim was arrested, tried, and found guilty. He was now serving time for attacking his daughter's rapist. He was content that he had sought vengeance. But for Ephraim, the sight of Leonid created instant internal rage and an intense desire for vengeance.

Words spread like wildfire and every inmate knew about Leonid's crimes. Ephraim thought to himself, 'Because of a son of a bitch, just like you, my daughter is now a vegetable in a psychiatric hospital. She'll never fully recover.' In the minds of these prisoners, raping and killing young ladies were two of the worst of all possible crimes.

Ephraim's thoughts continued, 'You raped and killed young women. I'm coming after you, you son of a bitch! You don't deserve to live. It's your type that destroyed my beautiful daughter's life. And she'll never be the same. She had a future and was about to enter the IDF. She was lovely and most importantly, she's my daughter.' This last thought opened the faucets of his eyes and Ephraim began to cry. He used his shirt sleeve to dry his tears.

In the courtyard, Ephraim made eye-to-eye contact with Leonid. Using his index finger against his own throat, he motioned that he was going to slit Leonid's throat.

Leonid was dressed in his workout clothes, and considering the mild outdoor temperature, he wore a short gym tee shirt of orange color. Leonid saw Ephraim's threat to slit his throat. He uttered loudly enough to be heard. "Go f*** yourself, you fagit idiot! Your daughter was probably a slut cwhore." He also gave him the middle finger. Leonid continued his modified workout. A bead of sweat appeared on his brow. He wished he could run but he was still recovering from the bullet wounds to his thighs – from the time that he had been shot by Shmuel. But Leonid felt invincible, like a cat with multiple lives.

"You're a f***** animal. You're a monster. I am coming after you! You deserve to die!" Ephraim voiced these words to himself.

The following day around eleven a.m., the guys were let out for their usual hour of fresh air and exercise. Orange-and-white-striped pants and a shirt were the official prison uniform the men wore. Today, about one hundred and fifty men congregated outdoors. Some talked to their fellow inmates, while others were involved in playing basketball or pumping iron. Leonid did the latter. Today, Leonid intended to bench-press two hundred and twenty-five pounds.

In the midst of his last couple of bench-press repetitions, Ephraim was seen hiding, kneeling quite low behind Leonid's head. He had arranged for many of the inmates to surround the bench-press area. He had positioned himself right behind Leonid and quite low to the ground. Ephraim remained hidden from being spotted by any of the guards. He lowered one of his socks and removed a homemade sharp metal object, a homemade knife with a several-inch blade. Suddenly, Ephraim slit Leonid's throat; he especially targeted at the carotid artery region. Then, he stabbed him in the heart and chest area. He made sure the knife was deeply imbedded. Ephraim aimed for Leonid's heart region. Instantly, the barbell came crashing down. His ribs were all instantly crushed. He stopped breathing. The home-styled weapon was lodged in Leonid's chest as the barbell came crashing down, squashing Leonid's ribs. Blood dripped towards the concrete floor below while the handcrafted knife was now deeply imbedded in Leonid's chest. Gurgling sounds were the very last sounds heard from Leonid as he choked on his own blood. A large amount of blood now pooled around the bench. He was pale white and lifeless as blood dripped down to the ground below. Suddenly, there was an air of silence as the inmates dispersed in different directions.

Ephraim smiled, feeling victorious and righteous about eliminating Israel's number-one lowlife – Leonid. 'You f****** loser rapist,' he thought to himself. 'You'll never ever do that again. This kill is in honor of my daughter; it's in her name's sake.'

But the cause of Leonid's death was repeated puncture stab wounds to his heart and the sustained throat slashing, causing him to choke. Ephraim blended with the other prisoners and no one dared snitch on him. Leonid was taken in ambulance to a nearby hospital but unable to be revived; a white hospital sheet now covered his entire torso, including his face.

The prison guards interviewed many of the inmates about this incident, but no one uttered a word. No one wanted to be a canary. An air of silence prevailed. No one wanted to spill the beans. In fact, many of the inmates admired Ephraim's behavior. Ephraim was considered a hero amongst them.

With a gleam in his eyes and a feeling of inward success, Ephraim was ecstatic about his own inner thoughts and feelings. 'Yes, payback is so, so sweet.' He smiled.

Chapter Twenty-Six

It seemed that good and bad news always traveled fast. While drinking his venti coffee, Yoni received a phone call from the prison warden at the Carmel-Haifa Prison. It was two p.m. in the afternoon when Yoni had just gotten off his phone and it rang again. He thought to himself, 'The phone hasn't stopped ringing today. My goodness!' Many of the calls had to do with Leonid. He wondered, 'What the dickens is going on?' Enjoying his late lunch, he took a bite of his sandwich. He answered his phone while still chewing bites of his turkey sandwich.

"Hello. It's Chief Detective Yoni Cohen. Can I help you with something?"

"Shalom, Yoni. My name is Eli Ben Canaan and I'm the head warden in charge of the maximum security prison in Carmel-Haifa Prison. I understand you're the lead detective in the case of Leonid Kozlov."

"Yes, I am. May I ask you why you're calling me?" inquired Yoni.

"I just want to inform you that Mr. Leonid Kozlov was stabbed in the chest area and his throat slit by one or more of the inmates. We don't yet know who did it. Leonid died two hours ago."

"So was it because of his stab wounds?" While on the phone, he smiled from ear to ear and thought, 'YES!' to himself. 'It's about time.'

"We are currently investigating this incident. It seems that one or more of the prisoners stabbed him while he was bench-pressing a barbell, with what appeared to have been a homemade knife. Someone must have stolen a butter knife and, with a rock, molded it into a sharp-pointed knife. We recovered this instrument of death. It looks like a homemade dagger. The knife was deeply imbedded in Leonid's chest, in fact right in his heart."

"Thank you for informing me. If I have any additional questions, can you provide me your contact information?"

"Sure." And with that, Yoni plugged his information on his cellphone number. He thought to himself, 'Ah, a knife that resembled a dagger? Indeed, payback can be so sweet.' Yoni smiled knowing his job was now complete. "And the threats to my Hannah's life are over once and for all. Oh, I did have a question. Did a physician examine and declare that Leonid had passed?"

"Yes, we have a resident physician in our prison. Leonid was examined. He had no pulse, no blood pressure, and there was no respiration – clearly, Leonid was dead."

"Okay, thanks for the information."

Yoni called his boss, Commander Levy, who stepped out of a meeting when he saw that Yoni was calling.

"Hi, Yoni. What's up?"

"I've got great news for you."

"Yea, what is it?"

"Our killer, Leonid, is dead now. Well, as of two hours ago."

"Oh really? No kidding. Wow! How did that happen?"

"He was hated by the other inmates, probably because they have daughters. One or more of the inmates fashioned a homemade knife and stabbed him in the chest's heart region and slit his throat while he was bench-pressing barbells. Our problem is solved once and for all."

"That's the best news I've had in a very long time. Thanks for letting me know. Yoni, your worries about Hannah and you are over. This must be such incredible relief for you."

"Honestly, you can't imagine what the stress has done to our home life. I was so worried about my Hannahle." Yoni began to weep while on the phone with his boss – just rehashing the family stress created by Leonid's ongoing threats to Hannah.

"Yoni, I do understand what difficult and challenging times you and the family underwent. Why don't you take a few days off and just be with your family? You deserve a break, Yoni. I just want you to know how much I appreciate your work on this case. You're one of our very finest detectives. Thank you for your service. Also, in a couple of days, I'll have a press meeting with you, your family, and Shmuel, Raffi, and Yitzchak. Oh, I would also want you to bring Sarah, Hannah, and Aaron. I'll also invite media and we'll give ourselves the credit we deserve as officers of the law."

"We'll be there, boss. Thank you for being supportive throughout this ordeal."

"You're welcome. No problem, Yoni. You're the best of the best!"

Yoni thought about the conversation and it turned out that his boss was a real mensch, a nice guy. He made a four-way call to Shmuel, Yitzchak, and Raffi. "Hi, Yoni. What's up?"

"Our killer is dead. Our problem is finally done with."

"Congratulations, but how did that finally happen?"

Yoni repeated what he had communicated to Commander Levy. "Basically, one of the inmates had intentions of killing him because his daughter had been raped."

The guys all said, "We need to go out and celebrate, Yoni. What do you think?"

"Sure, I'd love to. The drinks are on me, guys. Thank you so much for doing such a great job. Without you, I couldn't have done it by myself. Great team spirit, guys! Each and every one of you rocks! I also spoke to Commander Levy and he intends to have a press meeting party in a couple of days. How about we meet up that evening and go out and shoot the breeze? But as soon as I hear more from Commander Levy, I'll let you guys know."

In unison, they all said, "Sounds like a plan."

***

When Hannah left school at two forty-five, Yoni waited for her outside school. He held a bouquet of red roses, a dozen long-stemmed red ones. He left work early as per Commander Levy's statement that he could take some time off to be with his family.

Hannah wore her blue denim jeans with a yellow blouse with tropical flowers, like the hibiscus. She smiled when she saw her father home so early. The investigation of Leonid was so time-and-energy-consuming where frequently Yoni hadn't come home till late into the evenings.

"Abba, what a surprise to see you home so early! Why are you giving me flowers? It's not my birthday today."

"Yes, Hannahle. Guess what?" He didn't wait for her answer and said, "Leonid is dead."

They hugged each other.

"I was going to call you about that. When I ate my lunch and used a sharp knife to cut my sandwich in half, I had a brief vision that Leonid was stabbed to death. Wasn't his throat slashed as well? Wasn't he stabbed in his heart?"

"So you knew all about it from your vision? Amazing! Your insights never cease to amaze me. I think you know as much as I do. None of the other prisoners liked him. Many of them have daughters and the thought of them being raped made Leonid the most detested prisoner."

"So, Abba, what are the flowers for?"

"I just wanted to let you know how I much appreciate your help in solving this crime. Frankly, without your visions and leads, we couldn't have solved it by ourselves. So, thank you, my Hannahle."

She smiled and hugged Yoni. "Abba, I'm so happy. Wow! Now, I will be able to sleep well at night and be worry-free about his threats of killing me." Her face reddened and Hannah began to shed tears. "I was so frightened and it affected so many parts of my life, our family, my schoolwork, my inability to date anyone, and the fact that I had to keep it all of this information inside of me. I couldn't tell my friends and needed to leave town and live with Aunt Rifka. I mean, she's great and I love her. But all these changes, Leonid's threats and holding onto this big secret, it was beginning to get to me. Now, it's over. YES!" She loudly shouted, "HOORAY! YEA!" She smiled as the father and daughter repeatedly hugged each other.

"By the way, Commander Levy will have a press conference/media meeting and he wants all of us and my detectives to be present. I'm sure there will be some refreshments as well. He made a point of telling me to bring you and Aaron to this press meeting/celebration."

"Cool."

"Mom and Aaron don't yet know the latest development. Why don't we surprise them with this great news?"

"Yea, let's do it."

Sarah wore her kitchen's yellow cooking apron. When Yoni and Hannah walked in excitedly with a great big smile on their faces, they both blurted out, "He's dead! He's dead! No more Leonid."

Aaron walked around looking confused and said, "Who's dead, Abba?"

Yoni explained to Aaron that there was a very bad man who killed young women and it was daddy's job to find this bad man and put him in jail. "So my detectives and I finally arrested him. He was put in a prison with other bad people. There, while in jail, some guy killed him. This man has a daughter who was attacked by a guy just like Leonid. Finally, Leonid got stabbed in jail and died. This killer had made many threats to kill your sister, Hannah, and me, your Abba."

"What do you think of that, Aaron?"

"Oh, he's a very bad man to want to kill you and my sister, Hannah. Good, I'm happy he was punished by Ashem. If he was here in our house, I would beat him up. I would punch him in his nose!" Aaron made a fist as if he was about to punch someone. "He's a very bad man for wanting to hurt my family. No one will ever hurt my Abba or Hannah because I'll punch him."

Hannah and her parents came over to give Aaron the biggest hug ever. They overheard his vocalized sentiments.

"How about we all go out to dinner? Let's give Mom a break from the kitchen."

"That sounds awesome. I'm game," said Sarah.

"Let's choose. Who wants pizza? Who wants Chinese? Who wants Middle-Eastern food?" Yoni asked.

The vote was in, and Italian food at Ashkelon's local pizzeria was everyone's desired restaurant of choice. The family had eaten there and enjoyed their cuisine. The spaghetti and meatball, the marinara sauce, and the pizzas were second to none, and today the restaurant was not very busy. They liked several of the Italian dishes and its down-to-earth appearance and feel. They were seated at once. Prior to ordering their main meals, the server quickly brought out home-baked bread, parmesan cheese, freshly crushed pepper, and olive oil for dipping. Aaron wanted slices of pizza while Hannah ordered chicken parmesan. Sarah ordered chicken scampi-style while Yoni enjoyed his favorite eggplant parmesan.

For the first time in a while, Hannah smiled and felt worry-free. As she took a bite from a slice of pizza, she said, "Wow, I can breathe normally now and it's wonderful."

Chapter Twenty-Seven

Aaron was most comfortable in his shorts and sandals. "Ima, why do I have to get dressed in long pants and shoes? I like my shorts."

"Because today is a very special day. At Abba's work, they're going to have a party and we're all invited. Your father's boss will be there and we have to show respect by getting dressed a little nicer. Look, Ima, Abba, and Hannah, all of us are getting dressed up for this special occasion, Aaron."

"Oh, okay," Aaron said.

The family drove to Tel Aviv and took an elevator to the main police headquarters.

Aaron was amazed at how quickly they arrived at their destination. "Wow! That was quick," he remarked.

The Cohen family including Aaron, Shmuel and Leora, Raffi and Shoshana, and Yitzchak and Eranit as well as the press were all invited to police headquarters in Tel Aviv, Yaffa district, at 10:30 a.m. For this occasion, the conference table had been removed. Instead, there were several rows of chairs for people to sit.

Commander Levy wore his uniform, stripes, pins, and medals signifying his rank. Several newspaper reporters, photographers, and television reporters were all invited. This meeting was held in a large conference room which easily sat forty-plus people. He was standing in the front middle and to his immediate left was Yoni. To his right were Shmuel, Raffi, and Yitzchak. Yoni and his three detectives displayed their detective badge and an Israeli police gold star.

Commander Levy approached a wooden podium and began by greeting his detectives, media, and guests. "Thank you all for coming. I will entertain questions at the very end of my announcements and updates. The case of Leonid Kozlov has come to an end when he was killed while in the Carmel-Haifa Prison by one or more of his fellow inmates. On their end, the murder of Leonid is currently under investigation. Many of the inmates have daughters and they certainly didn't welcome a rapist of young women in their presence.

"Leonid Kozlov killed a young lady, stabbed another, and had intentions of killing several more, including a very special young lady, Hannah Cohen, who's in our presence here today. She happens to be my Chief Detective Yoni Cohen's daughter. She received many direct threats to her life. She was stalked and the family's home windows were shattered. Leonid Kozlov also threatened to kill my lead detective, Yoni Cohen, by stalking and burning his car and threatening to rape and kill his daughter, Hannah. On another occasion, Leonid Kozlov stalked Yoni while he drove to work. He burned and destroyed his car while Detective Yoni and his family were sleeping. Leonid and his boyfriend, Mr. Moyshe Stein, were involved in the recent Tel Aviv's police headquarter bombing incident. Mr. Moyshe Stein was arrested for aiding and abetting a criminal. He's awaiting his court trial. Leonid previously wrote death threat notes on the windows of the Cohen family and Hannah was directly presented a death threat note. Hannah, would you please stand up to be recognized?"

Hannah stood as her face blushed cranberry-red.

"I'd like to call you, Hannah, to come to the front of the room and please stand next to your father."

All of the detectives made room for her.

Hannah walked to the front but didn't know quite what to expect. She raised her shoulders as if to say, 'What now? What's going to happen next?' After all, she was not one of the police detectives. She wondered why Commander Levy asked her to join his team of detectives. Yoni knew his daughter was nervous being a part of a press conference. He took hold of his daughter's hand and held it.

"To continue where I left off, when Yoni Cohen was first assigned to the case, he informed me that his daughter had advance knowledge about the murderer, his appearance, and where and when the killing and stabbing will take place. I wondered and doubted how anyone could have such advanced knowledge about future killings. The answer is that Hannah's a psychic. She perceives advanced information because of her psychic abilities. When Yoni mentioned that his daughter was willing to help us with explicit details about Leonid Kozlov, my initial reactions were, 'Are you crazy? Have you lost it, man? Did you forget your forensic investigation training?' You can see how skeptical and annoyed I initially felt. However, I reluctantly said okay to Yoni and let his daughter's visions provide direction to our investigation.

"As he and I communicated about the progress of this investigation, I began to appreciate Hannah's lucid and brilliant case details. These were incredibly accurate and valuable to us. The case became even more perilous when Hannah's visions revealed that she was going to be Leonid's next victim. In fact, there were writings in lipstick on her bedroom window which confirmed Leonid's intent to kill this lovely young lady standing right here in our presence. Can you imagine the amount of stress the Cohen family faced? Also, she predicted her father's car burning as well as the bombing of our Tel Aviv Police Station."

When Commander Levy described the family stress, Hannah and Yoni began to relive the emotional rollercoaster times. Their eyes became teary. The emotions associated with all the extreme dangers to Hannah's life rekindled all of the recent emotional turmoil. Yoni took out tissues and gave some to Hannah. She dried her eyes while he dried his eyes as well. Commander Levy continued, "This was the most difficult case in the entire history of my department. All these detectives are exceptionally brave. But a very courageous person here is Hannah, and I was wrong about my initial misgivings about the investigation being helped by a psychic. I must conclude there's something uniquely amazing about being a psychic and how it helped our police work. On behalf of the citizens of Israel, I want to present Hannah a certificate signed by the mayor of Tel Aviv commending Hannah's help." And with that, Commander Levy handed her the signed framed certificate, shook her hand, and hugged her as well. "Without you, Hannah, apprehending this criminal would have been so much more difficult and perhaps many other young ladies would have perished. Thank you, Hannah, for your bravery and help in solving these murder sprees."

Hannah was so shocked by all the gratitude; she was unsure of whether to return to her seat. She began to go walk back to her seat when Commander Levy said, "Not so fast, young lady. One more surprise. As the commander of the police force, I have a certificate of appreciation for your help signed by myself as well as a gift for you. Thank you again. Would you like to say a few words?" He handed her the framed certificate of appreciation and her present, a gift-wrapped credit card for the equivalent value of one hundred and fifty dollars. Hannah was so surprised. He stated, "Happy shopping, Hannah."

Hannah blushed and said, "Wow! I never expected this. I'm not sure of what to say. What a surprise! Thank you, Commander Levy. I want to also thank my parents and my brother, Aaron, for their support. Being a psychic is often misunderstood as woo-woo-hocus-pocus type of trait. Some people even think clairvoyants are witches or gypsy quacks. However, it's being studied by many universities worldwide and some police forces in other countries use psychics to help solve crimes. As an example, look at Debbie Malone's psychic work in Australia which helped solve many crimes. But you know, I'm just a normal teenager who will graduate high school next year. Then, I plan to serve my country in the IDF. I love art and see myself developing my creative art skills by one day being a student at the Letzior Art College, that is, if I'm accepted. I'm not sure why I have visions. All I can say is that God must have given me this gift. I think your initial reactions about psychics, Commander Levy, are common among many people. It's normal because it's something so different, unknown, and intangible. There were times when my own parents doubted my having visions, but finally, they came around. My Ima and Abba have more than stepped up to the plate. They were very supportive of my having these frightening visions. Commander Levy, thank you for the recognition and your generous gift." She looked at her credit card gift as she turned to Commander Levy and said, "How did you know I like to shop?"

Everyone laughed.

She continued, "I will continue my education and just be a normal teenager. So, I think I said enough. The real nitty-gritty hard work was done by all these detectives in our presence. Thanks again." Commander Levy reached over to give her a big hug. She went back to be with her Ima and Aaron.

Everyone stood up and applauded while Sarah was now overcome with emotions and cried. She was so proud of Hannah. Aaron asked his Ima if she'd like to use his handkerchief to wipe her eyes.

"Ima, why are you crying? Was I bad or something?" asked Aaron.

"No Aaron, you're a very good boy. It's just that Mommy is so proud and happy for your sister."

"Oh, okay."

Commander Levy continued, "Thank you, Hannah, for your inspiring words. I do want to commend Detectives Yoni, Shmuel, Raffi, and Yitzchak for doing a tremendously professional job as they circled the wagons and finally apprehended Leonid." Commander Levy presented each with a certificate of accomplishment signed by him. "Last but not least, I want to congratulate and promote Yoni with these three silver stars that denote chief inspector status of the police. Yoni, now as chief inspector, would you like to say a few words?"

When everyone heard about Yoni's promotion, they all stood and applauded. Aaron screamed loudly, "Abba, you're the best! You're the best! I love you, my Abba!"

That drew considerable laughter. Several people in the crowd were heard whispering to one another, "Oh, he's so cute! Isn't he a darling?"

Yoni indicated, "Yes, I'd like to say something about apprehending Leonid Kozlov. Thank you from the bottom of my heart for this promotion, Commander Levy. It's quite unexpected but I'm very grateful to you. Thank you for your support, Commander Levy. This investigation was probably the most difficult one I've ever faced. I want to thank my daughter, Hannah. My wife, Sarah, deserves special praise for being so supportive. Commander Levy accepted my frantic phone calls when my family and I worried about our safety. Sarah lived through some of my crabby moods, being sleep-deprived and worried about Hannah's safety. Thank you, Sarah. Hannah, your visions helped drive this entire investigation. Thank you to my team of the very best ace detectives – Shmuel, Yitzchak, and Raffi. I think we need to applaud their efforts. Congrats to Shmuel for getting engaged to lovely Leora. And Raffi, Mazal Tov to you and Shoshana for the birth of your first son. Without my team, we'd be nowhere. So thank you, guys. You're the best of the best!"

Everyone stood and applauded for Shmuel, Raffi, and Yitzchak's detective efforts.

"My team of detectives is second to none. They're truly the best! Commander Levy deserves special thanks for his continued support during this investigation. Aaron, I promise you we'll now have more time to play soccer and take walks. Maybe, you can even try out for a children's soccer league. Wouldn't that be great? I'll now turn it back to Commander Levy. Thank you."

Aaron smiled and looked forward to have more time with his father. He was heard saying, "Abba, I love you too. You're the best father in the whole world!"

"Thank you, Yoni. I'll now entertain some questions, as we have a few minutes left."

A Yediot Haachronot Journalist Mr. Nachum Berg asked, "Commander Levy, throughout this investigation, what would you say was the most difficult challenge and how did you overcome it?"

"There were several challenges along the way. Leonid Kozlov was very illusive and he used a number of disguises. The first time Detective Raffi chased and shot him, Leonid escaped. He was a fast runner, knew the layout of the gym and later of the apartment building where he lived with his boyfriend. He was like a modern-day ninja, knowing how and where to jump from one building to another with dartingly fast speed. On another chase occasion, Yitzchak shot Leonid, and he was actually injured. Using one of his disguises, he convinced a trauma doctor to treat him in his medical outpatient office. He upped his tactics by lipstick writings on both Hannah's as well as her parents' windows. The windowpane writings were all threats to rape and kill Hannah. He was also a key participant in the bombing of our other Tel Aviv Police Station. While Yoni was sleeping, he received a call from a police officer that his car was trashed and burning up in fire. Later, a neighborhood police officer confirmed that he interviewed someone in a suit and tie. When Yoni asked the officer if he had a scar around his left cheek, the officer responded with a 'yes.'

"How did we overcome challenges? Perseverance, good team spirit, supporting one another and, of course, Hannah's visions and leads were incredibly helpful. Also, our detectives were determined and often sleep-deprived while being on a chase for Leonid. We're fortunate to have the best detectives." Commander Levy looked right at Yoni and the three other detectives.

A reporter from the Tel Aviv Gazette turned towards Hannah and asked, "Did you ever question the reliability and validity of being a psychic?"

She stood up. "No, I don't know much about statistics that measure validity and reliability. But I discovered my being a psychic when I was in kindergarten. Somehow, I was able to predict children's accidents and falls in school, ones that were about to happen, including some that would require stitches. One boy, I predicted in advance, would fall from the swings and break his arm. Indeed, it happened. Eventually, my school teachers and nurses began to take me seriously. Similarly, my parents and I also went through a process. I never doubted my gift, but other people did. In terms of being reliable and valid, every one of my visions has come true. Every vision became a reality. Have I conducted a statistical study? The answer is no. I'm just seventeen and have not yet graduated from high school. If you want to learn more about scientific studies, you might want to look at ones being conducted at the University of Arizona or at Duke University in the United States. You might want to speak to Ms. Debbie Malone about how her psychic abilities helped solve crimes in Australia. I have to believe that what I see and feel is valid and real. Also, there are organizations manned by psychics that help find missing people, some of whom turn out to be deceased. These organizations manned by psychics have a much higher success than do police departments. Some of them claim to have a forty-to-fifty-percent success rate versus police departments that have a six-or-seven-percent success rate. So, I hope I answered your question."

"Thank you. That's a great answer to a very complicated question. As a teen, your answer reflects maturity well beyond your age. Thank you again."

"Commander Levy. You mentioned there's an investigation as to Leonid's killing at the Carmel-Haifa Prison. Can you tell us more about it?"

"An investigation is moving forward by Warden Eli Ben Canaan at that prison. We were just informed a couple of days ago. There's nothing more I can say about it. You might want to inquire with Warden Ben Canaan, since it's an internal prison matter. Thank you all for coming. We have some refreshments in the back. Please feel free to help yourselves. And with that, I'll end this meeting."

Yoni mentioned eating lunch out as a family. And of course, the answer was, "Yes."

Yoni mentioned to Sarah that his detectives were planning to celebrate tonight. "Is that okay with you, Sarah? Do you need me around to help in any way?"

"No, no. Go ahead. Have fun with the guys. You know how proud I am of you. Yoni, just save some energy for us later. Okay?" She smiled and winked.

Chapter Twenty-Eight

In the evening around 9:00 p.m., Shmuel, Raffi, and Yitzchak met up with Yoni at the Zanzibar Club in Tel Aviv, located near the fashionable Dizengoff Street. This nightclub was a bit on the dark side, not well lit at all but had great atmosphere. Several guitars hung on the walls. Some of the nightclub patrons had been smoking, which created an overhead hovering cloud of grayish-white smoke. The detectives situated themselves in the back of the club to ensure they wouldn't be overly inundated by the loud sounds of the band, which was now playing, Stevie Ray Vaughn's, *The Sky is Crying*. Some of the band's previous songs were Jimmy Hendrix's *Foxy Lady*.

Shmuel turned to his detective colleagues and said, "It's funny. When Leora and I first began to date, Foxy Lady was one of the songs we sang while driving in my Mustang convertible."

The server came over and asked, "Gentleman, what are we drinking tonight?"

Shmuel said, "A Russian Mule."

Yitzchak said, "Rum and coke."

Raffi said, "A Bloody Mary."

Last but not least, Yoni asked the server, "What type of cognacs do you have?"

The server mentioned a few brands. Yoni decided on Courvoisier.

"Please make it a double one with water on the side, please."

"So, Shmuel, how's Leora? Have you guys decided on a wedding date?" asked Yoni.

"Yes, we have a date in mind and will shortly send out invitations. We talked about 27th February, an afternoon synagogue ceremony to be followed by an evening dinner and dancing at a nearby restaurant. Thank God, Leora and her mom are taking care of all the plans. I have no mind for that kind of stuff. Say, will you guys and your spouses be able to make it? Of course, you're all invited."

Unanimously, everyone said, "Yea, of course. Are you kidding? We wouldn't miss it."

Raffi poked fun roasting Shmuel. "So, the stud, our babe magnet, is finally getting married – tying the knot. Shmuel, lover boy, what are your thoughts about keeping your wedding vows? Ha, ha."

"Yea, of course. I love Leora. I totally intend on being faithful. Otherwise, I wouldn't get married. Besides, Leora is such a class act – pretty, smart, educated, has great common sense, and she'll make a great mom one day. She loves children. I have a nephew and a niece. You know, I'm a kid at heart, so of course I love children. Why? Why are you asking me that question?"

Raffi said, "I'm just teasing you because we all know you've been a babe magnet up until recently. Oh, just busting on you, not criticizing you. Just poking fun."

Shmuel smiled and said, "It means a lot to me that all of you will be there. After all, we're such a great team!" He thought momentarily and asked, "Oh, by the way, since Hannah and Aaron feel like they're a part of our team, we'll invite them as well. Is that okay with you?"

"Sure, I'm sure they'd love to come. I feel like we're all part of a large family. Hannah loves to dance and have fun, like a typical teenager. Finally, now she can laugh, dance, and be her normal self. Boy, Leonid's threats were so incredibly trying for her and for us as a family," Yoni said.

Shmuel said, "You know you're so lucky to have such a wonderful daughter. Man, she's such an outstanding young lady! And, what a knockout!" The other three detectives raised their drink as if to say, 'YES!' Unanimously, they all exclaimed, "Lechaim to Hannah!" They clicked their drinks together.

Yoni inquired, "What's new with you, Raffi?"

"Glad you asked. In three days, which is this coming Sunday, Shoshana and I are having a Brit Milah (a ritual circumcision) for our new baby boy, Shimon Ben Rafael. Of course, you're all invited. It's kind of short notice but–"

He was cut off when his colleagues all said, "Of course, we'll all be there. You can count on us. What can we bring?"

"Bring nothing, just your spouses and yourselves. Shmuel, please feel free to bring your lovely bride-to-be, Leora."

"What's new with you, Yitzchak? How's your family?" Shmuel inquired.

"Children are growing, becoming more chutzpadik, but it's all good. They attend a school in our neighborhood. My youngest is in preschool. The most important thing is that everyone is healthy. Right? My wife is finishing up her bachelor's degree in psychology. She wants to eventually get her master's degree in school psychology. Then, she'll hopefully work at a school. That's the long-range plan."

Everyone said, "Yes, for sure. Let's drink to that."

Yoni's detectives all remarked, "How pretty and well-spoken Hannah was today! She's quite a young lady – intelligent and beautiful. Without doubt, she'll go very far in life."

"Thank you. From your mouth to God's ears! It's been an amazing eye-opener over the years to have a daughter who's a psychic. As parents, we had to come to terms with that. It was an adjustment for all, including Aaron. Hannah definitely has a unique God-given gift. Oh, I forgot to mention to you that she was recently awarded a first-place prize by the Letzior Art College for her being the best high-school artist in all of Israel." Yoni smiled proudly as he mentioned Hannah's accomplishments.

Raffi, Shmuel, and Yitzchak congratulated Yoni on having such an incredibly talented daughter.

Shmuel said, "Wow! An artist, so pretty, and a psychic, all wrapped up in one, that's f****** amazing. Remarkable! Let's drink to Hannah."

He changed the subject for a moment. "Hey guys, can you imagine we're all done with this SOB Leonid? He's dead once and for all. Let's drink to that. Le-Chaim!" They lifted their drinks and gently touched them together.

Shmuel said, "I got to tell you, this was one hell of a stressful time for me. Leora wanted attention because she's becoming a new bride and I was one hell of a crabby guy being sleep-deprived. Yea, no sleep will do it, plus trying to apprehend this SOB so he won't kill any additional young ladies. Raffi, you shot at him several times and he escaped. Yitzchak, you shot and your bullets injured him. Man, that Leonid was like a cat with many lives. And finally, I shot him just above the knees. And the rest was history, you know, hospital and then being imprisoned."

Shmuel wondered and said, "Hey, did anyone ever investigate who shot Leonid with arrows in his shoulder and forearm?"

Yoni quickly answered, "It could have been anyone – one of the victims' family members or a community vigilante. But the SOB got what he deserved. He's dead. So, we can leave that behind us. The guy is f***** dead. Thank God."

They all agreed. The guys all enjoyed another round of drinks, schmoozed a bit longer, and then it was time to go home.

By the time Yoni saw Sarah, it was one o'clock in the morning. He slipped into bed but tried not to be noisy. He brushed his teeth to get rid of any alcohol smell in his mouth.

"I'm so proud of you, Yoni." Sarah wrapped one of her legs around him and drew him towards her. They rediscovered each other with amorous loving embraces. Receptive to his kisses, her breaths and sighs amplified. They made up for lost time, eventually drifting into a deep slumber. With their arms draped around each other, they experienced intimate feelings of closeness.

***

The Bat Zion High School lunchroom was crowded with students scurrying to get their lunches and sit next to their friends. Some were on line while others were already seated. It was loud and busy environment with several hundred teens chatting. This made it more challenging to hear one another.

Hannah spotted Yigal while she began eating her lunch. She looked up from her chemistry book and there he was. Yigal sprouted a big happy smile. Yigal was a tall and slender high-school senior wearing blue jeans, a white shirt, shortly cropped hair, and with sparkling blue eyes. Hannah could tell that besides all of the external signs of being handsome, he appeared to be sensitive and caring as well. In their last phone conversation, he took a great deal of interest in Hannah's art and school projects with questions like, "How do you decide on an actual theme for your paintings? How do you decide on which color you'll use?"

Because Hannah's picture and name appeared in several newspaper articles, she was an instant celebrity at her high school. Many of her friends congratulated her on winning first place at the Letzior Art Contest as well as her help in solving crimes.

She smiled and asked Yigal, "Hey, how about sitting down here? Would you like to join me? We still have some time to kill. It's nice to run into you today. What have you been up to?"

Sporting a smile on his face, he said, "Hi, Hannah. It's so nice to see you too. I see your fame hasn't gone to your head yet."

"What do you mean by that, Yigal?"

"Your picture and stories about helping to solve a major crime due to being psychic have appeared everywhere – newspapers and even television. That in addition to winning first place in art, which makes you famous; everyone knows about you. Hannah, you're a superstar! I should be asking you for your autograph." He paused and then, with a wink, said, "I'm just teasing you."

"Oh, come on, Yigal. Yes, this God-given gift helped solve a major crime, but did you know that I was about to be his next victim? I envisioned this in advance." She paused and then added, "Wow! I'm relieved it's over. It's been a nightmare from hell."

"Yea, I'm sure it was. And you could see all of that in advance?"

"Yea. But there were several great detectives, my father being one of them. As a team, they pursued and finally captured this killer. But I'm telling you, Yigal, I am a hundred percent sure that I would have been his next victim. He made numerous threats, including writing them on my bedroom windows. He stalked me."

"Oh my God!" Yigal looked sad about the prospect of losing his friend Hannah. He continued, "So, you read minds? Can you read my mind, you know, my thoughts?"

"Well, let me guess. You'd like to ask me out on a date. Right?"

"How did you know?" He didn't wait for her answer when he added, "Because I think you're very pretty. I've waited for the right moment to ask you out, Hannah."

"That's like the nicest thing anyone said to me in a very long time. And yes, I want to go out with you. Because I'm psychic, I knew you were going to ask me out." She paused and then added, "No, all kidding aside, I really did take a wild guess. If you wouldn't have asked me, well, I might have just asked you out. You know, our time has come as women that we're not afraid to ask guys out."

He sounded kind of shocked by this revelation. "Would you have?"

"Yea, I would have. You know women are more liberated today. Women have a larger, more equal voice today."

"Hannah, you just made my day. I've had a crush on you for months. It seemed like I've had this crush on you forever." Yigal's smile accentuated the dimples on his cheeks.

"Yigal, I also liked you for several months too. Now, I no longer feel mentally preoccupied and I can devote more energy to being in a relationship with you."

"Would you like to take a nice, long stroll along the beach, right after school? I'm done with all of my school-related projects," Yigal asked.

"Yea, sure, let's do it. We can leave our schoolbags at my house because I'm just a block away from the beach. We'll also fill up our water bottles."

"That's sounds awesome, Hannah." Even though it was a school lunchroom, he reached over to give her a big hug. He gently touched her face. Had it not for being in a school lunchroom, they might have shared their first tender kiss. Both Hannah and Yigal didn't care who might have observed their tender moment. They took a selfie together.

It was time to get back to their respective classes. They winked and hugged each other. Unanimously, they both said, "See you later."

Hannah quickly sent a text to her mom and father, saying that after school, she was going to take a walk along the sea with Yigal.

Sarah quickly texted her back, asking, *"Is he cute, Hannahle? Is he nice to you?"*

"Ima, yes, he's very handsome. He's tall, sensitive, funny, smart, and a great athlete. I know he likes me a lot." She paused and wrote, *"And I like him too. Here, let me show you our selfie."*

"Yes, he is so handsome but, Hannah, just be careful. I'd never want to see my baby getting hurt."

"Thanks, Ima. I love you too."

***

It was a picture-perfect sunny day where the crystal-clear blue waters of the Mediterranean Sea blended into the white sandy beach, pockmarked by various seashells and swept up broken coral. Small blue-and-gray-colored crabs were visible, just walking around. Hannah and Yigal held hands as they walked the shores with a breeze that caressed their face. Occasionally, Hannah bent down to pick up seashells, some round while others long. "Yigal, look at this one. What a shining surface! Look at the brown and tan colors. Nature is amazing, isn't it?" she said with excitement and wonder in her voice. She added, "Look, a red flag. Today's not a good day for any swimming. It's too windy – too many waves and strong undertows."

Yigal agreed. "Oh, look, Hannah. What a beautiful starfish shell. Wow!" They teasingly played 'catch me' while each darted across the sand. Yigal caught up to Hannah and grabbed her arm as they both dropped to the sand below. They romantically kissed each other as lovers do. They smiled, giggled, and enjoyed smooching with each other. They knew that deeper feelings will unfold in the very near future.

Yigal touched her face and said, "I'm so lucky to be your boyfriend. I've had feelings for you for a while now."

"We're both so lucky to have each other," Hannah said.

In a few months, they'd both be in the military as boys and girls must serve. They'd both face changes such as being in the IDF and be away from home. They wondered if their relationship will stand the test of time. Will Hannah's psychic gifts continue? Would there relationship continue in spite of being in the IDF for the next three years? They felt they should enjoy the moment now, as their future was difficult to predict. After enjoying a fruit snack of oranges and bananas, they both walked back, holding hands together.

"Yigal, I want to ask you a question."

"Okay, what is it?"

"I always had the feeling you were sad about something, but maybe I'm wrong. And I hope I'm not being too personal?"

"No, no. You're fine. My parents got divorced a year ago. My mother was just diagnosed with heart problems. I really think she has a broken heart about the fact that their marriage had not made it to the finish line. She loved my abba. We both think he had like a midlife crisis as he picked up with his secretary. But I'm not a hundred percent sure about that."

"Oh, I'm so sorry. That's got to be weighing heavy on your mind. So, is your father involved in your life now that your parents are divorced?"

"No, not really. Like I said, he's got a new girlfriend and he spends a lot of time with her. I rarely hear from him. When he divorced my ima, it seemed like that included me as well."

"I'm sorry, Yigal. It's not right for him to behave like that towards you. It must be difficult for you."

"Yes, it has been. How about you, Hannah, any family drama?"

"No, not really. My parents are happy with each other. My ima and abba are very supportive people."

"Hannah, what would you like to do in life?"

"I have a few things that I'm trying to sort out. First and foremost, I'm an artist and in the future, I would like to be a student at Letzior College. But I also think that what my abba does as a lead detective fascinates me. In the IDF, I hope I'd qualify for their intelligence unit. It's very hard to get into that unit." She smiled and then added, "I think I probably need a couple of lifetimes to accomplish all these goals. Ha, ha."

"What about you, Yigal? What do you want to be?"

"I think it would be cool to be a psychologist, you know, helping people, especially children with family problems."

"That's so rewarding to be able to help others." Hannah looked at her watch and added, "I think I need to get back home, as my parents expect me home for dinner. Sorry to interrupt your thoughts."

"Yea, for sure, no problem." He reached over to kiss her tenderly and added, "Hannah, you're very caring and sweet. I'm so happy we're in a relationship."

"Yea, me too. Now we can see each other frequently. I have feelings for you as well."

They got up off the sand and walked towards Hannah's home. An ice cream truck was parked nearby, selling ice cream. "Hey, what's your favorite glidda?" he asked Hannah.

Yigal ordered two ice creams, one vanilla and the other chocolate.

"Thanks, Yigal." She leaned over to kiss him. They both said their goodbyes.

"Hannah, I'll call you later."

"Cool."

Chapter Twenty-Nine

Hannah had just finished reading Aaron a children's book entitled Ima Mesaperet. Aaron had snuggled close to Hannah. A pot roast was broiling in the oven while Sarah was busy finishing up her potato pancakes – latkes. Hannah helped by cutting tomatoes and carrots to complete the dinner salad.

They sat down as a family to enjoy dinner. "What a relief to be done with Leonid! That case was so unbelievably time-consuming and emotionally difficult for us as a family," said Yoni.

"Yea, so glad it's over for all of us. What a relief!" Hannah said.

"Anyone wants to bring up anything to talk about?"

"Yes, Abba and Ima, actually there is something I'd like to bring up. I prefer privacy, so maybe Aaron can watch some television or play a videogame? Or perhaps after dinner, Aaron could go to his room and play with some of his toys?"

Sarah said, "Sure. After dinner, Aaron, why don't you go to your room, play, watch TV, or look at your videogames?"

"Okay, Ima. Did I do something that I'm in trouble?"

"Oh, no sweetie. We just want to have some grownup conversation with Hannah. You're not in any trouble, Aaron. Don't worry."

"Oh, okay. Bye." He had finished eating and he went off to his room to watch his children's videos.

"So what's up, Hannah? How are things between you and Yigal?" asked Yoni.

"He's very sweet and caring. No, things are going well between us. But there's something else I wanted to talk to you about. I mean, to share with you." She took several deep breaths to relax. This subject weighed heavy on her mind. "I would never want to hold any secrets from you."

"Another vision?"

"No, not quite." She sipped on her lemonade.

Aaron barged in. "Ima and Abba, we didn't have our dessert yet. When are we going to eat Ima's favorite home-baked cake with ice cream?"

"Aaron, give us a few minutes. We'll let you know when we're ready for dessert. Okay?"

"Yes, Abba." Aaron went back to watch his videos.

"So, what's up, Hannah? Is there something bothering you?" asked Sarah.

"Yes, actually there is. But it's really very difficult to talk about." She took another sip of her lemonade and then continued, "Do you remember when I last stayed at Aunt Rifka's place?"

They both said, "Yes."

"Well, I did something I shouldn't have, and I feel very guilty and shameful about it." She welled up with tears. She leaned over to take some tissues and blew her nose.

"Hannah, what did you do that you feel so bad about?" Sarah asked as she put her hand on Hannah's shoulder.

"Remember how Leonid threatened to rape and kill me? Remember the letter, the writing on my windows? Well, it all finally got to me, especially after Leonid bombed your police station and burned our family car. It just got to me."

"Yes, so what made you feel so guilty?" asked Sarah.

"I shot him with three arrows."

"You shot him with your bow and arrows?" asked Yoni with a raised voice.

"Yea, I shot him with my bow and arrows. But there was no intention to kill him – just wound and scare him." By now, Hannah had begun to cry. She knew her father was both angry and disappointed that she took the law into her own hands.

"Hannah, you realize you did the wrong thing because you interfered with the law, in particular my investigation. Also, you took the law into your own hands and you could have easily killed him."

"Yes, I realize that, but I honestly felt I was about to be killed. I felt it was a matter of self-defense. Also, there seemed to be no break in this case. Who knows how many other ladies he would have raped and killed, including myself? Abba, I did not mean to interfere in your work, but please keep in mind that it was a matter of self-defense."

"Yes, I understand how you feel, but you shouldn't have taken the law into your own hands."

"Yes, you're right, Abba. Please forgive me. I do believe you and your detectives did a fantastic job, but it was taking a very long time to apprehend Leonid. I definitely felt my actions were in self-defense. What about his written threats on my windowpanes? I honestly felt I was going to be killed shortly – any day then. I knew that I would have been kidnapped and killed."

Yoni shook his head in disbelief. "How could you take the law into your own hands?" His face was red and he was feeling angry at his daughter.

"Abba, I'm sorry. I know I've made you feel angry and disappointed in me. I'm so sorry. I never intended to upset you." There was quiet in the room, not a peep from anyone. "Ima, you haven't said anything. Why?"

"Your father is right. You shouldn't have taken the law into your hands. You're not even old enough to handle weapons. You're not yet in the IDF."

"Yes, I feel that I'm a huge disappointment to both of you, and I feel really guilty." Hannah now shed tears as she reached for tissues to wipe her eyes. Her face was red from shame and guilt. After some time, she said, "But in the Old Testament, it says, 'An eye for an eye and a tooth for a tooth.' Can you try and understand that I felt I had enough proof that I was about to be killed? In his note and in his writing on the windows, he said, 'You're next.' What am I supposed to do – just wait for the inevitable?"

"Yes, you're supposed to let police handle it. That's what you should have done," said Yoni. He continued to be angry.

"I appreciate everything that you and your detectives did, but his direct threats to my life made me do it. And in mind, it was questionable about why Leonid had not yet been captured. So, I'm really sorry that I offended you. When I shot my bow, I aimed for his shoulder and arm, not his heart or head areas. I wasn't out to kill him, just sting him and slow down his killing instincts."

"Still, you should have let us, that is, police handle it," said Yoni.

"Okay, well, I don't know how to get beyond the impasse between us. What would you like me to do? You want me to go to court and explain this to a judge? You want me to go to jail?"

"Let's just take a break, as your brother has waited patiently for dessert."

Sarah raised her voice when she asked, "Aaron, would you like dessert?"

"Sure," said Aaron.

"You'll excuse me. I'm not feeling well right now. I'll skip dessert. I'm going to my room." Hannah appeared tearful as she walked away from the family dining room. Clearly, she was shamed for her actions and the choices she made.

Once she reached her bedroom, she texted Yigal, *"My parents and I had a real bad fight. I don't know what to do to resolve it."* She lay down on her pillow and began to sob. She blew her nose loudly.

After a few minutes, her parents came into her room. Hannah was lying on her stomach face-down, still crying. As she heard them enter her room, her crying intensified.

"Look, if I made an issue about this, you'd have to possibly be arrested and go in front of a judge to answer criminal charges. This could affect your future career, your entrance into the IDF, and maybe even entrance into college. You would have a record. Depending on the judge, you might even have to spend some time in jail. It would create considerable doubts about why our police department allowed you, a psychic, to help us when you yourself took the law into your own hands. It would also continue to seriously undermine our relationship and the trust in this family. So what are your reactions, Hannah?"

Still sniffling, she said, "No, I mean in retrospect, I did the wrong thing. I'm asking for your forgiveness, Abba and Ima. I'm very sorry. It must have been stupidity." Her crying continued.

"As your father, I forgive you. I don't want you to have any of negative ramifications in your life, including possible jail time and a criminal record. But don't ever take the law into your hands again. Don't be a vigilante. I understand you felt that your life was threatened, and it was, but that's why police departments exist." He paused pensively to deliberate. He reached for Hannah's hand and pulled her towards Sarah and himself. "We love you, honey, but please don't ever take the law into your hands." They all hugged one another.

"I won't do that again. I love you and don't ever want to ruin our family trust." Hannah enjoyed languishing in her parents' arms. Can I have a piece of cake now? I'm so hungry/famished."

"Sure."

She closed her eyes with inner satisfaction while she devoured her second piece of cake.

Yoni inquired, "The IDF is a few months away. Any thoughts about that?"

"I hope I can qualify for the intelligence division. I feel ready to fulfill my responsibilities. After I complete my military responsibilities, I want to pursue my art studies at Letzior College. But I'm also impressed with law enforcement and may wish to be a detective just like you, Abba."

"You have sound plans, Hannah. The IDF is very selective when it comes to being in intelligence. I hope all your aspirations come true."

"Well, all I can do is try and do my best on the IDF psychometric tests. To change the subject a bit, Yigal and I might meet up after school. Would that be okay?"

"Yes, sure. Thanks for letting us know."

In the meantime, Hannah sent Yigal a text. *"U want 2 meet tomorrow after school? Maybe the beach again?"*

He answered her while she swallowed yet another bite of the cake. *"Sure. Let's do it. Look forward to seeing you tomorrow. Good night, honey."*

Hannah answered, *"Love you too, Yigal. Good night and sweet dreams to you."*

***

On this still sunny day, after school let out, Hannah and Yigal walked the beaches in Ashkelon. On the sea, a scuba-dive boat was visible with a number of novice and advanced divers. A buoy with the red and white scuba logo floated visibly a hundred meters away. Today, divers looked for lost historic treasures. In 604 B.C.E., Nebuchadnezzar, the King of Babylonia, invaded the philistine metropolis and ransacked the entire city of Ashkelon. There, Samson had fallen in love and was seduced by a philistine named Delilah. She cut his hair, he lost his strength, and he became a prisoner there. The story unfolded that when his hair grew back, the source of his physical strength returned. His physical might destroyed a philistine temple as he pushed the columns and brought the temple to rubbles.

Whenever Hannah walked past the ruins, she thought to herself, 'Wow! The temple destroyed by Samson is still evident right here in Ashkelon with its pummeled columns lying naked in the ancient sand. It's incredible to see such history unfold in front of my eyes.'

Yigal asked Hannah, "Are you okay today? Yesterday, you sounded very upset?"

"Yea, I was, but I'm in a much better place now. As a family, we needed to air some things between us. So, now I'm good."

"How about you, Yigal?"

"I finally heard from my dad who wanted to arrange a time and day to take me out for dinner." He paused for a few seconds. "I don't know. I haven't yet responded to my dad."

"What's holding you back, Yigal?"

"You know that for the past year, he totally disappeared from my life. He never responded to any of my calls or attempts to reach him by email. I was hurt and angry. That was a difficult time in my life, especially since my ima got diagnosed with congestive heart failure. It's hard enough to go through a divorce, but to be diagnosed with a life-threatening illness? Boy, it's been hard on her and me."

"Wow! I'm sorry you and your ima went through so much. With your dad, it sounds like you must have felt abandoned by him. No?"

"Yea, imagine if your father stopped all communications with you for nearly a year. It was tough because I grieved losing him in my life. I mean, I was sad, angry, hurt, and I also wondered if it was my fault. Then, one day, my feelings changed. I felt like I no longer wanted him in my life. Suddenly, I felt stronger and was okay about it all. So, now he wants contact, and I'm confused about whether to let him back into my life. Hannah, what would you do if you were me?"

"Yigal, I feel for you, you know, all that you went through this year. If I were you, I'd meet with him and ask him some questions about why he disappeared from my life. The other thing is that it sounds like it's hard for you to trust him now. What do you think?"

"Yes, absolutely, right on point. I mean, he'll definitely have to explain himself to me. I don't trust him anymore. It's not normal for a father to disappear for a year's time without communicating. In fact, it's so bizarre!"

"Yea, for sure. You'll need to ask to explain himself and how do you know that it won't happen again?"

"Exactly. I've lost all trust in him. There was a time we were close, but like I said the other day, he not only divorced my ima, he also ended his relationship with me."

"And I know you feel awful about it. I hope things change for you because the bottom line is that you need a father."

"Yea, I think you're absolutely right, but I will let him back into my life if he demonstrates that he can be nicer towards me and that we can have consistent contact. You know even though I'm hurt about his actions, the reality is that I still love him. Just to change the subject, let's find a place to sit or lie down."

They found a quiet, secluded area. Yigal had brought a big towel which he placed on the sand. He snuggled close to Hannah as they exchanged tender kisses. "Want some water?"

"Yea, sure," said Hannah.

"Hannah, what's your vision about our relationship?"

"I'm open to a relationship with you, Yigal. I mean, I'm open to have a closer relationship. How about you?"

"You must know by now that I have very strong feelings towards you. You're on my mind when I first wake up and when I go to sleep. We'll have some hurdles to overcome?"

"You mean when we get drafted to the IDF?"

"Yea."

"We'll manage and see each other when we can. We can text each other. Granted, it's not the same as seeing each other in person. But what can we do? If we each make an effort, perhaps we can make it work? No?"

"I'm willing."

"Yigal, what do you think about my saying I'm open to a closer relationship with you?"

"I love it. You know what? I'm crazy about you too."

Their inner passion took over. Suddenly, it seemed like time stood still as they kissed and continued their sensual exploration. Beads of sweat poured down their faces onto their necks.

She glanced at her watch. "Oh my goodness, I have to get back to my family. It's our dinnertime."

"Yea, me too. I'm sure my ima's wondering where I am. I love you, Hannah. Why don't we send them each a reassuring text?"

"I love you, my Yigal."

"I love you too, Hannah."

They kissed one more time to say goodbye for now. They sprouted huge smiles and hugged each other before each returned home.

***

When Hannah arrived home, her parents smiled. Seated on the living-room sofa, Sarah seemed animated as Hannah received a letter from the Letzior Art College. "Please open it, Hannah. We're so excited for you. We wonder what they have to say. It came as a registered mail."

"Yea, for sure. But first, I want to wash my hands and rinse my face with some cold water." Hannah went to their bathroom.

"Okay, ready? Here's what it says." She opened the envelope.

"Dear Ms. Hannah Cohen. Once again, congratulations on your first-place win in the yearly art contest sponsored by Letzior Art College. Your talent is clearly evident in your paintings. We'd like to offer you a full scholarship to our program for the duration of your four-year studies at Letzior. We understand that you will soon begin your IDF duties. Please note that this offer can begin upon the completion of your IDF responsibilities. We hope you'll seriously consider our program. Please let us know of your interest in us and understand that this offer by no means binds you to Letzior Art College. If you wish to study elsewhere, we'll understand. A commitment to art studies must feel like a right fit for all parties. We would be pleased to have you be a part of the Letzior family.

Sincerely,
David Schwartz, MFA, Ph.D.
Dean of Letzior Art College."

"Wow!" said Yoni. "What a generous and enticing offer! Congratulations, my Hannahle! My understanding is that they hardly ever offer any scholarships. They were clearly smitten by your art."

"Yes, it's generous, but I have to sort things out in my mind. Will I become one of those talented, yet starving artists? I mean, will I be able to make a living in art? It's kind of like acting. You can be very talented, but that doesn't guarantee earning a living. There's lots of competition out there." She paused and said, "I've begun to think practical about my future."

"We're so proud of you. Hannah, we love you in whatever you decide to do in life," said Sarah.

"Thanks. Yea, lot's to think about and decisions to make in the future. I'll write Letzior College a thank-you letter." She changed the subject. "Guess what?"

Hannah's parents both unanimously said, "What?"

"Yigal and I are in love. We're crazy about each other."

"It's nice to be in love, but please be careful."

"What do you mean when you say, 'Be careful?'"

"I mean, please watch yourself and don't get pregnant at this time in your life. You have so much to look forward to. You haven't yet graduated from high school and you have a full scholarship offer. Wow, that's so awesome!"

"I get it, Abba. But at the same time, have more confidence in me. I do use good judgment in whatever I do." Pensively, she added, "Leonid's threats to kill me and others were awful. Now, it's just so nice to be able to have candid conversations with Yigal, who I care about. He's such a great guy. He let it be known that he's also in love with me. Maybe you would like to meet him in the near future?"

"Of course, we would love to," said Sarah. Yoni shook his head in agreement.

"I'm glad. Don't worry, I'll keep up with all of my responsibilities. Getting through high school, the IDF and college are my number-one priorities. Then, if Yigal and I are still in each other's life, it could mean marriage. But in the meantime, we each have so much to accomplish."

***

It was now ten thirty p.m. Yoni and Sarah were about to fall asleep when Hannah knocked on their door. "Abba and Ima, I'm so sorry to wake you up. Can I talk to you? It's really important."

"Yea, sure." Yoni had put on his robe and stepped out to the kitchen area. "What's the matter, Hannahle?"

Her face was red and she began to hyperventilate. "I thought I was done with my visions, but I just had an extremely disturbing one." She patted her face with tissues to wipe away accumulating sweat beads on her forehead. Her face was beet-red. She took a long sip of her lemonade. "We're in for more problems, bigger than ever before." She took a couple of deep breaths and tried to slowly inhale and exhale. She rubbed her forehead and continued, "Did you know that Leonid has a first cousin by the name of Anatoly Kozlov? He's twenty-nine and is a computer engineer with a degree from the Moscow Technological Institute. After he completed university studies, he was recruited by the Soviet KGB spy system. There, he trained and became one of their very best assassins. He's amazingly knowledgeable about computers, especially when it comes to hacking. This makes him a formidable enemy; he promises revenge for the wrongful imprisonment and killing of his Cousin Leonid. He feels that Leonid was not even afforded a fair trial and that public opinion would not be fair. He claims strong collusions between law enforcement and prison authorities in his cousin's death and he vows to avenge his first cousin's death.

"I'm not yet able to make out his exact appearance, but I am sure he'll spell big trouble for police. What I do see is a resemblance to his cousin. Anatoly threatens to kill us, police officers, and he's bent on destroying Israel's police computer technology. He plans to jam it in a way that immobilizes police's IT. He promises harm to the prison authorities. While Leonid's weapons of choice were knives, Anatoly has the most sophisticated and dangerous weapons in his arsenal. He also has several ex-soviets KGB's willing and able to assist in his quest for revenge. He lives in Haifa and Tel Aviv, as do his KGB spy associates. Our Shin Bet intelligence police consider him to be one of the most highly trained sharpshooter assassins who surrounds himself with clever KGB spies. Remember, he too was a member of the KGB, and probably still is. He'll report to Russia and all classified police and Shin Bet documents."

"Oh, my goodness," said Yoni as he inhaled deeply. He rested his face on his hand while he looked towards the floor.

"When will Anatoly begin his revenge mission?"

"Now! Immediately!"

"Did you say now?"

"Yes, now, immediately! Abba, the prison, police, and the Shin Bet will all have your work cut out for you. If you thought Leonid was crazy, just wait, because Anatoly tops the list."

"Wow, I must contact my boss and begin a plan of action. Hannah, where would he begin?"

He'll look to assassinate detectives – your team and Commander Levy. He'll look to hack police and Shin Bet computer information. Anatoly and his men will kidnap my Ima and Aaron and demand a ten-million-dollar ransom; they'll also demand the release of five thousand five hundred Jihadists who are currently imprisoned in Israel. Abba, don't forget that Russia has helped arm Israel's enemies, including Syria, Hezbollah, and even Hamas." She paused. "Abba, this is a much bigger threat than was Leonid."

"Wow! In addition to Shin Bet and police, we might even need to coordinate with our IDF," said Yoni. He wiped his sweaty brow.

"Yes, Abba." She took sips of her lemonade.

THE END

Word Glossary in Alphabetic Order

Abba in Hebrew means father or dad.

Acre is an old city with ruins from the Roman Empire.

Anchoring is a technique taken from NLP – Neuro Linguistic Programing.

Ashem is one of the Hebrew words for God.

Ashkelon is a city near Gaza. They both face the Mediterranean Sea.

Babaganush is a Middle-Eastern dip and garnish made predominantly of squashed eggplant.

Babka is Jewish Eastern-European sweet chocolate bread cake, eaten as either a dessert or with coffee at any time. Babka has sweet crumbs on the top of the cake.

Banias Park – Banias (Paneas), or Caesarea – Philippi was an impressive Greco-Roman city located near a flowing spring – one of the sources of the Jordan River.

Baruch Hashem means thank God.

Ben Yamin, Geva Binyamin *(or* Benjamin Hill) is an Israeli settlement in the West Bank, located five kilometers northeast of Jerusalem.

Beera Schorah is a dark beer, like an ale.

Brit Milah is the ritual circumcision for new baby boys, usually on their eighth day.

Caesarea is a magnificent site, a national park where amazing ancient harbor ruins, beautiful beaches, and impressive modern residences sit side by side. Caesarea is originally an ancient Herodian port city.

Challah is a Jewish is a special bread in Jewish cuisine, usually braided and typically eaten on ceremonial occasions such as Sabbath and major Jewish holidays (other than Passover).

Carmel Mountain, Hebrew Har Ha-karmel, or mountain range, is located in northwestern Israel; the city of Haifa is on its northeastern slope.

Carmelit is an underground train in Haifa, one that also goes towards the top of Mount Carmel.

Chassid is an ultra-orthodox brand of Judaism with designated dress codes for men and women.

Chieken Chabab is broiled chicken chunks, usually with Middle-Eastern spices. Note that **Chieken** is a Russian pronunciation for chicken.

Chutzpadik is a Yiddish word derived from the Hebrew word, chutzpah, which means being fresh or someone who has overstepped the boundaries of what's considered acceptable behaviors.

Cupat Cholim is a local medical infirmary or clinic.

Deltoid is known as the shoulder muscles.

Dizengoff Street is a busy business area with several stores in Tel Aviv.

Eilat is a busy port and popular resort at the northern tip of the Red Sea, on the Gulf of Aqaba. The city's beaches, coral reef, nightlife, and desert landscapes make it a popular destination for domestic and international tourism. Especially noted are the coral reefs making it a wonderful destination for snorkeling or scuba diving.

Eilat Tanzenite is a semi-precious greenish stone used to enhance jewelry.

Elana or Eleyna is a typical is female name of Russian origin.

Ergos Platoon is an elite Israel Defense Forces (IDF), special forces unit specializing in guerrilla warfare, special reconnaissance, and direct action (military). Although, a part of the IDF Central Command's eighty-ninth Brigade (commonly referred to as the commando brigade), its operators undergo basic training with the IDF Northern Golani Command.

Galil is Northern Israel characterized by high mountain ranges and borders with Lebanon and Syria. It's also the name of a high-powered military assault rifle made in Israel.

Glat is a Jewish word which refers to adhering to be strictly kosher.

Glidda means 'ice cream' in Hebrew.

Golani Briggade is a commando, Special Forces unit of the IDF.

Haganah was Israel's first defense force.

Hamotzie is the Jewish blessing over bread and indicates a meal is commencing.

Hanukah celebrates the miracle of light; it is a Jewish holiday commemorating the rededication of the Holy Temple (the Second Temple) in Jerusalem at the time of the Maccabean Revolt against the Seleucid Empire. Hanukkah is observed for eight nights and days, by lighting a candle for each of the eight days.

Hermon Mountain is actually a cluster of mountains with three distinct summits, each about the same height. The entire range covers an area of about thousand square km, of which about seventy square km are under Israeli control. At its tallest point, it's nine thousand two hundred and thirty feet.

Ima in Hebrew means mother.

Ima Mesaperet means that Mom or mother tells stories to children.

IDF stands for the Israeli Defense Force.

Kalaniot is the poppy seed flower, often a beautiful reddish color.

Kafka is Middle-Eastern elongated broiled meat with a combination of beef and lamb. It is thought to have originated in Tunisia.

Ketzale is a term of endearment, meaning 'my little kitten' in Yiddish.

Kfar is a small town, such as Kfar Saba.

KGB was the previous Soviet spy system.

Kiryat Bialik is a town five kilometers north of Haifa with a population of about thirty-nine thousand people. Hayim Nahman Bialik is recognized as Israeli national poet.

Kfar Vradim is situated in Northern Israel; it is a town (local council) in Northern Israel with a population of fifty-eight hundred (2008). The homes are known for their beautifully manicured roses.

Kivun in Hebrew means to have a direction or a goal.

Krayot is plural for kiryat, which means 'towns.'

Kfar Gildani is a fictional name of a town in northern Israel, part of the Galil with incredible views of mountains and valleys.

Latkes means potato pancakes.

Lechaim it's also meant to be congratulatory.

Letzior College is a fictional name of an art college.

Tzion is the word for Zion or the nationalistic movement called Zionism.

Mah Pitom is a question of surprise that asks, 'why?' Or 'why now?'

Mazal Tov is a congratulatory compliment that means 'congratulations.'

Machanei Yehuda is a large open-air market in Jerusalem.

Magen David means the Jewish star.

Meltzar means a being sever or a waiter/waitress in a restaurant.

Mensch is a compliment that refers to someone being a nice guy or a nice person.

Meshugas or meshugene means 'craziness,' or 'emotional immaturity.'

Mikvah is the ritual bath.

Mishebeerach is a traditional prayer asking God's help in healing and wellness.

Merkava IV tank is a solidly built tank. The Merkava, or Chariot, was the first tank entirely designed and built by the Israeli Army.

MMPI stands for the Minnesota Multiphasic Personality Inventory. Clinical psychologists use it frequently to measure psychopathology, i.e., anxiety, aggression, and depressions, etc.

Moel is a religious individual trained to do ritual circumcisions.

Moyshe is a Hebrew name for Moses.

Nasheries means a sweet treat or treats to munch on.

Nahariah is a vacation town right next to the beach.

Ness means 'miracle.'

Neve Shannan is part of the Carmel Mountain Range.

Nooh is a type of an impatient question, like so?

Pisher means someone who is not yet toilet-trained when it comes to urination.

Qassam Rockets have been sent over to Israel for many years.

Ramat Gan is a neighboring town to Tel Aviv. It is home to one of the world's major diamond exchanges and many high-tech industries.

Rambam is the name of a large hospital in Haifa, named after a renowned Spanish physician.

Reframing is when you redefine an emotion in a much less self-critical manner.

Russian Mule is a drink with vodka. It's a bit of ginger and lime drunk in a copper mug.

Sapta means 'grandmother' in Hebrew.

Sayeret Matkal is a Special Forces unit in the Israeli Defense Force (IDF) to gather intelligence, conduct deep reconnaissance and undertake covert missions behind enemy lines.

Shekel is an Israeli currency. The cupronickel Israeli new shekel (properly 'new sheqel'), the present currency of the state of Israel.

Shekels is Israel's current money currency.

Shmates are old hand-me-down clothing, similar to rags.

Shin Bet is a law enforcement agency setup to both protect Israel's citizens from internal terrorism as well as from internal terror attacks.

Stromal is a large black hat worn by males who are Chassidm on special occasions like the Sabbath.

Simcha means a happy occasion, like an engagement party or a wedding.

Soshanna is the Hebrew name for 'rose.'

Tante means 'aunt' in Jewish but still frequently used in Israel.

Tzion is technically a hill in Jerusalem on which the temple was built but has become associated with the movement of returning Jews to their promised land of Israel.

Volga is the name of a large river in the USSR.

Yaffa means 'pretty.'

Yafo or Jaffa is an ancient port city in Israel, close to Tel Aviv. Jaffa is famous for its association with the biblical stories of Jonah, the whale and King Solomon.

Yediot Ha Achronot is fictional name for a newspaper of the latest news.